SWEET LIFE

SWEET LIFE

Britt Ekland

Translated from the Swedish
by Joan Tate

HEADLINE

First published in Sweden in 1993
by BONNIER ALBA under the title Det ljuva livet

First published in Great Britain in 1994
by HEADLINE BOOK PUBLISHING

10 9 8 7 6 5 4 3 2

British Library Cataloguing in Publication Data

Ekland, Britt
Sweet Life
I. Title
813.54 [F]

ISBN 0–7472–1023–3

Phototypeset by Intype, London
Printed and bound in Great Britain by
Mackays of Chatham PLC, Chatham, Kent

HEADLINE BOOK PUBLISHING
A division of Hodder Headline PLC
338 Euston Road
London NW1 3BH

To my friend Johan Pramell,
whose inspiration and help
made SWEET LIFE possible.

For my Mother.

Prologue

Prologue

In silence, Tanya and Robert took the lift down. Their grandparents had already left the hospital; they wanted the children to have a moment alone with their mother.

Robert looked at his young sister and felt an enormous tenderness for this tall, slim fourteen year old. He wrapped his arms round her thin body and she leant her head on his shoulder, crying. Robert fought back his own tears.

The lift came to a halt and, with their arms still round each other, they went out and across to the car park. Tanya looked up at this tall dark man who was her brother. He had a beautiful face, almost like a woman's, but his eyes were filled with sorrow.

'Where do you want to go?' he said, searching for the car keys, his arm still round Tanya.

Neither of them saw the man in a dark blue cashmere coat, a briefcase in his hand, hurry through the glass doors of the hospital the moment Tanya and Robert's car had disappeared.

1

Edward sighed loudly. Why was there so much traffic? It usually only took an hour from Hewitt Hall to Heathrow, but today it seemed an impossible task to get there. Not only that, the Land Rover was at the garage with a flat battery, so he had had to ask poor Mrs McDonald to take him to the airport in her Hillman Estate. He was doing the driving, but that made no difference. They were making little headway.

It was unlike Philip not to have things under control at the Hall, particularly the Land Rover which they used practically every day. True, Philip was his brother, but that was no excuse for not doing his job. Edward simply mustn't miss this plane, the only connection to Stockholm via Copenhagen. But the chances of catching it did not look good.

It was to be a very special weekend. Count Niclas Silferschiöld of Koberg had invited him to the first elk shoot of the year, and this time members of both the Swedish and the Danish royal families were to be present.

Edward always looked forward to going to Sweden in the autumn. It had become something of a tradition and he liked his Swedish host and hostess very much. Swedes might be thought rather stiff and reserved, but after a few drinks all that seemed to blow away and they got on well. They all spoke excellent English, a fact that impressed Edward enormously; he had decided the twins were to start learning French as a second language next year.

He glanced at the Cartier watch he'd inherited from his father. His plane was due to take off at five to four and it was already twenty past three. At last he spotted the signs for the exit road to

3

Heathrow and put his foot down, though with little effect. The car just coughed and continued at the same speed. Edward could feel the sweat breaking out on his forehead and upper lip. Again he glanced at his watch.

'If the worst comes to the worst can you get a later plane?' asked Mrs McDonald, who until now had suffered in silence beside him. The housekeeper had come to Hewitt Hall straight from her family home in Scotland at twenty years of age when Edward had been just a baby. Hewitt Hall was nowadays as much her home as that of the Hewitt family. On her fortieth birthday, she had insisted on being addressed as Mrs McDonald, and quite rightly. Even in her youth, people had reckoned she was nearly forty. Despite the fact it would soon be over half a century since she had left her home country she had retained her strong Scottish accent. Her generous heart had always been and still remained faithful to the Hewitt family.

At last they arrived at the terminal – twenty minutes to check in and board the plane. Edward grabbed his black leather case with the family coat-of-arms and his gold initials, took out his guncase and waved a quick goodbye to Mrs McDonald. Would he be in time?

The blonde ground hostess took his ticket and shook her head in distress.

'I suppose you know you're very late, Lord Hewitt? The economy class is fully booked, but you can go to the gate and try checking in there. It looks as if there are some seats left in first class. I can't promise anything, but it's worth a try.'

Never before had Edward run so fast. Out of breath, dripping with sweat and his shirt sticking to him, the ticket clutched in one hand, his guncase over his shoulder and suitcase in the other hand, he finally arrived at the gate. He managed to gasp out his name and gratefully took the first-class boarding pass.

An indescribable relief. Edward sank down into seat 3C with pleasure, fished a handkerchief out of his pocket and started mopping his forehead.

'My name's Monica. Would you care for a drink?'

Edward looked up and was met by the most beautiful face he

4

had ever seen. For a second or two, everything seemed to stand still. Speechless, he simply stared at the young woman.

'Oh, I'm sorry, I thought you were English. My name's Monica and I wonder whether you would like a drink after take-off?' she said in Swedish.

'Sorry.' Edward finally managed to get out, 'Scotch and soda. Not too much ice.' What a beautiful woman.

Monica took his order, her cheeks turning warm. She went straight back to the pantry.

'Katarina, who's the passenger in 3C? The rather red-faced man. I haven't got him on my list.'

Monica's colleague glanced down at the papers she had been given by the ground staff.

'Lord Hewitt,' she said in passing as she went to stand in the aisle to start the safety instructions.

Lord Hewitt, thought Monica as she sat down on the seat they used at take-off and landing. She was surprised he'd affected her so much, although they had exchanged only a few words.

Minutes later the plane was in the air and the pilot's voice came over the loudspeakers. 'We are now cruising at thirty thousand feet. We have a good tail wind and can expect to be in Copenhagen on time.'

Monica and Katarina had already begun to fix the drinks, but Monica could only concentrate on 3C. Scotch and soda. Not too much ice. Would two be too much? she wondered. Well, he could always take one out.

She served the passengers along the aisle, but stopped at 3C.

'Not too much ice, I hope?'

His face had returned to a normal colour. And he'd taken his jacket off and hung it tidily over the empty seat in front of him.

'Shall I take your jacket?'

Edward shook his head, staring intently at her.

She noticed that he had unusually beautiful hands with long slim fingers and singularly well-kept nails. He had a gold signet ring on his right hand and was wearing a blue shirt with white collar and cuffs. His tie was dark blue with a narrow gold-coloured stripe and something like a crown at the bottom. It looked like the

5

coat-of-arms on the ring, but she wasn't sure.

His face was handsome, even if the features were rather weak, with high cheek bones, deep-set dark blue eyes and finely drawn eyebrows. His nose was narrow and straight, his mouth friendly with generous lips in an otherwise thin face, with a sprinkling of silver in his dark brushed-back hair.

Monica couldn't help noticing his small well-shaped ears. She had a thing about ears, especially her own, which she hated. She always remembered when one of her friends had come to school with her whole head bandaged. Her friend's parents had understood and let her have an operation on her ears. How jealous she'd been. She had kept mentioning it to her mother and father, but they had just said she was pretty as she was.

Katarina woke her out of her daydream.

'Monica, there's lunch and I need your help.'

When she went to pick up Edward's lunch tray, he put his hand on hers.

'Excuse me,' he mumbled. 'What's your name?'

'Monica Forssgren,' she said.

'Here's my telephone number. Would you possibly consider having lunch with me next time you're in London?'

From the very first moment, he'd known he had to see her again. He'd finished his whisky but had only picked at the food. What could he do to meet this radiant, beautiful young woman again? Suddenly he'd leant over towards his jacket and taken out his gold pen and the small leather-bound notebook, torn out a page and written clearly on it: Edward Hewitt, Mayfair 1509. The phone number to his flat in St James's. To make sure, he wrote down the Hewitt Hall number as well.

He gave a sigh of relief as she took the piece of paper and, smiling rather shyly, removed the almost untouched tray.

'Weren't you hungry? SAS has a reputation for good food,' she asked quietly.

He shook his head and smiled, embarrassed. Then he leant back and closed his eyes.

It was now three years since Mary Elizabeth had died, and her last years had been very difficult. The cancer had spread so far that she was bedridden and heavily drugged with morphine. Not being able to help her had been terrible.

They'd had a wonderful marriage and when the twins were born, he had been overjoyed, though deep down his great hope had been that their first child should be a boy so that Hewitt Hall would have an heir. Anyhow, he loved his daughters, and he and Mary Elizabeth had thought they had time on their side. The idea had been to have more children. But after two miscarriages within two years, his wife's illness had been discovered, and slowly but surely he'd had to accept that his dream of a son would not be fulfilled.

The memory of the day when they'd had to take an agonised Mary Elizabeth to the hospital still pained him. After three days, which had seemed like weeks, and endless tests, the diagnosis had been made: cervical cancer.

Their whole life was shattered. He had been unable to grasp how this could happen to her. She had been an outdoor person, healthy all her life. She neither smoked nor drank, went for long walks every day with the twins regardless of the weather, was an excellent rider and had won many rosettes for dressage.

He remembered with horror their trips to the hospital for the radiation treatment which meant that she'd lost all her hair and how they'd gone to London to Wig Creations, who made a wig in the same colour as her natural hair.

For two years the doctors managed to keep her illness at bay, though both of them knew they were living on borrowed time. But they'd had those two years together and they'd made the most of every second.

He opened his eyes when he heard the captain's voice crackling in the loudspeakers. 'Smoking is no longer permitted. Please make sure your seat-belt is fastened. We shall be landing at Copenhagen Kastrup Airport in seven minutes. The local time is 18.50. We hope that you have had a pleasant flight and that you will fly SAS again.'

Edward got up and put on his jacket. On his way out he thanked Monica and gave her a questioning look.

The Chelsea Cloisters apartments where Katarina and Monica shared a furnished two-roomed flat was in Sloane Avenue, close

7

to the shops of King's Road and Knightsbridge. The flat consisted of a living-room with a sofa-bed, a bedroom with two single beds and a kitchen so cramped you could hardly turn around in it, though they had managed to squeeze a table and two chairs in below the only small window.

The colours in the flat were green, yellow and brown: forest green carpets, yellow curtains, brown corduroy sofa and two unmatched yellowish-green armchairs. To add to this mishmash, the bedspreads in the bedroom were yellow with a pattern of white daisies.

They had done their best to brighten up their horribly dreary flat in the Swedish way, putting candles in nearly every niche. To an English eye it looked like Christmas all the year round.

A photograph of Monica at her confirmation, and one of her parents, Gerd and Gunnar, stood in a red leather frame on Monica's bedside table. Apart from the photograph, there was an ocarina she had been given by her first boyfriend, Åke on her thirteenth birthday. It was her mascot and she always took it with her wherever she went. Despite all her travels, it was still intact, as was the gold heart on a ribbon she had once won at Tivoli.

Women's magazines, Swedish and English, were the only things on Katarina's bedside table. Katarina loved wallowing in the lives of the rich and famous society people and devoured beauty tips of all kinds which she delighted in sharing with an uncomprehending Monica. The bathroom shelf was crammed with innumerable jars and face masks, and Katarina would often wander round the flat like a ghost with a bright green face, or with hair and hands made sticky with olive oil, then covered with plastic bags – a recent tip from the beauty pages of one of her magazines.

One Friday afternoon Monica had come back from shopping in the King's Road to find Katarina in the bathroom, both legs wrapped in cellophane. The roll held high, she was attempting to wind it round her body.

'Thank God you've come home. I can't do this bit on my own. You have to wind it round your behind five times. Take a look,' she said, motioning towards the magazine. 'You'll see what you have to do.'

An open copy of *Vogue* with detailed illustrations was lying in the basin in front of her.

'You see,' said Katarina, oblivious to the stares of her flatmate and best friend. 'Then I have to put those on,' she went on, pointing to a pair of woollen stockings on the bathroom stool.

Laboriously, Monica helped her, not only with the stockings, but with a pair of thick pants as well.

'It says this is the best way to lose weight quickly,' Katarina announced, shuffling over to the bedroom. 'All I have to do now is go to bed, wrap up in blankets and sweat it out. Can I borrow yours, too?'

She lay down on the bed and Monica again gave her a hand. Suddenly she burst out laughing. She was used to her friend's peculiar ideas, but this time Katarina really had gone over the top.

Katarina was the complete opposite of Monica. She had long dark curly hair, brown eyes and thin lips which she accentuated with bright red lipstick. She was flat-chested, so always put double foam inserts into her bra. Once she had admitted she was green with envy at the thought of Monica's thirty-four size cups. Her clothes were always colourful, her favourites red, blue and green, preferably worn all at once. She laughed and cried with the same intensity and life was never dull with her; a quiet evening at home with the two of them would turn into a party.

Katarina was also passionately attached to red wine. Monica liked a glass now and again, but she thought it made her face red and left a nasty taste in her mouth. Not so Katarina. Without the slightest difficulty she could drink a whole bottle on her own.

'Monica, Monica. I need a glass of water.'

'But you just said you were to lie there and sweat it out. Surely you shouldn't drink a whole lot of water.'

Katarina had read in another magazine about the importance of drinking water, at least eight glasses a day.

Shaking her head, Monica got the water for her. 'You can get the other seven yourself,' she said. Monica had only one beauty preparation apart from soap and water, a Helena Rubenstein moisturiser. Her mother had given her the first jar for her

9

seventeenth birthday and she'd gone on buying the same brand ever since.

She never thought about her weight, just ate when she was hungry, surviving on sandwiches and airline food. She had been given her model figure free of charge – narrow hips, slim waist and, in relation to her neat body, large breasts. She was a natural blonde and wore her hair in a page-boy bob, but her greatest wish was to be able to let it grow longer. But as long as she was an air hostess that was impossible, as her ears would be revealed if she put her hair up as the regulations demanded.

Her eyes varied from blue to green depending on what clothes she was wearing, and she drew attention to them with a lot of mascara. Her nose was small but perfect: she'd never forget that time in Harrods when she'd heard two American women discussing her nose. 'That's the best nose job I've ever seen,' one had whispered rather too loudly to the other, and that wasn't the only time she had heard comments about her nose.

She had occasionally been offered work as a model, but out of shyness had always turned it down. She had chosen to become an air hostess largely because of her shyness, as it was a good way of making contact with other people. She had succeeded beyond all expectations. It had taken her only two years to be promoted to first class.

'Monica!' Katarina yelled again from the bedroom. 'Please come and help me up.'

Laughing, Monica took the blankets off and hauled Katarina up with both hands.

'Oh, I'm so sticky,' she said with some satisfaction. 'Must have lost at least a kilo.'

She waddled over to the bathroom, the plastic riding up between her legs.

'You look like a duck,' said Monica, teasing.

'I like that, coming from a spindly thing like you,' Katarina retorted, struggling to find the end of the plastic film to start unwinding it. Appealing desperately to the laughing Monica for mercy, she grabbed the nail scissors and started snipping wildly, stabbing herself several times and shrieking loudly.

Finally she gave up, exhausted. 'This is much too slow. Monica, I'll do anything, but please get the kitchen scissors and help me out of this.'

Giggling, Monica released her from her plastic wrappings with three snips. She couldn't have lost a kilo, but the film was certainly dripping wet. And the main thing was, Katarina was triumphantly happy.

'You see. It works beautifully. Now let's celebrate.' She started towelling down her legs. 'Guess what I've bought today?'

'Vino Chianti Classico,' chanted Monica, as if that were the most obvious thing in the world. The flat was full of empty raffia-covered Chianti bottles, useful holders for all their candles.

'But I also bought a baguette, salami and camembert. And a little bottle of Sambuca for after. How about that!'

'Have you had a rise?' grinned Monica.

'No, but I'm heartily sick of soup, crispbread and that smoked roe in a tube!'

Monica was lying on the sofa feeling a trifle woozy, Perry Como drifting from the loudspeaker. A whole week had passed since Edward Hewitt had given her his telephone number.

She got up and went to the bedroom to get the piece of paper from her handbag. Back in the living room, she asked Katarina if she remembered the man who had flown with them on that flight from London. 'The man in 3C? Lord Hewitt?'

Katarina looked at her as if she were crazy. Was she supposed to remember passengers from every flight? Of course she couldn't. She shook her head.

Monica started telling her about what had happened, and Katarina, rolling round on the pillows on the floor on to her back and lying with her hands behind her head, at once pricked up her ears.

'. . . And here I am with this telephone number and don't know what to do.'

'For heaven's sake, it's a real live lord. Are you mad? Phone!'

Perhaps it was the wine, or Katarina's powers of persuasion, but before Monica knew what was what, they were sitting on the bench by the telephone in the hall, each with a glass of Sambuca

11

and, despite the fact that Monica was trying to cut down on her smoking, an overflowing ashtray.

'Well, go on. That was what he wanted you to do. He's not likely to say no. Go on, take a big swig and pick up the receiver.'

Monica dialled Mayfair 1509. No reply.

'Try the other number.'

The candle in the Chianti bottle had almost burnt down, so before dialling the number, Monica asked Katarina to go and get another, thinking she really needed to be alone for this. But Katarina was not so easily deceived.

'Hewitt Hall,' said a female voice with a marked Scottish accent.

'May I speak to Lord Hewitt?'

'Who shall I say is calling?'

'Monica. Monica Forssgren.'

'One moment.'

The seconds seemed like minutes. With the heavy Bakelite receiver between her shoulder and her ear, she took a big gulp of the Sambuca.

'What's happening? What's happening?' Katarina was tugging at Monica's green jersey dress.

At that moment the woman returned. 'Lord Hewitt is just coming.'

Monica felt butterflies in her stomach. Then she heard him speak, his aristocratic tone of voice unmistakable.

'Monica, I thought you were never going to call.'

His words broke the ice and the conversation was soon in full swing. Katarina went back into the other room and poured out another glass. She had succeeded in getting Monica to phone, but she wasn't in the slightest bit interested in the actual conversation. The *fruits* of the conversation would be much more interesting . . .

Monica had started rather hesitantly by apologising, but before she had time to get into a tangle, Edward interrupted her.

'Promise you'll have lunch with me tomorrow.' And they had decided he would pick her up at midday outside her flat.

'What's the outcome? Lunch or even dinner?' Katarina called from the living room the moment Monica put down the receiver. 'Lunch, of course.' She nodded without waiting for a reply. 'God, how romantic.' And with that she curled up like a cat on the silk cushions.

2

Edward swung the car round and drove down the long avenue, past the lodge and out through the great wrought-iron gates. Both Philip and Lady Rose Hewitt had observed the car, Philip from a window on the first floor and Lady Rose from her beloved rose garden behind the cottage. It was just past ten.

Philip couldn't imagine what his brother was up to so early on Sunday morning though he suspected it might have something to do with the call Edward had received on Saturday night. He and Edward nearly always went to their mother's for Sunday lunch, to give Mrs McDonald time off to go to church. Then in the afternoon they'd go through the week's work and accounts together. Philip managed the estate. Much of the land was rented out to local farmers for grazing but the income from that did not by a long way cover the incredibly high costs of running the place. Philip took a minimal salary and ran the estate largely because he more than anyone else loved the place where he had grown up. Edward's income also went straight into maintaining the house and grounds. Like Lady Rose, both brothers had received a small legacy from Lord Hewitt, but death duties had taken most of the capital.

This Sunday, Philip had planned to have a serious discussion with Edward. The south wing was in urgent need of a new roof and the cost of repairs would amount to at least twenty thousand pounds, a sum Philip was only too well aware they did not have. But he had been farsighted enough to have the pictures in the hall and the carpet over by the library window photographed. The latter was a Kerman and he knew it would bring in a large sum.

15

He had also managed to find a buyer. All there was to do now was to get Edward to realise that their income was insufficient for the repairs required to the roof. It was also rather urgent, as it was already early October.

Although Edward was a financial consultant, he was nevertheless quite naive when it came to their own finances. He was a partner in Hewitt & Clarke Ltd, but his partner, Gordon Clarke, had such prodigiously extravagant habits that, despite his background, Philip couldn't understand how anyone could squander money in such a lighthearted manner. And Gordon's lavishness tempted Edward into believing he was also quite without financial troubles.

Every summer, Edward spent at least two weeks on Gordon's 150-foot yacht, *Gordanza*, which had four double cabins and space for a five-man crew. There was a motor-boat on the stern deck used for trips ashore and water skiing, and four little motor-bikes for getting along the quays.

Gordon also owned a chalet in St Moritz, where he usually spent his winter holidays, and he used his own helicopter whenever he went skiing. However, his permanent address was a penthouse apartment in Eaton Square, but whenever the weather was wet and miserable he took a trip to his property in Bermuda.

Philip was not envious. That was not the kind of life he wanted to lead. His passion was writing and he had already had eight novels published, all of them detective stories featuring Stuart Corke, a fumbling but observant detective, written under the pseudonym of Craig Stevens. He had written his very first book in the greatest secrecy after his national service, as he'd at first considered it inappropriate for an aristocrat to write fiction. Now Philip's publisher had told him that Peter Sellers was interested in buying the film rights and Philip wanted to discuss this with Edward. He presumed that if the deal came off, it might be very lucrative. In that way he would also be able to do his bit . . .

Edward had telephoned his mother at half past eight in the morning; not that that mattered to her, she was always up at the crack of dawn.

'Mother, I can't come to lunch today,' his familiar voice had said. 'I have urgent business in London.'

Lady Rose loved her Sunday lunches with her sons. Today she was giving them poached salmon and creamed potatoes, then for dessert she had prepared vanilla pudding with whipped cream. She was a good cook and her vanilla pudding was Philip's absolute favourite. She resigned herself to the fact that they would be only two today.

What was so important that Edward had to go off to London on a Sunday? she wondered. He usually spent the weekends away from the city, enjoying the quiet life of Hewitt Hall. Oh, how she longed to ask, but Lady Rose had learnt not to interfere with the private lives of her sons. Her thoughts were suddenly interrupted by the telephone. It was Philip.

'I saw Edward going off this morning. Does that mean he won't be here for lunch? Oh, I see, but when did he phone? Did he say where he was going? Yes, of course I'm coming. You know how I love your vanilla pudding.'

Edward swung on to the A4, acutely aware that his unexpected departure would arouse his mother's and his brother's curiosity, but this time he was not going to share his plans with them. All he could think of was lunch with Monica. Although he preferred discussions and news programmes to popular music, today he only had the concentration for the Light programme.

His weekend at Koberg had been wonderful but he hadn't been able to think about anything except Monica. He'd been the only one to have bagged an elk, and he would have liked to have brought the antlers back home with him. The Danish Crown Princess Margrethe and the young Swedish Princess Desirée, just introduced to the weekend party, had been there, together with a delightful woman, a lady-in-waiting called Mrs Brita Petersen. But Edward's mind had been full of the young air hostess he'd met on the plane.

He'd waited for a whole long week for her to phone and had almost given up hope when Mrs McDonald had come to tell him that a Miss Monica Forssgren was on the telephone. He'd been alone in the library when the call came through, which he was grateful for, as he had not the slightest desire to tell his brother about Monica.

To save time Lady Rose had, as was her habit, laid the table the night before. They usually ate at one and that way she had more time in the kitchen. One of her favourite occupations, apart from her famous roses, was to lay the table beautifully. When her husband, Lord Hewitt, had been alive and they had often had guests, she had been renowned for her beautiful table arrangements. She'd had to leave most of the porcelain at the Hall when she'd moved to the lodge, but she had taken with her the beautiful turquoise dinner service and some of the family silver.

Now she had to remove one place setting and she was wondering how to change it all. Usually her sons sat one at each end of the table with her in the middle. They were as different as it was possible for brothers to be. Philip was two years younger than Edward, and while Edward was tall, slim and dark, Philip was rather short with the beginning of a paunch. His hair was ash-blond and thin at the temples and his face could not be called anything else but round, the blue eyes he had inherited from his mother rather close together. He was often told he was strikingly like her, and there was no doubt he was her favourite son, something she was aware he sometimes consciously made the most of. The brothers were very popular in society, particularly as they were both considered to have quick minds and swift tongues. In contrast to Edward, Philip had never married, nor even come anywhere near it. He was a confirmed bachelor, relished his freedom and, his mother knew, would never submit to having to adjust to someone else's will. Perhaps it would be better now if she and Philip sat opposite each other on the long sides, Lady Rose pondered. Yes, that's what she would do.

She went over to the sideboard, where she kept a silver tray of sherry, Gordon's gin, Edward's favourite whisky, Chivas Regal, and vermouth. She was not the only one with a certain liking for gin. Philip always had a dry Martini. She took out a glass and mixed herself a light gin and tonic, took a sip, then went out to where her prize roses were still in full bloom.

Two years earlier, in 1957, she had received a special distinction for them from the Queen Mother at the Chelsea Flower Show. There had been a photograph in the *Telegraph* and she had ordered a copy of the original, now in the place of honour in a lovely silver frame on the mantelpiece. She carefully picked three yellow roses, a kind actually named after her – Lady Rose. She was going to put them in a silver bowl in the middle of the table. After a quick glance at the time, she hurried in, finished her gin and tonic and took the glass with her into the kitchen, where she checked that lunch was ready.

Philip could choose the wine from her small but well-stocked cellar. Sometimes they contented themselves with a drink before the meal and took only water with it. But Philip could decide that.

Lady Rose nipped into the bathroom and smoothed down the short blonde hair Sebastian, her hairdresser, carefully coloured once every four weeks. Her hair still looked good, as she had been to Sebastian's only two days ago for a shampoo and set – a ritual repeated every Friday, come rain or shine. She quickly ran her powder puff over her nose and carefully put a smear of Elizabeth Arden's 'Old Rose' colour on her lips; she didn't want to get lipstick on Philip's cheek when she kissed him. She kept a box of Curiously Strong Mints in the medicine cupboard on the wall and she swiftly popped one in her mouth. She certainly didn't want Philip to smell alcohol on her breath.

The noise of dogs barking heralded Philip's arrival.

'Quiet, Mopsy!' she cried, though the yapping could just as well have come from Topsy or Popsy. She adored her little Pekes, all three of them bitches, Mopsy the mother and the two others her daughters, all three identical. Not even Lady Rose could tell them apart. Philip knocked on the door and came in. She swallowed the last bit of the peppermint before affectionately embracing him and kissing him on the cheek.

'This way, please, Lord Hewitt.' Edward was a familiar guest at the Connaught Hotel. The head waiter pulled a chair out for Monica and she sat down.

'Would you like a drink first, or shall we just have wine?'

Monica didn't really know what to say, but in the end said she would have whatever Edward was having.

'Then we'll just have wine,' he said, turning to the head waiter to give the order.

They had the traditional Sunday roast beef and Yorkshire pudding, though Monica was so fascinated by Edward's life story that she could hardly eat anything. She was only interested in devouring what this increasingly captivating man was revealing to her.

What a sad life. To lose his wife must have been a terrible tragedy. As the meal went on the feeling became stronger: if she were only given the chance, she would do everything in her power to make him and his daughters happy again.

As they finished their coffee, Edward leant over the table, took her hand in his and looked into her eyes. 'Monica, I'm terribly glad you came.'

'So am I,' she said with a warm smile, wishing he'd never let go. Was this what being in love was like? Her heart jumped when she thought about how attractive, well spoken and sophisticated he was, and how happy she was that he was sitting there holding her hand.

After lunch they went for a long walk through an autumnal Hyde Park, Edward's arm laid gently round her shoulders. When he stopped, took her face in his hands and gently kissed her, a wave of happiness washed over her.

Here she was, in Hyde Park, twenty years old, being gently embraced by a man seventeen years older, a man whose background and experience of life were totally unlike her own. But Edward was a man she could look up to and respect. And for Edward, whom she had met only twice, she already had stronger feelings than she had ever had for any of her other boyfriends, even those she'd been a little in love with – like Kjell. This seemed to be the kind of love you only read about, the love she'd fantasised about so many times in her daydreams. And now it was reality.

What her parents would say did not even occur to her. Monica had always regarded herself as an independent and self-sufficient woman. She had her own flat in London. She did still live with her parents when she was in Stockholm, but she was seldom there and she paid for herself when she was. Why shouldn't she? She had a decent income now she'd been promoted. It hadn't been easy and she'd worked very hard to become a hostess in first class. But now that didn't matter any longer. She would gladly give up everything for this man – if he only asked her.

On his way home, Edward thought about Mary Elizabeth for the second time in a fortnight, both times in connection with Monica. After three painful years, he had at last begun to accept Mary Elizabeth's death and that there was nothing he could do to get her back. Life must go on, if only for the sake of the twins.

Edward had been unswervingly faithful to his wife during their marriage, and actually also to her memory. True, he had spent a lot of time with Margaret, a family friend, going to the theatre, enjoying exotic meals. Last summer they had even rented a villa in Brittany for two weeks. With Philip, Lady Rose, the twins and Margaret's son and daughter, they'd had a very pleasant holiday. The children in particular had got along well together as they were all about the same age. Among their friends, there was a good deal of speculation, but Edward had never let it be understood that they were anything more than just friends. Margaret had lost her husband under very tragic circumstances, so he regarded their relationship more as good friends supporting each other in their great sorrow. Philip, and others besides him, had implied that Margaret would be a suitable wife and a wonderful hostess at Hewitt Hall. And they were certainly right, but after a marriage such as his and Mary Elizabeth's, it was impossible to pretend love, tenderness and desire – all that he had experienced with his wife.

Lying in bed in the darkness, he often thought about the pleasurable moments of love he had experienced with her. Today was the first time he'd dared believe that he would ever experience those feelings again. Monica had succeeded in resurrecting emotions in him which had been deeply buried for the last three years. And when he kissed her in the park and felt her immediate

21

response, it had aroused a desire and a longing he hadn't felt for a very long time, and it had given him hope for a future together.

3

Lady Rose, Philip and the twins were on their way to Scotland to spend the weekend with Aunt Agatha, the girls' favourite great-aunt.

Philip was only moderately pleased. He would rather have spent the weekend shut up in his bachelor pad alone with his typewriter. He was in the middle of a new Stuart Corke story, but as he was stuck with writer's block he had promised to go with them to Scotland; all he could do now was to resign himself. Perhaps the change of environment would do him good.

They took the 7 pm train from Euston and, having put their luggage in the sleeper, were on their way to the restaurant car. Fortunately they had booked a table in time, for the train was full.

The twins were very excited. This was the first time for over a month they had been out of boarding school. They were in their first term and they missed their father, their horses even more. But all that was forgotten now the visit to Aunt Agatha was looming and as they watched the countryside flash past in the dark, they could hardly contain their happiness.

Lady Rose was on great form. As soon as the train had pulled out of the station, she had excused herself and gone to the toilet where she had taken out the big Milk of Magnesia bottle she'd filled with an extra strong mixture of gin and tonic, just to be sure. She had a similar bottle ready in her luggage in their compartment. She didn't sleep all that well in her old age and tonight she also had to share the compartment with the girls. It was going to be a long night.

Edward's Land Rover swung in through the great wrought-iron

23

gates and Monica's heart started to beat faster. She couldn't see the Hall yet, but they drove past a wonderfully picturesque Lodge.

'My mother lives there,' Edward pointed out.

He had already told her that the rest of the family were in Scotland with his aunt so Monica knew there would be only the two of them in the house. She also knew what that would entail and the thought both tempted and frightened her. But she was now certain that what she was feeling was genuine love.

Last Saturday they'd had dinner at Les Ambassadeurs and had danced close together. She'd sensed his desire, but nothing had happened. Edward was clearly a gentleman to the core. He had driven her to Sloane Avenue, kissed her goodnight and left her; all very different from what she was used to back home in Sweden.

As the Hall came into view Monica saw that the house was not quite as large as she had thought it would be. In her imagination she had seen a fairy-tale castle with pinnacles and towers. The sand-coloured three-storey building in front of her looked more like a large country mansion.

They drove round a pretty fountain and stopped by the steps to the front entrance. Edward helped her out, took her tapestry-patterned suitcase and carried it up the three steps to the front door.

The enormous wooden door with its ironwork fittings was opened as if to order by a thin little grey-haired lady.

'Let me take it, my lord.'

Monica recognised the Scottish accent she had heard when she had rung Edward for the first time.

'Monica, this is Mrs McDonald.'

'Very nice to meet you, Miss Forssgren.' She smiled at Monica with no particular curiosity. 'Tea is ready when you are.'

Monica simply had to stop and look around. The hall was so big, the ceiling so high, she felt as if she'd stepped into a church. The enormous chandelier was the most beautiful and impressive she had ever seen, the chains holding it covered with velvet. On her right was a long dark brown mahogany table, a tall vase of pink lilies on it. The walls were covered with pictures which she presumed were portraits of members of the family.

'That's my great-grandfather,' said Edward, when he saw her staring as a vast painting in a frame the like of which she had never seen before.

The painting was of a young boy in black velvet breeches wearing a beret. But it was the frame that impressed her most, all sprigs of laurel leaves and small berries, with garlands intertwined to bind together the leaves and berries to form an exquisite pattern in gold leaf. Monica stood for a long time in mute admiration.

'Shall I serve tea in the library?'

'Yes, please, Mrs McDonald. That'd be excellent,' said Edward, looking at his watch. It was exactly half past four. He picked up Monica's suitcase and together they went up the long stairs to the right.

On the first floor, he opened the door into a lavishly flowery guest room, dominated by a vast bed, its chintz bedspread in the same rose pattern as the curtains, cushions and tablecloths. The green wall-to-wall carpeting was slightly worn and a large dressing-table with a mirror stood against one wall, complete with an old-fashioned silver hairbrush and matching comb. A blue-green ceramic vase on a round lace mat stood on the dressing-table, also filled with pink lilies. Monica wondered whether they could possibly have been Mary Elizabeth's favourite flowers.

Opposite the dressing-table was a mahogany wardrobe with a faceted glass mirror in the middle and doors on each side. For a moment, Monica thought she'd stepped into a dream.

'Let's go down to the library for tea. Mrs McDonald will unpack for you.'

Monica was glad of her air-hostess training – packing neatly was one of the very first rules she'd learnt.

They went down the long stairs, past the picture of Edward's great-grandfather and in through the high double doors on the left. Edward walked so quickly through the light drawing-room, she had no time to look around before he opened the door into the library.

Mrs McDonald put the tea tray down on a table in front of the fire, and they sat down on a big brown chesterfield.

'Sugar?' he asked.

'Two, please.' He put two lumps in her cup with a pair of silver tongs.

He proffered the sandwich plate. 'These are egg and mayonnaise, those cucumber and those smoked salmon.'

She would have preferred to have taken more than three of the delicate offerings, for together they weren't even as big as an ordinary sandwich.

'Would you like a scone?' he said, taking the lid off a silver warmer. Then he put a small, apparently unbaked, white bun on her plate, cut it open and spread strawberry jam and whipped cream on to it.

As Monica took a bite, it fell apart in her hand. Edward laughed and helped her put the crumbs into her mouth. Perhaps he noticed her flushing at her clumsiness.

'I don't know who decided what scones should be like. They're almost impossible to eat, as you see, but they're good.'

Monica could see he was trying to smooth over her embarrassment and was relieved.

'Come on, I'll show you round the rest of the house.' Edward got up and held out his hand, but at that moment the telephone on a side table by the door rang. As he answered his face suddenly brightened.

'My darlings, how are things? Oh, so you've both had sweets. And you've eaten the lot! I hope you'll clean your teeth extra-specially well tonight. Don't forget what the dentist said. Was it fun on the train? Oh, you slept with Grandmother. And Uncle Philip played Scrabble with you, what fun. Hello, Mother. Have they been a lot of trouble?'

Monica felt very moved as she watched his face while he spoke to his daughters, and she realised how much he must miss them. It couldn't have been easy to send them to boarding school, she thought, although she knew his work in London kept him from being with them during the week, and the schools in the area were simply not good enough. He had told her he wanted his daughters to have the best education money could buy.

And how nice he was to his mother. She'd always heard you could judge a man by the way he treated his mother. In that case she was extremely lucky, because he appeared to be very considerate.

''Bye then. See you soon. 'Bye.'

How different from her own father. Of course he loved her, but she couldn't recall him ever speaking to her affectionately when she was small. The only things she seemed to remember were warnings and admonitions.

After going all round the Hall, Edward took her down to the stables to show her the twins' palomino ponies who happily munched the carrots and sugar lumps he had brought them. They tickled her hand oddly as they nibbled at the sugar lumps she held out, but Edward assured her they wouldn't bite – they just wanted some more. Monica rather reluctantly patted their soft muzzles, for they were very sweet, but her hands were sticky and she wanted to go to her room to wash. Edward put his arm round her and they walked slowly back up to the Hall.

When Monica opened the door to her room, she found her clothes all laid out on the bed, her pearl necklace with matching earrings neatly arranged on the dressing-table.

She decided to have a bath before dinner. She studied the many bottles along the edge of the bath and finally took a blue one smelling of lilies-of-the-valley, one of her favourite scents. She had brought one of Katarina's magazines, *Harper's and Queen*, with her; it felt rather comical that here she was in a mansion in her own suite with her own bathroom, reading about what the rest of English society was doing. But she was both contented and happy. She could relax in Edward's company.

Monica was just fastening her second earring when Edward knocked on the door.

'Come in. I'm ready.'

'How beautiful you are.'

She actually felt beautiful. She had dug into her holiday money and spent nearly a whole afternoon in the ladies' department at NK in Stockholm where she had finally found a black crepe dress with black satin rosettes on the shoulders and one in the cleavage. Her new shoes were also of black satin.

'Come on, let's go down to the library and have a drink before dinner.'

Unused to walking in such high heels, on their way down the steep stairs, she took his arm. For a moment she imagined she was Lady Hewitt on her way down to meet the evening's guests.

Dinner was wonderful. Mrs McDonald's chicken, her speciality, was exquisite and the purée of carrots and courgettes the best Monica had ever tasted. She had drunk perhaps just a little too much red wine, but they had toasted each other and laughed so much that she had lost count of how many times Edward had filled her glass. With the large silver candlesticks the only lighting, it had all been utterly romantic.

Now they were sitting on the big chesterfield in the library again. Edward got up to get a glass of brandy for himself and suggested that she should try a small glass of Cointreau. He leant over her holding out the glass, and when Monica took it, he kissed her affectionately on the nape of her neck. Her whole body trembled in expectation. They had met not quite a month ago and as yet he had made no approaches. But tonight she knew something was going to happen. She took a sip of the liqueur and coughed. Edward took her glass away and put it down on the table.

'Perhaps too strong for you,' he said, and bent down and kissed her passionately. Monica responded to his kiss with all the longing she felt.

The fire had burnt down and she suddenly shivered. Edward at once took off his jacket and draped it round her shoulders, then he took her hand and pulled her up off the sofa. All shyness gone, when her new shoes pinched on the way up the stairs, she took them off. Like a true gentleman Edward offered to carry them.

With her shoes in his hand, he opened the door to his bedroom. It was a truly beautiful bedroom, if somewhat masculine with all its dark furniture, the only feminine touch a blue floral bedspread with matching curtains.

He took his jacket off her and hung it over a chair, putting her shoes on the floor. Then he pulled down the zip on her dress and helped her out of it, placing it over his jacket.

Monica felt small and vulnerable as she stood there in nothing but her underwear. He kissed her cautiously on the shoulder and neck as he led her over to the big bed. Carefully, he took off her stockings and her thin girdle and ran his hands over her legs, making Monica shudder with pleasure. Then he quickly stood up and started unbuttoning his shirt.

'I'll be back in a moment,' he said and went into the bathroom.

Monica slid down into the bed, feeling the cool linen sheets against her skin. When Edward returned he was wearing a thin silk dressing-gown with an embroidered monogram on the pocket. In the faint light of the bedside lamp, she saw him take it off and let it fall to the floor. He crept slowly into the bed and she shuddered as she felt his naked body against hers. With one hand he eased off her briefs, she helping by kicking them off. She realised there was nothing she wanted more than to feel him inside her. He carefully unhooked her bra and she felt her body clench with pleasure as he covered her breasts with passionate kisses. Monica moaned loudly, his mouth found hers and one hand began to seek its way over her trembling stomach.

Monica could feel him hard against her thigh. She hesitated. She wanted to touch him so much, but didn't know whether she dared. Fumbling, she instead stroked his back, then slowly downwards. Then Edward took her hand and guided it to him. He groaned and took her hand away again. Then he rose a little and smiled, slowly parted her legs and with one single movement he was inside her.

Quite still, resting on his elbows, he kissed her face and ears. Monica began to move against him, but could feel him withdrawing.

'Wait,' he whispered.

Monica didn't understand his hesitation and pressed harder against him. He groaned loudly and a few seconds later it was over.

They lay quite still, intertwined, and she could feel liquid running down the inside of her thigh. Carefully he came out of her and lay beside her.

'Sorry,' he whispered. 'But it's been a long time.'

Tears welled up in Monica's eyes. Now she knew he was hers. She leant over him and took his face in her hands.

'I think I love you,' she whispered.

Edward smiled and switched out the light.

'Fasten your seat belts. Smoking is no longer permitted. We expect to land at Stockholm Bromma airport in fifteen minutes.'

Monica and Katarina removed the last boxes, then closed and locked the metal cupboards. Katarina sat down with the paper-work and tried to concentrate on how many bottles had been consumed on the trip and how much duty-free they had sold. She put down her pen and looked at Monica.

'You haven't said a thing about what it was like.'

'I haven't had a minute. Anyhow, you were out when I got back last night. And we hadn't time this morning.'

'Well you'd better make time. I want to know everything. You could at least tell me if you slept with him.'

'Ssh! Not so loud. Someone might hear you.'

'There's no one here who knows who he is.'

'I didn't mean that.'

'I know you slept with him. I can see it in your eyes.'

'Katarina! Not here, I said.'

'OK, then, but see you at Cecil's tonight? Nine o'clock?'

'Yes, yes,' said Monica as the plane landed. 'But don't be late. I hate waiting.'

'All right, all right. By the way, you must talk to Kjell. What are you going to say to him?'

'Do I have to say anything?'

'Of course you must. You've been seeing the poor boy for almost six months now.'

'Four, actually.'

They undid their seat belts, upended the seats and put on their pale blue coats and little hats.

'Thank you.'

'Thank you.'

She opened the door of the apartment and the smell of pork and cabbage rolls immediately struck her. For some reason, her mother had got it into her head that they were Monica's favourites, but it was really her father who loved them. At least two or three times a month, Gerd cooked 'her daughter's favourite dish'. Monica had nothing against the minced pork, but she always tried to conceal the cabbage it was wrapped in, usually putting a knife over it, or at worst taking her plate out into the kitchen herself, saying she was in a hurry. But then her mother always said she should sit down, she who had been on her feet all day.

She couldn't really understand her mother. As a child she had always been made to help clear the table and do the dishes. God knows, she had hated standing there in the kitchen drying plates. Now she was grown up and had no objections to helping, it seemed almost forbidden.

'Tell us a little about what you've been doing this week,' said Gerd as she put out the fruit salad and vanilla cream.

Her father wanted to light his pipe, but Gerd stopped him.

'Not until we've finished. Tell us all about it after I've brought in the coffee.'

Monica looked around the cosy little dining-room. She had sat there as a child, on the very same chair. Everything was just the same, Dad with his pipe and Mother fussing. After two years abroad, she had realised she could never live like this. If she married Edward she wouldn't have to.

Monica was an only child. When she was younger, her friends with brothers and sisters had envied her not having to share everything. Family life had been tremendously routine. They had rented the same summer cottage as long as she could remember, and every year during winter-term she had the week off school to go skiing, they rented a room at Widow Österlund's up in Härjedalen. On Tuesdays, they had brown beans and pork, on Thursdays pea soup and pancakes; in between a blessed mixture of potato dumplings, black pudding with lingon, sausage with mashed turnips and, sometimes on Sundays, her mother's pride, beef croquettes, boiled potatoes and brown gravy. And the home-made blackcurrant jelly, of course. Not that food in England was any better, but it was different. And she could at least decide for herself there.

For years she had listened to their quiet bickering. Poor Dad.

That he could stand it even felt sad. Gerd did nothing but vacuum clean, polish copper and silver, scrub the floor and the toilet, and iron. Monica remembered with horror the heaps of washing waiting to be ironed.

She wondered if they had ever loved each other. She had never seen her parents show each other the slightest sign of affection. The few times they ever had any kind of physical contact were at parties at Christmas and on birthdays.

Once a month, Dad went to the Oddfellows. All Monica knew about the Oddfellows was that they had had jolly Christmas parties when she was a child.

'Tell us now, dear,' prompted her mother.

Monica really wanted to keep it to herself a little while longer, but at the same time she wanted to share her newfound happiness with her family.

'I've met a wonderful Englishman. He's a lord,' she added cautiously.

'What did you say he was? A lord?'

'Yes, how can I put it. He's a nobleman. Like a count or something.'

'A count. Well I never. What do you say about that, Dad?'

Why did Mother insist on calling him Dad? She was Monica's father, not hers.

'He lives in the most fantastic country mansion outside London. He's got—'

'But, my dear child, have you been there?'

Her father, Gunnar, who would never ordinarily dream of interrupting her, or anyone else for that matter, was looking surprised.

'Yes, of course I have. Otherwise I wouldn't know what it was like, would I?' she said, irritable at being interrupted.

'Yes, but how long have you known each other? Your mother and I haven't heard a word about any count before.'

'We met a month ago at a dinner party with some mutual friends,' she lied. It would have been too difficult to explain the way things had really gone. She sensed her parents would find it hard to accept that she had been given Edward's telephone number on the plane, and she had actually phoned him. 'His wife died three years ago and he has twin girls.'

'Now Monica. Wife and children?'

Monica at once regretted mentioning them. She ought to have known her parents wouldn't understand. And what would they say about his age?

'How old is this lord?'

Monica stirred the watery vanilla cream and put a piece of pear into her mouth. Gerd and Gunnar stared steadily at her as she ate the fruit. Monica looked her mother straight in the eye.

'He's thirty-seven and I—'

'Are you out of your mind?' Gerd looked really upset.

'He's old enough to be your father.'

'He's not, Dad. Then he would have had me when he was seventeen.'

'Well, that's not impossible.'

'But, Monica, you're being really rather naive. He's quite clearly trying to exploit you.'

Monica could feel the tears rising, but was not going to show it. How could they be so narrow-minded? She got up swiftly from her place at the table.

'Monica, come back and sit down. We must talk about this.'

'I knew I couldn't tell you anything,' she cried, slamming the door of her bedroom behind her.

'Monica,' called Gerd.

'Let her be,' said Gunnar and lit his pipe.

Monica was sitting alone in a dark corner. It was nine o'clock and the Cecil was packed out. She had already been there for half an hour. Her parents' comments had been more than she could stand and in her loneliness she had drunk two Brandy Alexanders – she who was always so moderate with alcohol.

Katarina at last arrived, for once she wasn't late; it was Monica who'd arrived early.

'How long have you been here?'

'I've just arrived.' Monica didn't feel like telling her about her parents' reaction; she would be sure to burst into tears after having so much to drink.

'Tell me. No one's listening here. No, wait. We must order a drink first.'

'I don't know where to begin. So much has happened.'

'Yes, but did you sleep with him or not?'

'Yes, we made love, but it's much more than that.'

'Oh, is it? Are you getting married? Good. He must be stinking rich.'

Monica shook her head, confused. 'No, we've not talked about marriage. Yes, well, I suppose he has got money, but that doesn't matter.'

'Don't be silly. Of course it matters. Much better to marry a rich man than a poor man.'

Monica was looking round the ladies department at NK when a saleswoman came and asked whether she could be of service.

'Yes, please. I need a suit and a coat which could be used both in town and in the country.'

The sales assistant showed her a rack of expensive designer clothes and Monica looked with horror at the prices.

'I was thinking of something slightly less expensive.'

For such an exclusive department store, the sales assistant was unusually understanding.

'I think I know just what you're looking for,' she said, and showed Monica a tartan cape with a matching jacket and skirt.

Without even looking at the price tag, Monica decided to try it on. It fitted like a glove, but unfortunately there was a minute tear by the second buttonhole and one button was missing. When she pointed this out, she was told that this was the last they had in stock.

'But I'll talk to the supervisor and perhaps we could take something off the price.'

They took a hundred kronor off, and Monica left with her purchase feeling very satisfied.

Edward had phoned her in Stockholm and invited her to meet his family the following weekend, so she wanted to make a good impression. She had spent last Saturday night at his tiny flat in Angel's Court in St James's. She laughed at the memory of it; it had contained virtually nothing except a bed and a coffee-maker, but she knew he used it only for overnight stays.

She thought about her new purchase. Her holiday money had now all gone, but something told her that the holiday she was to take with Katarina would not now come off.

Outside, it was pouring with rain. Normally she would have simply taken the bus, or even walked, but with her new find, she thought she would stand herself the luxury of a taxi home.

The working week went by at a snail's pace, with nothing to look forward to except Edward's telephone call. He had promised to look in to the girls' flat on Wednesday, but at the last moment some business had got in the way. Oh, well, he would pick her up on Friday and introduce her to his family. Of that she was sure.

Philip was in the kitchen decanting the wine. Edward was on his way with 'the Swedish au pair', as Philip called her in his mind. He couldn't believe that his brother had fallen for a girl of twenty. And a foreigner at that.

He had always hoped Margaret and Edward would get together, particularly after the holiday they had taken together last summer. With her background and especially her money, all Philip's financial problems with the estate would be solved. So much more than just a new roof was needed.

'Philip,' his mother called from the drawing room. 'Come and keep your old mother company and get me a drink.'

In the drawing room, he poured her a gin and tonic and mixed a dry Martini for himself, a task at which he considered himself an expert.

Then they heard a car stopping outside and Mrs McDonald opening the front door. Lady Rose would have liked to take a peep but managed to control herself. She would meet Edward's air hostess in good time.

Edward opened the door to the guest room, went in and put Monica's suitcase down by the dressing-table. The first thing her eye fell on as she went in was an exquisite evening dress lying on the bed. Black velvet, modest neckline with a white organdie collar.

'I wanted you to be extra beautiful this evening, so I took the liberty of buying it without really knowing your taste or size.'

Monica flung her arms round his neck and kissed him tenderly.

'Oh, it's lovely. I'm sure it'll fit me.'

'How long do you need to get ready?'

From his tone of voice she realised that she should take no time at all.

'Will ten minutes be enough?' he asked.

Heavens, she thought. She had been up since five this morning and was dying for a bath, but she didn't bring that up.

'Of course, Edward.'

'Fine, I'll knock on your door.'

She rushed into the bathroom, flung off her clothes and left them in a heap on the floor, then swiftly wet a flannel and rubbed it under her arms and between her legs: a whore's bath was what Katarina called it.

As she was putting the dress on, she couldn't help noticing the label. Bellville Sassoon. It must have been expensive. Luckily she didn't need any make-up. A little Peach Blush would do. She usually wore lipstick, but tonight she decided on lip-gloss. Her mascara was still all right since this morning.

She put on her pearl necklace and earrings. The image that looked back at her in the wardrobe mirror made her shiver with delight. She was ready to meet the family at last.

There was a knock on the door and Edward came in.

'I see it really did suit you. You look fabulous. Come on.'

She had to lift her skirt to avoid tripping on the way down the stairs. She was not used to full-length dresses.

'Monica, I want you to meet my mother, Lady Rose Hewitt.'

'Call me Rose,' said Lady Rose, taking Monica's hand in both hers.

'My brother, Philip.'

'How do you do. A pleasure to meet you.' Monica felt a distinct chill coming from Philip. 'Would you care for a drink?' Philip went on in the same icy voice.

Monica looked appealingly at Edward, who came to her rescue.

'I think Monica would like a little sherry. Another, Mother?'

Edward was busy being bartender.

'Only a small one, and not too strong. You know how careful I am.'

Suddenly there was the sound of children's voices and Edward's twins came rushing in.

'Daddy, Daddy!'

Edward lifted up both girls, one on each arm, and gave them each an affectionate kiss.

'Girls, this is Monica.'

'How do you do. I'm Sarah – and I'm Emma,' they both said at once.

Monica politely shook hands with the two well-brought-up children, then went over to sit beside Lady Rose. She accepted the glass Edward handed her and took a sip of the sherry. Edward sat down in the big wing chair with a girl on each knee. Lady Rose broke the silence.

'Edward tells me you're an air hostess. How brave of you! Once when I was to fly to Deauville, I'll have you know there was almost a disaster. We flew via Paris and there was a terrific storm . . .'

Edward interrupted her.

'Mother dear, that was years ago,' he said. He had heard this story far too many times and wanted to spare Monica; the tale was more or less endless.

Standing slightly apart, Philip watched this family scene. She was certainly beautiful and his mother seemed to have taken to her immediately. But so young. Just a child. What was Edward thinking of?

'Dinner is served.' Mrs McDonald came in to take the twins with her to the kitchen.

'See you tomorrow,' they both said at once as they vanished through the great door.

Monica watched their departure with surprise.

'They aren't going to have dinner with us?'

Philip answered quickly. 'No, they always have their meals in the kitchen.'

37

Monica flushed. She had no idea how the English aristocracy treated their children.

The dinner was extremely good and not at all as formal as Monica had imagined it would be, thanks to Lady Rose, who hardly touched her wine but all the same seemed to be in high spirits or even slightly tipsy.

After the dessert, Mrs McDonald came in with a bottle of Dom Pérignon. Monica gasped as the champagne cork missed by a hair's breadth the big brass chandelier hanging from the ceiling. Having filled their glasses, Edward turned to his mother.

'Mother, Philip – Monica and I are getting engaged this evening.'

As he spoke, he took out a small leather box containing a sapphire and diamond ring, then went over to Monica and put it on her finger. Monica turned scarlet, speechless. Why had he said nothing about his plans?

'Congratulations!' said Lady Rose, picking up her glass of champagne.

'To you, my darling,' said Edward, and he kissed her on the mouth.

Philip seemed less delighted by these rapid developments and nodded briefly.

'I suppose I must congratulate you,' he said, the dissatisfaction in his voice only too evident.

Recovering slightly from the first shock, Monica was now gazing happily at the beautiful ring. If she were dead and this was the kingdom of heaven, then she had no desire whatsoever to return to earth. Her head was in a whirl, but one thing she was perfectly sure of – she had never been happier.

'Oh, Edward. I just wish you'd said something before. It's so sudden, but I do love you.'

Philip was again quick with a comment.

'Hadn't you talked it over before? Then I can quite see why it came as a surprise. You must be as shocked as we are.'

Monica did not quite grasp the implications of his words, but Edward glanced sharply at his brother. Why couldn't he be pleased at their happiness?

38

The rest of the evening passed in a fog. Bemused with happiness, Monica scarcely took in what was going on around her. She could hardly believe how sweet life could be . . .

When Monica came down to breakfast the next morning, Edward was already in the kitchen with the twins. When they saw her coming, they rushed up to her like excited puppies and pulled and tugged at her.

'Are you going to be our new mummy?'

Edward laughed, pleased his little girls already had such trust in his future wife. He knew nothing could ever replace their real mother, but the time had come for the twins to be able to turn to a younger woman. Until now they'd only had their grandmother and Mrs McDonald.

'Can we look at your engagement ring?' they both said at once.

Monica held out her hand and the twins admired it with wide open eyes.

'When we get engaged, we're going to have exactly the same rings as this one.'

'I'll remember that,' said Edward, feeling a glow of paternal pride. 'Shall we go down to the stables?'

'Yes, let's,' smiled Monica, 'but I must first call my mother and father to tell them the wonderful news.'

'Of course. Then we'll wait.'

Finally the exchange informed Monica that her call to Stockholm had come through.

'Mother, are you sitting down?' Monica had decided she might as well get straight to the point, remembering only too well their last conversation. 'Edward and I got engaged last night. Yes, I'm at Hewitt Hall now. Yes, he's standing just beside me. He's given me the most beautiful engagement ring, a sapphire with diamonds all round it. Yes, of course, he can.'

Monica turned to Edward.

'My father wants to speak to you.'

'Hello, Mr Forssgren. I want you to know that I love your daughter with all my heart and will do everything in my power to take care of her.'

He handed back the receiver to Monica. Again she heard her mother's worried voice. 'Monica dear, you're not pregnant, are you?'

'No, of course not, Mother. I must go now, Mother, but I'll be back in Stockholm the day after tomorrow and I promise you I'll tell you all about it. Don't worry. But please be happy for me instead. Yes, I love you both, too. 'Bye then.'

At last, thought Edward. Now they could go down to the stables. He had been waiting like an impatient child to show her his surprise.

Philip had not slept well. He had still not got over the fact that his brother had got engaged to a twenty-year-old Swedish girl, and not only that, hadn't even discussed it with the family. That was hard to take.

How long had he known her? Everything seemed to have been done so hastily. Was she after his title? Or did she think he had money? What was the power she had over him? It was not like Edward to behave like this. Naturally he knew Edward was not nearly as strong a character as he was, but this time things really had gone too far.

Although it was only eleven o'clock, Lady Rose was sitting on her sofa surrounded by her three dogs, a gin and tonic firmly in her hand. She was in a good mood. She loved parties at the Hall. Yesterday they'd had a dinner party, and tonight there was going to be another one.

Of course, the girl was far too young to marry her son, but on the other hand she could see the advantage of a younger woman. She herself longed for company in the daytime and she would be able to teach her so much. They would be spending lots of time together. For that matter, she hadn't seen her son looking so happy for several years and he thoroughly deserved it after all the suffering he had gone through after Mary Elizabeth's death. The girl was pretty, too, and seemed well mannered and unpretentious.

Lady Rose got up and went to get herself another gin and tonic. The book lying open on the sofa was called *Baby, No Return*, by

Craig Stevens. She was very proud of her younger son and liked reading his detective stories. Stuart Corke was such a fascinating character. However had Philip thought him up?

Monica hadn't believed her eyes when Edward opened the stable doors. Alongside the girls' ponies and his own black Arab was another, a golden yellow palomino.

'It's yours, darling,' he had said, and the twins had screamed with delight.

They had spent most of the morning trying to teach her to ride, and she knew the girls were looking forward to the day when they could all go out riding together.

And now, here she was putting clothes on to a complicated paper doll while at the same time the twins kept wanting to hold her hand.

Although Monica was an only child, she could understand their dependency on each other. The girls were identical and as alike as two peas in a pod. Not only did they both talk at once, but they also seemed to finish off each other's sentences. It was impossible to distinguish between them, even their own father found it diffi-cult, and the fact that they dressed alike did not make it any easier. No one could say they were pretty with straggly reddish blonde hair, thin faces and deep set eyes. But their wonderfully open personalities meant that their appearance was soon forgotten.

All three of them were quite unaware that Edward had been standing in the doorway for a while. He had not seen his daughters so full of life for a very long time. It had struck him that he ought to have told his children about his plans before carrying them out, but now he could see with his own eyes that he need not have worried. He had unearthed a jewel in Monica.

A blue Aston Martin DB3 suddenly screeched to a halt in front of the Hall and Edward sprang to life.

'It's Gordon! Come on, you must meet my partner and best friend, Gordon Clarke.' Edward took Monica's hand. The twins had already rushed down the steps.

'Uncle Gordon, Uncle Gordon,' they were shouting.

Mrs McDonald was quickly outside the front door and taking

care of his luggage. Gordon had a very special place in her heart, largely because after every visit he made a habit of putting a clean five-pound note on the dressing-table in the blue guest room, together with a few lines of appreciation.

The girls were equally fond of Gordon. He never came to stay at Hewitt Hall without some surprise for them. This time he held two boxes of chocolates behind his back and let the girls guess which hand he had them in.

'Now for God's sake don't go eating them all at once. You know your father will blame me if you get a stomachache and you don't want your Uncle Gordon to get into trouble, do you?'

The girls giggled and Gordon kissed them on their foreheads.

Gordon didn't only spoil Mrs McDonald and the children. Every time he stayed at Hewitt Hall, he brought with him six bottles of Dom Pérignon. Gordon never made a great show of bringing expensive gifts with him, but this time he had surpassed himself. He whispered something in Mrs McDonald's ear and gave her a brown paper parcel. Edward had no idea that Gordon had just given Mrs McDonald a kilo tin of Beluga caviar, the best in the world.

Monica kept slightly in the background while Gordon was holding court, fascinated by this charismatic man and his expensive presents. He was not only attractive in appearance, she noted. His charming, extroverted manner left no one unmoved. He was in his late thirties, tall with thick dark, slightly curly hair brushed straight back, his brown eyes framed by thick eyelashes. He had a perfect body, the fruits of sporting activities which Edward had told her he assiduously practised wherever he found himself in the world. He was clearly very interested in clothes and appeared to be verging on a perfectionist when it came to his own image. He smelt strongly of Guèrlain Habit Rouge. He smelt, Monica thought, of money.

An exclusive set of Gucci black leather suitcases with red and green stripes was lined up by the car. Gordon was not the kind to be content with one or possibly two suitcases when away for the weekend. Although he was a habitual traveller and ought to have learnt simply to take the things he would be using, he always had his butler pack at least four or five changes of clothing, regardless. You never know, was Gordon's philosophy. Something might turn up to change your plans . . .

Gordon greeted Monica by kissing her hand.

'Very nice to meet you,' Monica managed to say, hoping her blushes didn't show.

'The pleasure is entirely mine.'

He was gazing into her eyes, which didn't help her rising embarrassment, looking her up and down, discreetly glancing sideways at her as he talked to Philip, who had just come sauntering down the stairs into the hall.

'Gordon, I'll have to buy some more aftershave for you tomorrow,' he said smugly. 'From the amount you must be wearing you can't possibly have any left.'

The year before, when he had been a guest on Gordon's yacht in St Tropez, he had himself been the victim of a similar remark and he had waited until now to make use of it. Gordon smiled at him. This was just the kind of humour he appreciated. Now he would have to take some kind of verbal revenge. Sooner or later he would get him. He turned to his friend and partner, ignoring Philip.

'This will be fun, Edward. Especially getting to know your delightful future childbride. Well, don't look so surprised. A little bird by the name of Philip twittered in my ear.'

Philip shot Gordon an angry glance. He had told Gordon in the greatest confidence, although he had known Edward wanted to tell him about Monica himself.

'By the way,' said Philip, turning to Edward as they went upstairs with Gordon's cases, 'I've invited Margaret to dinner tonight.'

'Oh, why?' said Edward with ill-concealed irritation. He and Margaret hadn't seen each other since last summer when they had shared a house in France.

'I thought it'd be nice to make up the numbers.'

On her way to her room, where she'd decided to take a bath, Monica heard quite clearly Edward's agitated voice.

'What do you mean by inviting Margaret? I don't understand

you. Yesterday you were rude to Monica and today you've invited Margaret of all people.'

'I don't consider I was rude. But seriously, have you thought over this situation? You go rushing headlong into an engagement with a little foreign air hostess. What has she got to bring to Hewitt Hall? I've always regarded you and Margaret as a couple. She is just what we need here. You can't possibly think that Monica will be accepted in our circle?'

Monica closed her door without a sound, tears rising. Wasn't she grand enough? And who was this Margaret? Her thoughts swirled round in her head as she threw herself down on the bed in floods of tears.

After dinner, coffee was served in the drawing room. Philip and Margaret were on one sofa and Lady Rose and Monica on the other. Edward and Gordon were standing over by the drinks.

'What would you like to drink, Margaret?'

'A Grand Marnier, please.'

'And what can I offer my dear brother? Armagnac?'

'No thanks, I'm all right.'

'Mother?'

'A very, very small gin and tonic, please.'

'Monica, dear heart, what can I get you? A Crème de Menthe perhaps? I'm sure you'd like it.'

Was he trying to make up for having neglected her at dinner? Monica had felt like an outsider from the outset. The conversation had circled round Edward, Philip, Gordon and Margaret all the time. They had seemed to be deliberately mentioning names of people she didn't know. And although her English was excellent, it was hard to keep up when they used expressions she'd never even heard before. Edward had certainly been generous with Gordon's champagne and caviar and now and again his lips had brushed her cheek, but after that he immediately joined in the others' conversation again.

The whole evening had been filled with anecdotes and stories she didn't understand. They all seemed to have a great deal in common and had talked about childhood memories interspersed with recent stories about friends and acquaintances currently in their social circle.

At first she had done her best to keep up with the conversation, if it could be called that when you just laughed when others did and smiled in the right places.

Lady Rose had been the most spontaneous and had for a while devoted herself to Monica, telling her about her great passion for gardening. But it wasn't long before Margaret had attracted Lady Rose's attention with some up-to-date information about some neighbour's apparently scandalous divorce.

Monica had carefully studied Margaret over dinner. What had her Edward and the woman sitting across the table from her had together? She was sure she would've instinctively disliked her even if she hadn't happened to have heard Philip's hints about her relationship with Edward.

The woman's face was as white as a sheet, her lips blood-red and her eyes black. Her equally dark hair was drawn smoothly back into a chignon and her long diamond earrings glittered in the candlelight. A diamond brooch in the form of a flower was fastened to her short-sleeved silk dress, so large and glittering that it had surely been placed there to conceal the fact that she lacked any bust. She had carelessly draped her chinchilla stole behind her.

Having sought consolation in champagne and wine at dinner, Monica now made her apologies and left the drawing room. She needed a breathing space. She ran up the stairs to her bedroom and sat in the darkness thinking with loathing of the hours that had just gone by. When she closed her eyes, she could clearly see Margaret's affected expression in front of her and she was suddenly, absurdly, struck by her likeness to Dracula. Only the cloak was missing.

She glanced at the little gold watch Gunnar and Gerd had given her when she had graduated from high school. The face was no bigger than a shirt button, so she had to make a great effort to focus on it, perhaps because of all she had drunk that evening. She'd been upstairs almost ten minutes. She would have to clench her teeth and go back into the fray. Suppose they were talking about her in her absence? She could imagine Margaret making disparaging remarks and Philip adding his bit so that Edward would at last be convinced . . .

No, pull yourself together, Monica. She got up and pushed those thoughts aside. She shouldn't have drunk so much. That always made you imagine things.

'Darling, you were gone so long,' Edward said when she walked back in. 'We were beginning to wonder . . .'

Why did he speak to her as if she were a child? She was usually touched by his consideration, but now she couldn't help comparing it with the way he spoke to Margaret, as an equal.

Monica fingered her engagement ring. Lady Rose and Margaret were looking at a photograph album, but Monica didn't really want to know what was in it. She wanted the past to disappear so that only she and Edward existed.

'Edward,' she pleaded, 'I'm so tired and my legs ache terribly. It must be all that riding and all the fresh air I've had today. Do you mind if I go to bed? Don't misunderstand me. I love Toto, my horse, but . . .'

'Of course, darling,' Edward broke in. 'I'll be up soon.'

He kissed her lightly on the lips and she went back up to her room, hoping in her heart of hearts that Edward would forgive her absence.

Exhausted, she crept down between the sheets. The room was cold, so although she usually slept naked, tonight she'd put on her pink flannel nightie. Suddenly the floral wallpaper seemed to be coming towards her. She kicked off the covers, sat up and switched on the light. Her head was spinning still and with a sickening lurch she ran to the bathroom and threw up. She wiped her face and felt a little better. Then she cleaned her teeth and splashed cold water on to her face – she didn't want Edward to know what had happened.

The door slowly opened and she could see Edward's silhouette in the strip of light in the doorway. She was glad the wallpaper was no longer moving.

'Dear heart, are you asleep? I've been longing for you so.' He started undressing, but instead of putting his clothes on the chair as usual, he left them lying on the floor and came to bed.

'Monica, my heart, my sweet little heart.'

He kept repeating the words and she realised that he had also had too much to drink. She could smell his breath as he clumsily kissed her. He had at least cleaned his teeth. He was pulling at her long nightdress and finally managed to get it over her hips.

'I love you, Monica,' he mumbled, his hand wandering up towards her breast.

At that moment, she felt nothing, but she knew she had to let him have what he desired. He was quickly inside her and this time he held out longer than the first time. She wished he would come soon.

He lay over her without moving, and she was unsure whether it had happened or not, but the weight of him meant she could hardly breathe.

Edward was asleep.

4

Hewitt Hall was preparing for the wedding. The little chapel at the back of the Hall was going to be used for the first time in years and Lady Rose had taken on the task of putting it in order. The walls needed re-plastering, some of the pews needed replacing and the mullioned windows also needed looking over. Unfortunately she knew only too well there was not enough money to restore the beautiful murals.

She had asked John, the rather simple handyman, to come and work full-time for a few weeks. He usually came once a week to help Mrs McDonald with the floors, the bathrooms and the big windows. He also washed the vehicles and polished them so that you could see your reflection in them. If there was any time over, he used to help in the stables. John loved horses and the love was mutual.

On 28 December, Monica flew to London, this time as a passenger. As she was a stewardess, she could fly for free, provided there was a vacant seat. She was in luck this time and had a seat in first-class.

She had missed Edward, although they spoke on the telephone every day, and she could hardly contain herself until she was back with him. She'd spent Christmas with Gerd and Gunnar as arranged, but she and Edward were going to see the New Year in together, and she was on her way to London with Christmas presents for Edward and the girls in her luggage.

Philip had been more difficult. The last time they'd met, he had been quite courteous to her. She still couldn't understand what he

49

had against her, and she presumed his sudden politeness had something to do with Edward. To show that she bore him no grudge, she had bought him a present of a traditional wooden Dala horse.

She had found two small glass domes for the girls, each containing a Santa Claus and a sledge. When you shook them, it snowed. Edward was to have a dark blue cashmere scarf from Harrods, and her future mother-in-law a lovely book on English gardens. For Mrs McDonald she had bought a small bottle of Floris bath oil.

After she'd told Katarina she was going to get married and would no longer be sharing the flat with her, she had moved all her belongings to the Hall. At last she had been able to legitimately share a room with Edward: they were engaged, after all, and were going to be married imminently.

Since she'd met Edward, she'd tried to learn something about the lifestyle of the aristocracy. But she could sense she was still not really accepted, though she hoped things would change once she became Lady Hewitt.

Tomorrow she and Lady Rose were going to Norman Hartnell's, the Queen's dress designer, to try on her wedding dress again. Made of thick white satin with a fairly high neckline and half-length sleeves, it went right down to the white satin shoes, slightly longer at the back. The bodice was embroidered with small pearls and on her head she was going to wear the traditional bridal tiara that had been in the Hewitt family for centuries. With that as the starting point, Hartnell had created a veil with pearls and silk flowers.

Although the dress had not been quite finished the last time she had tried it on, she could see from the sketches it was just as she had wanted it. She would not just look like a lady, but like a princess. Lady Rose agreed with her on that score. Monica was actually very grateful for Lady Rose's support in coming with her; what's more, she had such excellent taste.

The plane landed and she went through customs, out into the arrivals hall and there was confronted with Katarina.

Monica was extremely surprised. She'd thought she would have to take the train on her own this time, as Edward was stuck in the office, though Mrs McDonald was going to meet her at the station.

'Katarina? What are you doing here?'

They had spoken on the phone, but as Gerd had fallen and broken her arm when cleaning the small crystal chandelier in the living room, Monica had had to help with all the Christmas preparations, so they hadn't had time to meet over the holiday.

'You don't sound particularly pleased. I'm here to spend a few days with my best friend before she gets married.'

Monica suddenly realised Katarina wanted to go with her to Hewitt Hall, and she just couldn't explain that she would have to speak to Edward first. Katarina wouldn't know how the English aristocracy functioned. There were rooms to put in order and housekeepers who had to be informed. But then why not, she thought, rebelliously.

'Come with me,' she said. 'I'm sure Edward would have no objections.'

The two friends boarded the airport bus to London. Then they had to take the train from Paddington and Mrs McDonald would meet them at the station and she would explain that her friend was going to stay for a few days.

Philip was more than just surprised when Mrs McDonald, Katarina and Monica came in through the front door. Who was this apparition, he wondered in appalled astonishment.

Katarina's long dark hair was hanging round her shoulders like a cape, her thin mouth bright red as usual, like the polo-necked jersey tightly stretched across her padded breasts. She was wearing a green and blue striped skirt that reached almost down to the ground, and round her waist she had tied a floral shawl instead of a belt. On top of it all she had a dark blue cape with a red flannel lining. Red gloves and boots completed the outfit.

Monica hadn't given a thought to Katarina's appearance. She was so used to her friend's imaginative creations, she had never even considered they might be inappropriate. But to judge from Philip's look, she realised that things weren't exactly as they should be. So she acted quickly.

51

'Philip,' she said. 'This is my friend Katarina. She's staying for a few days. Mrs McDonald, would you be so kind as to put the pink guest room in order?'

For the first time, she wanted to show Philip she was going to be Lady of the Manor. She had never seen him look so astonished before, and the sight secretly pleased her.

'Mrs McDonald, could you please also set the table for four. Philip, you'll have dinner with us this evening, won't you?' Even Monica was surprised at her own new-found authority.

'Come on, Katarina. I'll show you your room. See you at dinner,' she added, turning swiftly to Philip, then she hurried on, not waiting for a reply.

Philip was dumbfounded. How dare she behave as if she owned the place? For a moment he had actually forgotten she was his brother's fiancée and that the wedding was to take place in ten days' time.

Monica remembered her wedding through a kind of fog. The little chapel was lit entirely by candles, just as she had requested, with pink lilies, Edward's favourite flowers, decorating the chancel. The ceremony had been simple, but important to them both, and when they exchanged rings and he then kissed her, she'd had to fight down her tears of joy.

She hadn't dared glance at the front pew where Gerd and Gunnar were sitting because she knew her mother's face would be tearful, just like Lady Rose's. The twins had been bridesmaids in long pale green dresses with wreaths of flowers on their heads and had behaved throughout like little angels. Philip had sat rigidly upright, looking as if he wished he were somewhere else a long way away. Gordon had been Edward's best man. Perhaps that was why Philip had been so awkward?

The wedding dinner had been small and intimate, with only a few guests apart from her parents. She would have liked to invite Katarina as well, but after her riotous behaviour the weekend before the wedding, she could hardly ask Edward and Philip to accept Katarina's presence.

However, she had to admit that she had really enjoyed that last, hilarious weekend although she would never have dared admit it to the family. She was also certain Lady Rose had enjoyed herself in Katarina's irrepressible company. If Monica had not known that Lady Rose was extremely careful about alcohol, she could have sworn she had been rather under the influence that evening.

She'd had to go upstairs and throw up, though thank goodness Edward hadn't noticed anything, but she hadn't been feeling all that well recently. Presumably all the preparations for the wedding had made her nervous and stressed, as she'd also lost her appetite.

They spent their honeymoon in Bermuda, at Gordon's villa on the beach. Apart from the cook, they were looked after by five servants who had obeyed their slightest wish.

Monica usually worshipped the sun and could lie for hours on the beach, but she was troubled by the heat and stayed indoors most of the time. Edward loved water-skiing and tennis, so he'd been in seventh heaven. However, every afternoon they had swum in the heated pool and afterwards had enjoyed exotic drinks. They seldom went out, as everything they needed was within reach.

Edward had been more loving than ever and had wanted to make love every night, but somehow Monica had lost the desire to, although she said nothing to Edward. To be perfectly honest, he probably hadn't noticed any difference, either.

She'd also begun to be irritated by the slightest little thing and on several occasions she found herself biting her lip to stop herself from bursting into tears.

She remembered when Edward had come back with a coconut and insisted they should drink the milk together. It had revolted her to the extent that she felt sick. She had never drunk coconut milk before and had no idea why she reacted to it so fiercely.

But then she had not known she was pregnant.

5

Monica had quickly adapted to her new rôle as mistress of Hewitt Hall, and during the years that had passed since the wedding, she'd been busy, occupied with her family.

Robert was now four and demanded a great deal of attention and the twins came home for the school holidays. Monica could no longer keep count of how many times they had tried to teach her to jump with Toto. She loved riding but simply couldn't master jumping. Either she stood too high in the saddle and fell over the horse's neck, or she leant too far back and lost her balance.

But today Sarah and Emma had challenged her. They had constructed a course with a number of low jumps and they were sure she could manage. Monica studied the course and reckoned she could manage the first four, but the fifth and last looked rather too high.

'Girls, you'll have to lower that last one.'

'Oh, Monica, you can manage that. Toto's such a good jumper.'

'Well, you start and I'll study your technique specially thoroughly this time.'

The girls set off. How simple it looked. They seemed to be floating through the air.

'See how easy it is,' they said in unison when they got back.

Monica thought to herself that the time really had come when they should stop talking at the same time in that way.

'Oh, well, look out then. Here I come.'

She dug her heels gently into Toto and he responded by setting off at an easy canter. Monica stood up in the stirrups and leant forward. The first jump went well. Toto increased speed slightly. He liked jumping, she knew that.

'No, steady, Toto.' She pulled on the reins. The third and fourth jump went fine; the fifth looked further away, and this time she let the horse increase speed.

She was feeling sure now, leaning forward and preparing herself, but at that moment Lady Rose appeared and her three dogs rushed barking at the horse. Monica had no time to see what was happening, but Toto suddenly refused the jump. Head first, she was flung off straight into the heavy wooden bar. She heard the girls scream but after that she remembered nothing.

Monica woke with a terrible headache. Thank goodness she was in her own bed. She hated hospitals. When she tried to turn her head to look at the little blue enamelled clock on the bedside table, it hurt so much she immediately abandoned the idea. The doctor had suggested she should take only two Panadol for the pain, but he'd given her a prescription for her nausea. Thank goodness she didn't have to feel sick and have a headache at the same time.

To think she was pregnant again. Of course she ought to have recognised the signs, but what with Robert to look after and the girls home for the summer holidays, she'd simply had no time to think about it. Also, Mrs McDonald had been away the week before, so she'd had much more to do than usual. With all the household chores, she hadn't had enough sleep and given little thought to her tiredness and nausea.

Gerd had come over from Sweden to help, but as her English was not particularly good, Monica'd had to be around all the time to interpret for her, especially with the twins who were so talkative. Also, unfortunately, Edward disliked her speaking Swedish with Gerd, but heavens, what else was she to do? Her mother's school English was hardly more than thank you and goodbye.

Edward's attitude meant the relationship between her and her mother was always rather strained when he was around, which saddened Monica very much. She simply had to get him to understand that just because they spoke their own language, it didn't mean they were talking about him. She couldn't understand her husband on this score. He had a number of minor odd whims which she was able to tolerate, but that anything as natural as speaking to your mother in your own language should be a problem, she simply couldn't comprehend. So Gerd seldom came to stay with them at the Hall. Instead, Monica preferred to go to Stockholm to be with her parents. But today Edward must have been grateful that Gerd was there after all.

It had just struck one o'clock and Edward was thinking of asking Mrs McDonald to take a tray up to Monica, but he wasn't sure whether they ought to wake her.

To think he was to be a father again. He would go through fire and water for his children, but with the uncertainty of his present financial situation, he wished they could have waited another year or so. But at least he'd just completed some transactions which he hoped would be profitable within the next eighteen months.

The running costs of the Hall were astronomical and most of the small trust Lord Hewitt had left had gone to his mother. Then there were the twins' school fees, and now they were beginning to develop an eye for clothes. Every day they seemed to want money for something new.

Mrs McDonald's salary had certainly not been raised for many years, so the time had come for that. Good heavens, how awkward it would be if she came and asked for a rise now. Nor were four horses cheap to keep although he had been able to dismiss the full-time stable girl when it turned out that John was more than capable of doing the job.

And then there was Monica. He wished he'd told her about his financial situation when they'd married, but she'd been only twenty, and anyhow Philip had been fiercely against it. That wasn't the kind of thing you talked about. But his wife was not exactly extravagant. He had given her twenty pounds a week plus an account at Harrods, but recently he'd asked her not to use it, as he had problems paying their bill.

It had been a relief to confess what the situation really was. Monica had been very understanding and only a few months later she and his mother had started organising private tours round the Hall and the famous rose garden. After the tour, Mrs McDonald served coffee and home-made ginger biscuits. For all this they charged ten shillings per head. His mother's and Monica's tours contributed more than they knew towards keeping things afloat.

On his side, Philip had made numerous trips to Christie's and Sotheby's. Together, the two brothers had spent many a night arranging the pictures in both the hall and the south wing so that the empty spaces shouldn't be too visible, and, in some places, they had got John to fill in the holes left by the hooks. It was no fun seeing the family treasures going under the hammer, but there was no other way out. Hewitt Hall was like a bottomless well when it came to money.

Sometimes Edward was actually envious of his brother. As a confirmed bachelor, he had no one else but himself to keep and the income from his books was his own. Edward was sure it came to several thousand pounds a year. True, Philip no longer took a salary from the trust, but Edward still thought he might offer to make a contribution now and again.

Philip knew only too well what the financial situation at Hewitt Hall was. He did the accounts and it pained him every time a picture or a carpet was sold at auction. But what could they do? That was the only way they could keep the Hall. Otherwise it would have to be sold or the National Trust persuaded to take it on.

He had read that Lord Bath at Longleat House had turned a part of his land into a lion enclosure and the public paid to drive through it. Philip hated his mother's and Monica's tours round the Hall. The very thought of people snooping round their home was repugnant to him. At Longleat at least they stayed out of doors.

His books had sold very well a few years ago and he'd had great hopes at the time when Peter Sellers had enquired about the film rights. But it had all dragged on and then he'd heard no more about it. He had just found out that Sellers had played the part of a certain Inspector Clouseau in his latest film, and he had had a dreamy vision that that character might equally well have been Inspector Corke. He wanted to see the film in case there were any similarities.

In the Fifties, he had had two books in the best-seller list, maybe not at the top, but all the same . . . Sales had now gone down markedly and his agent had told him his style was far too old fashioned and that he must find another or that would be the end of Stuart Corke.

Pride had forbidden him to tell Edward about his tangled finances, so his dear brother still lived in the belief that he earned big money from his writing. He had simply been unable to argue about the matter when Edward had pleaded with him not to draw a salary for his work at the Hall.

And Edward ought to know what trouble there had been with Jackson's recently when Philip had dealt with the payment for the last twelve deliveries. Where did all that wine go? Mother drank practically nothing, and he was quite content with a cocktail before dinner then going on to water. He couldn't help wondering just how much Monica and Edward really drank.

Edward got up out of his armchair in the library and went along to the kitchen. He was relieved. The doctor had assured him that both Monica and the expected child were all right. All Monica needed was to rest in bed. She was young and she was also only in the second month.

According to Sarah and Emma, she had just been approaching the fifth jump when his mother's dogs had come rushing up and barked at Toto. The horse had been frightened, refusing the jump at the last moment, and that was how Monica had been thrown.

He must get Mother to discipline her dogs better in future. This time Monica had come out of it with nothing worse than concussion and a few scratches, but it could have been much more serious.

He opened the kitchen door and looked in. He didn't often set foot in there, for these were Mrs McDonald's domains. His mother-in-law was sitting at the table with Robert on her lap.

'Daddy, Daddy, listen! Yog hater Robet.'

'What does that mean?'

'It's Swedish for "my name is Robert".'

Gerd seemed to be extremely happy. She worshipped her

grandchild and had just heard the good news that Monica was expecting again.

'Um – um – how is my dotter?'

'She's still asleep. I was just about to ask Mrs McDonald to take up a lunch tray.'

'Yes, yes,' said Gerd, though she hadn't understood a word.

Edward found it very difficult to communicate with his mother-in-law and couldn't make out why she went on asking questions when she couldn't understand the answer. Gerd was a simple woman with no great pretensions and she preferred the kitchen to any drawing room. But today, at least, Edward was glad she was there.

'Daddy, can I come with you to see Mummy?'

'Me also?' said Gerd with an appealing smile.

Edward nodded briefly.

'The tray's ready,' said Mrs McDonald.

'Oh, thank you. I'll take it up.'

The housekeeper looked very put out. That had never happened before, and was not at all appropriate.

'Are you sure?'

'Quite sure.'

Together with Gerd and Robert, he left the kitchen and crossed the great hall.

Monica had eaten as much of the vegetable soup as she could, but still had to leave half of it. She had taken two Panadol, so her headache was better, if not quite gone. Thanks to the other tablets, she no longer felt so sick. If only she'd had those miracle pills when she'd been expecting Robert.

The morning sickness in her first pregnancy had started on their honeymoon in Bermuda, then had simply got worse. She had spent most of the first three months in bed to avoid the waves of nausea. Naive as she was, she thought nothing could complete a relationship quite like having a child with the person you loved.

Reality had been different. With Edward in London most of the week and Rose as her only company, meals were the only bright spots of the day. She loved going to see Rose in her warm little cottage, the dining room with its dark ceiling beams, the long sideboard laden with beautiful silver, and Rose's drinks tray. She had spent many amusing evenings there, and that was where she had discovered Rose's secret.

When Monica had first come to the Hall, her impression had been that Rose was very moderate with alcohol, but after a few years of lunches and dinners with her, she now knew better. Apart from the drinks Rose was served, she always added some from her own store and Monica had found this out quite by chance.

After one long dinner with guests from Edward's circle of friends, she'd come across Rose with the gin bottle in one hand and a medicine bottle in the other. Rose had looked round but hadn't noticed Monica in the doorway. Then with a practised hand she had quickly filled the medicine bottle and stuffed it into her black handbag. Now Monica understood. This explained Rose's high spirits at innumerable dinners when she apparently only sipped at her wine. Oh well, her secret would stay safe with Monica.

Over the years, Monica had won Rose over completely to her side. But for some peculiar reason, Philip still disliked her intensely and on occasions had tried to make her life as miserable as possible. She had taken the matter up with Edward, but he had waved it aside, saying that it had nothing to do with her personally. Philip was probably under pressure from having to run the estate at the same time as think up exciting situations for his books, he said. Night after night he sat up in the little study he had fixed up in the attic, and the light in there could sometimes be seen at four or five in the mornings.

'Imagine yourself sitting up half the night and then doing accounts in the daytime. No wonder he's irritable.'

Being up half the night was something Monica knew about only too well. When Robert was born, he had at first woken up every other hour. She had not had enough milk and had to bottle-feed him, so she had a refrigerator installed in the bedroom, and kept the night's supply of bottles ready for heating up. They had an electric kettle in the bedroom, and when Robert woke up crying, she took a bottle out and warmed it up from the kettle. When

Edward was at home, she fed Robert in the bathroom so as not to disturb him.

Most of the women in their circle had also become friends of hers, although it had been difficult at first, as it had taken some time for them to accept her, for despite everything, she was a foreigner. But her Swedish upbringing and open, unaffected manner soon meant she was much liked, even popular.

Many of her new women friends had expressed surprise that she had no nanny. But Monica had told them that she and Edward wanted to look after their first-born son together without help for the first couple of months. Of course they would get a nanny later on. But that had not happened.

Later she had realised that they were never going to have a nanny, and that Edward had no intention of helping to look after his child. Instead Mrs McDonald had to work harder than ever. But the proud father was overjoyed at having a son and an heir to the title and Hewitt Hall.

When Robert was born he was the most beautiful child imaginable with his thick dark hair, Edward's dark deep-set eyes and his mother's nose and mouth, enchanting everyone who saw him. In time, his hair had grown fairer and at four it was brown. Monica refused to have it cut and to Edward's great embarrassment they often heard people say how pretty their daughter was.

Monica loved her son above everything else and because Edward was away so often, the boy gave her all his love and affection. At weekends when they had dinner parties, she always let Robert stay up to greet their guests, despite her husband's protests. On nights when Edward was away, Robert was allowed to sleep in her bed, an impossibility when Edward was at home.

'Mummy, I love you,' Robert often whispered, crawling into bed next to her, and with his small arms round her neck, they fell asleep together.

Edward's and her sex life had never been all that marvellous but now that she had Robert, she didn't let that worry her much. Edward was usually tired when he got back on Friday evenings, and their many social engagements over the weekend meant their sex life suffered. There was always someone to lunch or dinner at weekends, and there were shoots in the autumn. Edward liked shooting, using his treasured gun. His father had given it to him for his eighteenth birthday.

Sometimes their life together seemed to be based on how many parties they could give or go to, but it became more and more difficult to get credit from the local butcher and Jackson's in London. To be able to accept invitations, they were also very aware that they had to invite people back. If it had not been for Gordon, it would never have worked.

His generosity seemed to be limitless and he often stood them the cost of their parties. Monica was genuinely fond of him and admired him for the social creature he was. Edward often complained that Gordon disappeared sometimes, not just from the office, but from his flat. Days could go by when he was inaccessible and no one had any idea where he was, though despite this, the firm apparently flourished.

Every time Edward complained, Monica always defended him.

'He's a bachelor and doesn't have to consider anyone else. Anyhow, you're at the office to make sure everything ticks over. Be grateful instead that he relies on you to run it all.'

However, her defence of him had little effect. Edward would usually mutter something like, 'Maybe you're right', but as soon as Gordon vanished again, he made the same complaint. Monica realised it had something to do with the fact that Edward didn't consider himself Gordon's equal, but as an employee, which in fact he was. She had found that out by chance the year before.

Together with Gordon, Monica had been very busy arranging Edward's fortieth birthday celebrations. They were going to have a surprise party at Les Ambassadeurs in Park Lane and had been secretly planning it very carefully for two months.

Edward wasn't in the habit of celebrating his birthday and nor was this year to be an exception. But as a result of Monica's stubborn pleading, he had reluctantly agreed to have ten or so close friends to dinner on the Saturday after his birthday. Consequently he was taken quite unawares when on the Wednesday evening, Gordon suggested they should have a glass of champagne at Les Ambassadeurs to celebrate his real birthday.

63

The club was packed and Edward was taken entirely by surprise. Monica and Gordon had succeeded in getting together two hundred friends and acquaintances right back from Edward's schooldays at Eton.

Ordinarily it would never have occurred to Monica to rummage through her husband's papers, but she had to find address books and old school newsletters to trace people from Edward's past. She'd found a folder of documents dated from long before they had married, a number of authorisations and some correspondence between Gordon and Edward. An agreement concerning the firm showed that Edward received twenty-five per cent of the profits, while Gordon was the sole shareholder. So Edward was indeed only an employee.

The fact that Edward had not told her the truth about his relationship with Gordon had come as a severe shock to her. He had expressly told her on several occasions that he was Gordon's partner, and there was no reason to doubt the information, as the firm was called Hewitt & Clarke Ltd.

She had never taken it up with him. She didn't really know why, but she had realised that it was a sensitive subject. But why Gordon had agreed to call them partners was quite beyond her. Not that she understood their business at all, but this did seem to be somewhat odd.

True, at a very early stage she had got used to things not always being as they appeared to be. Gradually she had come to see that despite their fine titles and great estates, members of the aristocracy were often short of cash.

Being Lady Hewitt was perhaps for many people an enviable position, but in Monica's case it was largely a matter of attending as many charitable events as possible, sometimes her physical presence apparently quite unnecessary as long as they could use her title on their letterheading.

Mrs McDonald knocked cautiously on her door.

'May I take the tray, my lady?'

'Of course, Nettie. Come on in.' Monica seldom used Mrs McDonald's first name, but she'd heard the consideration in her voice and felt a surge of affection for the elderly lady.

Mrs McDonald held her hand in hers and said how glad she was things hadn't been any worse and that the expected baby was not hurt.

'Don't worry about Robert,' Mrs McDonald went on. 'He's having great fun with his grandmother. It's amazing how children communicate despite the language barrier. Do you want anything else before I take the tray down? Maybe you'd like me to remake the bed?'

'No thanks, Nettie. All I want is to rest for a little while.'

Mrs McDonald closed the door behind her and seconds later Monica was sound asleep.

Monica awoke from the anaesthetic and the first thing she was able to focus on properly was an open fireplace and a glowing mock-coal electric fire. On the right of it was an armchair covered with floral cretonne, behind that a tall window with curtains in the same material. She was in the Welbeck Street Nursing Home, a private maternity clinic.

Her baby was due on the 19th February, so two days beforehand she had moved into the tiny flat in Angel's Court with Edward. She would have preferred to stay at home in Wiltshire until the pains started, but Edward had insisted she should be near to the nursing home.

She had reluctantly left Robert. He had been impatiently waiting for a little brother or sister to play with and had been given a labrador puppy as a stopgap which Monica and Edward had agreed he would look after himself, so that he wouldn't feel neglected when the new baby came home.

Robert loved Ruffi, a name he himself had decided on. Monica had been fascinated by the responsibility a four year old could feel towards another living creature. Robert took him for long walks, sometimes all the way down to the lodge. He had never before gone that far and Monica would have preferred him not to, but Edward had told her she was being overprotective.

She used to stand watching as he eagerly ran down the drive, and the sight filled her with happiness. How big he'd grown. Suddenly she was able to feel how she longed to be holding the new baby in her arms. Edward had assured her that, after the birth, he would spend less time in London and more with her and the children.

The expected day had come and gone and Monica had impatiently paced the little flat in Angel's Court. To try to start labour, she'd taken long walks in Green Park and on the night of the twenty-first, at last her waters broke.

Edward had driven her at top speed to the clinic and she was installed in a room as unlike a hospital ward as it could be. It reminded her of a smallish living room with an open fire and comfortable armchairs. The only thing that revealed what the room was used for was the bed with its green bedspread and characteristic frame.

The labour pains had been moderate, but had gone on all night, so she hadn't slept a wink. At half past five in the morning, the contractions had been coming very quickly, every third minute, and soon after that every thirty seconds. The pains had been unendurable and she knew she couldn't take much more without some kind of painkiller. It felt like someone had taken a pair of iron tongs and twisted her insides.

'Give her gas,' the doctor had ordered, and the nurse at once put the mask over her face.

'Press down,' she heard the doctor and the nurse say through the mist.

'Push hard, I can see the head.'

Monica had greedily breathed in the gas. She'd still felt pain, but it seemed to belong to someone else's body. Both the doctor and the nurse had urged her to press down. And pressed down she had, as best she possibly could. Dripping with sweat and with a heartrending scream, she had pushed out the head. The doctor had helped by rotating the child so that its shoulders should be in the right place and the little body would come out more easily.

'Push, now, push hard,' they had urged her in unison.

And so with all her strength she had pressed as hard as she could and a few moments later felt the baby being born.

The doctor had cut the umbilical cord. She collapsed totally exhausted, and when she came to again, she noticed both the doctor and the nurse had gone. Where was Edward?

Monica knew he'd been in the waiting room. He'd come in now and again, but when the pains had been too severe, he'd left the room, unable to bear seeing her suffering.

Now just as she reached out to push the bell, the door opened and a totally strange nurse came in.

'Lady Hewitt, Dr Grant has asked me to give you an injection.'

'Injection? Why?' Monica said dully. 'Where's my baby?'

'I don't know,' the nurse answered to both questions.

Monica could just make out Edward and the doctor in the doorway, behind them the nurse with the baby wrapped in a large hospital blanket. Monica still felt dazed, but pleasantly so, almost as if she'd left her body. She'd opened her mouth to speak but was now so relaxed her lips wouldn't move. Was it the injection making her feel like this?

Then Edward stood above her. 'Monica, my darling. I don't know how to tell you.'

She saw his eyes fill with tears and then he swallowed, struggling for words, but unable to get any out.

My baby? Is my baby alive? she wanted to ask, knowing she'd seen the nurse with the baby in her arms but the drug had done its work and she was too dazed to get a word out. Slowly, she was beginning to feel desperate, for not knowing was worse than anything.

Dr Grant put his arm round Edward's shoulders, and now Monica could see quite clearly that Edward was crying. She had never seen him cry before.

What's happened? Why doesn't anyone say anything? Her thoughts whirled. She was imprisoned by the drug and the pleasant feeling had now turned to panic. At all costs, she had to get out of bed, but her arms were too heavy and she was unable to lift them. She let out a moaning sound, as if appealing for an explanation.

Dr Grant sat down on a chair by her bed and took her hand in his. Monica realised that something had gone very wrong.

'Monica, my dear,' Dr Grant said in a soothing voice.

Then the doctor and Edward floated together into one person

and she saw herself, as if from above, reaching out for her baby, but the nurse refusing to hand it over.

The room suddenly started revolving, the floral cretonne floating like a sail in front of her eyes and she heard someone calling her name time and time again. Then everything went black.

6

'Where the hell have you been? Gino has been fine-combing the whole place looking for you.' Eddie was boiling with rage and jealousy. He'd seen Katarina dancing, pressed up against that young Brazilian all right.

'I only went out to get some hash for later, so we could ease off. You know how randy you get from hash, and tonight I've got a surprise that'll make you crazy with desire. Do I have to say more than that I was down at the sex shop in Wardour Street.'

Katarina walked straight across the little office and sat down on his lap. With obvious right of ownership, she put her hand on his crotch and massaged it a little. She soon felt it hardening.

'Darling, don't you trust me? You were the one who wanted me to dress provocatively and dance with the guests. We agreed on that.'

'Come off it. I saw you pressing up against that Brazilian.'

'For Christ's sake, Eddie, lay off. He's nothing but a kid. You don't think I'm so bloody stupid that I go necking with a little schoolboy on the dance floor, do you? Tease them a bit, yes, but why should I go further when I've a stud waiting for me later?'

She cautiously licked his neck and put her tongue in his ear, rubbed her hand up his thigh; he was really hard now. She ran her nails over it and clearly saw he liked that. But he stopped her by putting his hand on hers.

'Yes, but where did he get to? I saw you wriggling away at him, and minutes later you were both gone.'

'Eddie, just give over, will you. You don't mean you want me to keep track of where our guests get to after they've left the club as

well? I met Diana on her way to a guy to get some hash. I was in a
hurry and couldn't see you anywhere. So I left without saying
anything. I thought you'd be happy I'd fixed something for
tonight, not go on like this about a Brazilian I can hardly
remember.'

'Where is it then?'

Katarina took out a small brown piece, wrapped in plastic, not
much bigger than a coin.

'Are you joking? You left here just to get that? Hardly even
worth smoking. What the hell did you pay for it?'

'Come off it. I know it's not much, but Diana said he had loads
and when we got there, there was only one cake and we had to
share it. If I'd known, of course I wouldn't have bothered, but I
wanted to make you happy, and I need it for what I'm going to
do tonight.'

Eddie didn't really know what to believe, but he certainly
wanted to know what she'd planned for later on. He recognised
that misty look and knew from experience it was promising. Perhaps he'd just imagined it? The idea that she'd dragged that boy
back home, screwed him, then come back was absurd, but you
never knew with Katarina. He'd taught her a lesson once, so she
bloody well ought to look out.

'Yes, OK, but for Christ's sake make sure you tell me next time
you leave the club like that. Out you go. We're not closing for
another hour.'

Katarina was just going back out into the smoky, noisy club
when Eddie called.

Hell! I thought I'd made it, she said to herself. As long as he
doesn't go on asking questions.

'Come here,' he said.

Katarina went confidently over to him.

He suddenly got up, pulled her to him and rubbed his loins
against hers.

'Your little surprise tonight better be fucking good.' His eyes
were now fairly steely and he smiled his crooked smile.

'You can bet it is,' said Katarina, pressing back up against him.

It had been a close thing. The scar from the burn mark was a memory of his jealousy etched into her forever. She had been in the club's *chambre separée* with two young Italians, drinking champagne. The atmosphere had been high and so had she and it wasn't long before the two of them were all over her. True, this was forbidden territory, but she hadn't intended things to go so far. One of them had been stroking her shoulders, his hand well on its way down her cleavage, while the other was concentrating on her thighs, both of them whispering seductively into her ear what they were going to do to her.

Then the door had crashed open and Eddie was there. He hadn't even had time to look surprised.

'Fucking whore!' he had yelled, so it echoed round the room, and she had leapt up, straightened her skirt and started making clumsy excuses.

In the course of a few seconds, he had slapped her hard in front of the two Italians and shouted for Gino, who was always somewhere around.

'Gino, these two guys are just a bit overheated. Cool them down for me. Get out of my way.'

Katarina had never found out what his 'way of cooling people down' was, and neither did she want to. It was enough to know what he'd done to her.

'Now I'll show you what happens to tarts like you,' he'd hissed, twisting her arm so hard she thought it would break. He had dragged her behind him straight across the dance floor. Tears were pouring down her cheeks, and she fought back the urge to scream. He'd hauled her into the office and literally thrown her on the sofa. Katarina had pleaded to be allowed to explain.

'Let's hear what you have to say then,' he'd said without even glancing at her as he locked the office door.

Katarina had been shaking with terror. She'd seen Eddie in a rage before, but this time his eyes were insane. Her voice trembling, she'd told him she'd thought the Italians had lots of money. She'd tempted them into letting the champagne flow. He could check that himself from the bar bill.

By this time, Eddie had sat down in the armchair opposite and lit a cigarette. He'd looked fairly collected; she'd told him a truth with some modification, certainly, but for a few moments she had really thought he'd bought her version.

Eddie had leant over her and without the slightest warning stubbed out his cigarette on her left breast. The pain had been unspeakable.

Katarina always wore thin, almost transparent chiffon dresses, with plunging necklines. After that horrible incident with Eddie, she'd often thought of having the ugly burn mark tattooed over. Meanwhile she let a scarf hide it as best she could.

Tonight Katarina was wearing her favourite dress of black chiffon. The skirt went down to her ankles and was transparent. All she had on underneath was a pair of black panties and the outlines of her long slim legs were clearly visible. The straps of her sandals, laced almost up to her knees, were also visible through the thin material. She had tied a black shawl with silver fringes round her waist and although her top was also black, her nipples were just discernible.

She also wore lots of silver chains round her neck hung with charms, crosses, turquoises and corals, a leather band with an ivory claw tight round her neck and a bunch of silver bracelets rattling on each wrist. Her hair was hennaed and came down to her waist, naturally curly – when she was younger, she had spent hours trying to straighten it, but now she just let it dry naturally, as that look had become fashionable.

She had made her brown eyes even darker with the aid of a kohl pencil. Nightclub life and drugs had affected her previously pure white skin and she had dark shadows round her eyes, though her lips were as scarlet as ever.

When she'd met Eddie Malakundris, the Greek nightclub owner, he had initiated her into the world of amphetamines. To manage the tempo of the club until five or six in the morning, he had suggested she should try some white tablets to keep her going. At first Katarina had had nothing to do with drugs. But she now loved the effect amphetamines and alcohol had on her. They not only kept her wide awake, but also gave her a kind of new self-confidence. Although as an air hostess she had been used to looking after other people, in fact deep down she'd had little self-confidence. Now drugs had wiped out all trace of that.

Of course it was difficult to go to sleep in the early hours of the morning, but that was where the hash came in handy. She and Eddie smoked every night; it was the simplest way of coming down.

Another plus was that all sense of hunger vanished. For years, Katarina had struggled with various diets and mostly failed. Whether that was the fault of the magazines they came from or her own lack of character was uncertain, but now she'd found the easiest way of all.

At first, since she'd met Eddie, she'd taken a pill at about seven or eight o'clock in the evening and that kept her high for a couple of hours. But she had gradually started taking them earlier and earlier in the day – the earlier, the less food, and the slimmer Katarina became.

She had left SAS almost two years ago, after she'd met David. He ran an art gallery in Albemarle Street, and she'd fallen helplessly in love. In order to spend every possible moment with him she had resigned from her job. He'd been her great love, but eight months later he had broken her heart by having not one but two affairs on the side. Katarina had flown back to Sweden. After a brief spell as receptionist at Nyman & Schultz travel agency and putting on a lot of weight, she decided to go back to London after all. After four years abroad, she found Sweden and Swedish men far too limited for her taste.

Back in London she worked as an assistant in a boutique on the King's Road; one of the other girls at work had suggested she should come with them to a newly opened place called The Spot. That was where Katarina had met the owner, Eddie.

She opened the office door and went out into the club, where they were playing 'P.S. I Love You'. As it was a slow number, the dance floor was like a snakepit of intertwined bodies.

'Hi, Katarina!'

Arnaldo, the young Brazilian she had just spent a phenomenal half hour with, was coming towards her from the crowded bar.

'What happened? We were supposed to meet here half an hour ago.'

He put his arm round her shoulders, but before he had time to attempt a kiss, she'd taken his glass and tossed back the contents, then she grimaced fiercely. She had never learnt to like whisky, however high she was. Carefully she removed his arm and glanced back at the office door, terrified Gino or Eddie would see her with Arnaldo again. At the same time she was just as scared of frightening the boy off. He was clever with his tongue, and she couldn't get enough of it. Fortunately he had a room in Soho Square, only a couple of blocks away from the club.

Katarina sensed that come what may, she must get out of here.

'Lover boy,' she whispered with a little smile. 'I must go to the ladies, but don't worry. We'll be seeing each other.'

Her silver ornaments rattled as she quickly went to the ladies room. Inside, she took a few small pills out of her black velvet purse, popped them in her mouth, leant over the tap and swallowed them. When she looked up, her eyes opened wide with shock.

'Monica!' she cried. The blonde hair, the narrow hips, the conservative clothes. It all fitted. It must be her. 'Don't you recognise me? It's me – Katarina.'

'I beg your pardon. Are you speaking to me?' The blonde woman turned to her and when they were face to face, Katarina realised it wasn't Monica at all.

She hadn't seen Monica for at least three or four years, not since that fatal party at the Hall with Gordon. She had never forgiven Monica for not inviting her to her wedding after such an insignificant blunder. Clearly, it was mutual, as they'd heard nothing from each other since.

But Katarina had followed Monica's fortunes. Hardly a month went by without a photograph of Monica appearing in Katarina's favourite magazines, either at a ball, a party or some charity event. The only common factor in the photographs was that Monica was always smiling that same pained smile. It would be fun to meet her old friend again, but Monica would probably not even recognise her now.

Suddenly Katarina's heart began beating fiercely, the pills taking effect. Now she needed a quick vodka and lime and then she would dance.

* * *

Eddie adjusted his crotch in his tight black garbardine trousers. He was going to do a round of the club, not only to keep an eye on Katarina, but also to see what the guests were up to. There had been a row the other night between two women and he had seen something he'd never seen before during his many years as a nightclub owner. The women had fought with their fists and one of them had had a bloody nose. Gino had to intervene to separate them and he'd also received a wallop, poor guy. Whether it was over another man, or possibly a woman, he didn't know, but he couldn't have fighting here. You never knew whether there were plain clothes police in the place and they had been trying to close down his club for several years.

The Spot was his third club and Eddie was very careful to keep on the right side of the law. Although born and brought up in England, his parents were immigrants and the police were always particularly careful to check anyone considered to be an alien.

Every Friday, Inspector Sackville came and collected the brown envelope with five hundred pounds in notes inside it. Nothing was said except their permanent little joke: 'See you next week, same place, same time.'

That was how it came about that the club took in seven hundred punters when other clubs which had the same capacity could legally take only four hundred and fifty.

Lately, however, another cloud had loomed on his horizon. It was 1964 and the young people coming to his club seemed to be of a different calibre from those of four or five years ago. A cloud of hash would often hang over the premises, and sometimes he had to ask Gino to escort some high little girls out.

Eddie himself had been taking amphetamines for half his life. In this profession, a man had to be on the alert all round the clock. But he was forty-five now and had begun to feel the time had come to reduce his consumption somewhat. Also, Katarina complained that he couldn't get it up, not an unusual effect of the drug.

Although he used a sunlamp almost every day to keep his dark complexion, drugs and late nights had left him with bloodshot eyes and deep furrows in his face. The fact that he also chain-smoked didn't improve matters, his forefinger and middle finger were always stained yellow with nicotine. In recent months he'd let his wavy hair grow to just below his ears, thinking it gave him a more youthful appearance. Anyhow most men grew their hair longer these days.

Eddie fingered the thick gold chain with its gold cross and St Christopher medallion round his neck. The black silk shirt was unbuttoned down to his navel to show his extremely hairy chest. He glanced quickly at his gold Rolex as he looked around for Katarina. Ah, there she was, just coming out of the ladies.

'Darling, I need a vodka and lime.'

They would be closing soon. Eddie could hardly wait to get home and claim his surprise.

7

Gordon and his new girl-friend were on their way to Bermuda. She clearly preferred the warmth to the chill of St Moritz, and that was just as well.

Edward was used to Gordon changing girl-friends in the way other men changed shirts. And why not? He was wealthy, success-ful and unmarried. But this time he had truly surprised Edward, for Gordon's new girl was black. Born in England, yes, but orig-inally from Jamaica. Edward was grateful for her choice, as that meant he and his family could spend Christmas at Gordon's chalet in Switzerland.

The house was at their disposal over Christmas, staffed by a cook, a butler, who also acted as chauffeur, and two maids – all of whom appeared as they drove up to the snow-covered space outside.

The chalet was a magnificent three-storey timber building. Snow had been falling all week and lay like a white blanket on the roof, long icicles hanging from the eaves, almost touching the great drifts the wind had driven up against the walls.

'Welcome, Lord and Lady Hewitt,' said Percy, the English butler. 'Lisen,' he went on, turning to one of the girls. 'Please show our guests to their rooms. I'll see to the luggage.'

Monica gazed round the hall. She hadn't been there for a couple of years and had quite forgotten how large it was. Apart from the seven bedrooms, there was an enormous living room with a library and television room on one side and dining room on the other. All the main rooms had picture windows facing the lake, and huge beams in the ceilings.

The walls of the living room were covered in an intricate patterned fabric, and the beams were painted in the same design. Two
large sofas stood opposite each other in front of the open fireplace, a low glass-topped table on the wolfskin rug between them.
Groups of chairs and sofas were scattered round the room and by
one of the picture windows was a games table for everything from
bridge to backgammon.

They went upstairs behind Lisen.

'This is your room,' she said, turning to Monica and Edward and
opening the door to a gigantic bedroom. The vast hardwood four-
poster had a blue and white striped silk canopy with matching
draperies, and fluffy sheepskin rugs lay on each side.

In this combined bedroom and living room, there was also an
open fireplace, the fire crackling invitingly, a vase of long-stem-
med roses on the low table in front of it. The staff had not only
decorated a twelve-foot Christmas tree down in the main room,
but had also done the same to a beautiful little tree here.

Robert squealed with delight at the sight.

'You come with me, young man.' said Lisen, taking his hand.

When she showed him the room next to his parents, his eyes
opened wide – it was every small boy's dream. Gordon must have
done this, thought Monica, touched. Where there was usually a
double bed was now a single bed in the form of a fire engine, and
along one wall a large panel of wood with a train-set mounted
on it, and underneath a small Christmas tree were at least ten
colourful parcels.

Monica was almost embarrassed at such generosity.

The twins' room had been similarly redecorated to delight the
two girls whilst Lady Rose's room was all in pink, a veritable
dream of pink roses – wallpaper, bedspread, curtains – all in rose
patterns and white lace, even the parcels under the little tree pink.

Lady Rose turned to Monica, stunned by all these fantastic
things Gordon had arranged for them. It already seemed almost
too much – and they hadn't yet opened their presents. However
would they be able to thank him?

Their modest Christmas present to him had been a silver frame
from Asprey's containing a colour photograph of the whole

family. They'd had it engraved with 'To Gordon, with love from the Hewitt family, Christmas, 1967' along the top of the frame.

'Monica,' Edward called from their bedroom. 'Percy can drop me off at the Palace. I'd like to go down to the bar to revive old memories. I'll ask him to pick me up in time for dinner. You don't mind if I push off for a while, do you, darling?'

Monica laughed and shook her head. She knew it was going to be a wonderful Christmas, and they certainly deserved that after the difficult years which, thank goodness, now lay behind them.

She hadn't yet taken off the mink coat Edward had given her when they'd first met – it had belonged to his first wife, but Edward had assured her that Mary Elizabeth had never had a chance to wear it. At first Monica had not wanted to take over his dead wife's personal belongings, but over the years she had realised that there would be no money to buy her a new fur coat. Now she wore it gratefully.

The tour of the house now over, Monica went to her room and took off her mink. With Robert fully occupied with his trains and Edward out, she decided to have a lovely foam bath.

Every time Edward had been to St Moritz, he had always gone to the Palace Hotel for a drink in the late afternoon. According to him, that added some spice to life. The best thing he knew was to sit by the big fire with a whisky and soda, simply enjoying his own company.

The owner of the hotel, Mr Badrutt, always gave him a warm welcome, even though he wasn't staying there. Edward presumed Gordon had told him who he was, for over the years the hotelier had introduced him to Onassis, Maria Callas and Gianni Agnelli, the Fiat magnate, just to name a few. Edward was not really grudging by nature, but he couldn't help feeling envious; just think what he could do with Hewitt Hall if he had even a fraction of their fortunes.

Once or twice, he'd been invited to go helicopter skiing, but he'd always felt bound to decline as he knew the day would come when he would have to ask them back and there was certainly no possible chance of that kind of spectacular extravagance. Edward was very much aware that in these circles it was presumed he was a very wealthy man, for not only was he a peer of the realm, but also a partner and good friend of Gordon's, quite enough for people to think he was a multi-millionaire.

Edward sank into the armchair by the fire in the enormous hotel lounge. Mr Badrutt had welcomed him as usual, and he was now waiting for his whisky and soda to come, then he could relax completely.

He had been truly looking forward to Christmas this year. He'd never before celebrated Christmas anywhere else but at Hewitt Hall, and although it felt slightly strange, on the other hand this way Monica had been relieved of all the Christmas preparations. Mrs McDonald had been very pleased to be able to spend Christmas in Scotland with her relatives for once, and only John was left at the Hall. Edward had told the local police they were away, and they in their turn had promised to keep an eye on the place.

The young Swiss waitress brought his drink on a tray and put it down in front of him together with a small bowl of olives and another of salted almonds. Edward took a mouthful of whisky.

Even today, he still found it difficult to relax. Since Amanda was born, he'd been dogged by one misfortune after another and was almost beginning to believe some kind of curse lay on the Hewitt family. He'd often spent sleepless nights worrying about how they were going to make ends meet and had done everything to keep the true situation from Monica. Naturally she knew by this time there were no great sums available, but he wanted to spare her the worry of just how critical the situation actually was.

She had difficulties enough without being burdened with the financial side. It had taken her a long time to get over the shock of Amanda's birth. The much longed-for baby daughter had been seriously brain-damaged. Edward had to struggle to keep back the tears whenever he thought about it.

The shock of being told that her baby girl was severely brain damaged had sent Monica into a coma for three days. After that, she had become deeply depressed, and the doctors had prescribed Librium, at first thirty milligrams a day, but when she was at her worst the dose was increased up to about eighty. She'd gone round the house like a zombie. Lady Rose had had to take sole charge of the tours and bookings for the banqueting room.

And poor Robert hadn't understood at all what had happened to his little sister. During the late stages of Monica's pregnancy, he had been allowed to feel her stomach and they had talked about what fun it would be to have a little brother or sister. It had certainly not been easy to explain to him what had happened, but in the end Edward had decided on a half-truth and had told him that God had taken his little sister and that one day they would meet again in heaven.

Edward had been very anxious that this lie should not only be shared with Robert, but also with all their friends and acquaintances. In his eyes, giving birth to a deformed child was something to be ashamed of, and could destroy the façade of happy family life that was so important. What happened behind closed doors was one thing, what showed outwardly was quite another.

Monica wouldn't have agreed to this version of the truth, at least not without a struggle, had she not been in such a daze from the drugs she'd been given. By the time she'd woken from a year of fog, it was far too late to change anything, for by then everyone knew the official version.

Edward had decided on his daughter's future together with Dr Grant. As it would be impossible to care for Amanda at home, the doctor had recommended St Mary's Institute for Children, where she would receive all the care she needed. The damage to her brain was so severe, Dr Grant assured him it was meaningless for them to go to see her. She would not be able to recognise them or even communicate. He didn't think she'd survive for long.

If it hadn't been for Robert, Monica would certainly still have been dependent on anti-depressant drugs. Edward had tried but failed to help her and had suffered from seeing his wife so deeply unhappy and utterly incapable of dealing with the situation. The only way out she had was to numb herself with drugs. She, who had always been so healthy. True, they both liked a drink before meals and some wine with dinner, but when it came to drugs, he had never seen her take as much as even a headache pill.

The turning-point had come when Robert had thrown himself

down on the floor in front of her, weeping and screaming: 'You don't love me any more!'

Monica had barely reacted.

By chance Edward happened to be passing the bedroom door when this scene was going on. He'd rushed in, grabbed her by the shoulders and yanked her up from the bed where she'd been sitting listlessly.

'Don't you see, Monica?' he'd said, shaking her limp body. 'Look what you're doing to our son.' Then he had gone to her bedside table and taken the large bottle of Librium and made her go with him to the bathroom, where he had ruthlessly flushed away the entire contents before her very eyes.

'Not another tablet is to come into this house. Over my dead body. I've had enough!'

He had left a shocked Monica trembling and sobbing by the basin, and taken the weeping Robert with him.

'Mummy's not feeling very well, you see, but of course she loves you. More than anything else in the world.'

Then he had closed the bathroom door behind them.

At the time Edward had not realised how severe Monica's addiction had actually become. She was extremely ill, sweating and shaking, diarrhoea combining with a terrible nausea. Mrs McDonald had sat up with her for several nights when Edward had to stay in London. In the end Dr Grant suggested she should be admitted into hospital. He had said that coping alone with breaking the habit after such large doses was almost impossible, and it had taken her six months to get rid of her addiction.

Gordon had suggested that Edward should be at home with his wife rather more during the most difficult time, and he'd stayed at the Hall for several weeks at a stretch. Not until Monica was free of her dependency had he had time to work on his own grief and think about his own problems.

He'd been so harassed with worries about finding a place for Amanda, Monica's depression, and looking after little Robert, there had been no time to think about himself. Edward worried continually about what things were like for the poor little creature in that home. They had assured him that she was all right, and that she was not capable of understanding what was happening round her, but to have to say their child had been stillborn weighed heavily on his conscience – all their friends' sympathy and the dreadful lie about the funeral they were supposed to have had for family only in the little chapel of the Hall were difficult to bear.

He suddenly felt tears rising again and dug a handkerchief out of his pocket. Here he was, a grown man sitting weeping at the memory of his lost daughter when he ought to be grateful things were now looking brighter for his family.

Edward blew his nose hard into the well-starched handkerchief and decided that he needed another drink. This time he ordered a straight whisky with no soda. He seldom drank anything that strong, but at all costs he had to dull the pain. Anguish was not something you could automatically shut off when it could no longer be handled.

He glanced absently through the newspapers lying on the table in front of him. Maybe there was something in them to catch his interest and disperse the gloomy thoughts that kept so obstinately obtruding. He was just looking through the previous day's *Financial Times* when the young Swiss girl put his double whisky down in front of him.

'Is this all right, sir?' she said in broken English.

'Thank you, that's fine.' He looked up at her and she smiled sympathetically.

He grimaced as the whisky burnt in his stomach, but it also filled him with warmth which was just what he needed. He took another gulp, surprised at his own impetuous drinking. He usually made a drink last by sipping at it cautiously.

The look in the eyes of the waitress had stuck in his mind and he wondered whether she might have seen his tears, or perhaps simply the desperation in his eyes. Anyhow, it had been quite clear how sorry she was feeling for him.

Edward watched her as she went between the tables, taking orders and serving drinks. She couldn't have been more than twenty, but with a curvaceous body and he could clearly see her swelling breasts beneath the silky blouse. Her skirt was almost indecently short, but the girl had nothing to be ashamed of; her long shapely legs reminded him of his wife's.

He was surprised at himself looking at a woman in this way, then felt a sudden tension in his loins, the first longed-for reaction for a whole long year.

Since Monica had started getting better they had begun to enjoy each other again, then he had quite unexpectedly become impotent.

At first he hadn't been able to make out what was wrong. He had waited so long for the love from his wife he'd renounced during her illness. They had tried only once in a whole year when she'd been sick but in the middle of the act, Edward had noticed she was so distant, she hadn't the slightest idea what was going on. But his desire had by no means diminished. On the contrary. Then, when she'd come back from hospital and life had slowly begun to return to normal, he had surprisingly been incapable.

At first Monica had actually admitted relief that her own desire was in fact infinitesimal, but when he had urgently gone on trying, she'd started blaming herself. Was there something wrong with *her*?

They had turned the problem over and over, but had come to no solution. They had decided neither of them had a particularly strong sexual urge, but what you cannot have, you often strive for most, and still they both felt dissatisfied.

During one night of yet another failed attempt, Monica had even taken him in her mouth, something she would normally never have dreamt of doing. Her well-meaning but clumsy attempt had produced no result, apart from giving her self-confidence another knock. Why, as a woman, could she not arouse her man?

Finally, Edward had sought professional advice. The doctors had told him the most likely explanation for his lack of reaction was that the physical and mental strain of recent years had created an imbalance in his body and his mind. In a self-obliterating way, he had tried to sacrifice everything for his wife and son and helped them overcome their problems, so had been unable to work on his own grief. A delayed reaction had set in and was expressed in impotence.

The doctor's advice had reassured them both.

Monica finally acquired some perspective on life and had begun to accept her child's handicap and the fact that in the eyes of the family and their friends, the child was dead. There was an unspoken agreement among them all never to mention Amanda's name.

Her already fierce love for Robert had if anything become even greater, and she gave of her all to him in an almost self-negating way. She could sit for hours in the window watching enraptured while her son played in the garden.

Edward had done his best to rouse her interest in other things, becoming involved again in the tours round the Hall, for instance, now still in the hands of Lady Rose. He'd pointed out that his mother was getting on in years and certainly needed the help. In his persistence, he had thought he'd appealed to her need to feel wanted, but unfortunately Robert fulfilled that more than enough. He was becoming more of a mother's boy with every day that passed.

'Excuse me, sir.'

Edward was jolted out of his thoughts by the waitress pointing out politely that he was sitting with a burnt-out cigarette in his hand and that ash had fallen on the arm of the chair and the sleeve of his jacket. Embarrassed, he brushed himself down and mumbled something about his having been in another world. It was time to set off home again.

At midday, the cook had served a traditional English Christmas dinner, but before that they had all opened their Christmas presents from Gordon. Robert had been standing by his parents' bed at seven o'clock that morning, demanding, 'Can I open my presents now?'

With the twins, Lady Rose and Philip, they had gone from room to room and opened the presents. Monica had been given a lovely pink cashmere shawl and Lady Rose a similar violet one, Edward and Philip identical gold Dunhill lighters engraved with their initials, and the twins a brushed-steel Rolex each. Little Robert had almost drowned in a sea of toys.

After lunch they had all gathered in the main living room in front of the fire and dealt out the family Christmas presents. Philip suggested playing the children's simple version of charades, an idea accepted with enthusiasm all round. Even the twins seemed keen, a rare thing these days, and they offered to go first. They placed themselves in a pose that was supposed to be a horse and carriage. To Robert's delight, he guessed right first time. Now it was his turn.

'Mummy, Mummy, help me. What shall I be?'

Monica was just about to whisper a suggestion to him when Edward stopped her.

'No, darling. Let him think up something for himself.'

Monica glanced nervously at her son. She always worried about him not managing something he had set himself to do, then being upset about his failure. She knew she over-protected him, though she was quite unable to stop herself.

But it was all right. Robert decided he was a crab, and his grandmother guessed right. Then it was Lady Rose's turn.

Edward and Monica looked at each other happily, Monica fingering the gold bracelet studded with small diamonds Edward had given her for Christmas.

Philip caught her eye and smiled. He had actually been with Edward when he'd bought it at Garrard's in Regent Street. He had wondered how Edward was able to afford to spend four hundred pounds on a bracelet, but after all the awful things that had happened to the family recently, he presumed that for once he ought not to question it.

They'd had an alarming number of bills before Christmas and Philip had endless sleepless nights. How on earth were they to conjure up the money their creditors demanded? Miraculously enough, at the last minute Edward had paid all the bills. Philip had stopped worrying about how his brother had managed to scrape up the necessary. It was not possible to have raised that sum out of his salary at such short notice, so he suspected that Gordon had a finger in the pie somewhere.

Philip waved goodnight when Edward and Monica got up to go to bed.

'Can't I stay up a little longer, Mummy?' said Robert, gazing hopefully at Monica.

'We promise to look after him and put him to bed,' said the twins in unison. 'Don't worry, Mummy.'

Sarah and Emma had started calling her Mummy when Robert was born, but Monica had never got used to it. However much she tried she couldn't feel any real maternal feelings for them. She liked them, of course, but she was Mummy only to Robert.

It had been a wonderful day and just as wonderful an evening, though Monica guessed that Edward had had rather too much to drink.

Edward stumbled on the top stair and Monica took his arm.

'Darling, I think I've had a drop too much, but it's been a fantastic Christmas. Did you like your present?'

'It really was a surprise, Edward. I simply love it,' she said with perfect honesty. Apart from her engagement ring, this was the first piece of jewellery Edward had given her since they had married. She had access to the family jewels, but many of the finest pieces had gone under the hammer, among them the beautiful tiara she'd worn for her wedding. She hadn't worn it all that often, but in the hall there was a portrait of Lady Rose wearing it, and she knew it had been in the family for several generations.

Edward put his arm round his lovely wife and kissed her passionately.

'Oh, Edward,' said Monica, laughing.

He quickly silenced her with another kiss.

'You know perfectly well they're all down there.'

Monica had always been very particular about the conventions and kissing on the stairs like a couple of teenagers was definitely not done. But Edward ignored her reproaches and continued just as persistently.

But Monica refused to give in so lightly: 'Edward, anyone could come.'

He took her resolutely in his arms and carried her into the bedroom.

It was a passionate night. They had never made love so intensely before and Monica achieved an orgasm for the first time in many years. If she had only known it could be like this, she thought in amazement, she would gladly have done it every night.

They lay in each other's arms, Edward asleep, snoring lightly. She eased herself out of his arms and put on one of the thick bathrobes Gordon had thoughtfully hung in every bathroom.

She simply had to go and take a look at Robert. She couldn't be sure the twins had really made him brush his teeth properly, especially after all those sweets he had eaten today, or wash his face and hands. Monica sat on the edge of his bed and looked closely at his sweet face as he lay there sleeping peacefully.

She kissed him lightly on the forehead and, satisfied, went back to their room. It had been a wonderful Christmas. At last they were a proper family again.

Monica fell asleep with a smile on her lips.

8

Percy the butler had sent a telex to Bermuda to inform Gordon of Edward's death, and he had immediately put his helicopter at the family's disposal and left for London.

Monica had flown back from Switzerland to England with the children and Lady Rose, while Philip drove the car back through Europe. The memorial service was to be held in four days' time. Philip would be tired after the long drive, but she couldn't do anything about that. She had more than enough to do looking after herself and Robert. Her grief knew no bounds. It had all been so totally unexpected.

It had been snowing intermittently and grown very misty. So Monica had decided not to go skiing that day, but to stay at home by the fire and read. The twins had taken Robert with them to try out some new snow scooters and Lady Rose and Philip had been out shopping, planning to go to Hanseman's afterwards for tea and cakes.

Edward didn't want to miss a single opportunity to go skiing, so he left the house at nine in the morning to meet friends at the Palace Hotel. Well, friends – they had met only the night before over drinks in the hotel bar. Monica had felt almost awkward in comparison with these sophisticated women with their Buccelati jewellery and draped sable and chinchilla stoles. The only thing she had that seemed to impress them was her title, probably the one commodity they couldn't buy. They had been planning to go up on one of the peaks by helicopter and when Edward was invited to go with them he had for once accepted with enthusiasm.

When Monica heard the weather forecast early that morning,

she had asked him not to go, but he'd assured her that it was only in the valley that the weather was so bad. It would be much better on the top. It always was, he said.

He had also suggested that the two of them should meet at the Corviglia Club and have lunch there, but she had declined. If he was determined to go, she wanted to take full advantage of the opportunity to be alone for a while; she so very seldom had time to herself.

She was aware now that her grief over Amanda and all the drugs she had taken had stolen two years from her. Now she was well again, she wanted to enjoy life and was looking forward to the New Year – 1968 was going to be her year and the year of her family. She had taken neither drugs nor alcohol for almost two years and on Christmas Day Edward had teased her that a glass of champagne wouldn't hurt, but she had refused. At last she had control over her life, and that meant everything to her. And time alone with herself was important.

Sometimes, she reflected, she found it really difficult to understand her husband. Nowadays he was so vague, it seemed that she was the one who made things work, and it was certainly she who also decided things at Hewitt Hall. Then there were those constant schisms with Philip. What had he really got against her? She had shown him a thousand times that their marriage was stable and that she loved Edward above all else. She had also provided the estate with an heir. True, Philip had seemed to make some effort over Christmas, but that was rare. Though it could be he was turning over a new leaf . . .

Gordon's cook brought a lunch tray into the living room – what luxury – ham, toast, real bread, Emmental cheese. She asked for some tea instead of the wine she'd been brought, and a little fruit cake for dessert: her content was complete.

She hadn't been so calm and comfortable for a long time. After lunch she dozed for a while on the sofa in front of the fire and then suddenly Percy was there.

'Your ladyship, there's been a terrible accident. An avalanche . . . Lord Hewitt . . .'

She was no longer listening . . . 'My husband,' she'd screamed.

'Is he . . .?' Then she remembered no more. She must have fainted and when she came to the cook and Percy had been standing over her. Slowly, Percy told her how the accident had happened.

'We've phoned the doctor,' he said finally. 'He'll be here in five minutes.'

'Where are Robert and the twins?' she asked, as the truth gradually sank in.

'They're not back yet. But we'll go down to the lake to get them. We thought perhaps my lady would want to tell them what has happened.'

Summoning all her courage, Monica had broken the news to the rest of the family. Edward had skiied into an unmarked area off piste despite the notices warning of the dangers of avalanche. His friends had followed him down the steep slope which, covered by the new snow, soon hid Edward's tracks. His companions had kept close to the piste, so when they heard the roar of the avalanche, they had had time to get back on to the marked slope. But it had been far too late for Edward, the avalanche had buried him completely.

His body had still not been found, but Monica instinctively knew he'd never had a chance. Both Philip and Lady Rose persuaded themselves that as long as the body hadn't been found there was still some hope of his being alive. For all of them, the fact that he had gone was impossible to take in; it was as if he would come through the door at any moment to give the twins and Robert a hug.

As they had come down at Heathrow the helicopter had shaken and shuddered, and reporters and photographers were waiting when they landed.

'Lady Hewitt.'

One man had marched resolutely up to her and she'd felt tears rising again, but Lady Rose had intervened.

'Please leave her alone,' she'd said in a firm voice. 'Lady Hewitt has just lost her husband, I have lost my son and the children their father. Have you no shame?' Lady Rose had not even deigned to glance at the journalists as she took Monica's arm and led her over to the arrival hall.

Monica had never seen this side of Lady Rose before, so strong, so completely in control of the situation; at the Hall it had always been Monica who was in control.

But those days at the Hall were now just a memory. As the body had not been found, Edward could not be certified dead, but when Robert finally took over the title, they would have huge death duties to pay. Philip had explained that there was insufficient actual cash and so the Hall would have either to be sold or handed over to whatever organisation would accept it. He was in despair. Hewitt Hall had been in his family for centuries. As yet, Edward's will could not be read, nor could his life insurance be redeemed. In itself, that was only twenty thousand pounds and would not even cover the new young peer's education, but it would be something. Philip was grief-stricken – losing his brother and the Hall as well was more than he could bear.

Lady Rose willingly looked after Monica on their way home, but had now shut herself up in the lodge. Robert found it hard to understand why his father would never be coming home again, but with the help of his mother and the other members of the family, he seemed to be managing to live a fairly normal life. The twins, on the other hand, having now lost both mother and father, were turning to each other even more, while Monica struggled with her grief on her own. It would have been easy to revert to Librium and disappear into a daze, but she was determined never to do that again. Thank goodness for Gordon.

He had returned to London and had been waiting for her at the Hall: he'd been at her side – if not in person then on the phone – almost every day since. It was really touching to see the way he looked after them all.

Two months had gone by since Edward's death. Mrs McDonald had not received her wages, nor had John, who was now living in at the Hall. The fodder for the horses had to be bought on credit.

Monica and Philip had already gone through all the remaining valuable objects and sent them off to auction, but the money from that would definitely not last for very long.

Gordon spent more and more time in the blue guest room and

had generously provided them with ten thousand pounds to tide them over the most urgent bills. They had often sat up late to discuss the future, after Robert had gone to bed. How could they exploit the Hall more commercially to make it more lucrative? It was difficult in the winter, because then it was closed to the public, and so was the rose garden. What was needed was something that brought in money all year round. Nowadays the banqueting hall was available for hire, but it was not used to the same extent in the winter as in the summer. Gordon had suggested that they should lay out a nine-hole golf course. Monica approved of the idea, but knew there were no resources to finance it. However, they agreed that if Gordon would find the capital and take a certain percentage of the profits, then it might be possible.

Gordon had suggested that Monica should come with him to Paris for a weekend. She had hesitated for a long time. Wasn't it rather inappropriate so soon after Edward's death? But not even Philip, who never seemed to approve of anything she did, considered that to be the slightest bit odd. Gordon was after all an old family friend and to get away was just what she needed.

Since the accident, she had woken up every night bathed in sweat. She kept having nightmares, if not about Edward and the terrible accident which she'd now seen in a hundred variations in her dreams, then they were about the Hall being taken away from her, or she was being harassed by creditors.

Nothing was the same any more. Lady Rose was taking to the bottle more than ever and now made no attempt whatsoever to conceal the fact. And Philip, who had supported Monica at first, had definitely reverted to his usual hostile attitude.

Perhaps Gordon was right. She needed to get away, even if it did mean leaving Robert for a few days, though he would be in the safe hands of Mrs McDonald.

Monica thought back again to Philip's reaction to the trip. She couldn't help but be puzzled that Philip didn't seem to have anything against her going away with Gordon. On the contrary, he almost seemed to be encouraging them to go.

Gordon had booked a two-bedroomed suite at the Plaza Athénée and they had had a wonderful dinner on the first night at Chez l'Ami Louis, a small bistro with only a few tables. Then they had strolled along the banks of the Seine. The next day they had gone for a long walk in the Bois de Boulogne and Gordon had insisted on taking her to Dior in Avenue de Montaigne, where they had ordered a lovely fawn spring suit with a matching hat and a dark blue and white satin evening dress with a cape in the same material.

Monica had never possessed anything so expensive before. She had been almost embarrassed when Gordon had laughed at her delight. He really was a wonderful man and he had kept his promise that they would travel just as friends. That night they had had dinner and then taken a trip on a Seine Bateau-Mouche.

Monica was glad she had accepted Gordon's invitation. Although it was now only three months since the accident, to her it seemed like three years. She was grateful she'd been able to sleep at least for a few hours each night.

The nights were her greatest enemy, and she always stayed up as late as possible before going to bed. She knew she would lie there sleepless, twisting and turning, and then her darkest thoughts would return.

Sometimes she longed desperately for a sleeping pill, but that would have meant falling back into her old habits. The detoxification she'd gone through had been such a terrifying experience, she had no desire to go through it again.

But Paris had made her look on life more lightly – at least temporarily, and Gordon made her laugh. All too soon they were on their way back to London, the plane racing calmly through the cold March air.

'Would you care for some champagne?'

As Monica asked for her usual orange juice instead she looked up at the young air hostess. It seemed like only yesterday when she herself had stood in exactly the same way, and yet it was a very long time ago. Now she was a widow with a child, no, three children, to look after. How would she manage?

The financial situation was in no way under control. On several occasions Gordon had asked how things were, but he had always contributed more than generously, most of all with that ten thousand as an advance on Edward's life insurance. She didn't really want him to know the truth and it would simply be painful to accept any more from him. So she'd told him that thanks to him they were back on their feet.

'Penny for your thoughts,' said Gordon, putting his hand over hers and stroking it with small light touches.

'Oh, nothing special. I was just daydreaming.'

'Monica, I can see something's weighing heavily on you. Are you thinking about Edward?'

'Yes, a little perhaps. But let's drink to a wonderful weekend and the best friend anyone could have.'

'And to the most beautiful woman on earth and . . .'

He didn't finish the sentence, but took her hand, lifted it to his lips and slowly kissed it.

Once again it struck her what a perfect gentleman he was.

Monica had just completed a tour of the rose garden with a group of German visitors and was on her way to the Hall when she caught sight of Philip. He was hurrying towards her across the open space in front of the Hall.

'How much longer will you be?' he said. 'I'd like a word with you.'

'I'll be ready in about twenty minutes. Is it something important? Nothing's happened, I hope?'

Philip didn't answer, but simply turned on his heel and went back into the Hall.

Every time Philip asked to have a word with her, she suffered agonies. It was always to do with the Hall's finances and she was tired of hearing how bad they were. She did her best and sacrificed everything to make things go round, but the place seemed simply to swallow money.

Sometimes she almost wished they could hand it over to the National Trust, but they would also expect money for its upkeep and there wasn't any. If someone took it over, her constant worries would be over. But then she thought about Robert. He would have the title, and the Hall would be his in the future. That was his heritage and a tradition he would carry on. But she couldn't remember when she had last bought anything for herself or Robert.

Philip's latest book had not sold as well as the publishers had hoped, so it was doubtful whether he would get another advance. The publisher had suggested that Philip should start writing under his own name. The publicity that it was an aristocrat who had written the popular Stuart Corke novels would ensure an increase in sales, they said, but Philip had stubbornly refused.

But at least the plans for a golf course had been approved by the planning authorities and now it was a question of finding a good landscape architect. Gordon was searching around and it looked as if the work could begin in August and the course open as early as the following spring.

According to the estimates, it should bring in a good income. Philip had always been against the tours of the Hall and the rose garden, but he did an about-turn when it came to the golf course, realising it was necessary and they were dependent on Gordon's financial support. He hadn't even protested when the proud name of the Earl Hewitt Golf Club had been suggested.

The heavy kitchen door screeched when she opened it. She must remember to ask John to oil it sometime.

'Have you seen Philip, Mrs McDonald?'

'Yes, he asked me to tell you he'll be in the office.'

Monica detested going up the back stairs to Philip's office. Philip looked very composed as he sat behind his desk, but from his mouth she realised that she could expect no good news this time, either. Before she had time to ask, he told her bluntly that Edward's body had been found.

'I suggest we hold the funeral as soon as possible. The body will be brought over to England in two days' time.'

Her grief and pain returned in a sickening wave and Philip's cold way of telling her made things no better. She started shaking, then burst into tears, for once making no attempt to control herself. She wept openly in front of her brother-in-law, who sat watching her without emotion.

'Where did they find him?' she managed to say through her tears.

'Pull yourself together, and I'll tell you.'

She wanted to rush out of the room and slam the door behind her, but she knew it was useless. Whatever she did he would feel neither sympathy nor compassion. He never did for anyone, least of all her. There was no point in making a scene. They had to live under the same roof; she had to face him every day.

The search for Edward's body had begun again after the snow had melted at the end of May. Although foot patrols and helicopters had searched the area, they had found not the slightest trace. But some climbers had come across the body in a crevice and had alerted the police. To reach the place, they'd had to go by helicopter, then Mr Badrutt of the Palace Hotel had identified the dead man as Lord Hewitt.

'I'll phone our solicitor first thing tomorrow morning, so we can meet as soon as possible and have the will read,' Philip said. 'I suggest we do it here. The twins really ought to be here, but as their term doesn't end until next month, we'll have to inform them afterwards. Then we can hope to have the funeral on Friday in the chapel. Just family, of course.'

Suddenly Monica could contain her fury no longer.

'Here you go informing me of all this. How dare you arrange things without asking me first? It is my husband we're talking about and I think you're forgetting that it is my son who is now Lord Hewitt, not you. And as Robert's guardian, I decide things here at the Hall. I'll telephone the solicitor myself tomorrow. And I require a few days to arrange the funeral, but I shall let you know when it is to be held.'

With those words, she turned on her heel, went out and slammed the door.

For once Philip was speechless.

Sir Hugh Grenville of Grenville, Warren & Buckel in Gray's Inn, had opened his black attaché case and was taking out a red file secured with both cord and seal.

Philip and Lady Rose were seated on one side of the dining table, Monica and Gordon on the other. Monica had phoned and asked Gordon to be present at the reading of the will. She had also asked Mrs McDonald to take Robert with her to the village, and she could hear the car chugging down the drive. She had a feeling all this was going to be very unpleasant.

It was a fairly ordinary will. The Hall and the title went to Robert, with Monica and Philip as guardians.

Monica felt a stab of anxiety in her breast. She had certainly not reckoned on that and simply couldn't understand Edward. Hadn't he trusted her? He had known perfectly well she and Philip did not get on, and now she was caught in this situation until Robert came of age. Not that she had thought of asking Philip to leave the Hall, but it would have been easier without him.

Philip was smiling to himself with satisfaction and after one glance Monica avoided looking at him.

Lady Rose was naturally to stay on at the lodge until her death, then it was to be incorporated back into the estate. The same applied to the apartments Philip had at his disposal. Should he marry, then he would naturally vacate them when Robert came of age. As far as the twins' future at the Hall was concerned, that would be Robert's decision when he was of age. The trust money their grandfather had left for them when they were born would be paid out when they came of age. Ten thousand pounds each was to go to their education.

Sir Hugh met Monica's questioning look impassively. Finally, he put the red file back in his case and took out a white one. In total silence, he started reading aloud. What they heard was utterly shocking.

Apart from the life insurance of twenty thousand pounds, there was nothing but debts, and all owed to the same man – Gordon Clarke.

It turned out that the total came to £403,492 exactly.

Monica caught her breath, almost unable to breathe at all. Philip, usually so under control, turned deathly pale and Lady Rose asked to be excused. There was no doubt what for, and Monica felt a great longing to walk out with her. How could Edward have kept all this from her for so many years?

Finally she spoke. 'Gordon, why did you lend us another ten thousand when you knew we had no hope of repaying it? And,

Philip, did you know anything about this? I suppose you were also in on the transactions.'

For once she was wrong about Philip. He gloomily shook his head.

Gordon took Monica's hand. 'Monica, my dear. Don't worry about this now. I'm sure we can sort it out to the satisfaction of all parties.'

Monica jerked back her hand. 'And how do you think we can do that? Perhaps I'm to win a lottery?'

They did have a few Reynolds and Arthur Davies' paintings left, but she had hoped to be able to keep those for her son. Now she could see no other way out but to sell them. Unfortunately they were not likely to bring in four hundred thousand pounds.

'Gordon,' said Philip harshly. 'I'm very surprised you've never informed me of the real state of Edward's finances. You know perfectly well I'm in charge of the finances here.'

'I acted according to Edward's wishes.'

The lawyer interrupted them by formally telling them what the death duties were likely to amount to. At that he closed his case and got up.

'I think with that, my task here at Hewitt Hall has been completed and I beg to wish you good-day.'

Philip got up and followed him to the front door.

Monica and Gordon were left alone in the great dining room.

'For eight years of my life I have been living a lie. To think Edward trusted me so little he couldn't tell me about his debts. And you, Gordon. I'm speechless. I thought you were my friend. The least one could ask was that you had told me. What do you think it's like finding out like this?'

'I know, and I'm sorry. I've often thought of asking you how much you knew about Edward's affairs, but then I didn't think it appropriate.'

'Naturally you must have his life insurance. I think that can be paid out as soon as this week. Then I shall sell some paintings, but that'll take time, and . . .'

She was interrupted by Philip's return. Before she could

continue Gordon got up and quietly asked them to listen to him for a moment.

He looked calmly at Monica. 'No, thank you, I don't want the life insurance, and nor do I want to hear anything about selling any paintings. I'm sure that as long as the golf course comes about, money will start coming in. So why not wait until then before paying back the debt? There is no hurry whatsoever. On the other hand, I'm now in a hurry. Duty calls,' he smiled disarmingly. 'I ought to be at the office.'

He kissed Monica's hand, nodded curtly in Philip's direction and disappeared through the door.

The twins wanted nothing better than to go to their aunt, Catherine Rawlings, in Australia for a year. Catherine was their mother's sister and when very young, she'd gone 'down under' and married a sheep farmer. Monica had been corresponding with her over the last year, but the twins had kept contact ever since their mother had died.

Catherine and Monica had considered that the most economical way Sarah and Emma could get to Australia would be if they took jobs as waitresses on a ship: Catherine had a friend who was captain on a liner and would keep an eye on them. On the fifth of August, they sailed from Southampton.

Gerd and Gunnar had come to the funeral, then stayed on for another month. Robert had thought it wonderful to have his grandparents to stay. Neither Lady Rose nor Philip had much time for him, and during the summer when it was high season for tours round the Hall, Monica was also busier than ever.

She was truly grateful for Gerd's help with Robert. Lady Rose no longer offered to look after him nowadays, and her involvement in the tours had also become markedly less. Monica wished she would seek help for her drink problem, but she also realised that for a woman of her age, it was not easy to admit to her dependency.

During the autumn, Monica had travelled quite a lot with Gordon. Nothing more had been said about the debt but, although she enjoyed his company, she had begun to realise that the friendship on his side was developing into something more. She had been panic-stricken when once in a gondola in Venice he had put his arm round her and tried to kiss her.

And although they did not talk about it, her financial situation was as difficult as before, if not worse. It had struck her that the simplest way out would be if she married Gordon. Philip had become considerably friendlier since she'd begun spending more time with Gordon, so he had probably also reckoned that would be the only way to save the Hall.

Robert was very fond of Gordon and the three of them had good times together. But she did not love Gordon. And she knew she never would. The very thought of being together with another man apart from Edward was almost impossible, most of all with Gordon, her dead husband's best friend.

Sometimes however she couldn't help thinking that Philip and their friends thought they were already having an affair – she, who had thought of Gordon only as Edward's friend, a friend who always rose to the occasion and had regarded it as his duty to look after his partner's grieving widow. But marriage to Gordon would definitely save their finances, no doubt about it. The constant threat that the Hall would have to go would be lifted, as well as the problem of Robert's school fees. But to marry someone she did not love for money, that would be breaking with everything she believed in; there was something terribly immoral about it. She didn't know if she could do it.

On 5 December, in a suite at the Plaza Athénée, Gordon went down on his knees and asked her to marry him. He took out of his jacket pocket a wine-red leather box containing a ten carat pear-shaped diamond ring, then he drew her wedding ring off the third finger of her left hand and threaded the engagement ring on in its place.

'You must put this on your other hand, my dear,' he said, kissing her passionately.

Monica responded to his kiss. She had decided to accept his courtship and she knew that tonight, after their light but delicious supper of caviar, lobster and salad, the inevitable would happen.

She also knew that to get through this she would have to drink the Dom Pérignon Gordon had ordered. She had not touched a drop of alcohol for three years, but her fear and nervousness over going to bed with a man she did not love meant she needed something stronger than orange juice.

Gordon told her how much he loved her and after a glass or two, she told him she felt the same. It was less than a year since Edward died, so Gordon would have to understand that she still missed her husband. This was not going to be easy for her.

Gordon opened another bottle of champagne and took it with him into the bedroom. Only one bedside lamp was on and the room was in semi-darkness.

'Here, my darling,' he said, handing her another glass.

Monica excused herself and took the glass with her into the bathroom. Once inside, she leant back against the closed door and for the first time looked at the big stone on her finger.

It was the largest diamond she had ever seen. She gulped down the champagne and turned on the hot tap.

The champagne had done its work. Monica was feeling slightly drunk but had made her decision. She slid out of the black Dior dress, took off her tights but kept her black bra and petticoat on. She glanced in the mirror and drawing a deep breath, she turned off the tap.

Gordon was sitting on the sofa beside the bed, looking very happy. Monica was everything a man in his position could desire, he reflected. He'd had enough of young girls. And he had no need to neglect any of his other pleasures just because he was getting married.

Monica was still young and had a good figure, and as Lady Hewitt, she was a well-known hostess with high social status. She had no money, it was true, but he had plenty. What she had was Hewitt Hall and as Robert's guardian she had the right to stay there regardless of whether she remarried or not.

Love? Yes, in his way he loved her.

Monica closed the bathroom door behind her and went over to sit beside Gordon. Without a word, she held out her empty glass to be refilled.

Smiling, he gazed at her as she drank half the glass in one go.

'Do you like the ring?'

Monica put a finger on his lips and whispered: 'I love it.'

He saw that she was slightly drunk, but that didn't worry him. A great many of the young girls he used to know became unpleasant when they drank, sometimes spending most of their time in the bathroom. But not Monica. He took her glass and put it down on the table in front of the sofa. Before he had time to take the initiative, she was on his lap. He was both surprised and pleased, and, with a kiss, carefully undid her bra and took it off. Her big breasts had not been affected by her pregnancies. He took them in his hands and kissed the stiffening nipples.

Monica trembled. No one had touched her since Edward.

'Darling, go to bed and wait for me,' he whispered.

When Gordon had closed the bathroom door, she leapt up and grasped the champagne bottle, almost choking over the bubbles. Her black petticoat fell to the floor, but she kept her briefs on and crept down into the big bed to wait for her new fiancé.

With nothing but a towel round his waist, he came out of the bathroom. Monica couldn't help but admire his well-trained body. It was hard to believe he was in his late forties and she stared with fascination at his hairy torso.

At the edge of the bed, he dropped the towel and slid in beside her. All her inhibitions now completely gone, she invitingly parted her legs as he ran his hand down her stomach. She rose on one elbow, leant over him and kissed him, her hand resting on his hairy chest, then running down over his stomach and muscular thighs. She could feel a certain excitement and quite unexpectedly she found she really did want to make love with Gordon. It was a long time since she'd been with a man.

She was breathing heavily and slowly slid her hand up between his legs, then gasped. What she felt was incredible. At that moment Gordon's hands slid to her hips and he pulled her over on top of him.

9

At a quarter to five, Katarina made her usual daily phone call to
Sandra. They always phoned between four and five every day and
God have mercy on anyone who didn't. Not even illness was
sufficient excuse. The only time that was legitimate was if they had
their period, and Sandra kept careful track of when that was
to happen.

'Katarina, I was just sitting here expecting you to ring.'

'Were you now? What fun have you got for me tonight, then?
No Sauerkraut again, I hope.'

'If you're good, it'll be cous-cous.'

'Mm. Arabs. Money, Honey!'

'Steady on now. The job isn't yours yet. He wants three, but as
usual I have to send more. Last time he was so dissatisfied with
two of the girls, this time I'm sending six.'

'You're sending up six? And he only wants three. Who are
the others?'

'You'll see when you get there. You're to be at the Imperial
Garden Hotel in Kensington. On the dot of half past seven. He
doesn't like if it you're late. Suite 1239–45.'

'Does he want anything special? Nothing lesbian, I hope.'

Sandra didn't reply.

'Hm, I thought as much. And you said it was going to be cous-
cous. Doesn't sound up to much.' She sighed dramatically. 'God,
how boring having to lie wriggling about pretending with another
girl.'

Sandra interrupted her. 'Half past seven, then. On the dot. If
nothing comes of it, I've got another on the go.'

She had two and half hours. Katarina opened her wardrobe and spent a long time looking through her evening dresses. Arab, Arab, Arab, she thought, then took out a bright green full-length silk dress with slits all the way up to the waist and a deep cleavage both front and back. She examined it thoroughly. It was very important that it was spotless. She scrutinised the black silk shoes that went with the dress with the same precision.

She decided to take a shower and took the dress with her into the bathroom. Steam always freshened up clothes. She started soaping her slim legs. The amphetamine had begun to work. She could feel herself speeding up. Although she was in the shower, the hairs rose on the back of her head.

She had sniffed speed for a month or two last year, but it was beginning to ruin the membranes in her nose, so she'd gone back to pills. Anyway they were much easier to get hold of. All she had to do was to visit a certain doctor in Harley Street every other week between one and two when the nurse and secretary were out for lunch.

Dead easy. He got what he wanted and she got prescriptions for Mandrax and amphetamine. Since Eddie had died, she hadn't smoked so much hash. She preferred pills now. But of course if anyone offered her any she didn't exactly refuse.

Eddie, yes. She didn't think about him very often these days. She'd done her best to suppress memories of the terrible thing that had happened. She shuddered whenever she thought about how poor Gino had found him. They could just as easily have got her as well.

Not only had they cut off his head and placed it on his desk, but they had then stuffed his amputated penis into his mouth. She still felt sick at the very thought of it. No trace whatsoever had been found of the rest of his body, but all the indications were that one of the Soho gangs had carried out the bestial murder.

Eddie had not wanted to share his profits and thought he could manage without their protection. He'd had several warnings. His Mercedes had quite inexplicably exploded outside the club one day, and a month or two earlier there had been a similar explosion, in the kitchen this time. Katarina was pretty sure he knew who lay behind it all, because he'd never gone to the police.

Not until after his death had she found out that the gang had been after him for several years. Gino had told her that he'd begged Eddie to pay them, but he had flatly refused.

Gino had suggested that she would be wisest to go back to Sweden for a few months. Katarina had taken his advice, but Sweden had been deadly. As if it were not enough living at home with her parents at thirty years of age, she'd had neither work nor amphetamines. The latter had been the worst.

She had taken the underground to Sergels Torg, a well-known hang out for drug pushers and junkies, every day and did occasionally manage to score, but she needed to go back to London. She'd rung Gino, now working at the Club dell'Aretusa, and he'd said it was OK to come back and suggested she should contact Sandra Hailey, the owner of the most successful escort agency in London, if she wanted to make easy money.

Eighteen months later, she was one of the best the agency had, because Katarina did everything – from S&M to lesbian games. Many of the other girls refused to be exposed to violence, but that was no problem to Katarina. As long as she was paid well and her access to speed and Mandrax was unlimited, it was okay by her.

Money was no problem and she was literally wallowing in it some nights. She'd bought herself a brand new red Jaguar with beige upholstery and she shared the house in Baywater Street, off King's Road, with two other girls who also worked for Sandra. She had always felt most at home in Chelsea.

Katarina was smoking in the lift on her way up to the twelfth floor. Ping! The doors opened, she dropped the cigarette and stepped out, crushing the cigarette with the tip of her shoe.

The green silk dress fitted like a snakeskin on her slim body. She had a goodly supply of amphetamines and Mandrax in her black silk bag. These jobs could take several days. Just as well to be prepared.

She could do with a drink. She shook her mane of long henna-coloured hair, put her nose in the air and headed for the suite. The door was opened immediately and she was shown into a salon by a liveried servant.

Hm, this bodes well. Servants!

There were already three girls in the salon, among them a small but big-busted blonde called Lola. Katarina knew her very well, but she had never met the others before.

'Hi, Lola. What are we sitting here for? Where's the action?' She nodded at the other two. 'I'm dying of thirst.' She indicated to the servant that she would like something to drink.

'Champagne, Miss?' he said, as he held a tray with champagne and glasses in front of her.

She downed it in one go and held up the glass for a refill. The servant poured it without the slightest change of expression. Katarina lit a Salem and took a puff, and at that moment a door opened and a shapely black girl in an orange minidress came out. She did not look happy.

'Miss.'

Another liveried servant appeared and showed Lola in through the door. Katarina winked at her.

'See you in bed,' she whispered.

The two of them had often played at being lesbians to the delight of a great many men. Lola did not come out when the door opened again and the dark-haired girl on the sofa was shown in. She came out almost equally quickly.

'What the hell's he doing in there? Has he taken Lola hostage?' she whispered to the blonde, flat-chested ex-mannequin sitting beside her. Katarina knew very well who she was – she had been a big name as a photographer's model in the early Sixties, but what do you do to survive? At least this was a job.

'Sandra said he's terribly choosy,' said the blonde.

'Miss.'

The servant had opened the door again and now it was the ex-model's turn. She got up and smoothed down her dark red crushed velvet minidress. Uhuh, thought Katarina. Now there's only me left. She rummaged in her silk bag for a pill and got hold of a Mandrax, not what she wanted, so she went on searching and found what she wanted. She popped it into her mouth and waved to the servant to bring her another glass of champagne.

She just had time to swallow the pill when the door opened and it was her turn. She knocked back the remains of the champagne and followed the servant into a large bedroom decorated in beige and gold. Lola and the model were sitting on a sofa by a window while the Arab prince lay stretched out on the vast bed.

He was in his fifties, with grey hair and a jet-black beard and moustache, rather corpulent and wearing a dark red paisley dressing gown with a shawl collar and a monogram on the top pocket. Underneath he had on green pyjama trousers.

He watched as Katarina joined the other two on the sofa, then examined the three girls, one redhead and two blondes. He said something in Arabic to the servant, who vanished into the living room, only to return almost at once with a large suitcase which he put on the bed. The prince opened it and Katarina saw that it was full of money. Her eyes widened. The prince took out a bundle and counted. Then he gave the servant three similar bundles and the servant in his turn handed them to the girls.

'His Excellency says this is for this evening,' he said, closing the suitcase, picking it up and retreating.

The prince had hitherto said nothing except in Arabic, but now he slapped the bed and waved the girls over to him.

'Girls, come and join me. Let's have some fun.'

They had had three successful days. The champagne had flowed, the caviar had been copious, too. The prince had turned out to be a very generous man. His problem was that he was virtually impotent. However good a blow job the blonde model gave, he never got a real hard-on, but it was clear he enjoyed Katarina and Lola's famous lesbian games. Lola had groaned and breathed heavily while Katarina lay giggling between her legs, then they had changed places. The model had been sent home the very first night, but Katarina and Lola had stayed for two more days. On the third day, they at last got it up.

The prince had sat stark naked on the marble floor of the great mirror-lined bathroom. Lola and Katarina were in black rubber suits with holes for their breasts and bottoms, black masks over their eyes. On the floor beside them was a basket filled with semi-rotten fruit. Their task was to fling the fruit at the masturbating prince.

Both of the girls found it difficult not to laugh, but at last he'd come. Afterwards he had collapsed like a burst balloon and lain groaning gratefully on the rotten fruit.

So he should be grateful, thought Katarina, when he got up. It had taken him three days.

'Girls, girls, I love you. You must come back next time I'm in London.'

'We love you too. You know where to find us.'

Katarina and Lola had left him in the bathroom and gone back into the bedroom to change into their own clothes. They had dressed in silence, not even looking at each other, for they both knew they would then explode into laughter. The prince was a gold mine they had no desire to lose.

On their way out of the bedroom they had been met by the liveried servant who handed them two more bundles of pound notes.

'His Excellency was very pleased with your performance,' he had said, then bowed and showed them out.

On their way home, she and Lola stopped off to have a cup of coffee. Katarina bought a packet of Salems and a *Daily Mail*.

At the café they could at last have a good laugh at the odd kinks of this generous prince. Katarina leafed absently through the newspaper and suddenly her eyes fastened on a headline in David Wigg's column: LADY HEWITT MARRIED AGAIN TO MILLIONAIRE GORDON CLARKE.

Katarina eagerly scanned the report. They had married at his property in Bermuda and then spent their honeymoon cruising in the Caribbean on his hundred and fifty foot yacht, *Gordonza*.

She showed Lola the photograph of the couple, Monica in a Chanel suit with a large collar of pearls round her neck.

Katarina went on reading the article. Monica's engagement ring was the famous ten carat pink Neider diamond. After their honeymoon the newlyweds were to live alternately at Hewitt Hall, Wiltshire and in Gordon Clarke's luxurious penthouse in Eaton Square. The couple had engaged a well-known interior decorator to renovate Mr Clarke's already fabulous apartment to the taste of his new wife.

Katarina laughed aloud and Lola looked at her, wondering why Katarina was so interested in these society people.

'What are you laughing at? Is he an old customer, or what?'

'Well, you could say that, but I never got paid. In retrospect I should have had at least a million for that night.'

'What are you saying? The man's smashing looking. I'd give him one free if I had the chance.'

'I hope Monica knows what she's letting herself in for. We shared a flat when we were air hostesses in the Fifties. Then she met a lord who was in business with that Gordon. I was invited to the Hall one weekend. That was before they married. Monica and the lord, I mean. Gordon Clarke was there too. After the dullest dinner imaginable – the lord was a real bore – Gordon and I ended up in his bedroom.

'We'd drunk buckets of wine, but thank goodness he had some bottles of Dom Pérignon with him. He was as drunk as a lord himself and to tell you the truth I wasn't far off that, either. Without the slightest warning he disappeared into the bathroom and came back stark naked. That is, apart from a white towel he'd put on like a baby's nappy. He had his thumb in his mouth so you could hardly hear what he said. Daddy, daddy, I thought he kept mumbling. He pointed at his clothes on the bathroom floor and hissed: "Put them on."

'Uhuh, I thought. He wants to play "daddy and child". He wants to be dominated. Fun, this was something new. I was so drunk I actually did put on his clothes. They were rather big for me of course and his shoes were just laughable, but I put my hair up and painted on a moustache with my kohl pencil. *Et voilà! Un papa.*' She giggled at the memory.

'Gordon was lying on the bed kicking like a baby when I went back in. He was also gurgling. Then he said he wanted to go down to get some baby gruel, at the same time pointing at the empty Dom Pérignon bottle. I realised there must be more downstairs and I remember thinking I hoped I wouldn't have to carry him down.'

Lola lit a cigarette and stared at Katarina.

'Go on. Tell me more.'

'I realised what he wanted and went along with it. I was so drunk I didn't care if we were discovered. Downstairs, we found the champagne and "daddy" opened it. But instead of glasses, Gordon insisted on lying on my lap and sucking on the bottle as if it had been a baby's.

'He suddenly fell with a thump on to the Aubusson carpet and wailed like a real baby. I was so astonished I dropped the cigarette I was smoking and was so drunk I forgot to pick it up. But I was at least sober enough to understand that he wanted me to look into his nappy.

'Drunk as I was, I ripped it off and then came the best of all. Lola, you won't believe it. The man had a hard-on, but you needed a microscope to see it. It was the smallest one I'd ever seen.'

'How small?'

Katarina held up her thumb, and the two friends laughed until they choked.

'But then he tore off my briefs and I rode him. And that wasn't at all bad considering how little he had to offer. After that I don't remember very much until the next day when I woke up with a terrible hangover. Before I knew what had happened, I was on the train back to London. I've never heard a word from Monica since. I wonder what that shit said to them. There must have been a big burn in the carpet.'

10

'House of Dior. Good afternoon. Would you please hold?'

'No, I won't.' Monica's voice rose an octave. 'This is Mrs Clarke speaking. Mrs Gordon Clarke.'

'I beg your pardon, Mrs Clarke. If you would just hold one moment, I'll see if you can speak to Madame Dessange.'

Monica put another Rothman into her gold Cartier cigarette-holder. Gordon didn't smoke and thought it would be a good idea if she gave up, but there was no question of that. Her life had changed so drastically compared with the eight years she'd been married to Edward, she herself occasionally found it difficult to keep up. Apart from the smoking, Gordon simply encouraged her extravagances. And she needed her cigarettes.

She had ordered a pink suit from Dior, but now she wanted the same model in three different colours, and she needed them quickly as they were going to Germany the following week. Then there was Ascot, and Wimbledon. Not that she was exactly short of clothes . . .

Madame Dessange came to the phone.

'Mrs Clarke. What can I do for you?'

'I need a white, a pale blue and a yellow suit the same as you delivered yesterday, and I need them by Friday.'

'But, Mrs Clarke, that's impossible.'

'When you have money, nothing's impossible,' said Monica shortly. 'I expect them to be delivered here on Friday at four o'clock at the latest.' With that she put down the receiver.

The year that had passed since Monica had remarried had changed her completely. From having lived with constant financial problems, she now found herself in a position where money didn't matter in the slightest. Gordon had opened an account for her at Coutts' in St James's and put a million pounds into it. Naturally she had arranged for Hewitt Hall to receive whatever was necessary and Philip had been overjoyed to at last be able to have the so long-neglected repairs and modernisation done. Gordon loved spending weekends there, and he arranged his business dinners at the Hall as well. As Robert was away at prep school, Monica spent the rest of her time in London.

Monica loved her new status. She'd had no idea what it meant to spend money in this way; now she didn't even have to use a cheque book. They had accounts at Harrods, Peter Jones, Fortnum & Mason, Harvey Nichols and other large stores. When it came to jewellery, she didn't have to ask. Gordon showered her with diamonds, emeralds and rubies. And as his wife she had plenty of use for them for she always had to be well dressed in order to do the social and business honours. They ate out at least six times a week, although they had a full-time cook. Gordon also had a valet, Roberto, and Monica had a maid of her own. All she had to do was to tell Maria what she wanted to wear and the clothes were laid out on the bed. When they went away, Roberto and Maria always went with them. Nowadays she couldn't imagine how people lived without servants.

Monica had begun to drink, more than she really wanted to. She liked Gordon very much, but she did not love him, and she found their sex life very difficult without drinking. Fortunately, Gordon had no great sexual drive, and sometimes he disappeared for several days at a time, but she didn't mind. Or rather, she chose not to demand an explanation. Explanations seemed superfluous in this dream-like existence.

As often as she could, she went to see Robert at boarding school. He clearly missed her, but he was also enjoying the challenge of managing on his own although he was only ten. Monica was so busy in her rôle as the wife of a wealthy man, she spent less and less time at Hewitt Hall, and as a result left the practical running of it increasingly to Philip.

She loved seeing her name in print these days and had all the newspapers brought to her every day, even having Maria keep a scrap book of the articles where her name and photo appeared. If they were for some reason not invited to a society ball, she complained to Gordon, who was usually able to explain that at that particular time they'd been abroad. There was always a good reason.

Her call to Dior over, Monica picked up the receiver of the big white telephone and pressed the intercom button for Maria.

'Yes, Missa Clarke,' said her Spanish maid.

Maria's inability to speak correct English always irritated Monica – the girl might at least learn to pronounce Mrs Clarke.

'Tell Dennis to have the Rolls ready. I'll be down in five minutes.'

She glanced at her diamond-studded Piaget watch. God, she thought. I mustn't be late.

That night a charity ball was being held at the Grosvenor House Hotel and as a patron she simply must be on time. But it was already half past two and she ought to have been at Michaeljohn's in Albemarle Street to have her hair done by now. John had promised to create a totally new coiffure for her to match her pink and black satin Yves Saint-Laurent dress.

Ordinarily she swept her long blonde hair up into a chignon. She still sang the praises of the day Dr Holmes-Bay at the Harley Street Clinic had operated on her ears, and why she'd waited so long she didn't really know. It had hurt horribly and she had looked ridiculous with her whole head in bandages, but she'd planned the operation for Easter, passing the ten days it had taken for her ears to heal at the Hall. Only Robert, Mrs McDonald and Maria had seen her. Robert had been an angel, spending all his time with her apart from when he was out riding.

She truly loved her son above all else and longed for him to come and live with her and Gordon in Eaton Square. But both Philip and Gordon had said that Robert was now the new Lord Hewitt, and a young man in his position needed a good education, so after his prep school he would eventually be going to Eton.

Philip had changed a great deal compared with a few years earlier; he could even be quite pleasant occasionally, possibly

115

because she made it quite clear where the money came from. Her financial support for the Hall was on behalf of her son, the young lord. She was the one who had the power and the money.

Monica had neither the time nor the inclination to devote much attention to the Hall. The rose garden was still renowned though, and Lady Rose liked showing it to people as long as she was given notice, so Monica had insisted that a girl from the village should cycle there to help.

Lady Rose had aged markedly recently. She was finding it more and more difficult to get around and had almost completely lost her appetite, though she drank more than ever before. Monica was genuinely fond of her and wished there was something she could do for her. Without telling Philip, she'd made sure Lady Rose's allowance was increased a little.

The Rolls glided towards Hyde Park Corner, up Piccadilly and stopped at the red lights. At Dover Street they turned left. Monica glanced nervously at her watch. At last they stopped outside Michaeljohn's. Dennis came round and opened the door. She was twenty minutes late.

Although predictable enough the charity ball held one surprise: Edward's old flame – though flame was perhaps an exaggeration. Margret had stared goggle-eyed at Monica's couture dress and the diamond and ruby tiara. Nevertheless Monica had waved in recognition to her through the crowd from her place at the top table.

She had drunk too much champagne and leant towards her husband. Occasions like this were just what he had married her for, Gordon thought. Monica was perfect, but he did wish she didn't drink quite so much.

Gordon studied his wife. She was beautiful as well as having exquisite taste. But to date she'd cost him over two million pounds and he still found he had to seek out professionals. Their sex life was as good as non-existent. Monica seemed to be quite uninterested and he was tired of having to hide his inclinations.

One of the reasons he'd married her had been his wish for a child. Recently he had found out that Monica was on the pill, so he'd spoken to her about his longing for an heir. Gordon knew this was a sensitive matter, as Monica's last child had been still-born, but that was never discussed. Together, they had gone to Mr Gordon Bourne, the Queen's gynaecologist, and after a thorough examination, the doctor had said there were no obstacles whatso-ever to Monica becoming pregnant again and giving birth to a normal child. Mr Bourne had suggested that Monica should stop taking the pill and then after at least three months she could reckon on becoming pregnant again. But, given the frequency with which they had sex, the likelihood seemed limited.

Gordon was horribly bored by the ball as he mused on this unsatisfactory state of affairs.

'Darling, why don't we go to the White Elephant and play baccarat?' he asked suddenly.

'Of course, darling, if you really want to. Though I'd prefer to go to Annabel's. Everyone at Gerald White's table is going there. Let's play baccarat another night.'

'You go with them, I'll play for a while and join you later.'

Gordon draped the sable round his wife's shoulders and, smil-ing, escorted her through the crowded ballroom.

The Rolls stopped outside Annabel's in Berkeley Square.

'Dennis, wait here for Mrs Clarke,' he instructed. 'I'll walk to Curzon Street. I won't be long, darling.'

Gerald White and his party arrived at that moment in two chauffeur-driven Daimlers. Monica took Joan McInnes' arm and, laughing, the two women went down the stairs to the club.

Two hours later, Monica had had enough. She'd danced and drunk far too much and now she wanted to go home. It didn't matter that Gordon hadn't turned up. That was nothing new. In the Ladies' room she took a pound note out of her oval Bulgari bag and when she tried to close it again, she simply couldn't. God, how she detested that bag – no room for anything but a lipstick, the powder escaped all over the place from the little compart-ment, and she could never shut it properly. Some things in this new life of hers seemed so ridiculous!

When she came out from the club, Dennis helped her into the car.

'I'm tired, Dennis. Home, please.'

'Yes, madam.'

Back in her bedroom, Monica rang for Maria. It was half past three in the morning, but, heavens, what did you have a maid for?

A very sleepy Maria appeared.

'Ah, there you are. Help me out of my dress, would you? And don't forget to hang it up neatly. Then get me a bottle of Malvern water. And I need two Panadol, too.'

Monica had a splitting headache. Sitting in front of the mirror, she started taking out hairpins. John must have put hundreds into my head, she thought. No wonder I've got such a headache.

She took off her flimsy tights and bra and thankfully put on the cool pink silk dressing gown from the White House in Bond Street. She bought nearly all her nightwear from them.

Maria put down a silver tray with the water and the Panadol.

'May I go now, Missa Clarke?'

'It's Mrs Clarke. Missis. You must learn that. Missis. Do you hear?'

Maria looked wide-eyed at her, then quickly retreated. It was not the first time her mistress had been bad tempered lately.

Monica was putting her heavy diamond earrings into the safe, not even aware of Maria leaving, when suddenly the telephone rang. Her heart leapt into her throat. Who could be phoning at this hour?

Nervously, she lifted the receiver.

'Mrs Clarke?' a man's voice said.

'Yes,' she replied.

'This is Inspector Greystone from Notting Hill Gate police station. We have your husband here and suggest that you come and pick him up.'

Monica felt faint; she hadn't even given it a thought that Gordon wasn't at home. Her husband was at a police station?

'What's happened?'

'I suggest you come on down.'

'I'm not dressed.'

'Then I suggest you get dressed, Mrs Clarke.'

'Are there photographers there?'

'No, but we could arrange that, I suppose.'

She heard the crude laughter of the inspector's colleagues in the background. Slowly, she put down the receiver and in a daze went over to the wardrobe. What should she wear? She chose a pair of black Cacharel trousers and a black sweater, then grabbed her sable coat, and rang down to Dennis, who eventually answered.

'Dennis, bring the car round at once.'

'But, Mrs Clarke—'

'No questions,' she interrupted him abruptly. 'I'll be right down.'

They drove through the deserted streets to Notting Hill Gate. As they approached the police station she told Dennis to park and come inside with her.

She couldn't remember ever being in a police station before. What had happened? Had Gordon got involved in a fight? That would be quite unlike him.

They rang the night bell and a constable immediately opened the door and let them in. Monica went straight over to the hatch.

'I am Mrs Clarke,' she said nervously. 'My husband . . .'

'One moment,' the policeman interrupted.

She heard voices and footsteps in the distance and suddenly a side door opened. Inspector Greystone came in and introduced himself.

'Mrs Clarke,' he said. 'You have no need to worry. This is not a chargeable offence, but we couldn't let your husband go in this state.'

Another constable behind the inspector was supporting Gordon. When Monica saw him, she had to suppress a scream, but Dennis immediately stepped forward and led his boss firmly out and down the steps to the waiting car.

Monica could feel the blood in her veins draining away and the nausea coming in waves. She wasn't quite sure what she'd just seen. Was it possible that that had been her husband? Suddenly she had to have some air. Hand to her mouth, she rushed out into the street, leant over the gutter and threw up, tears pouring down her cheeks. When she'd calmed down, she felt Dennis's arm round her shoulders.

'I'm sorry, Mrs Clarke, I really am.'

11

Monica slowly opened her eyes to a sickening nausea; it was the 20th August 1972, her birthday. She carefully reached out for a dry biscuit on her bedside table. She knew she couldn't even move until she'd had one. This was her third month and her morning sickness was horrendous.

Maria knocked on the door. Thank God, here was her tea.

'Good morning, Missa Clarke.'

God, thought Monica, will the girl ever learn to say missis? Monica tried to be tolerant, only today she was feeling particularly vulnerable. It was her birthday and Robert wasn't at home.

Gordon had insisted that he should go to an exclusive camp in Boulder, Colorado, where he was to live in a tent, ride, and go hiking every day and build windbreaks whenever he had to spend the night in the open air.

Monica was appalled at the thought of her son being involved in anything unpleasant, but she knew that Gordon was right. He not only paid for Robert's school fees, but he'd begun to take a hand in his upbringing as well, for Gordon thought the boy was far too weak.

Gordon himself was at their property in St-Jean-Cap-Ferrat to supervise the renovation of their new house. Everything was supposed to be ready by September, when they were going to spend a few weeks there. That is, if Monica felt well enough. She'd have preferred to spend the rest of the year in bed.

Gordon was due back that afternoon and they'd planned a large birthday dinner at Tiberio's. Monica felt sick at the thought of having to eat Italian food, all that garlic and olive oil. She reached

121

for another biscuit. At least the truce prevailing between them had been working and Gordon was very considerate to her now she was pregnant.

Maria put the big tray on the bed, helped her sit up and put more pillows behind her back. Then she put a couple of newspapers and some telegrams on the bed and poured out a cup of tea with plenty of milk. Monica gulped it down.

'How do you feel today, Missa?' Maria said kindly.

'Fine, thanks.'

Monica had no desire to hear about Maria's difficulties with her children all over again; she'd already heard them a hundred times before. She swiftly turned back the delicate Porthault sheet covered with pink hearts, put the starched white table napkin across her stomach and did her best to eat her breakfast – food had been horribly difficult these last two months.

Halfway through breakfast, she opened one of the Sunday papers. She loved reading all the shabby revelations.

She bit absently into a piece of toast and read that Roger Moore had signed a contract for the new Bond film. She had always thought Sean Connery made the perfect James Bond, though Roger Moore really was wonderful as The Saint. That series had long been her favourite television programme. Watching television was one of the few things she could spend her time on now she was pregnant, as both shopping and lunching out had become impossible.

She sipped at the cold tea, and as she turned the page, she almost broke the delicate china cup by putting it down with a crash, her eyes glued to the headline:

GORDON HAD ME FOR A DIRTY WEEKEND

In a state of shock, she read on: 'Sexy Katarina Hove speaks about her past.'

The photograph was indeed of her old friend from her SAS days, but this time she was wearing a black corset, suspender belt, fishnet stockings and sky-high heels. She was posing on a fur-clad bed with her husband, the long-haired rock star, Robert Hove.

How her old friend had changed! Monica could hardly take it in as she skimmed through the painfully detailed article. Had Katarina no shame? Then her eyes fastened on what she had been so feverishly looking for.

'I'll never forget my weekend at Hewitt Hall. My ex-room-mate, Monica Forssgren, who later married Lord Edward Hewitt and became Lady Hewitt, had an engagement party at the Hall. The well-known society millionaire Gordon Clarke and I were the only outsiders at the party. It was probably the most boring dinner I've ever been to, but when the host and hostess retired, things began to happen. After several bottles of Dom Pérignon, Gordon and I ended up in his bedroom, where the champagne flowed freely. In the middle of it all, Gordon disappeared into the bathroom and I could hardly restrain myself from laughing when he came back dressed in nothing but a baby's nappy.'

The sensational Mrs Hove laughs heartily at the memory of this sight and goes on to tell me that after his appearance, Mr Clarke asked her to put on his tailor-made suit and the evening was concluded downstairs on an Aubusson carpet "where I rode him like a pony". His physical assets were pretty well non-existent. And as this is a family newspaper, unfortunately we cannot print the rest of Katarina's story.

The newly married Mrs Hove really has had a colourful past. Read on next week about her two-year relationship with a well-known nightclub owner and her sensational nights with an Arab prince. Not to mention her ultra-secret relationship with a member of the House of Commons.'

Monica pushed away the breakfast tray. She simply had to be sick, but this time it had nothing whatsoever to do with her pregnancy.

Afterwards, she rinsed her face thoroughly with cold water, and sank to her knees on to the marble floor of the bathroom.

Good God, what would people say? Tonight? She'd never be able to show herself either at San Lorenzo's, Meridiana's or any of the other restaurants where she and her friends usually lunched.

So that's what had happened that evening! Edward had made sure Mrs McDonald had driven Katarina to the station before Monica had even woken. The official version had been that Katarina had been so drunk she'd burnt the carpet and then woken poor Gordon to try to get him to come down with her to have some more champagne and God knows what else.

Edward had said that that was the last time she'd ever invite her friend to Hewitt Hall. Katarina's behaviour had been truly inappropriate.

So now, over ten years later, she'd found out what had really happened. God knows, she knew Katarina's story was true, except that it hadn't been their engagement party. But everything else was true. How could she ever forget the sight that had confronted her at Notting Hill Gate police station?

Her husband had come towards her, dead drunk and mumbling, dressed in a black corset, her own full-length dark red velvet skirt, long black gloves and an expensive chinchilla stole draped over his shoulders. In a bright red wig, his lips scarlet, and eyes that would have made Elizabeth Taylor look unmade-up, he'd stood there swaying between Dennis and a police constable, trying to give the impression that Monica was his girl-friend.

'Monica darling,' he'd shrieked. 'How nice of you to come and see your old girl-friend!' And his lips had pursed into a scarlet snout.

Until that moment, she'd had no inkling whatsoever of her husband's odd inclinations. It had been a terrible experience and her whole world had collapsed, but that had been only the beginning.

Quite suddenly everything had become clear to her. He'd been doing this for as long as she'd known him. She clearly remembered Edward's annoyance whenever Gordon unexpectedly disappeared. When he returned, Gordon just made out nothing had happened. And she'd frequently been unable to find her full-length skirts but had presumed they were at the cleaners, though she hadn't given the matter much thought. To find out that her husband was a transvestite had been so shameful, she'd thought she'd never get over it . . .

124

When they got back home on that appalling night, Dennis had helped Gordon to bed. Monica had taken two Mandrax to get through the remainder of the night and the following day she'd locked herself in her bedroom saying she had a migraine, though she soon saw that would solve nothing. So she'd asked Gordon's valet, Roberto, to tell Mr Clarke that she would like to see him at dinner.

She remembered with horror his self-righteous expression. He had been sitting in the living room with a bottle of Malvern water, an ice-bucket and a glass with a slice of lemon in it, with apparently no trace of shame over what had happened the night before.

'Sit down, my dear. I think it's time we had a little chat. May I offer you a glass of water? Or would you prefer champagne as usual?'

The irony in his voice had not been wasted on her. She'd been expecting him to apologise for his shameless behaviour, but he'd just sat there, comfortably leaning back in his armchair and looking her straight in the eye.

'No, thank you. I think I'll wait a while for champagne.'

'I thought you would. Water never was much to your taste, was it? This is the first occasion for a long time I've seen you without a glass in your hand. That's an expensive habit you've acquired since you married me, is it not? As Lady Hewitt, I suppose it was mostly water, if I'm not wrong.'

Monica remembered biting her lip and feeling her cheeks burning. Yet she hadn't really been able to believe what she was hearing. Why hadn't he humbly begged her forgiveness for the shame he'd brought on them both? Instead of just sitting there commenting on her drinking habits?

'Gordon, I'm devastated—'

Before she'd even finished the sentence, he'd broken in.

'Shut up and listen. Since we married, I have showered you with money. You were given an account of your own of over a million and that's nearly all gone, according to the bank. You have more jewellery than the Queen of England, and judging from your collection of furs, half the animals in the world are naked. You have a maid and a chauffeur, two Rolls-Royces at your disposal and one of the largest apartments in Belgravia. You had a decaying country mansion, but that is now in good order. In addition, your dear departed husband owed me half a million, which I have written off. Where did you think you got all that money from? You can't have thought your husband was famed for his business acumen? No, I was after his name and title.' He smiled at her, as if pleased with his own ruthlessness.

'I married you because I loved you in my own way,' he went on. 'You were humble and grateful for the slightest thing, and it gave me great satisfaction to see your delight every time you opened a present. But now it has all degenerated. What have I got out of it? An alcoholic, spendthrift fashion-plate who is also a wretchedly bad lover.'

Monica had fought back the tears. The last thing she wanted him to see was how hurt she was by these accusations. She started to get up.

'Sit down!' Gordon's voice cut like a whip. 'I've not finished yet. I am a transvestite and have been for as long as I can remember. Up until last night, no one except Dennis knew where I went when I "disappeared". I have always taken care of my own business and looked after my family. To the best of my ability, I have hidden my disposition from you, and when the desire has been too great for me, I have always been very discreet with my activities.'

'Discreet!' Monica had almost screamed. 'Do you call it discreet when I have to go and get you, painted, tarted up and drunk, from a police station at four o'clock in the morning? I'm so ashamed, I could die. And as far as my jewellery and clothes are concerned, you yourself created the "fashion-plate". That was the sort of wife you wanted. I could easily go back to the life I used to live.'

The moment she'd said it, she'd known that it was a terrible lie. But she'd gone on.

'I don't think I have ever seen you as drunk as you were last night. You were disgusting.'

'Possibly. What happened last night was unfortunate, I agree. And naturally, it will not be repeated, but there was a black woman who . . .'

'A black man, you mean.'

126

'Let me finish . . . who offered me some marijuana and as it is several years since I last tried it, I had quite forgotten that it doesn't agree with me. I prefer cocaine now and again.'

A transvestite and a drugtaker, she thought. What kind of man have I married?

'Now that you know my secret, you are part of it,' Gordon had declared as she had fled from the room in tears. It had sounded almost like a threat.

In a daze, Monica got up from the bathroom floor. How long had she been sitting there, sunk in the past, a past that was as hard to bear as the present?

To have a newspaper article flung in your face without warning was the most vile birthday gift she could have imagined. She went back into her bedroom and rang for Maria. The breakfast tray had been upset all over the bed.

'Yes, Missa.'

'Please change the sheets,' she ordered.

While she was waiting for Maria to finish, she sat in the chair by the window, looking down on to a sunlit Eaton Square.

Since Gordon had been told Monica was pregnant, his whole attitude had changed. If she hadn't known better, she might have believed that he loved her. His astonishing delight over at last becoming a father at the age of fifty-one had meant that at least an outsider would think he had fallen in love all over again. His consideration for her knew no bounds. She herself hated the prospect of being large and clumsy, the swollen breasts and constant backache. Thank heavens she could spend most days in bed. It had been quite different when she'd been expecting Robert. Then she'd had only poor Mrs McDonald to help and she'd had to manage on her own as best she could. But then Edward had been wonderfully supportive and she'd genuinely loved him.

'Your bed's ready, Missa Clarke. I help you?'

'I'm not an invalid, Maria. I'm just pregnant.' She got up and went over to the bed. 'Maria, how many times have I told you not to use these sheets? I simply hate them.'

Monica stared angrily at the blue and white striped linen sheets she'd clearly forgotten to throw out when she'd refurbished

Gordon's bedroom. She couldn't imagine where Maria had found them.

'Maria, go and get my Porthault sheets. There must be at least ten pairs in the linen cupboard. I never want to see these again.'

She sighed heavily and shook her head. She was feeling quite drained, although she'd done nothing at all. It must be the shock. Wearily, she went back to the window and sat down.

Gordon had been away almost a week. Thank goodness. If he hadn't spent so little time at home, she could never have made it this last year. The humiliation and abuse she was exposed to was not of this world. Ironically enough, their marriage was considered ideal by their friends, but today, after that article, the bubble would burst.

The thought of their fine façade collapsing from something as embarrassing as that newspaper article made her feel like crying. The only reason why she'd stayed with Gordon was that she'd no means whatsoever of her own. Although the Hall was now in good order, Gordon hadn't replaced any of the valuables they had been forced to sell during Edward's last years. Stupidly enough, she hadn't even thought of saving some of the money Gordon had put in her account. These days he only put in a thousand or two occasionally. Enough to pay for her lunches. She could still buy as many clothes as she liked – the bills from them went straight to Gordon – ready cash was another matter.

She'd once gone as far as to ask for a divorce, but Gordon had just smiled arrogantly and pointed out that as they had married in Bermuda, according to their laws she had no right to a penny of his fortune. He'd also gone on to explain that without his financial support, Hewitt Hall would decay and Robert's future would be ruined. Robert was a model pupil and the thought of him not being able to go on to Eton meant Monica continued to endure the constant humiliations Gordon so brutally exposed her to.

So it was not only her own expensive habits that meant she stayed with her husband. Most of all, it was to ensure a future for Robert, for whom she would go through hell.

She was going to pick him up at Heathrow in less than two weeks, and thankfully she'd have him with her for a whole week before he was due back at school. They hadn't been on their own together since Easter, when they'd been at Hewitt Hall and Gordon had been skiing in Colorado with some friends. Although she'd grown up in Sweden, she was not that keen on skiing and after Edward's accident it had been unthinkable to go skiing anywhere.

For that matter, she thought, this was the first year she hadn't gone back to Sweden in August.

She insisted that Robert should spend at least a week or two in her old country every summer, as it was important that he also knew about his Swedish roots. Gerd and Gunnar usually joined them in the ten-roomed villa with its wonderful view over the sea she rented at Värmdö. She loved crayfish and always looked forward to the traditional parties held at the beginning of the season. Gordon did not, she was glad to say, share her passion for the small red delicacies, so she always left him in England.

Gerd and Gunnar had very little contact with their new son-in-law. The only time Gerd had been to stay with them, her mother had been terrified by the thought of bumping into one of the delicate pieces of art-glass and lamps which filled the apartment. She hadn't said more than two words to Gordon, who'd gone away the very next day.

The telephone on her bedside table rang and Monica sat up.

'Joan. Of course I'm up. I presume you've read that awful article about me and Gordon in the *News*. I can't think where that creature got all those lies from. We're thinking of suing. I think we flew together once or twice in the Fifties, but I can't remember her ever being at Hewitt Hall. The papers pay for anything these days. What? That much? Well, then it pays to tell lies. Tonight? Of course. Why should it make any difference? Yes, but honestly, Joan, you know he never had anything to do with someone like that. How many are we going to be? Well, if the Rothschilds don't come, we'll be eighteen. No, I haven't got anything yet. He's coming back from the South of France this afternoon. But I expect it'll be something from Cartier. What are you going to wear? Oh, yes. Ah, then I certainly won't be wearing black. Oh, yes. He'll be back the week after next. We're going to Hewitt Hall. There's a seven hours time difference between London and Colorado, so I expect he'll phone early evening. How can you ask me how I am? I'm as sick as a dog in the mornings. I hate being pregnant, but Gordon so very much wants someone to take over the firm and it will be great for Robert to have a brother or sister. No, no. I'm just going to forget the fashion shows this autumn. I've no intention of flying to Paris fat as a cow. To be honest, can you see me dolled up in a pink Chanel suit at five months? But perhaps I should ask them to design my maternity clothes. That doesn't sound a bad idea. Monica Clarke's maternity wear by Chanel.'

The two friends laughed.

'No, to be serious, I can't think about clothes at the moment. I already feel like a sow. Yes, I understand. Hurry then. See you this evening.'

After her conversation with Joan, Monica at once felt much better. Of course it was all a pack of lies, the whole lot. If she told herself that firmly enough she'd believe it. She decided to take a walk in Hyde Park.

'Run my bath, would you?' she called to Maria. 'And tell Dennis I want the blue Rolls. I'll drive myself. And, Maria, tell the cook I want something to eat.'

Monica drove round Belgrave Square, past St George's Hospital and turned left at Knightsbridge. Oh dear, she'd taken the wrong turn. Then she'd have to go into the park by Sloane Street. Lucky there wasn't much traffic on Sundays.

She parked the car on South Carriage Drive and took her big sun hat off the back seat, leaving her handbag behind. She put the car keys into the pocket of her silk dress and started walking slowly towards Park Lane. A bunch of Americans were playing softball on her left and further on some kids were kicking a soccer ball about.

This was her thirty-third birthday and she was living an apparently golden life. Not even her closest friend had the slightest idea what she had to go through.

After that night at the police station, Gordon had been transformed into a Dr Jekyll and Mr Hyde. From being a considerate and accommodating husband, he had turned into a madman. It was true she'd never really enjoyed their sex life. On the contrary, she had found it a torment. That was one of the reasons why she'd started drinking. But she really had tried. To give the bedroom some atmosphere, she had lit candles everywhere and she'd dressed up in lovely sexy négligés, but all the same she had sensed that Gordon was never really satisfied.

But now. The dam seemed to have burst since she'd been given a glimpse of his secret world. Gordon had swiftly drawn up the guidelines for their future life together and she could do nothing but adapt if she wanted to stay.

She never knew when it would happen. It could come at any time, and she lived in dread of the telephone call from Gordon which always consisted of the same sentence.

'It's girls' night out tonight.'

That meant the staff would be given the night off and instructed to stay away from the apartment. But before the cook went, she was to prepare 'a feminine meal'. That could be, for instance, vol-au-vent, and a salad with vinaigrette dressing, cold lobster with Krug Brut Reserve champagne and a light dessert.

The ritual was always the same. Gordon, now to be called Georgina, would come into her bedroom wearing women's clothing and a wig he'd selected for that evening. Then Monica's task was to sit down with Georgina at the dressing table and exchange make-up and beauty tips. He loved the feminine atmosphere which, after considerable quantities of champagne, she managed to conjure up. Georgina usually insisted that the two girl-friends should share another bottle while they giggled together at the dressing table.

Naturally Monica had to do Georgina's nails and sometimes she had to re-do them several times before they found the right shade. Apart from the wig and make-up, Monica had to get out her jewel case. He usually chose thick, heavy gold chains for his neck and wrists, and heavy, dangling earrings.

Then, draped across the big pink four-poster and, with the television quietly on in the background, giggling, he would ask how things were with Monica's husband. He loved questioning her

131

about Gordon, and Monica always told him how wonderful her marriage was and how generous her husband was, and of course what a stud he was in bed, how she could never get enough. Georgina always tittered over the latter.

'I wish I had a husband who loved me like that. But you know how deadly Herbert is. I should be pleased he's rich and is away a lot, as sex with him is—' He finished the sentence with a shrug. 'Perhaps I should get myself a little something on the side.'

On these occasions Monica never really knew whether it was Gordon or Georgina talking. Did he really have a man called Herbert in his life?

The very first time, she hadn't understood how important it was that she played her part with empathy. She had laughed hysterically at his appearance, but she'd learnt never to do that again, for that night he'd almost killed her. Now she surprised even herself at the professional way she performed her rôle as Georgina's girl-friend.

The next phase came after dinner. Georgina would thank her for the meal and complain that unfortunately she had to go home to boring old Herbert. She hoped that Baby Gordon wouldn't wake up and keep her up all night. Monica always assured her that he was such a good baby and slept all through the night.

Then she had to go back to her bedroom and change into a dark blue or grey suit Gordon had selected. There was no question of underwear. She'd put her hair up inside a cap and get out one of her Gucci crocodile belts. When she heard Gordon's baby wails, she knew that it was her turn again.

She had to go downstairs to the living room where Gordon would be lying kicking like a little baby, in nothing but a nappy. To see a grown man with well-trained muscles lying gurgling on an exquisite velvet sofa among beautiful art and furniture was absurd, but Monica knew what was expected of her.

'Baby Gordon, quiet now. Mummy's here.'

But he would go on wailing, louder than ever.

'If Baby Gordon doesn't stop, then Mummy will have to give him a spanking.' Then she would take out the belt and strike him hard across his naked body.

Baby Gordon would snivel pitifully and Monica would have to console him by stroking his head, now lying in her lap. But then he would begin screaming again and the procedure would be repeated. That could go on for at least half an hour, until Gordon indicated he was ready. Then he would tear off the nappy, pull up her skirt, bend her face down over the sofa, and brutally penetrate her anus. That was the only position that would really satisfy him. Fortunately he usually came fairly quickly, but the pain for her was always excruciating.

But worst of all was the humiliation of having to go through this bizarre ritual. It was always exactly the same, every single time, the only difference the colour of the wigs and clothes. Gordon would always go on a business trip the following day, and when he came back again a few days later, he behaved as if nothing had happened. The one thing that still surprised her was when Gordon demanded perfectly ordinary sex. Then he preferred her to ride him without the slightest suggestion of foreplay. Sometimes she wondered however she'd got trapped in this strange, topsy-turvy life . . .

As she strode along, Monica began to feel stronger. She ought to go for walks much more often. In the past, she used to ramble for hours round the grounds of Hewitt Hall, but usually her 'walks' were limited to the brief distance between car and party, restaurant or one of the many designers she visited several times a week.

Monica stopped for a moment to enjoy the dazzling greenery all round her. When she turned away from the buildings of the city, she might have been in the countryside round Hewitt Hall or even in Sweden.

She felt a stab of nostalgia when she thought about her own country.

She had only gradually grown to love London and sometimes regarded England as her 'new' country. Her attitude had been a subject of irritation to Edward: she'd always talked about going home when the destination had been Sweden, and on their way back she'd always referred to it as England. He thought it should be the other way round.

'England is your home now, darling.'

Edward's voice now echoed strangely inside her.

It suddenly struck her how seldom she took time off to think, to look at her life. It was actually years since she'd given either Sweden or Edward a thought. Where did all her time go?

Her new life took up every ounce of her energy and God knows, it wasn't always easy. The changes over the last few years would have thrown the most harmonious person off balance. The façade she'd had to show her friends had become solid and impenetrable. She'd become a fully-fledged champion at changing reality to suit herself, even if that entailed occasionally modifying the truth.

She took out a Rothmans from her gold Cartier case and mechanically lit the cigarette.

The cigarette case was the first present Gordon had given her, and he still lived in the belief that it was the same one. How wrong he was! Monica had lost count now, but she'd mislaid at least five of them and replaced them with identical ones. They must have had some fun at her expense at Cartier, because they never even asked what should be inscribed on the back – they knew it by heart: 'To Monica. I will always be there when you want me. Your friend Gordon.'

How she wished it had stopped at that *your friend* and not developed into the nightmarish situation she now found herself in. At the time, he really had been a good friend, supporting her when things were difficult.

Monica felt much better for the fresh air, but she'd hardly smoked half the cigarette, when that all too familiar sense of panic began to come over her.

Usually the feeling did not make itself felt until she'd put down her book or newspaper and switched off the light to try to sleep. But this hadn't exactly been an eventless day, she could still see that headline: GORDON HAD ME FOR A DIRTY WEEKEND.

She was again seized with panic, this time fiercer than ever, the desire to scream overwhelming. She managed to control herself. She could feel the sweat running down her spine, the thin silk sticking to her body; her mouth was dry. The thought of being pregnant and feeling like this sent further waves of panic through her.

How awful, she thought. I must have put on several pounds since last week.

She hadn't been to Lotte Berk's in Manchester Square for at least six weeks. If not more. In her mind her thighs and arms had turned into wobbling fat lumps. At least, that's what it felt like. And she had always had such a slim figure.

God knows, how she hated being pregnant.

She actually missed Lotte's voice. 'Girls, the fucking position, please.' The fucking position meant lying on your back with your feet firmly on the floor, knees bent and stomach tucked in, then making small sexual intercourse type movements.

Slightly disorientated, she looked around the park, then she spotted the blue Rolls through the trees. Luckily she'd parked it in the shade.

Her feet had swollen in her thin Charles Jourdan sandals and the straps were cutting into her feet for every step she took. If only she could take them off, but what would that have looked like? Mrs Clarke barefoot in Hyde Park!

How stupid of her to go for a walk on a hot August afternoon in London.

Again she was seized with panic, her heart racing, she felt herself sweating profusely again. What would become of her life if this was how she was coping with its pressures?

She fumbled with the keys and managed to open the car door despite her shaking hands. The heat, mixed with that special smell of leather particular to Rolls-Royces, struck her the moment she got into the back. She at once wound down the window.

From her dark blue Hermès handbag she took out a white silk handkerchief with her monogram in one corner and wiped her hairline and under her arms, then she stuffed it resolutely between her legs and left it there.

There was a walnut-veneered bar mounted in the back of the front seat, inside were three crystal decanters containing whisky, brandy and fresh water, which Dennis filled every morning. Monica drank the water as she feverishly searched in her bag for the little round diamond-clasped Cartier pill box. She took out the Gucci address book. The attached pen had fallen out somewhere in her bag. Then her gold compact, and lipstick.

At last she found the round box she'd been looking for so frantically. No, damn, it was that blasted keyring. Damned tortoise. The ring was shaped like a tortoise, made of gold and enamel. Gordon had given it to her some years ago, jokingly pointing out that she'd come out of her shell like a tortoise. She threw the keys angrily on the back seat. The panic and the sweating attacks had not subsided. She must find that damned pill box. She leant quickly forward and opened the window on the other side in the hopes of some kind of cross-draught.

At last!

She'd meant to take only one, but in her haste it became three and she felt the water helping them slide down her throat.

With the Valium, she reckoned she would get through the afternoon. In any case it was high time she went home, but she chose to lie back and wait for the effect of the drug.

She was fully aware her doctor would question her judgement. From the very beginning, he'd emphasised that she should keep off pills of any kind, though he'd assured her that Valium wouldn't cause damage to the foetus. But what had happened to Amanda lived with her forever.

Once again she thought about the newspaper headline and with panic rising and her hand trembling, she half filled the glass with brandy, drank it and put the glass back.

'Dear Lord, forgive me. As long as I don't damage my baby, but I really need it.'

A few minutes went by and the Valium settled like cotton wool round her mind, the problem fading at the same pace as her movements.

Slowly she moved to the front seat. Her gold Piaget said quarter to five. Soon she was on her way home.

London was really showing its very best side this late summer day. The car glided along the street and she again passed St George's Hospital, at last feeling completely calm. With a vague feeling at the back of her head that something wasn't quite right, she turned into Belgrave Square, in such a daze it never occurred to her to look right.

The crash was deafening.

Monica was thrown against the windscreen and the wheel struck her in the stomach. She fell unconscious across the front seat with blood running down her face.

The chauffeur of the big Austin Princess got out unhurt and, frightened, hurried across to the totally crushed wing of the Rolls. He looked in through the window and saw Monica's body.

God Almighty, he thought. Is she dead?

12

It was half past one in the afternoon and Earl's Court was throbbing with life. Katarina had forgotten to pull down the blind, so
the sun was shining straight into her eyes. How could she have
been so bloody stupid?

Her head felt as if someone were shrinking it and her tongue
was like a dry leaf in her mouth. Eyes only half open, she looked
down at her apparently lifeless husband. They'd taken the same
amount last night. She closed her eyes. Oh well, if I'm alive, no
doubt he is, too.

She reached for the sticky glass of water and took a gulp, then
her fingers eagerly felt for the pack of cigarettes. Relieved, she lit
the first one of the day with the gold lighter Rob had given her
when they first got together.

She coughed desperately after the first puff and her thin body
shook, her headache devastating. She put the cigarette out in the
glass of water and, with her hand over her eyes, got out of bed and
shuffled over to the bathroom to find an aspirin.

She opened the medicine cupboard and took out two Panadol,
filled the pink toothbrush mug that hadn't been washed since she
had bought it, with water and, grimacing, swallowed the pills.

She never seemed to learn. The effects of cocaine, alcohol and
Mandrax were always the same – a horrible headache and pains
all over that took hours to get rid of.

But, Christ, what fun they'd had. Rob had been in the studio
when Katarina and the other girls had met up about twelve. The
routine was always the same when Rob and the band went into
the studio to make a new album. At four thirty he went to the

studio, and at midnight the girls were allowed in.

Rob was very special. When he was putting down his vocals he demanded that the studio should be empty. No one could be there except the producer, who'd often operate the mixing board himself. Then the rest of the band would pop down to the pub or have a game of billiards on the table in the foyer.

The owner of the studio sometimes let groupies in to meet the band, though not entirely from benevolence, as he made sure his own needs were satisfied before the girls were let out into the foyer. But of course it was Rob they were after. At midnight, when Katarina usually swept in to join her husband, she always gave the girls a condescending glance to make sure they realised it was Mrs Hove arriving.

She was fully aware that she was the oldest of the girls. Rob was thirty-one and at the peak of his career, and some of the guys in the band wondered why he'd married a flat-chested thirty-four-year-old ex-call girl. But as long as Rob was happy, they were.

Robert Hove came from a typical working-class background. His father was a fishmonger who had to get up at four every morning and his mother worked in a newsagent's. Despite Rob's success and his wish to buy them a new house, they refused to leave their home in Brixton.

The Rob Hove Band had been playing together for five years. From being a typical pub band who made their living playing covers, two years ago they had signed a contract with Arinome, a new record label looking for raw talent.

The band's first album had sold pretty well in Britain, and had become very popular in West Germany. There was hardly a German club the RH Band hadn't played.

They were also famous as a party band and wherever they went there were always plenty of willing girls, amphetamines and more beer than they could ever drink. One of the reasons for their success was that they seldom contented themselves with one or two shows a night but often went on playing until five or six in the morning.

Their single, 'I'm Hot On You, Babe', had been released in time for Christmas, 1971, and had quickly climbed to number seven on the UK hit list. The album was released in February the following year and a tour hastily planned.

The first time Katarina had seen Rob Hove was at the end of January on *Top of the Pops*. She had at once known he was the one she wanted.

Behind the sleazy dark brown hair under a black leather cap, the grey-and-black striped shirt hanging out, the obligatory black leather waistcoat and patched jeans, she saw a hungry body she knew she would be able to satisfy.

There was something vulnerable about him, perhaps his expressive green eyes, that had attracted her. Perhaps it was something else. His hollow cheeks and long chin made his nose look bigger than it really was. Big nose, big . . .

When the tour reached London on the 3rd of March and the band was playing the Hammersmith Odeon, Katarina had been there, both in front and eventually backstage. And that night she had found use for all the skills she'd learnt during her years as a 'professional'. No wonder Rob insisted that she should come with them on tour when the coach went on to Wales the next day.

They had been together day and night ever since, and on the 24th of June, they'd been married at Chelsea Registry Office.

Katarina had sent Mel out for the Sunday papers. He lived more or less permanently in the other bedroom when he wasn't touring with the band and functioning as Rob's personal roadie. Otherwise he was everything from their drug pusher to cleaner and general handyman.

Despite her headache, she managed to get to the kitchen and switch on the electric kettle. She opened the dishwasher, took out three dirty cups and put them under the hot tap, then whisked round each of them with the brush. Yesterday's coffee stains remained, but to hell with that, she thought as she put the wet cups on the draining board and took down the big jar of Nescafé. She put two heaped spoons in each cup and opened the refrigerator – it was empty except for two bottles of milk and ten cans of beer.

Katarina grimaced and thought to herself that as soon as Mel got back, she would have to send him out again. For a second she thought of having a beer, but stopped herself and put some milk in a pan on the gas stove. When it had almost boiled she poured it in the cups and then topped the lot with some water from the kettle. She put four spoons of sugar in one cup and stirred, then took it to the bedroom and put it on the table next to Rob.

She tried waking him with a kiss on the mouth, but he just grunted and pulled the pillow over his head.

'Silly ass,' she said tenderly, and went out again.

With a cup in her hand, she sank down on the sofa in the big room, which also functioned as a dining room, and looked at the coffee table in front of the fire. The sight and smell of the overflowing ashtrays, empty beer cans and an empty whisky bottle was disgusting.

The rattan table with its glass top was sticky from the night before and right in front of her was the razor blade. She covetously ran her finger over the glass surface and a line of greyish-white powder formed along it. Quickly she rubbed her finger along the gums of her top jaw.

The cocaine mixed with ash almost made her sick, but the effect wasn't at all bad. Her mouth at once went numb and a few seconds later she felt the familiar racing of her heart.

She took a gulp of the coffee and screamed. Her mouth may have gone numb, but her throat still felt what was hot and what was cold. Quite unexpectedly she began to feel sick and rushed to the bathroom, but nothing came up. The cocaine mixture must have done that.

I never seem to learn, she sighed to herself as she put her face under the cold tap.

'Mel, did you buy all the Sunday papers?' she yelled as she heard the front door open.

'No, they hadn't got the *People*.'

Ordinarily she would have sent him out again for the food and the paper, but as she wanted him to clean up the living room, she held her tongue. She loathed the sight of full ashtrays.

'Mel,' she said softly. 'I've made some coffee for you. It's out in the kitchen. I hope it hasn't gone cold.' She knew perfectly well it had.

To get him slightly more interested in doing the shopping and cleaning, she thought she might soften him up with a little conversation.

'Just look at the table, Mel. What really happened here last night?'

'Last night was a right bloody rave-up. We went from the studio to a party at Marc's in Hampstead. Don't you remember?'

'Marc?'

'Marc Bolan.'

Ah yes, the memory suddenly came back. They'd all come back here afterwards.

'But where did all the beer come from?'

'I don't bloody know. Do you want one?'

Well, why not, she thought. Things couldn't get worse.

'Do you know if there's any coke left?'

Mel just looked at her, but didn't reply.

Katarina shrugged and asked him to help her take some of the things out into the kitchen.

Mel went to the refrigerator and took out two beers, ripped off a ring with his teeth and handed it opened to Katarina, who looked steadily at him as she gulped back the cold beer.

'Mel, I know you. You're a mean bloody Scot. Where have you hidden the rest of the coke? You think I don't remember, but I saw Rob give you at least two hundred pounds yesterday.'

'I know, but when Rob wakes up he'll have some left.'

'Doesn't matter,' she said. 'You know where there's some more. Rob won't wake for an hour or two.' She picked up a blue and white towel and wiped the table top carefully. 'Come on, hand it over,' she commanded.

Mel disappeared into the little bedroom beyond the kitchen and came out with a knotted plastic bag partly filled with white powder.

Katarina's heart started racing even faster. What an asshole, she thought. Had he really thought he could keep all that for himself, or was he so faithful to Rob that he was hanging on to it?

She took the plastic bag and, with the beer in her other hand, sat down on the Habitat orange and red striped sofa. She'd actually been partly responsible for choosing the damn thing – it was good to look at but damned uncomfortable to sit on.

She plumped up the orange Thai silk cushions, carefully opened the plastic bag and, with the help of the razor blade, divided the cocaine in two lines. She looked round for the short silver tube, but it suddenly occurred to her that last night they'd used a rolled-up hundred-dollar bill. Who the hell had nicked it? Not that she remembered whether it had really been theirs, but all the same.

'Mel!' she yelled.

She could hear the tap in the kitchen running and realised he had started on the dishes.

'Mel!' she yelled again.

The tap was turned off and Mel appeared with a towel slung over his shoulder. 'You called, madam?' he said slightly maliciously.

His sarcasm was lost on her.

'Last night there was a hundred-dollar bill here on the table. I remember quite clearly.'

'Yes, that's absolutely right, but it wasn't yours.'

'Oh, then whose was it?'

'It was Marc's, and he took it back.'

Bastard, she thought. She could have done with it. She loved her husband, but he could hardly be called generous. A hundred dollars would have been enough for a new dress.

'Here you are,' said Mel, pulling the silver tube out of his pocket.

He knew exactly how far he could go with Katarina. Although she was not the one with the money, he knew that she decided who should stay and who should go. And he liked the room off the kitchen. There were always drink and drugs, and sometimes, when they were alone and Katarina was drunk, she told him marvellous stories about her past.

She was not bad to look at. Tall and slim, with long dark red hair, she made out she was thirty-one, but the lines round her mouth and eyes told another story. He also knew with certainty that her next birthday was her thirty-fifth. When he'd been getting visas for the US tour in May – the band were only going on a short promotion tour – he'd been the one to put in their applications and he'd had confirmation of his suspicions in black and white. He didn't know whether Rob knew her real age, but on the other hand it didn't really matter.

Mel had been with Rob for almost seven years and he had never seen him happier than he was now. Katarina had also turned Rob into the very attractive rock star he undeniably was today. She had taken him to Vidal Sassoon, who had trimmed his shoulder-length hair and put some blond streaks in it. Katarina had also seen to it that Rob had a tailor make all his clothes. All he had to buy was his shoes, and she went with him for those, too, to make sure they were right. Mel realised how important Katarina's influence on Rob actually was.

As he saw it, Rob was The Boss and Katarina was his Missus.

'Do you want some?' said Katarina as she stuck the silver tube into her nostril and drew in the whole line. 'Oh!'

Mel heard her out in the kitchen, and that was only one nostril, he thought as he wiped the draining board. Christ, why not, it was Sunday after all. He flung the dishcloth in the sink.

Katarina opened the bag again and repeated the procedure. Mel took his line and went over to the stereo to put on the latest Slade record. He knew Katarina liked them: the Rob Hove Band sounded not dissimilar. Or perhaps that was why?

He sat down in the green corduroy armchair and reached out for one of the Sunday papers.

'Mel, would you be an angel and get another beer for me?' said Katarina, taking the paper out of his hand.

She nervously leafed through the *News*. She'd done it because they'd paid five hundred pounds and guaranteed they would mostly stick to her exciting life with Rob and how happy they were together. They had insisted on being allowed to write a bit about her background but at the same time had assured her it was not that angle they were after.

The headline that hit her was not exactly what she had expected. Panic began to set in. Supposing Rob saw this: GORDON HAD ME FOR A DIRTY WEEKEND.

The telephone rang shrilly. She at once knew who it was. Who else but Alex Debenham would ring at this hour on a Sunday morning. Well, it was half past two, but all the same.

'Katarina? Oh, so you're up early. What's this shit I've been reading? Has Rob approved it?'

She could feel the effect of the cocaine and for a moment thought her heart was going to burst. She was gasping, the sweat beading her top lip as she spoke very rapidly.

'Alex, Rob was there at the interview. Of course he knows what went in. But the bastards promised it would be about us and his career. It's not my fault!' The words were tumbling out of her mouth.

She hadn't read the whole article, it was true, but the headline implied the contents were about her and her past rather than Rob and his present success.

She reached for her beer and took a gulp. 'Rob's in the shower at the moment, but I'll have him call you as soon as he's out.'

Katarina threw down the receiver and quickly read through the article. It contained everything she'd said but hadn't thought they would print. When she looked up, Mel was standing in front of her.

'Is it good?' he said.

Katarina glared angrily at him. 'I'm thirsty, I need another beer.'

Mel obediently went to the kitchen and got her a beer.

Katarina leant back against the cushions and pulled her black kimono more firmly round her body, then put the beer can down with a bang and rushed out into the bathroom. Once there, she looked at herself in the mirror.

Good Christ Almighty, she thought when she saw her own reflection. She had forgotten to take off her make-up last night, she who had always been so proud of her good skin. Now she had dark rings under her eyes and lumps of mascara in the corners. Her bright red lipstick had gone, but there was still a faint trace round the edge of her lips.

When the basin was full of hot water, she soaped her face thoroughly all over. She hated seeing herself the day after. She rinsed her face and rubbed in some Clinique daycream, brushed her hair and cleaned her teeth.

Her heart had calmed down and she knew what she had to do.

146

First she would send Mel to Safeway's round the corner and then she would go in and wake her husband in her own special way.

She took the flannel and rinsed it several times before carefully washing between her legs. When that was done, she went out and closed the bathroom door behind her.

'Mel,' she said ingratiatingly, 'would you mind doing the shopping? I want to get a good lunch for Rob, and you, of course.'

Mel went to the front door, put on his leather jacket and disappeared down the stairs.

As soon as the door had slammed shut, Katarina went into the bedroom and let the kimono fall to the floor. She pulled back the blanket, lifted the pillow off Rob's head and resolutely sat on his face.

13

Sister Lisbeth showed Gordon the door to Monica's private room.

'She'll be confused. She's had a concussion, and as you know, she lost the baby. It's possible she will have a scar on her forehead where she hit the windscreen, but that's hard to say at the moment.'

'Is she awake?'

'Yes, but she's sure to be feeling very poorly, so please don't stay too long.'

Gordon stayed where he was for a few seconds before going in, out of habit straightening his tie. After all, this was a business meeting.

What had happened had hit him hard. He was a man who had everything and was used to getting everything. And now, when at last he was to have what he most desired and what he could not have bought for money – a child . . . He hadn't been concerned about the child's sex. To him a male heir wasn't necessary. A woman could take over his business just as well.

His anger rose. How had Monica dared risk the life of their expected child?

He slowly opened the door and saw Monica's pale face and the bandage round her head. She was asleep and breathing heavily. Impatiently, he wished she would wake up. He had no desire to stay any longer than necessary in this dismal place.

He stared intently at Monica and she slowly opened her eyes. Gordon sat down on the chair by the bed.

'Monica, my dear.' He looked into her eyes. 'We both know what has happened.'

Monica was trying to shake off the effects of the anaesthetic and could only hear Gordon through a fog.

'I'm so thirsty. Could you give me something to drink?'

'Of course,' he said. He poured out a glass of water from the carafe on her bedside table, then got up to help her drink. When she had finished, he sat down again and straightened out the creases in his pale grey gabardine trousers.

'I've spoken to the doctor, and as far as they can make out, there are traces of sedatives and alcohol in your blood. According to Dr Stanley, it is possible that the combination reduced your ability to react and so was probably a contributory cause of the accident.'

He got up abruptly and started striding to and fro, then stopped suddenly and turned to Monica, his face scarlet. He had controlled himself long enough.

'My child! You've killed my child! You knew perfectly well how much I wanted this child. And now you've murdered it.' He spat out the words.

Monica dropped the half-full glass and backed up towards the bedhead, terrified of what her husband was going to say and do next.

Gordon started towards Monica, who desperately fumbled for the bell that called the nurse, clutching at the little box.

'Touch that and I'll kill you! Do you hear? To hell with the consequences. You've murdered my child.'

Her terror of Gordon had shaken Monica out of her daze. Her heart was thumping. She knew he meant every word he said. She dropped the bell box, picked up the empty glass off the bed and leant forward.

'Gordon . . . Gordon, I . . .'

With a sweeping gesture, he struck the glass from her hand and grabbed at her white hospital shirt with both hands.

'You listen to me . . .'

Monica felt sick and put her hand to her mouth, the nausea rising and heaving her whole body.

Gordon at once let go and hastily pulled back. He straightened his jacket and strode over to the window facing Knightsbridge. He took a silk handkerchief out of his inside pocket and dabbed his forehead. Then he drew a deep breath. He could hardly recognise himself. It was most unlike him to lose control completely.

He bowed his head and let out a sigh, full of grief over the loss of his child. Then he looked up, straightened his shoulders and turned back to Monica, still lying with her hand over her mouth. Her pupils were enlarged from the narcosis and terror: she looked like an old-fashioned china doll.

'Monica . . .' Gordon's tone of voice had changed completely. He was now in full control again. 'I am quite aware of the content of that article.'

Gordon had to mobilise all his strength to appear unmoved. The *News* was not the kind of paper he usually read, but he knew only too well his wife's childish delight in that type of tabloid gossip.

When Dennis had met him at the airport, it was already seven o'clock, as the plane had been over an hour late. Now that he had acquired a villa on the Riviera, he realised the time had come when he would have to get his own plane. He had just been looking through some brochures on the new Lear executive jet. It had eight seats and since the villa was ready, he had decided to order one. He had even amused himself with the idea of putting the Hewitt coat-of-arms on the side of the plane.

With the brown suit bag over his shoulder, he'd hurried through customs, glancing at the clock and realising he would never get to Tiberio's on time. He would call Franco and ask him to give his guests some well-chilled champagne while they were waiting for his and Monica's arrival.

'Mr Clarke, there's been an accident.' With those words of greeting, Dennis had taken the Gucci bag off his shoulder. 'Mrs Clarke is in hospital.'

On his way to St George's, he had read the newspaper article and was disgusted by the contents. How could the woman write about his private affairs, about something that happened almost twelve years ago? He had completely forgotten the episode with Monica's friend, but that she should reveal something as intimate as that . . . and then have the nerve to describe his sexual inclinations!

Dennis told him that he didn't know how the accident had

happened, but from Maria he had learnt that, well, yes, Mrs Clarke had seen the article too.

As the London streets flashed by Gordon decided on a course of action. He had previously bought three cruise ships to run between Florida, the Bahamas, Bermuda and Barbados beginning in January, 1973. He hadn't thought of personally supervising and marketing the line, but the situation being what it was at the moment, he decided to spend the coming months in Bermuda.

Now, as Gordon looked round the sterile hospital room, the thought of Bermuda was more tempting than ever. Monica was lying with both arms down her sides, quite still, her eyes avoiding his.

'Naturally the content is very unfortunate, and I know how important it is to you what other people think. How you handle the situation is up to you. I am going to Bermuda until Christmas to supervise my new cruise line. I'm sure your friends will have forgotten this unnecessary episode by then. I want you to listen very carefully to what I have to say.'

He opened wide his cold unemotional eyes.

'I'll be back by Christmas and expect us to spend it together at Hewitt Hall. After that I'll take Robert skiing with me to St Moritz. I see no reason to change our habits. And, as usual, I presume you won't be coming with us. But now I'm going to say what I really want you to understand.

'I am fully aware that you do not love me, but at the same time, I know how much you love my money. In the four years we've been married, I have spent an equal amount of millions on you. All I have wanted in exchange has been a child. I have loved you in my way, but you needn't worry, that feeling has gone completely. From now on, this is nothing but a business arrangement. You have two alternatives. One is that we try again after Christmas. Dr Stanley has assured me there is no reason why you should not become pregnant again. If you give birth to my child within eighteen months, counting from the New Year, I'll put a million into an account for you in Switzerland. Tax-free, of course. Meanwhile you can go on living as you're used to and you need lack for nothing. Also, neither this accident nor the newspaper article will ever be mentioned again.'

Monica was in a cold sweat. So what he wanted was to turn their marriage into a business transaction? Georgina, she thought feverishly. What'll happen about Georgina?

Gordon interrupted her thoughts.

'On the other hand, you can choose divorce. But as we married in Bermuda, I don't have to pay alimony. If we go our separate ways, that'll leave you with nothing. I know what you're thinking. You can always return to Hewitt Hall. Am I right? But according to my calculations, you would only manage the costs of upkeep for a while. After that, the Hall would have to go. Then we have Robert's education. I don't think you have the slightest idea what his school fees are. How would you manage that in future especially when he's at Eton? I presume you want to complete his education? Anything else would be disgraceful for such a promising boy.'

Monica suddenly realised why Gordon had insisted on the wedding being held in Bermuda. She would have preferred Paris, but he had persisted. How naive she had been.

'I'll be back tomorrow, and I want you to think carefully over what I've said. If for nothing else, then for Robert's sake. And you must agree that it's a generous offer. By the way, congratulations on your birthday.'

He put a red Cartier box beside her on the bed.

'Your answer tomorrow will settle whether all the nice things will stop with the contents of this box or whether there will be any more . . .'

He turned on his heel and left a dumbfounded and confused Monica fingering the jeweller's box.

Philip's career had picked up. After Stuart Corke, he had found it difficult to think up a new hero that his publisher would accept as sufficiently modern. He had let Stuart make a magnificent exit. In the book he'd had a wealthy shipping magnate die quite inexplicably of a heart attack, with nothing suspicious arising from the post mortem. Stuart had been the only one to listen to the daughter and continue the investigation on his own long after the police had closed the case and the third young wife had walked away with the entire fortune.

Stuart Corke had fought for a second post mortem and in the end a pinprick had been found in the man's navel. It was established that ricin had been injected, an extract from the plant world which caused internal bleeding or heart attacks without leaving a trace behind.

Stuart Corke had the grieving widow convicted, the fortune went to the daughter, and he himself left the book as a hero.

But, despite his problems in coming up with a new character, last spring, Philip's latest book had been published and this time featured two detectives, one of whom was actually a lord. It had always been against his principles to make use of his background, but finally the idea had been so tempting, he had been unable to resist it. Now ITV had bought the rights and were to make a television series out of it.

Recent years had been very profitable for Philip. Gordon had been extremely generous, but neither he nor Monica had spent much time at the now almost totally renovated Hall and Philip and Lady Rose had mostly been there on their own. During the school holidays, Monica came to be with Robert, and about once a month Gordon and Monica came down with their staff for large business dinners.

He was amazed at the change in Monica recently. He had never approved of his brother's choice of second wife, but he had to admit she had worked hard to keep everything together during the difficult years. But now she didn't seem to be able to lift a finger and even had a maid of her own.

Their relationship, which had never been good, was now limited to a few polite phrases. But he was well aware of the advantages of Monica's marriage, indeed he had contributed to bringing Gordon and Monica together. Otherwise it would have been the end of the Hall. He didn't like admitting this, but Monica had been good for Edward, and the fruits of their marriage had undeniably been a handsome son, the twelve-year-old Lord Hewitt. But what did she really know about the English upper classes and their habits? When Edward had first introduced her, Philip had jokingly referred to her as 'your Swedish au pair'. He had never seen his brother so angry before and after all these years, Philip could still clearly hear his brother's furious words ringing in his ears. 'I never ever want to hear that phrase again. Do you hear?'

The fact was that even today Philip couldn't understand why Monica had always aggravated him so. She had been a good influence on the twins, who adored her, and old Mrs McDonald had nothing against her, either. And Lady Rose had taken to her from the very first moment. Was he really the only one to be so old-fashioned?

As Philip did his usual Sunday inspection round of the Hall, he had to admit that in recent years, thanks to Gordon and Monica, it had never looked better. But poor Mrs McDonald had rheumatism and two weeks earlier she'd broken her hip. Monica had appointed a new housekeeper who had moved in temporarily, but Philip was not pleased with her cleaning.

He drew a finger sceptically along the bottom of one of the gilt frames. Just as he'd suspected. Nothing had been dusted for at least a week. He was perfectly aware that it was difficult to dust the elaborately decorated frame, but not impossible. She was simply careless.

The picture of his great-grandfather as a child was not exactly one of his favourites; Philip had always thought the figure stared so unpleasantly down at the onlooker, and also he looked so horribly world-weary despite his youth.

How he wished he could get Gordon to see how important it was to retrieve some of the works of art and objects they'd had to sell before. Philip knew they could easily buy back some of the pieces that had gone under the hammer. Perhaps he should get Monica to help persuade Gordon to open his wallet. As long as she was in a good mood, there were never any difficulties about getting her to spend her husband's money.

The sound of a car made Philip glance at the Cartier watch he had inherited from Edward, who in his turn had inherited it from their father. The handsome face said two o'clock. That must be Monica and his nephew. He really had missed Robert this summer.

Philip lifted the iron latch on the enormous wooden door and went out on to the steps where a cream-coloured Mercedes was just drawing up. He stared at the open car in surprise; he had rarely seen anything so luxurious. He went down the steps towards his sister-in-law. Her linen dress matched the upholstery in the two-seater sports car to perfection. With false enthusiasm he held out his arms and lightly kissed the air on each side of her cheeks.

'Wonderful to see you again. You look radiant. And the car – never seen anything so elegant.'

'It's my birthday present, Philip. Isn't it pretty?'

Philip stared at the red scar on Monica's forehead. She seemed to be unusually fresh and lively for someone who had just lost her child. He wondered how Gordon had taken it, but on the other hand, with such a generous birthday present, things must be all right between them.

He flung his arms round his nephew and gave him a great hug, a very unusual gesture for him. But over the years since Edward's death, Philip had become something of a father-figure to his nephew. He had been the one to contribute to the intellectual side of his upbringing, while Gordon had encouraged Robert to take part in as many sports as possible. And Robert, always an emotional child, seemed to bring the best out of his uncle.

Anyhow, Philip was overjoyed to see the boy again. Although they had only a week together, and that week had to be shared with Monica, he was sure the two of them would at least have a few hours together on their own.

'Pity Gordon couldn't come. I gather he'll have to spend the whole autumn in the Bahamas with his new cruise line.' To Monica's ears Philip sounded sarcastic as he went on: 'I'm sure you must miss him.'

Monica turned her head away. He clearly knew what had happened between her and Gordon, but she had no desire to give him the satisfaction of seeing how hurtful his words were.

'Yes,' she said, with a fixed smile as she opened the luggage hatch. 'Robert, help us, would you?'

Philip took out two identical cream-coloured leather suitcases with the initials M.H.C. in gold and the coat-of-arms just below.

She still called herself Monica Hewitt Clarke and always used the Hewitt coat-of-arms on her notepaper, and now, he noticed, on her luggage as well.

'Isn't Maria coming this time?'

'No, I thought I'd do everything myself.'

Philip was surprised. What could have happened? He hadn't seen Monica do a hand's turn for years.

'Mother's invited us to dinner tonight. Half past seven, on the dot. You know how she hates being kept waiting.'

Monica was about to tell him what an officious bastard he was, but she didn't. This was after all only the first day of their stay and it would be stupid to spoil it from the very start. Time enough for that.

She looked around. It was still wonderful to be back at Hewitt Hall. After Gordon's dreadful ultimatum, she had realised their loveless marriage would have to go on if her son was to have the upbringing and the future he deserved.

It certainly hadn't been easy, but thank goodness she did not have to see her husband until Christmas. That was a long time off and she would have to face the problems when they arose. Things would work out somehow or other. She was looking forward to this week with Robert and a wonderful dinner with Lady Rose this evening. She looked affectionately at her tall handsome son. Although he was only twelve, he looked much older, and with his dark wavy hair and sunburnt skin, he was almost indecently good-looking. In a year or so the girls would be after him in droves. Monica was not looking forward to the day when she would have to share him with some spotty giggling girl-friend.

She turned to her brother-in-law. 'Philip, I heard you'd sold the rights in your book to ITV. Why do you persist in remaining anonymous? Everyone knows who wrote it. But Craig Stevens does sound very American, so I suppose that sells better?'

So – good, she'd also got a crack in at Philip and his self-importance. She knew he hated discussing his books. Monica was pleased with herself as she quickly went up the steps.

Touché, thought Philip. Not here, not now – but just you wait.

157

14

The *Queen Elizabeth II* sailed out of Southampton harbour at six o'clock, the sunset that evening exceptionally beautiful.

It had rained most of the day, but from the bridge, Captain Kent Cooper was now able to survey with pleasure his first-class passengers down on the foredeck where they were all standing with glasses of champagne, full of expectations for the trip.

Captain Cooper was fifty-eight, tall, thin and with distinguished greying hair and beard. His dark blue uniform led the ladies still further to compare him with Gary Cooper, and he certainly had no objections to that. He loved his profession and crossed the Atlantic at least ten times a year.

The magnificent ship had everything a fastidious passenger could ask for. The two restaurants in the first class served every kind of food, whether Arab cous-cous or Swedish meat-balls. The chefs on board were prepared for anything between heaven and earth, and the wine list would make the most enthusiastic connoisseur drool with envy.

The crew and the staff were all specially trained and it was a matter of honour to provide the very best service. Passengers paid what were heinous sums to spend five days crossing the Atlantic.

Evening dress was obligatory in one of the dining rooms. There was a casino and cabarets, in themselves not to everyone's taste, but both singer and dancers had been hand-picked and were extremely good. Nightlife on board provided a number of opportunities to make new acquaintances, as there were at least half a dozen bars.

Every evening the captain invited guests to dine at his table,

159

and of course to be invited was a much coveted honour among the passengers. Captain Cooper always went through the passenger list with the purser, who was then instructed to go round to the passengers and personally deliver the invitations.

Before dinner, by tradition drinks were served in the captain's cabin – a suite rather than a cabin. Apart from his sleeping cabin, he also had a charming living room with a small office next to it. Here guests were offered sherry or mixed drinks with canapés. He rarely offered wine or champagne. In that respect he was very old fashioned: the tradition of a cocktail had to be maintained.

He had seen from the passenger list that Mr and Mrs Clarke were occupying the Somerset Maugham suite, the largest of the four suites named after famous authors. To judge from Mr Clarke's requests, he appeared to be a very wealthy man. He had asked for a butler with round-the-clock service, and also, apart from the well-equipped bar, a constant supply of Dom Pérignon and Cristal Brut.

As if that were not enough, Mrs Clarke, once Lady Hewitt, had ordered a massage for two every day at four o'clock, a manicure and pedicure for one on Tuesday and a hairdresser available at any time of the day. As well as all that, they had booked an extra room in which their enormous wardrobe was to be unpacked and pressed, then laid out as the garments were required by their maid.

It was not all that unusual for passengers to have a great deal of luggage, but when his staff told him of the vast quantity this couple was taking with them to New York, he had to admit it was a record. Especially as he noted they had booked their return journey on British Airways flight 800 only a week later. Captain Cooper was truly looking forward to this evening's cocktail party and the dinner to follow.

As he went down to his private apartments to see that everything was in order for the evening drinks he looked round the tastefully equipped room, feeling full of satisfaction. The panelled walls were the only clue that they were actually on board ship. He always laughed at guests who complained of seasickness: it was impossible to feel the sea whatever the weather was like, the ship was so well stabilised.

This first evening, he had also invited Earl Whyte and his wife. She was the famous film actress Eve Crawford. He had seen her in several films, but it was now many years since she had retired from the bright lights, presumably because of her marriage. It wasn't quite the thing for someone with her title to be an actress.

Then there was the Austrian industrial magnate Sachs von Furn with a young woman many people took to be his daughter, though the lady in question was actually the latest in a long line of mistresses. Carl-Otto Sachs von Furn had become a good friend and made at least two trips a year, always in the Ernest Hemingway suite. Captain Cooper wondered how old the girl with him this time was. The staff had speculated wildly and reckoned she couldn't be more than eighteen. Though Carl-Otto could hardly be described as ugly, he was grossly overweight. But he was charming and the von Furn millions certainly helped his appeal.

Still curious about the Clarke couple, Captain Cooper called the purser.

'Mark, make sure the canapés and ice are ready in ten minutes. By the way, the Clarkes? What were they like when they checked in?'

'Well, sir, Mrs Clarke is a very shapely lady with all the right attributes, if you know what I mean. But I think she won't be easy to please. There were clearly problems of the non-existent kind even before they checked in. On the other hand, Mr Clarke seems more cool and collected and to have the situation quite in hand.'

'Hm, yes. Well, I'll just go and change my shirt. See to it that everything's in order. I won't be more than five minutes.'

Eve, Countess Whyte, gazed in admiration at the magnificent apparition that was Monica. The low neckline of her full-length Dior dress, in black lace over a close-fitting skin-coloured silk bodice was completed by the most eye-catching diamond necklace and accompanying earrings the countess had ever seen. But her attention was particularly riveted by an enormous pear-shaped diamond on her right third finger, and a bracelet that seemed part of the set.

As a celebrated actress in the Forties and Fifties, Eve had worn

161

garish jewellery in many of her films, but this outshone almost anything she had ever seen. The impact was all the greater because the woman wearing those fantastic jewels was both tall and slim and held herself beautifully. Eve held out her hand as the captain introduced her, and smiling, Monica shook it.

'How nice to meet you. I've always admired your films.'

'Mrs Clarke.' Captain Cooper's voice interrupted them. 'What can I offer you? We have sherry or cocktails.'

'No, thank you. Only champagne for me. Dom Pérignon or Cristal.'

The purser intervened to save the situation. 'I'm sorry, Mrs Clarke. Captain Cooper doesn't serve champagne at his cocktail parties. It's a tradition.'

'Then I think it's high time to break that tradition. Of course, if you haven't any available, we've plenty in our suite. I'm sure you wouldn't mind going to get some.'

Monica did not even deign to look at the man.

The captain gazed at her with astonishment, but then collected his wits. This had never happened before.

'That – er – won't be necessary,' he stammered, somewhat confused. He was not often thrown, but faced with this forceful woman he was speechless. 'You, too, Mr Clarke?'

'No, thank you. I'd like a Martini.'

'Gin or vodka?' said Mark.

'Gin,' said Gordon curtly.

His wife's behaviour did not amuse him. Like the captain, he thought traditions were there to be upheld, not to be demolished.

'Ich auch,' squeaked the young blonde at Carl-Otto's side.

Eve turned to the pale little girl in the low-cut black crepe. She looked like a thin copy of Marilyn Monroe.

'I'd like a whisky and soda, with a little ice.' Carl-Otto sounded very definite.

'Gin and tonic for me,' said Desmond, Earl Whyte.

Amused, Eve turned her attention back to Monica and the two women spent most of the evening in mutual admiration. Despite the difference in their ages, they seemed to have a lot in common and soon decided to lunch together the next day.

The Monroe-like blonde clung nervously to Carl-Otto all evening. Gordon and Desmond seemed to have quite a good deal to
talk about, and for once the captain felt left out. This was his
dinner, after all!

After dinner, at which the champagne really had flowed,
Monica and Eve decided to go and play baccarat. They got up
rather unsteadily and thanked the captain for a wonderful dinner,
then Monica looked at Eve in dismay.

'God, I haven't got a penny.'

'Nor have I.'

Gordon never carried cash so he went with the ladies to the
baccarat table and ensured they were given unlimited credit.

Carl-Otto excused himself. The blonde seemed paler than ever,
the champagne having clearly gone straight to her head. Gordon
laughed quietly to himself. There would be nothing doing there
tonight. She was much too drunk.

After Gordon had quietly watched his wife lose ten thousand
pounds in less than an hour and her new-found friend even more,
he decided to break up the game. The two ladies seemed to have
no control over money whatsoever, whether because of the champagne or their total ignorance of the game, he chose not to specu-
late. Not that he minded about the money, but the table was
beginning to be somewhat noisy. Gordon always drank moderately when he was out and he had no desire for Monica to make a
scene on their very first night.

'Darling,' he said, touching her elbow. 'Shall we take a little
walk up on deck?'

'That's a jolly good idea,' Desmond piped up. 'Let's join them,
you old bag.' Earl Whyte had definitely drunk too much.

'Desmond, sweetheart,' his wife replied, 'you only call me an
old bag when you're drunk.'

The four new friends were walking slowly up to the foredeck
when Monica turned round shivering. 'Oh, I'm cold,' she said.

Quickly Gordon seized his opportunity. 'Please excuse us.
Monica and I are going to retire.'

'See you tomorrow.'

With his arm round her shoulders, Gordon propped up the now

163

rather drunk Monica. He had decided that tonight they would make the child he wanted so much.

The cold sea air had sobered up Monica and she at once understood Gordon's plans, but she was in such a good mood and the evening had actually been so successful, not least with the thought of her new friend, she decided to fall in with him.

Gordon locked the door behind him and went over to Monica, now lying face down across the big double bed. With practised hands, he took off the diamond necklace and earrings, pulled down the zip on the dress, turned her over and carefully eased her out of her clothes.

Monica lay quite naked on the bed with her eyes closed. Gordon took off the bracelets and ring and put them all on the bedside table. When he himself had undressed, he turned out the top light, leaving one of the side lamps on.

He leant over the apparently lifeless Monica and kissed her on the mouth, slowly whispering into her ear.

'Tonight, my darling, we'll make our child.'

His face burrowed into her breasts, he sucked gently on her nipples, his tongue tracing over her body, and Monica suddenly started breathing faster. Weakly, she tried to protest. This wasn't Gordon she could feel. He had never done this before. But the pleasure was too great and she leant back.

Gordon's tongue was as rough as a cat's as it ran back and forth over her swelling clitoris. She could feel a wave of pleasure washing over her and suddenly knew she could no longer resist. His tongue worked faster and faster and, with a weak moan, she let him know she was quite satisfied. He pulled himself over her body and with rapid fingers pushed his throbbing penis into her. The thought of having satisfied his wife so successfully meant it took him only a second or two to come.

He collapsed on top of Monica with a deep breath. His slack penis fell out of her well-filled vagina and with a light kiss he lay down at her side.

'Goodnight, darling. Sleep well.'

Monica was confused but at the same time fulfilled. It had been so long since the last time. What had happened? And why just tonight? Before she could finish her thoughts, she was falling asleep.

Gordon listened to his wife's breathing. He was also feeling fulfilled – tonight he knew their child had been created.

It was a wonderful spring day in New York. Monica walked slowly down Fifth Avenue, absently glancing into Tiffany's before crossing the street to Bergdorf Goodman's.

She had half an hour before meeting Eve at the Russian Tea Room on the corner of 57th Street and Sixth Avenue and she'd seen a pair of really lovely diamond earrings and a négligé in apricot silk with marabou feathers at the wrists. Perhaps she could take Eve there after lunch to see what she thought.

Yesterday afternoon they'd had tea together at the Plaza Palm Court hotel after they'd been to Bendel's. Before that they had tremendous fun at Serendipity. Although they had all the money in the world, there was only one small thing they had wanted to buy. Who on earth were all these things made for? They had also looked in at Fiorucci's and Monica had tried on a bright yellow T-shirt with two huge strawberries across the front and had laughed so much she'd cried when she'd seen herself in the mirror.

Despite the almost twenty-year difference in their ages, Monica and Eve had become friends in a very short time, something very unusual for Monica – she was usually extremely reserved and reluctant to let anyone come close to her.

She glanced down at her new gold Rolex. Gordon had been a veritable angel and given her whatever she'd pointed at. A new wristwatch was not what she needed at the moment, but it was sporty and watertight. Not that being watertight was much use. The only time her hands ever came into contact with water was when she washed them.

Monica crossed 57th Street and walked past Bendel's. Their windows were always tempting, but she had been there the day before and bought most of the things she'd wanted. They were all now lined up on the dining-room table in the suite at the Hotel Pierre. Even Gordon had been surprised at the amount she had purchased, but he had chosen to say nothing.

In her pale green Chanel bouclé suit and massed Chanel pearls, Monica opened the door to the restaurant. Her black and beige Chanel shoes were rather difficult to walk in, so it would be good to take a rest. Eve was already there and had left her coat in the cloakroom. She kissed her friend lightly on both cheeks and together they sat down in the dark smoky room and ordered a bottle of Dom Pérignon, blinies and Beluga caviar.

The two friends toasted each other in the ice-cold champagne. Monica felt enormous admiration for Eve. She had been married to the same man for almost twenty years, and had given up a Hollywood career to have his children. They had two boys and a girl.

Eve had obviously had a fantastic figure. Monica remembered her from her youth when she'd made a lot of films with both Cary Grant and Clark Gable. She'd had a very narrow waist and a big bust, and her dark red hair had hung seductively over one eye. She still looked very striking, but now it wasn't just her bust that was large. Her hips and thighs were also of considerable proportions. But her face was as beautiful as ever and her eyes shone with a happiness and fulfilment Monica had unfortunately never seen reflected in her own. Not only was Eve happily married to a man who worshipped her, but he was also one of the wealthiest men in England. Monica gazed wistfully across the room, wondering how this woman had got everything so right.

'Monica, where are you?' Eve put her hand over Monica's.

'I was just thinking how wonderful it must be to have lived a life like yours. To have been a famous movie star in Hollywood, and then to fall in love with a man you still feel the same about twenty years later.'

'Excuse me.' The young waiter put the plates of blinies down in front of them.

'Well, I suppose that sums it up. But what about you? You and Gordon seem to have found a lifestyle that suits you. God knows, it's not always easy to be married. It's just a question of finding the right man.' She raised her glass and winked at Monica. 'We must meet in London. It's Ascot in a month's time, then Wimbledon and the Henley regatta. I *love* tennis.'

Alas, thought Monica, I don't. A new suit. A new hat. It was simply a matter of being seen. That was probably the only thing she liked about those events.

'And I hope you're free on June the eleventh, because that's when we always have the Whyte Ball. As in our name, but you'll both have to dress in white.'

Monica smiled happily and raised her glass. Balls were always fun. That meant new clothes, long dresses. Although she didn't like sunbathing any more, she would perhaps spend a week in the new house near Cap Ferrat. Gordon would be pleased if she suggested it. She still hadn't set foot in the house, but a tan against a white dress would certainly look good.

Monica asked for a telephone. 'Shall we take my car?'

'Yes, let's do that. Or I could call Desmond and he could send ours.'

'No, no. It's fine. I call the hotel and they'll send a limousine.'

Eve had suggested they should go down to the United Nations building after lunch. God knows why, Monica had thought. But as long as she was back in time at Bergdorf Goodman's before they closed she didn't mind. Her American Express card was burning a hole in her Chanel bag. She simply had to have that négligé.

Maria appeared in the doorway of the bedroom.

'Missa Clarke . . .'

Monica looked at her reproachfully, but actually she had stopped being annoyed over Maria's inability to pronounce Mrs properly.

'Your bath's ready.'

Monica went to the bathroom and dropped the bathrobe to the pink and grey marble floor of the mirror-lined bathroom. She put her fringe on a roller and the rest of her hair in a pink towelling turban.

With a deep sigh, she sank down into the big bath tub, feeling very contented. She studied her newly manicured nails intently through the foam. They were really good at these things in America. Elizabeth Arden in Bond Street didn't do them half as well.

It was only half past seven. At half past nine she was meeting her husband at the 21 Club. Gordon had been at meetings all day and hadn't even had time to get back to change. She felt really sorry for him. They'd had a swift lunch together at the nearby Plaza Rib Room, then walked down to David Webb's on 57th Street.

It was all so pleasant. Everything she liked was only a block or so away from the hotel. They had chosen a fabulous ring with an emerald cabochon on a bed of diamonds. It was very big, but fun, she thought. Actually, she had chosen and he had paid.

Robert had telephoned. He was missing her and wanted her to buy something for him at Hammacher Schlemmer's, some kind of army knife you could only get in the States. She had promised she would, although she wasn't all that keen on weapons of any kind.

How different her life was now from that of last summer and that terrible day when Gordon had delivered his ultimatum. She hadn't thought it possible for anyone to hate like that, or that one could feel so humiliated. Today, just over seven months later, Gordon seemed a changed man.

She had indeed thought his proposal over long and hard. Most of all she'd wanted to flee from her hospital bed, from everything, but the thought of Robert and his future had been decisive. The worst of it was that Gordon held all the trump cards. He knew she would be ruined without his financial help, and the truth was that he had saved Hewitt Hall when Edward had died, and had kept it going ever since. Monica couldn't conceivably allow Robert to break off his education and spoil his chances in life, especially since the young lord would not even be able to keep the Hall that had been in the Hewitt family for centuries.

The autumn had gone by with no major problems. She'd spent as little time as possible in London and retreated from the social life she'd enjoyed so much, and in Gordon's eyes, largely lived for.

He had telephoned Hewitt Hall every week and asked how Robert was getting on. Once or twice he had also spoken to Philip. She had tried to sound cheerful, but was always thankful when the conversation was over and done with. How good it had been when he was so far away. The thought of escaping 'Georgina' for a few months, at least until Christmas, had helped her agree to his proposals. Despite the hot bubble bath, Monica felt cold shivers running down her spine at the thought of her husband made up and scented and dressed in women's clothing.

She and Lady Rose had become even closer that autumn. Monica had increasingly felt she had neglected the wonderful old woman. The rose garden had also suffered, but together they had pruned and replanted it and Monica was sure that in the summer it would once again be as resplendent as before though, of course, Lady Rose no longer needed to show it to the public.

On the minus side, Philip had been his usual unpleasant self, and despite the money that had been poured into the Hall, his attitude had remained the same. He might have shown her a little more gratitude, as without her the Hall would have been ruined by now. His books hadn't all been on the bestseller lists. Just as well they were going to make a television series out of his new one. Then there was his snobbish reluctance to appear at interviews and press conferences. She couldn't understand why he had to hide behind the pseudonym of Craig Stevens.

It had been with a rising sense of panic that Monica had realised Christmas was approaching, and Gordon with it. But against all her predictions, it turned out to be surprisingly painless.

Gordon had kept his distance and not once touched her – not even tried. He had been pleasant and generous to the whole family, including Monica, and not tried to press her into anything. On Boxing Day, he had as usual taken Robert off skiing to St Moritz and Monica had thanked her lucky stars for another week's respite. As soon as they were back from their skiing holiday, Gordon had flown straight back to Bermuda. Clearly some problem had arisen with his new business, and Monica couldn't really believe her luck. It wasn't until the end of February when he made the attempt to take up their sex life together again.

During this time, Monica had avoided both alcohol and tranquillizers, feeling that this time she had to break her bad habits to have the strength to return to a life with Gordon. She knew she could no longer rely on drugs to see her through, though to her surprise his demands were far less outlandish now. But baby

Gordon's wails still echoed in her ears, and it was difficult to get rid of the vision of him in nappies when she again sat astride him – the position they always used for Gordon to come.

However it was now 26 April and she had until now been spared Georgina. The remarkable thing was that something had happened to Gordon. Since that first night on board the *Queen Elizabeth II*, she had even enjoyed their sex life together. Perhaps she had been worrying unnecessarily. Perhaps it was simply that he now respected her after that night. He had treated her with lots of consideration and even love.

Monica ran her hands down her soft body and played a little with her nipples under the bubbles. She was actually looking forward to seeing her husband this evening. It was an eternity since she had felt like this. Sexy. Almost like being in love . . .

The thought of what dress she was to wear made her sit up in the bath. There were so many to choose from.

She got out of the bath and swept the huge bath towel round her. The apricot-coloured silk négligé she had bought earlier tempted her enormously, but where was it in all those parcels? Carriers and boxes were scattered all over their suite. She dried herself and rubbed lotion all over her body, then splashed a little Joy between her breasts and behind her ears. She wasn't all that keen on Joy but it was Gordon's favourite and tonight she wanted to please him.

She picked up the bathrobe and put it on. She *had* to find the négligé, the feel of the cool silk against her naked skin and the fluffy feathers was just what she wanted. And apricot was a new colour for her; she mostly stuck to beige, or white.

She ran to the dining room trying to find the right bag. She found the Bonwit Teller carrier with its purple flowers, boxes from Saks Fifth Avenue, bags from Bendel's and a few others from Bergdorf Goodman's, but no négligé. She tried to think back in case she'd left it behind somewhere. She'd had to run from the limousine to get to the store before they closed. She and Eve had spent much too much time inside the UN skyscraper although there was really nothing to see in there. Had the chauffeur forgotten to have it sent up?

On her way back to the bedroom, she had a glance at the rococo clock on the mantelpiece. Quarter to nine. She was panic-stricken. She really mustn't be late tonight. It was their last evening and she and Gordon were going to do the town.

Maria had already laid out three black, almost identical cocktail dresses, but Monica was determined to find the négligé so that she could at least try it on while she was doing her make-up.

She opened the wardrobe doors. God, she certainly had been shopping, she thought. Maria wouldn't find packing easy tomorrow, not that that mattered. She had bought a whole set of Louis Vuitton suitcases at Saks. She didn't know what had got into her because she usually preferred Gucci.

There it was – the Bergdorf Goodman bag. Why on earth had Maria put it in Gordon's part of the wardrobe? Oh well, that didn't matter.

She threw off the bathrobe and eagerly started undoing the tissue paper. But instead of the silk she expected, an orange dress with a low-cut neckline and a tulle underskirt fell out. Monica was absolutely certain she had never bought anything that colour, as she looked terrible in it. And also, the dress was enormous. There must be some mistake. She looked through the bag to see if she could find the receipt. She found it and saw Gordon's signature on the American Express copy.

She sank to the floor, a cold chill racing through her naked body.

'No, no!' she screamed, covering her face with her hands.

At that moment she knew she would never be free from the one thing she feared most of all: Georgina.

15

Monica was late and was aware she was exceeding the limit as she drove to pick up Robert from school; it was already ten past one and she had to be there by two at the latest.

It was Friday 6 June and she and Gordon had arranged a family meeting at Hewitt Hall over the weekend. Dennis was on his way to Heathrow to pick up Mr and Mrs Joseph Clarke who had flown in from their tax haven in Guernsey. Since Mr Clarke had retired fifteen years earlier, he and his wife had been living on the island and enjoying life in the autumn of their years, having worked hard to build up the finance company Joseph had now handed over to his son.

At the same time, Gerd was on her way from Stockholm and was due to land only half an hour after the Clarkes, so Dennis had orders to drive all three of them straight to the Hall.

Gordon had a business meeting in town and was coming down by helicopter. He had promised to be there by seven, as Monica had wanted them all to have dinner at eight; older people did not like eating too late.

Monica slowed the Mercedes down, the spasms in her lower abdomen contracting into one great pain. She would have to stop to take a painkiller.

When she'd woken that morning, the bed had been stained with blood. Gordon had fortunately already gone to the office. She didn't dare even think about what he would say. He had been so wonderfully generous and understanding and had even managed to convince her that she was pregnant. This time she had been looking forward to it. Her period was almost two weeks late.

173

Monica stopped, opened her Chanel bag and took two tablets out of the prescription bottle. She put both hands on the top of the wheel and rested her head against them, breathing deeply to try to get rid of the pain. God, what'd happen when he found out? Panic rose in her. She opened her bag again, but this time she took out a bottle of Valium. Although she seldom took it nowadays, she always had some with her. But then, with the thought of what the next few hours were likely to bring, she put the Valium back in her bag.

Robert was thrilled to see his Swedish grandmother, she had always had a special place in his heart. For Monica it was a joy to see them together and although they still could barely understand each other, the language barrier didn't seem to stand in their way. Today Robert was eager to show her all his new things, his horse and the stables . . .

Monica was touched to see the two of them setting off towards the stables and for a second the thought of her period faded. She didn't know how she was going to tell Gordon she wasn't pregnant. He'd had no doubts at all and had treated her as delicately as if she were in the ninth month of a difficult pregnancy. He had actually been so sweet and kind for the last couple of months, she'd occasionally found herself missing him, sometimes even nervously expectant when he'd returned from a trip or just from work.

But now she could feel deep in her bones that he would be shattered to hear he would not be becoming a father this time round either. Monica didn't dare think about the consequences.

'Monica darling, there you are. I've been looking for you all over the place.'

The sound of Gordon's familiar voice went through her like an electric shock. The moment she turned round, she decided she would postpone the problem for a while. She simply couldn't face a confrontation just now.

'Gordon, I didn't hear you coming.'

'How pale you look, darling. Aren't you feeling well? Or aren't *we* feeling well?' Gordon's eyes were mischievous as he put his hand over her stomach.

Monica felt sick and took his hand firmly away.

'Don't be silly, Gordon. I'm fine, but you know I've had a lot to do. Mother's arrived, as well as Gertrude and Joseph.'

'Where are they?'

'I think they're in the drawing room. You go and see them and don't worry about me.'

Monica was relieved when he gave her a quick caress on the cheek and turned towards the Hall. Why this weekend? When Gerd was here, and Robert . . . Monica simply could not go on thinking about it. Her longing for a drink was almost irresistible, but she didn't want to risk anyone smelling it on her breath.

Dinner passed in a fog. Monica did her best to smile in the right places and nod whenever necessary, but her thoughts were miles away from the beautifully laid table.

When Gordon raised his glass, looking straight into her eyes and toasting her, it was almost too much.

'To us, Monica.'

If it hadn't been for Lady Rose, the dinner would have been a disaster. She must have had her first drink at breakfast, for she was on great form.

Monica looked at her affectionately: she was so full of life and as eager as a child to take part in the conversation. They'd never be bored as long as Lady Rose was one of the company. She was always so sensible and wasn't afraid to give full rein to her striking sense of humour. Poor Gerd though was not really completely with them. She had great difficulty following the conversation and was always very tense, terrified someone would ask her something. Her English had not improved since the first time she had visited England.

Coffee and liqueurs were served as usual in the library and after that Lady Rose, eager to show Gordon's parents her home, suggested they should all go down to her place for a nightcap. As they walked together across the park towards the lodge Lady Rose took Monica on one arm and Gerd on the other.

It was very cosy and pleasant. Lady Rose gave them all a drink, herself included. These days she was less particular about revealing her fondness for a drink, at least at this hour of the night. Gertrude and Joseph were the first to leave, announcing, 'Tomorrow is another day,' as they said their goodnights.

Monica felt a lump in her throat when Gordon fumbled for her hand on their way back to the Hall. She knew she would have to tell him.

Monica spent an unnecessarily long time in the bathroom, sensing how impatient Gordon was.

She put in two Tampax and a pad on top, then she gathered up her courage. She was trying to think of what she was going to say, although in fact her nightdress said it all: a pale red cotton shift with dainty white lace at the neck and wrists. Not exactly what one wore if planning a lovemaking session.

Her head felt heavy. She had taken too many painkillers that day and now felt quite nauseous, her whole body aching. If only she could just lie down and go to sleep without any explanations and excuses.

'Darling,' she heard Gordon saying from the bedroom as she opened the bathroom door. 'Are you feeling all right? I know it's been a hard day, what with picking up Robert and preparing dinner. But I'm really proud of you. The food was superb. My parents were delighted, and that's not usually their first reaction to anything. The whole evening was a great success.'

Monica sat down at the edge of the bed and Gordon jokingly tugged at her long nightie.

'What are you trying to hide under there, darling? You've never looked more beautiful.'

He slid his hand under the thin material. Monica quickly pulled away, but it was too late. He had already felt it.

'Gordon . . .' she said, genuinely distressed. 'I got my period this morning and have been feeling bad all day. I didn't want to spoil the day for you when your parents were here and . . .'

Gordon's face turned ashen, anger and disappointment in his eyes.

'Gordon – it isn't my fault.'

Without a word, he got up, went out and slammed the door hard behind him.

Monica couldn't think where he'd gone. He wasn't going to leave her alone, was he? What would she say to his parents? Tearfully she crawled into the bed, opened the drawer of her bedside table and took out her sleeping pills. All she wanted to do was to sleep. She took two Mandrax although her doctor had warned her that they were so strong she was to use them only in an emergency. Well, this was an emergency if anything was, she thought, putting them in her mouth and swallowing. She leant across the bed and switched off Gordon's light first, then her own.

He'd probably gone down for a whisky to pull himself together, she thought. When he came back she would be sleeping so soundly she wouldn't hear anything. All she wanted to do was sleep.

She was just dozing off when the telephone rang shrilly. Monica saw the internal light blinking. Who could be disturbing her this late?

'Yes,' she said groggily, not bothering to turn on the light.

'Hi, Monica! It's me, Georgina . . .'

Monica dropped the receiver, unable to believe what she'd heard. It couldn't be possible. Not here at Hewitt Hall. Not while his parents were just down the corridor. And Robert . . .

She fumbled for the receiver. 'One moment,' she said.

She had to throw up. She reached for the Kleenex box and grabbed a handful. Then she switched on the light and sat up. Perhaps Georgina would understand if she explained the situation.

'Georgina,' she began cautiously. 'I'm not feeling too good at the moment. I've actually already gone to bed.'

'Oh, have you?' Gordon's artificial voice replied. 'But I'm sure if I drop by we can fix it so that you feel better. See you in about quarter of an hour. It's been a long time. We've lots to catch up on.'

The sleeping pills were beginning to work. Monica was feeling dizzy and rather absent, but she had to get ready. She knew now that nothing on earth would stop Georgina.

How she managed to get to the bathroom she didn't know, but once there she was violently sick.

Coffee, she thought, stumbling round the bathroom. But how on earth would she be able to get all the way down to the kitchen? Her head began to spin and she sank down to the floor by the bath, leaning her head against it. The chill cleared her mind for a moment.

A shower was the only answer. She managed to get her nightdress and panties off. Trembling, she got in under the hot stream of water. Then she had to mobilise all her strength to get out of the bath. Her next task was to concentrate on what to wear. The respectable grey suit she usually wore when Georgina called was in London.

Hastily she pulled on her underwear, and fumbled in the wardrobe. She had never imagined Georgina would ever come to Hewitt Hall, so there was nothing suitable here. In the end she found an old tweed suit intended for long walks in the country. But at least it was faintly similar to what she usually wore.

Her reflection in the bathroom was blurred and she had to peer in the mirror to attempt to comb her hair. The comb got caught in a knot and fell to the floor. She bent down to pick it up and struck her head hard against the edge of the basin, cutting it slightly. Blood started running down her face.

With a wet towel pressed to her forehead, she attempted to put some lipstick on and spray perfume over the suit. The high-heeled patent leather shoes she'd found in the wardrobe completed the outfit.

There was a knock on the door. Monica shuffled over to the bathroom door and to her surprise found no one there. Of course, she thought hazily, she had to open the bedroom door. This would never work, never. To play her part properly she should have made the bed, and had things more or less presentable. Her ears were singing and her head spinning round. Not to mention her thirst . . . but the show must go on.

'Oh, there you are,' said Georgina, smiling. 'I'd begun to think you weren't going to let me in.'

He closed the door behind him and locked it, then placed the key neatly on the bedside table.

After various polite remarks, Georgina came to the point.

'I've bought a new dress and as you see, I don't know what make-up would go well with it. But you, Monica dear, have such sure taste. Help a poor confused friend. And my hair! What do you think?'

The sight of Gordon dressed in the orange evening dress he'd bought in New York, tights, high-heeled shoes, and added to that a dark red wig, was too much for Monica. She started laughing hysterically, but stopped abruptly when she managed to focus her eyes on Georgina.

'Georgina,' she said in a slurred voice, the words tumbling over each other. 'That colour is fantastic.'

He looked icily at her, but his features smoothed out as Monica showered him with compliments. She suddenly sensed this was a matter of life or death.

'Come on,' said Monica, pointing at the dressing table, the realisation of the seriousness of their game giving her a few moments' clarity. 'Sit down. You need something different with that dress. But we must have something to drink first. I think my husband has some champagne in the refrigerator in his dressing room.'

Georgina nodded.

Monica managed to get herself into the dressing room and came back with two glasses and a bottle of champagne. She knew she would never manage to get the cork out.

'Can you help me? I've hurt my hand, you see.'

'Not just your hand,' Gordon noted. 'What's happened to your forehead?'

'Oh, I stupidly tripped just now. It's nothing.' She could feel how stiff her smile was.

Georgina poured the champagne out so carelessly the glasses overflowed. Georgina giggled and Monica, trying to appear involved laughed, tossing back her head. A singularly stupid idea: the room spun round and she closed and opened her eyes in a huge effort to focus.

She sat down beside Georgina at the dressing table and started picking up brushes and jars, finally selecting a purple eye-shadow. She forced herself to her feet and, standing behind her husband,

179

started in the corners of his eyes, brushing the purple eyeshadow below the strongly marked eyebrows, then mixing in some shimmering gold shadow. Thick layers were needed to get some colour into Gordon's weatherbeaten skin. Georgina smiled with delight at her own reflection.

But Monica wasn't finished yet. She anointed Georgina with mother-of-pearl blusher then in a commanding voice said, 'Stay there. We need a very special lipstick for this.' Monica selected three colours, a shocking pink, an orange and a bright red. With a practised hand she mixed the colours together with a little gold brush. 'There we are. Now you're nearly ready.'

There was no mistaking the satisfaction in Georgina's expression.

'But, Monica dear, oughtn't I to have some mascara?'

'Of course. Try this green. It's new, Madeleine Mono. It'll look fantastic with your dress. You put it on.'

She didn't dare herself. By now her hand was shaking so badly, she was afraid she might stick the brush into his eye.

She began to feel sick again.

'Your hair looks terrible,' she said hastily. 'Wait a minute. I'll get the brush and some spray.'

She put down the champagne glass and rushed to the bathroom, turning both taps on full so Georgina wouldn't hear, then crouched down and threw up in the toilet. She wiped her mouth, cleaned her teeth and put on a little lipstick. Then she walked calmly back with the brush and spray.

Georgina had noticed nothing and was still sitting expectantly on the chair studying her reflection.

Monica, trying to ignore the bizarre sight in the mirror, busied herself with the short red wig.

'Careful, dearie,' Georgina rebuked her, 'not so hard. You know how sensitive I am.'

Monica was suffering, unable to pretend any longer this wasn't happening. Every moment she had to take part in this charade was humiliating. She just wanted him to get on with what he was here for, so that it was over and done with – at least for the time being.

Georgina suddenly rose from the dressing table and Monica knew the moment had come. She watched her husband as he went over to the bed and spread himself out in a seductive pose.

'Come here and sit down, Monica dear. We've got so much to talk about. We see far too little of each other, don't you think? We must do something about it. A friendship like ours has to be nurtured, doesn't it?'

Monica swallowed and cautiously sat down on the edge of the bed.

'No, no, come and sit here beside me. You aren't afraid of me, are you?'

'No, Georgina. Why should I be? I've no reason to be, have I? We're friends.'

Georgina put her glass down on the bedside table and before Monica knew what was happening, he was suddenly looming over her, pulling up the tweed skirt and dragging off her panties. As he lay over her propped on his elbows, he looked straight into her eyes.

'Tonight, Monica,' he said in his ordinary voice, 'we won't be making any children. Tonight I'm going to fuck you. Fuck you, do you hear?'

He shoved her off the bed and made her crouch on all fours on the floor, then with terrible intensity, he drove his small erect penis into her anus.

The pain was hideous, every thrust a dreadful degradation. Oh, how she hated herself for not having the courage to leave this man. How could she have been so stupid to think that he would ever change?

He clung roughly to her hips as his thrusts grew harder and harder. Monica cried out in confusion and pain.

'Shut up,' hissed Gordon, slapping her bottom hard.

The more she cried for mercy, the harder he hit her. This was something new. He had never done this before, but from his grunts and groans and the brutal obscenities he was hurling at her he seemed to be enjoying it.

Suddenly Monica's head was on the floor. She clasped her hands. Dear Lord, please let him come soon, she prayed silently, I

can't cope with this much longer. She didn't know which hurt most
– his thrusting, the blows or the shocking things he was panting
at her.

But then it came. With enormous force he thrust into her and
groaned loudly, hitting her with one hand and digging his nails
into her with the other. To her terror, everything inside her
seemed to be being moved around.

He collapsed over her back. At last it was over.

Monica hoped her cries hadn't woken his parents sleeping two
doors further down the corridor.

She waited for him to get up and go, gasping as Gordon's
suffocating weight pressed down on her.

'Gordon,' she whispered cautiously. 'You're hurting me.'

But she got no answer. Instead, to her horror, he pressed harder
against her and his penis began to grow hard. Before she knew
where she was, he had slapped her hard across the face.

'Shut up, you fucking whore!'

The blow was like a lash from a whip, but she was too shocked
to feel any pain.

'I'm going to give you something you won't forget in a hurry.'

With that he began again and this time, both the blows and the
jabbing thrusts were even worse.

Monica wished she was dead. Anything was better than this.

Someone was knocking persistently on the door. At first Monica
didn't know if she were dreaming or whether it was real. She made
an effort to wake up, quite unaware of where she was.

'Who is it?' she called. Her head felt as if it would burst at any
moment and her mouth was as dry as a dead leaf. She reached out
for the familiar glass and after a couple of gulps she heard
Robert's thin voice.

'Mummy, Mummy. It's me.'

Naked, she pulled the sheet up to her chin, but then saw the
tweed suit lying on the floor and with her hands holding her head
she managed to kick it under the bed. She didn't dare look for
bruises on her body.

'One moment, my darling.'

She ran into the bathroom for her dressing gown.

'Come on in, sweetheart. I've got a terrible headache, but it's OK.'

Her son came into the darkened bedroom and jumped up on the edge of the bed.

'Did you have a party last night? Was it you and Gertrude or . . .' Robert asked, nodding towards the champagne glass.

'Gertrude?' said Monica in confusion.

'Who else would use such bright lipstick?' said Robert with a giggle. 'You didn't even finish the bottle. What a waste.'

What a funny little old man he seemed sometimes. He always noticed small details, but she couldn't believe he'd spotted the glass with lipstick straightaway.

Monica laughed apologetically. 'Yes, we had a chat together.'

'Mummy, I've only come to tell you I'm going out riding with Gordon today. I don't think we'll be back for lunch.'

Monica was disappointed as she had planned a picnic, and now Robert was going to be out all day. With Gordon, to crown everything.

'I'm sorry, Mummy. You know how I love riding and I hardly ever have time for it. We can't at school . . .'

She melted as he looked appealingly at her.

'All right. But I would have liked . . . well, off you go now and have a good time.' She would do anything for him ordinarily, but at the moment all she really wanted was for him to leave. 'Don't forget we're having dinner with Grandmother tonight.'

After he'd gone, Monica dragged the covers over her head and burst into tears. Then she pulled herself together and pressed the intercom to the kitchen.

'Maria, I would like my breakfast in bed.'

'But Missa Clarke, everyone's having a big breakfast in the dining room. Your mother is here, and Mr and Mrs Clarke . . .'

Monica interrupted her. 'I want it here, do you hear? Now!'

Monica was at least glad she would not have to see Gordon today. He usually disappeared altogether after 'Georgina', but as his parents were here, he couldn't.

She knew the whole situation was totally impossible. What

had happened last night was the worst ever. What would come next?

At seven they all gathered in the library for a drink before going together down to Lady Rose's for dinner. All except Gordon. Monica replied vaguely and evasively to questions about where he was, just managing to behave normally, hoping that no one would notice anything was wrong. She was simply grateful for every minute, even every second, she didn't have to see her husband.

She had no idea what Gertrude and Joseph had been doing all day, but she was aware that Gerd had spent most of it in the kitchen, and had felt it her duty to look in on her occasionally. Conversation between them had become more and more forced. Gerd had said nothing to her daughter, but she complained to Gunnar that evening on the telephone. 'I don't know what it is,' she said worriedly. I can't seem to get through to her.'

Gunnar had suggested she should talk to Monica which Gerd knew would be the best thing to do, but she couldn't bring herself to confront the problem immediately.

Monica had decided she would just have to pretend as best she could that evening, not least for Gerd's sake. It worried her that she barely succeeded in behaving normally: if they had all known what purgatory she had just been through they would perhaps have been more understanding. How much easier it would have been if she'd had someone to talk to. Having to struggle with the problem on her own was destroying her. She asked for another drink, and out of the corner of her eye saw Gertrude nudging her husband with a meaningful gesture. Yes, it was her third glass of champagne in less than half an hour, but Monica hadn't the energy to conceal it. She needed every single drop to be able to face Gordon, who would be coming in at any moment.

It was nearly half past seven and time to go.

'Well, time we were off,' said Philip. 'Where's your husband, Monica?'

'Don't let's wait for him,' she said lightly. 'He's probably on the phone as usual. He'll come as soon as he can.' Smiling, Monica took Gertrude by the arm.

It was early June and still light outside, and for England it was unusually warm. The three women walked down the gravel path and were soon overtaken by Robert. Monica was in high-heels and knew she was ruining them with every step she took. She was doing her best to keep up the happy façade, but it became more and more forced the nearer they came to the lodge. Her thoughts were going round and round. Supposing Gordon didn't turn up? What explanation would she find then?

Robert opened the gate and they went through the rose garden and up to the house. Without knocking, the boy rushed in through the front door, the others following him.

When Monica entered the living room, she found she needn't have worried. Lady Rose and Gordon were seated on the sofa, each with a gin and tonic. Monica tried not to show her surprise.

'Gordon, how on earth did you manage to get here before us?'

Monica sat down as far away from him as she could.

'What would you all like to drink?' said Lady Rose, who had clearly had rather more than enough already. Although she made a great effort to be the perfect hostess, her unsteady gait rather gave her away. 'Champagne all round?'

'That'll be fine, I think.' Monica looked round to see if anyone would prefer something else. 'Is that all right, Mother?' she said in Swedish to Gerd.

'You decide, dear.'

Monica wished her mother would be a little more forthcoming.

'Actually, I think I'd rather have a little sherry,' said Gerd, sensing her daughter's impatience.

'Why don't you say so then?' snapped Monica, regretting it the moment she said it.

Gerd looked shamefacedly at her.

Although Joseph didn't understand the language, he had grasped what was going on.

'I'd rather not have champagne, if you don't mind,' he said, trying to help. 'Far too many bubbles. Gin and tonic for me, please.'

A beaming Robert helped his grandmother put the food on the table. It was wonderful to see how well they got on together,

Robert with his old-fashioned ways and Lady Rose so childish, Monica thought. Both of them were glowing with pleasure, which made Monica very happy but at the same time worried her a little. She did wonder whether Gerd would be hurt that they had such a close relationship. Not that Robert didn't love Gerd, but the language barrier meant he couldn't have quite the close understanding he had with Lady Rose.

She had placed all her guests round the table and made it quite clear that Robert was to sit next to her. He played his part as dinner partner with great aplomb, pulling out her chair and helping her sit down. The meal was lively and Lady Rose as usual entertained them all with amusing stories from her past.

When they were again back in the living room, something occurred that had never happened before. Lady Rose was heading unsteadily over to the drinks tray when Philip suddenly got up, went quickly over to his mother and with a determined gesture took the glass away from her.

'You've had enough, Mother. Don't make a fool of yourself.'

Shocked, Monica glared at Philip, trying to attract his attention.

But he ignored her. Almost scarlet in the face, he said: 'It's quite clear you've had enough for tonight.'

They all held their breath. It really was unlike Philip to act so insensitively.

'Philip, give me back my glass,' demanded Lady Rose in a slurred voice. 'How dare you speak to your mother like that.'

Gordon intervened. 'Rose, I'll get you a drink.'

'You keep out of this, Gordon. Mother's had enough for this evening.'

Gordon was not used to being opposed and pursed his lips as he got up. 'Well, perhaps it's time we left. Come on, Monica. Mother, Father? You can stay if you want to, Philip.'

Monica did her best to mediate. 'Yes, perhaps we'd better be off now. We were late yesterday, and we're all rather tired. Come on Robert, say goodnight to Grandma.'

She glared angrily at Philip, thinking he would live to regret this. He was right, of course, but it was unforgivable to expose Lady Rose in front of everyone else like that. She went over to Lady Rose and gently stroked her cheek, whispering to her that she shouldn't bother about what Philip had said.

'I'll stay for a while,' said Philip.

Swaying a little unsteadily again, Lady Rose said: 'Oh, don't go yet. Not yet. We were having such a nice time.'

Monica kissed her on both cheeks.

'I think we'd better. Go to bed now and forget it. We'll see you tomorrow. Don't bother about the washing up. I'll send Maria down in the morning and she'll see to it all.'

The atmosphere was gloomy as they all separated back in the great hall.

'You go on, Monica. I'll just have a drink with Father in the library.'

Monica couldn't decide whether she was relieved or not that Gordon had stayed downstairs. Part of her wanted to put an end to the tension, felt ready for some kind of resolution of the situation. Philip's clumsy action had annoyed her and, her spirit roused, she was ready to tackle Gordon.

She had decided. Whatever the consequences, this was the end. She was going to tell him tonight. She knew what he would threaten her with, but there simply had to be a way out for her and Robert. She could stand it no longer.

Her thoughts were going round and round in circles. She sat down by the window in the bedroom sipping at the glass of white wine she'd taken from the fridge in Gordon's dressing room. She watched Philip sauntering up the path and wondered what he'd said to Lady Rose after they had gone. Poor old Rose.

Lady Rose got up off the sofa. She was terribly hurt by Philip's cruel words and decided to disperse her thoughts by clearing up a little. Monica really didn't have to send Maria down. She took a firm grip on the glass which had provoked the incident and gulped down the contents, Philip's words echoing in her head.

She looked at the table. The candles in the silver candelabra were still alight, throwing a beautiful glow over the room. It wouldn't take much to clear this little lot away, she thought to herself, going over to the sideboard for another drink.

187

With the glass in her hand, she sank down at the table, suddenly feeling desperately tired. Still seated, she started collecting up plates, but dropped some of the cutlery. As she bent down to pick it up, one of the buttons in her cuff caught in the beautiful embroidery on the white linen cloth and as she pulled it, plates and candlesticks crashed to the floor.

She quickly stood up, desperately trying to get free, but the button was caught fast. To her horror she saw the scattered linen napkins catching fire and she started waving her hands about in panic. The flames rose and then the cloth caught light.

She tried vainly to free the button tangled in the lace of the cloth, her free hand flapping desperately at the flames. But the more she tried, the faster the fire spread.

'Help! Help! Please help me someone!' she cried as the fire took hold on the sleeve of her blouse.

But there was no help. No one heard the old lady.

Monica opened the wardrobe door and put on her dark blue silk dressing gown with a rich red border on the sleeves and the family coat-of-arms on the top pocket. It was an exact copy of Edward's and had hung there for many years.

She had decided not to take any pills that night. She had to be clear headed when she settled things with Gordon. It was true she'd already had quite a lot to drink, but it should be all right.

She could hardly wait to see Gordon's expression. He was so insufferably certain he had her all tied up. But he was right in that it would be tough without his financial aid. She would simply have to lower her standards, as long as Robert could complete his education. Perhaps she could sell her jewellery . . . well, that would come later.

She could hear Gordon in the other room.

'Gordon, could you come in here for a moment? I need to talk to you,' she said, deliberately keeping her tone of voice formal.

Monica took a deep breath and tightened the belt of her dressing gown. Without even looking at him, she went over to the window. The curtains were still drawn back and the brisk summer wind was blowing in.

188

She wondered why Maria hadn't drawn them, then realised how absurd it was even to think about such a trivial matter when she was about to make a vital decision about her life.

'Gordon, I've been thinking,' she said, looking out at the drive and the great circle of gravel.

How odd? Somewhere down the drive, yes, she thought she could see a light, like yellow flames. It couldn't be possible. It seemed to be coming from the lodge. No, it couldn't be true.

'Gordon, Gordon! Come here! What's that? Down there?'

Gordon walked slowly over to the window and Monica shouted at him to hurry.

He stiffened as he looked out.

'My God, can't you see there's a fire?'

'A fire . . .?'

Both quickly headed for the stairs and halfway down they heard the fire alarm. Someone had made the same discovery. They could hear footsteps everywhere.

A bewildered Gerd looked out.

'What's going on? I don't understand . . .'

Monica didn't even bother to answer.

Gordon's parents came out from their room looking worried and Philip rushed down from the other side of the hall, closely followed by Robert. Even Mrs McDonald emerged hobbling from her room.

'There's a fire,' said Gordon, 'and it must be the lodge. I'll phone the fire brigade.' He had swiftly taken command.

'Grandmother, Grandmother . . .' Robert rushed weeping towards the front door.

Monica made a fruitless attempt to catch up with him as he raced down the drive.

'Robert, wait . . .'

But Robert was running as fast as he could, breathless and weeping. Philip, passing Monica, was soon close behind him.

It was just as they had feared. The lodge was ablaze. Philip rushed forward, but was at once driven back by the heat.

'Mother, Mother!' he shouted at the top of his voice.

The fire engine appeared at that moment, its siren wailing.

'Get back. Get back, everyone.'
But Philip refused, hysterically trying to fight his way through.
'Get back, sir. This is dangerous.'
A man in uniform literally lifted Philip outside the gates.
Water was now pouring on to the flames. Monica collapsed in a heap with Robert in her arms and began to sob. It wasn't easy for him to have to see this. Somewhere at the back of her mind she knew she ought to take him away.
This was the end, she knew that now.

The funeral was held a week later, a family occasion at which only Philip, Robert, Monica, Gordon, Gerd and a handful of friends were present. Mr and Mrs Clarke had gone back to Guernsey to leave them alone with their grief.
Philip had tried to contact the twins in Australia but they had been on a camping trip and by the time they were told it was too late for them to get back for the funeral.
For the first time in years, Monica was back in the little chapel. Rose was to be laid to rest alongside her husband and son and not far from where they had told the world Amanda was buried.
The service was simple and emotional. Everything had happened so quickly, no one could believe that Lady Rose really had gone. The ruins of the lodge were still there, however, a constant reminder of the grim truth.
Philip was inconsolable, blaming himself for his mother's death.
'If I'd kept my big mouth shut, she'd still be alive,' he said, repeatedly, to anyone who would listen. Weighed down by his sense of guilt and talking openly about it, this was a side of Philip Monica had never seen. She was used to regarding him as a man who was either incapable of feeling anything, or else a master at concealing it. She now felt some genuine compassion for him.
Gordon was less involved. When the simple service was over, he at once flew by helicopter back to work in London. The remainder of the family gathered at the Hall to have coffee with the vicar and Lady Rose's closest friends.
The atmosphere for the next few days was unbearable. Robert locked himself in his room and was utterly inconsolable in his

grief. Monica was too dazed to have any real grasp on the situation and she kept swallowing handfuls of pills at regular intervals, closing her eyes and waiting for them to take effect. Philip stayed on his own in his room, drowning his sorrows in whisky and not even appearing at meals.

Gerd had gone back home. There was no real reason for her to stay, so Monica had not protested when she had said she was leaving. Mrs McDonald did her best to console Robert whenever he emerged from his rooms.

The confrontation Monica had planned with Gordon had had to be postponed to a future date. Robert, she realised, would not be able to cope with another blow. He looked up to Gordon and there wasn't the slightest chance of explaining to him why his mother and Gordon had to go their separate ways. So her life would go on as before.

Georgina visited her more and more often during the rest of the summer. Monica had given up worrying when or where she would appear. She played her own part so routinely and with such quantities of drugs and champagne that sometimes she had to search her room the next day for clues in order to remember what had happened.

Monica felt like an Egyptian mummy, cocooned in a layer of tranquillisers. Robert was at school and Lady Rose had gone, so there was no longer anyone to turn to. What did it matter what happened to her? Before, she had taken to secret drinking and tranquillisers only when she was alone, but now it didn't worry her if she started the day with a glass of wine and a few Mandrax. The game of pretence was over. With sufficient anaesthetic, the pain became almost non-existent.

Philip had decided they should bide their time and not rebuild the lodge. It had been underinsured and he refused all financial help; presumably, Monica thought, he was working out his sense of guilt. Mrs McDonald told her that he often went down to the ruins and then stayed there all day.

Monica could no longer feel compassion for his suffering. Nor did she derive malicious pleasure from it. Many a time in the past she had wished she could have pricked a hole in his self-importance, but now that he was a broken man, she actually felt nothing at all. The reason for his misery was far too tragic.

Monica longed to get away, but didn't know where to go. It had occurred to her that she could go to Sweden, but there was really no one there to see except Gerd and Gunnar. How she regretted that she hadn't kept contact with her childhood friends, but her present life had taken up all her time.

For a brief while, she considered the houses in the Bahamas and St-Jean-Cap-Ferrat, but neither tempted her. She had christened the place where she was living her life 'the Valley of the Dolls'. For the time being she would stay there.

Gordon decided that Robert should spend a month of his next summer holidays on a cruise ship sailing to Australia. Once again, Monica had only a week with her son. Of course, she could have said no, but Gordon had more or less taken over Robert's upbringing and insisted he needed more of the outdoor life. In Gordon's opinion, Robert was far too weak, and Monica had been too feeble to protest. One of Gordon's arguments was also that Robert should have the chance to see his half-sisters.

'That's only right, you must see that, Monica. Robert needs contact with his sisters.' Monica could do little but agree.

The months of waiting for her precious week with her son had gone by painfully slowly and when it came she'd been so befuddled she had spent most of it in bed at Hewitt Hall. Philip had taken Robert out riding and shooting. Monica had felt left out but had not protested for her son's sake. What could she offer him in her present state? He was very attached to his uncle, she told herself, and it did them both good to be together.

By the autumn, Monica didn't even know what day of the week it was, and kept asking people in the same way others asked the time. Weeks went by without her even going out. She rarely bothered to answer invitations to social events she had so keenly attended before, and not even shopping tempted her any longer. Never had she felt such apathy and depression.

Christmases had been celebrated at Hewitt Hall as usual, but the absence of Lady Rose had settled like a heavy cloud over them all. Family occasions would never be the same without her.

Her sex life with Gordon was now limited entirely to the humiliation she was forced into with Georgina. His desire for a child seemed to have vanished completely. Instead, he seemed to be doing his utmost to degrade her: there was no hint of his attitude to anyone else, and once or twice he told her that no one would ever believe her if she told them. He was unfailingly charming and attentive whenever they were with other people.

In early January, Gordon had some important business colleagues visiting London, and he made it quite clear to Monica that she must be there with him for the first week. He needed her at his side as hostess and wife to make a good impression. Monica realised this was an important occasion, as all his preparations beforehand were minutely carried out.

She did her best, although she now took up to sixty milligrams of Valium a day.

Through his secretary, Gordon had told her that on Thursday evening, they were having dinner at San Lorenzo's in Beauchamp Place at exactly half past eight. She made up very carefully and dressed as stylishly as she could. Recently she had been in the habit of going around in her dressing-gown. She discovered it was rather exciting having her hair done at Michaeljohn's again. She looked at herself in the mirror for a long time and was pleased with the result. Her red and black woollen suit looked good against the black silk polo neck underneath.

She pulled the full-length sable tighter round her and got into the dark blue Rolls ahead of Gordon. Gordon said little during the short journey to San Lorenzo's but he did at least tell her she was looking stunning that evening.

Lorenzo greeted them in Italian and his wife Mara waved in the background.

As three Japanese men joined them they sat down. Monica gratefully accepted a glass of wine and made fruitless attempts to memorise the strange Japanese names.

'The usual Mozzarella pomodoro con basilico,' Monica ordered as bottles of the house wine were brought to the table, as always at San Lorenzo's.

Gordon appeared to be in an extraordinarily good mood and even managed to come up with a word or two in Japanese. Monica, feeling the effect of her Valium, found it hard to keep up. She took a sip of the cold white wine and looked round. Immediately across the room was a company of very cheerful people, and in the seat corresponding to hers, his back to the restaurant wall, was a long-haired, bearded man. He kept staring intently at her.

Suddenly he raised his glass and looked straight into her eyes. Did he really mean her? She glanced in both directions to see if there was anyone else responding, but there was no one else. His eyes were fixed steadily on her.

Instinctively she looked away and took a sip of wine. When she looked up again, he was still staring. What was he up to? She felt herself flushing like a schoolgirl. She couldn't remember when a man's look had last affected her like this. If ever. His gaze had sent her into a kind of trance. She excused herself and went to the cloakroom, feeling dizzy. She needed to move.

Who was the man? she thought as she walked towards the door. She turned off towards the ladies without looking in his direction, her heart thumping so hard she had to stop and take a deep breath.

In the ladies, she pulled out some paper towels, soaked them in cold water and pressed them against her burning cheeks. She looked hard at herself in the mirror, took out her diamond-studded compact, powdered her nose and cheeks, but make-up couldn't hide the flush.

On her way back, she bumped into the stranger. Strong arms caught hold of her.

'Oh, sorry I'm in the way,' he said, smiling.

Monica stared into his eyes, unable to say a word.

He let go of her and held out a piece of paper.

'Here's my telephone number. Please phone me . . .'

He had a dark, sensual, velvety voice. He kept staring intently at her as he pressed the paper into her hand and held it there for a second before turning on his heel and without a word going back to his table, leaving an astonished Monica behind.

Monica unfolded the paper. Just a telephone number. No name. Nothing more. She quickly put the paper into her bag and tried to collect herself, but her thoughts remained with this mysterious man. She knew she would have to meet him again.

'Crispin Que,' said the voice that had echoed in her head for the last few days. There was no doubt it was the man from the restaurant on the other end of the phone.

'Hello,' said Monica, feeling her way.

'Oh, it's you. At last. I've been expecting you to ring. What about lunch today?'

Strangely, Monica didn't hesitate for a moment to accept, and nor was she particularly surprised that he had made the suggestion right at the beginning of the conversation.

'Let's meet in Hampstead. There's a little restaurant called Keats off Hampstead High Street. I'll be there at quarter past one.'

Monica's heart beat faster. Today, so soon, she was to meet the man who had been in her thoughts since she had first laid eyes on him. There was something magical about his gaze that had etched itself on her mind.

She had thought about him day and night, but Gordon hadn't noticed any change in her behaviour. He was used to his wife wandering around in a daze. But this time it was another kind of daze . . . She tried to cut down her Valium intake.

She drove past Lord's Cricket Ground in her cream-coloured Mercedes, past Swiss Cottage, left up towards Hampstead High Street. As usual there was a traffic jam and she drummed her fingers uneasily on the wheel. She really didn't want to be late for this lunch.

She was simply dressed. It was late January and the wind was cold. Her clothes had been carefully selected. This man would not be interested in her wealthy look, hence the black slacks and a black cashmere sweater.

But the cold made her take her fur coat. She pulled the full-length mink round her as she got out of the car. She seldom wore it these days, as it was so heavy compared with the sable, but she thought it looked less expensive.

There were no parking spaces in sight as the restaurant loomed ahead of her.

She eventually parked, very badly, on a corner but reckoned

she didn't have time to go round the block again to find a place. She glanced back at her car parked halfway up on the pavement. The worst that could happen would be that she got a ticket, or perhaps towed away.

He was already there, sitting in a booth at the back, a bottle of red wine in front of him. When she came in, he immediately got up and came towards her with his arms out.

'I'm Crispin. Crispin Que. And you are . . .'

'Monica Clarke.'

'Come and have a glass of wine with me.'

She could feel herself trembling all over as he took her hand, guided her to the booth and smiled as she eased her way into the table.

He had long hair down to just above his shoulders, slightly wavy, a beard and moustache. He was very tanned for the time of year and was wearing blue jeans, brown cowboy boots, a black and mixed colour jersey and a denim shirt that stood up a little at the neck.

He reached across the table and took her hand again.

'When I saw you at San Lorenzo's I knew I had to meet you again.'

He neither let go her hand nor took his eyes off her, and an electric shock seemed to go through her body.

The waiter gave them each a menu.

The lettering leapt up and down in front of Monica's eyes. She hadn't the slightest desire to eat anything.

'I suggest we have something light then go back to my place. I've got so many pictures I want to show you. By the way, I'm an artist.'

Monica was entranced. Was this love at first sight?

He ordered a cheese and spinach omelette for both of them without consulting her any further. But it didn't matter – whatever he wanted, she wanted the same.

The omelette came and vanished equally quickly, and half an hour later they rose and went out to her car. She drove and he directed.

Suddenly he asked her to stop the Mercedes. It was misty and almost three o'clock. Monica did as he said and pulled into the pavement. He took her in his arms and kissed her more passionately than anyone had ever kissed her before. For a few moments she thought she was going to die. She had never had a feeling like it in her life before.

'Crispin.' She made a half-hearted attempt to protest, but soon gave in to his kisses. They became more and more intense and she responded to them with the same intensity. Then he drew back.

'Let's hurry back to my place. This is only the beginning. I want all of you.'

Before she could blink, they were there. Time and space no longer mattered. They stopped the car outside a tall narrow blue house with white windows.

Crispin went round and opened the car door for her.

'Allow me,' he said and took the car keys out of her hand and locked the Mercedes.

He lived quite alone in the blue house. Wherever she looked she saw paintings and drawings. On the floor, leaning against the wall, on the wall, everywhere.

Crispin took off her mink coat and hung it over the banisters. Then he took her hand and led her upstairs. On the right was a small living room full of pictures, sketches and statuettes.

But Crispin took her with him to the left – to the bedroom. He lay down on the bed and slowly stroked the bedspread beside him. This is where I want you, he seemed to say. Without a thought, Monica kicked off her shoes and lay down beside him.

Once again he put his arms round her, kissing her the same way he had in the car. Monica didn't dare open her eyes, afraid that this was only a dream. He pulled the black cashmere sweater over her head and undid her black bra. Monica said nothing. Then he stripped her of her slacks, black briefs and tights.

She lay, quite naked on this stranger's bed, trembling. He wrapped her tenderly in the bedspread before unbuttoning his denim shirt. Monica sighed deeply: she was totally at his mercy. She would do anything for this man. She turned to him and before she knew where she was he was inside her. But he didn't move.

Once more time seemed to stand still. Slowly she began to

move against him, but he did not respond to her movements. Monica could only feel him inside her, his lips against hers in passionate kisses, still without moving.

'Crispin,' she whispered.

Slowly, slowly, he began to move slowly, upwards, inwards . . .

Monica pressed against him and clung on hard, almost convulsively as if afraid he would disappear out of her arms. He increased pace. Monica moaned louder as his movements grew quicker and quicker. Then quite unexpectedly he slowed down. Monica wanted more, but he did not allow it. She begged him, but he was restrained.

'Crispin, please . . .'

With a few simple thrusts he soon brought her to a climax. He knew exactly what to do. Monica came with a force she had never experienced before.

Afterwards she held on to him like a small child and fell asleep in his arms.

Cautiously she opened her eyes and looked at her watch. Quarter to five. God, she thought. I must go home. Gordon will begin to wonder.

She looked round, but Crispin was nowhere to be seen. Where was he?

She called his name and he at once called back. Suddenly he was there in the doorway, naked in front of her. With a laugh he jumped down on the bed and buried his face in her lap.

Monica grabbed at his hair. 'Crispin, I must go. My husband . . .'

He raised his head and looked into her eyes.

'Your husband. Your husband, my dear, will soon be your ex.'

Confused, she got off the bed and, naked and quite unembarrassed, walked through Crispin's house, chatting with a foolish happiness as she dressed.

She was to go home to hell, but now she had found love. There was no doubt about it. It was the only thing that mattered. Crispin's words rang in her ears all the way home: '. . . will soon be your ex . . .'

Monica smiled to herself and felt stronger than ever before.

16

The great purple fluorescent bus with the image of the Rocky Mountains painted along its side and a large head of a Red Indian on the back was roaring through the night along Route 66. They had left Kansas City, Missouri and were on their way to Tulsa, Oklahoma.

At four in the morning, Katarina was reclining at the back with Rob. They had a small separate living space, with two long upholstered benches that served as sofas and a table between them. A door separated it from the rest of the bus.

Sleeping accommodation on the bus consisted of small berths along the sides, four on each side with curtains for privacy. The toilet was contained in such a minute space that you could actually sit on it and take a shower whilst you cleaned your teeth over the basin, a triumph of compact design.

Up front in the bus was a small kitchen with all the essential equipment, and it was round the kitchen table the members of the band usually gathered.

In the driver's seat was Big Daddy with his great cowboy hat. An old hand at the game, he'd been driving this kind of tour bus for over twenty years. He never had to hesitate over how many Dexedrine he needed to keep awake for twenty-four hours of driving and he knew the freeways of the United States like the back of his hand.

Katarina had been on the road now for three weeks. She had flown with Rob from London to New York, and from there on to Spokane, Washington, where the tour had started, after which it went on to Canada, then back through the US, with Los Angeles as the last stop.

199

Rob's latest record, the single 'I'm with You', had climbed to number four on the Billboard Chart in the States, and an American promoter had arranged the tour. They did a town a night; at least that's what it felt like. It was a matter of playing as many towns as possible during this compressed tour. As soon as a gig was over, they only had to wait for the roadies to get the gear off the stage, load the van which followed them, and then set off to the next place.

Katarina was the only woman on the tour, and she found it difficult spending all her time with the band. The difficulty was mutual, but naturally no one said anything. She was the old lady of the L.V., the lead vocalist's wife. He was boss and no one questioned his wishes.

At first being on tour had been exciting. This wasn't her first tour, but here in the States things seemed very different. The fans were more hysterical, more devoted than in Europe, and there also seemed to be more girls at the concerts. She loved the excitement of standing in the wings, watching Rob out there with hysterical fans clapping and screaming, wanting nothing but to have him there and then.

But what pleasure lasts for ever? After three tremendously intensive weeks, her excitement had slowly but definitely faded and she was now longing to be able to stop in one place for a few days, to unpack . . .

The bus rolled into Tulsa, where they had a gig tomorrow, or rather today; it was half-past five in the morning and the atmosphere in the bus was tense.

They stopped outside the hotel and Bucky, the tour manager, went in to get the room list. He came back to the sleepy group, impatiently stamping and stretching their legs, aching to get inside for a few hours' much-needed sleep in real beds.

'Back in the bus,' he ordered. 'The rooms won't be ready until nine.'

Katarina could have cried. It just couldn't be true. Back to that sofa in the bus again. She and Rob had been up until the coke had run out. They hadn't a grain left. They'd used all they had and she had spent the last hour raving about getting in to the hotel, showering and feeling like a human being. She hadn't slept at all. Her heart had been racing from the cocaine and her body was flaked out, while her brain was working overtime.

She was surrounded by complaining band members and road-ies, with no energy left to express her dissatisfaction. She bit her lip fiercely as she got back into the bus. This had happened so many times during this tour. But all they could do was accept the fact. They all went back to their bunks, but Katarina knew she would never be able to sleep. All she could do was to count the hours until they could get into the hotel. She looked at Rob. He had fallen asleep at once and was now snoring quietly. It didn't matter how much coke he took, he seemed to be able to fall asleep at any time.

When, back in London, Rob told her about the coming tour she had seen it as nothing but partying; it had not turned out quite as she had envisaged. The other side of the coin was duller than she could have imagined.

It was certainly fun to be the centre of attention being the wife. In each town the promoter would swan up to her asking whether everything was okay, anything she wanted . . . The room behind the stage was usually very small, but the rider was always the same, vodka, Matteus Rosé wine and a cold buffet of ham, salami, pressed turkey, cheese, rolls and fruit, plus Heineken beer and big bowls of salted peanuts.

On the road the days merged into each other, sometimes it was impossible to tell them apart. One day's routine was identical to the next, all hotels looked alike, so did all the clubs, all the promoters.

They either played at clubs to audiences of between six and nine hundred, or at civic centres. Tonight in Tulsa it was at the Ol' Lady on Brady. They were going to be here for two days, so fortunately there was time for Katarina to get the laundry done. She usually took a taxi to a laundromat and then sat there waiting for it to be done, tired, hungover, in sunglasses and dressed in black. She noticed people raising their eyebrows and wondering what she was doing there. Life as the wife of a rock star was not always glamorous, though she knew it could be in the big cities like New York, Chicago and Boston. She sat there dreaming about Los Angeles. How she was looking forward to going there! LA was her goal and her dream. Everyone had told her how wonderful it was.

Thanks to the success of the single, this was a forty-day tour, but if that also turned out to be a success, it might be extended, something she regarded with mixed emotions. She didn't know how much more she could stand. It didn't matter how much coke they took, it was still tough going. Problems arose with the band when they lived on top of each other like this and, what was worse, there were problems with Rob. On the whole, they'd not had a single minute to themselves, and they were always followed everywhere by the others. She didn't know quite what the next few weeks would hold . . .

The first thing Rob had given Katarina when they had got to New York was a laminated backstage pass emblazoned with her married name. The pass gave her access everywhere, on and off the stage.

There were girls wherever she looked, drugs too. There was always someone in town who knew the best nightclub, and a large table was invariably reserved for them in a corner of the club, with champagne or drinks on the house. Then up to the office with the club owner, or to the bathroom, with someone from the record company – there was always cocaine. This life meant dressing up, tired or not.

Every time the band played Katarina was there, on the side of the stage. She had her own style, lycra tights, sky-high boots, wide belt and long-sleeved tops, with a long black or leopard-skin cape and a black top hat. She had to be seen. Not just Mrs Hove, but also as the most envied, the best dressed, the most exciting, having the most fun.

Katarina hardly ever met anyone except the band, and if she did, it was only fleetingly. Alex, Rob's manager, always watched his client like a hawk. He would certainly have liked to see the goose that was laying his golden eggs with a younger and more co-operative person than herself was. He had a brain like a cash register, and it was he who had insisted they should stake everything on being a success in the States. That was where the serious money was. He saw everything in terms of money, and any subject of conversation was turned towards it. Undeniably, he'd made huge efforts to create the Rob Hove Band and they were now doing well. And that meant he had the opportunity to wallow in his favourite occupation, buying the most expensive clothes possible. He indulged in tailor-made suits, Valentino, Gucci – the list was endless. He could never have enough designer clothes.

Alex was the ultimate chameleon, Katarina had decided. Whatever Rob thought, Alex agreed with, but all the same, he always managed to get what he wanted. He put everything in a way that made Rob think it was he who had actually made the decision.

Katarina knew Alex didn't approve of the British papers writing so much about her in connection with Rob's success. But then he ought to be more pleased with the situation here in the US, where she was unknown. He often manoeuvred her out of the way at photo calls and press conferences, making sure Rob was photographed instead with beautiful models and bimbos rapidly rounded up.

He also insisted that she should stay at the hotel when Rob and the band went to record store signings, and radio stations. She made it clear she didn't like this and she and Rob bickered more and more often about it.

Then there was the band's tour manager, Steve Buckley, called Bucky. It was a standing joke that his great task in life was to lay every fourteen-year-old girl who came his way. As soon as a thirteen or fourteen year old came into sight, the band yelled: 'Bucky, Bucky, there's one you've missed.'

Ian played the drums. Katarina didn't like drummers: they sat all the time and got big arses, not at all attractive. Ian spent all his time off stage doing crosswords. No one had ever seen him with a woman, but on the other hand nor had he been seen with a man either, so no hasty conclusions were drawn. He was very quiet, dear Ian, and kept his private life to himself. He was also a tee-totaller and as far as she knew had never touched a drop. Really dismal.

His opposite was Kevin, on bass. He was an open book,

everything he did happened upfront. At twenty-nine, he was the youngest member of the band and its great charmer. Always with a devilish glint in his eyes, he looked delicious with his long blond hair and almost perfect features. He dressed in crushed velvet, lace and tights, and the girls fell like skittles for him. The boys, too, for that matter . . .

Kevin was never sober, but had the amazing capacity to consume any amount of alcohol without getting blind drunk or becoming impotent: no one was at all surprised to see three different girls per day slipping out of his hotel room.

You could never be sure with Kevin. He always had some practical joke on the go. In New York, he had spread clingfilm over everyone's toilet seats. The result was just as devastating whether you were man or woman, to Kevin's great delight.

Then there was Mike, who never hurt a fly. He played keyboards and spent his free time ploughing through every comic book on the market. Katarina would often watch with amusement as Mike tried to find the mouth of a beer bottle without taking his eyes off his comic, nudging Rob or Kevin when he missed.

Yes, Katarina reflected, as she sat in the laundromat, they were a colourful lot and she had a great deal of fun with them all, but there was no mistaking the fact that they always kept her at a distance. There was no genuine warmth between them. They tolerated her because she was Rob's wife and they would probably like anyone in that position. That frightened her. In the past Katarina had been the focal point around which everyone else circled, like flies round a sugar lump. And after all, she was the one who had created Rob. Alex had contributed, but Rob would not be who he was today without her. She had taught him everything and had always been at his side, day and night; the only thing he possessed was talent.

As she watched him on stage, surrounded by hundreds of fans, she was filled with a bitter mixture of pride and unease. He had always been so dependent on her, asking her advice on the slightest thing. Now, he was feeling more secure and realising his own worth. She didn't like it.

'Big Daddy, how much longer?'

'Take it easy. We'll be there in an hour.'

Big Daddy knew Katarina was impatient to get to Los Angeles, and she was certainly not the only one. He put his foot down a little harder and exceeded the speed limit.

The champagne cork popped and Kevin was the first to hold out his glass for the bubbly. Music was blaring out from loudspeakers and they were all looking forward to stopping in LA for three whole days. After being on the road all this time, three days seemed like an eternity.

The small paper envelope made out of a page from *Vogue* was lying in front of them on the table. Katarina opened it with practised fingers. It was an art slitting the packet from one side and then poking the contents over the other side before opening it entirely.

Nothing was to be wasted. With the aid of Rob's American Express card, she scooped out the cocaine on to the already much-used mirror on the table. The waste paper basket was full of beer cans, wine bottles and two small crumpled envelopes, the contents of which had already gone up their noses. They'd had a good time for hours and this was now the finale before their arrival in LA.

'Make a snowdrift,' yelled Rob.

'Mm, it has to be big enough to ski down . . .' Kevin laid on his wolf smile.

They referred to cocaine as Charlie. 'I'd like to meet Charlie this evening' or 'I was with Charlie all night'. And they had reworded the old expression 'my mouth's watering' to 'my nose's watering' . . .

Katarina could hear the boys' banter but felt as if she were in a trance. She was concentrating on cutting up the cocaine and getting rid of the lumps: this was their last gram before they got to LA and Rob looked uneasily at the contents.

'Christ, there's almost none left and Big Daddy says it'll be an hour before we get there . . .

'To hell with that, there's lots of big lumps here. If we cut it up, there'll be at least half a gram left.'

Katarina poked inside the packet and showed him the lumps to calm him down. It was always the same. This nagging fear it would run out.

With great care, Katarina made six lines and after studying them for a moment or two and deciding the two in the middle were the largest, she pushed back her long dark hair, put a rolled-up hundred-dollar bill to her nose and sniffed hard, first into her left nostril, then into the right. They joked about their status, having worked themselves up from pound notes, to hundred dollar bills. They'd come up in the world . . . Then Katarina gathered up the remains on the mirror with her finger and rubbed it into her gums, took a gulp of champagne, drew an equally deep puff on her cigarette and felt her teeth going numb.

'Good coke.' She nodded and handed Rob the rolled up hundred-dollar bill, now slightly wet at the end.

A few lines later, they swung off the freeway at the Sunset Boulevard exit, travelling towards Beverly Hills. She shivered with delight. The streets marched past – Rexford Drive, Beverly Drive, Rodeo Drive, Canon Drive. The Beverly Hills Hotel was like a pink fairy-tale castle on the left. As they drove by they raised their glasses in a toast to Hollywood.

Katarina, Rob and Kevin went forward to the front of the bus joining the rest of the band sitting in the 'kitchen' doing crosswords or reading comics. As they drove along the Sunset Strip with all its small hippie boutiques and restaurants, they could see the Roxy ahead of them and only a few blocks further on, the Whisky, where they were playing that night.

Big Daddy told them that their hotel, Hyatt House, was only a stone's throw away. It was nicknamed the 'riot house' and there was probably a good reason for it. They were certainly going to help preserve its reputation!

The Whisky had been packed, and as usual the majority of the audience were girls. Katarina was in a great party mood, tossing back beer after beer as she stood at the front of the stage with Sue Cameron, assistant to one of the guys from the record label, appointed to keep Katarina company.

Katarina swayed in time with the beat, now and again singing at the top of her voice. She knew every single word of all the songs. A pair of blonde Californian twins was standing, or rather bouncing

ecstatically beside her. They must have been about seventeen and
were breaking all records when it came to enthusiasm. Katarina
nudged Sue, and together they watched the two girls – both
dressed in identical clothes.

Afterwards there would be the usual crowd from the record
label and assorted liggers in the dressing room and Katarina went
into a corner backstage to refresh herself with a few lines before
going upstairs.

It was incredible how thirsty coke made you, and you could
drink as much as you liked. It was a treadmill. When you felt you
were too drunk, you took a line to sober up, and when you felt
you were too high, you took a few drinks to get drunk and cool
down.

It turned out that they were all going to a party in Laurel
Canyon, and the limousines were lined up outside The Whisky.

She sat with Rob, Mel and Kevin in the first one, the black
partition separating them from the driver's view. More lines were
fixed and there was plenty of wine and beer in the limo's bar.

The party was in full swing when they arrived and she had soon
lost them all. There were people in every corner, drinking or
smoking marijuana, and Katarina went from room to room to find
someone she knew. The music thumped.

Suddenly a man was standing in front of her offering her
cocaine.

'The best in LA. Believe me, I know.'

His words were music to her ears, particularly as Rob had
apparently been swallowed up by the earth.

The man with the generous offer had swept-back black hair,
long sideburns, black leather trousers, snakeskin boots with high
heels and a black silk shirt and black leather jacket. Round his
neck he had a thick gold chain with a small spoon hanging from it.
He led her up the stairs and into a small room, the walls of which
were covered with gold discs, guitars and stuffed animal heads,
and which to her surprise was empty.

They sank down on the tartan-patterned carpet. He had a bottle
of red wine with him but only one glass, so they took it in turns to
drink, taking enormous lines between rounds. Katarina loved this

man, she decided: he had a whole plastic bag of cocaine, at least eight or ten grams in it. She wanted more than anything else to nick some of it, but she couldn't.

Katarina had completely lost track of time when he suggested they should go and see how the others were. 'All right, but let's have one for the road first.'

She pulled at his shirt. He fixed two more lines on the back of a copy of *Cashbox* they were using, one for her and one for him. Katarina, however, was quicker than that. Before he could blink, she had sniffed them both.

By the time Katarina opened the door and went out, she'd spent over an hour in there with a man whose name she didn't even know.

Weren't they the twins from that evening's concert slipping down the stairs in front of her? She couldn't be sure. Suddenly she had to stop by the wall, propping herself up with her arm, sweat running down her forehead, her heart racing and her head spinning.

'Katarina, I've been looking for you. Where have you been?'

Rob came up behind her and put his hand on her shoulder. She was on the verge of panic. The nausea was so severe, she thought she was going to throw up there and then, and her hands were trembling like aspen leaves. She wiped away the sweat with the handkerchief she almost always carried with her in a cramp-like grip, then she blew her nose and looked carefully at it to see if her nose was bleeding. Thank goodness it wasn't.

She thought Rob was looking at her with a rather nasty searching look, and for once she realised she had taken far too much.

'Rob, please take me home?'

Rob laughed.

'What's up with you? You usually know the art of partying. Come on, let's go down and have a beer.'

But Katarina couldn't move an inch. She watched Rob's back as he slid down the stairs with his swaying, jerky gait, then she collapsed on to a step and sat with her head in her hands. A few minutes later, she had gathered enough strength to get up, stumbling now and again and grabbing at the banister rail, her lifeline. If she let go she'd fall over and roll to the bottom of the stairs.

'How could that bastard leave me when I'm feeling so fucking awful?' she mumbled, cold sweat pouring down her face.

Through the crowd, she could just see Alex and Rob in the middle of the combined bar-kitchen, Alex with a glass of champagne and Rob with a bottle of beer. She managed to elbow her way through to them and grabbed hold of Alex so as not to lose her balance, trying to focus her eyes on Rob.

'I need something to drink.'

Mechanically Rob handed his beer.

It was Budweiser, which he knew she detested. She didn't really like any of the American beers, but she was too far gone to protest.

'Rob, I really do need to go home.' She felt as if she was going to faint.

'OK, we'll all go back.'

Rob turned to Katarina. 'Go out to the limo and wait. I'll just help Alex find Kevin and the others. We've got the white stretch.'

Katarina found the cape she had carelessly left over a chair on her way in. With a jerk and without a word to the woman sitting on the chair, she yanked the cape up and swept it round her.

'How the hell's it supposed to go?' she mumbled, staggering.

They looked with surprise at this pale woman with enormous pupils struggling to get her cape on straight.

The white limousine brightened up the rather foggy January night and the black driver opened the door for her. She sat in one corner and suddenly felt freezing cold, her teeth chattering and her nose running. She pressed her scarf to her nose and snivelled. Why didn't they come? He'd promised they would go back to the hotel. She knew she'd throw up any minute.

The limousine doors were jerked open and in came the twins. They smiled rather absently at Katarina and sat down. Then Rob and Alex came.

'Katarina, these are friends of Alex's. They're coming with us to have a drink.'

Rob and Alex talked about tomorrow's gig, but Katarina heard the voices as if from a distance. Something about the KLOS radio broad-casting live from the concert and something else about a soundcheck.

The moment the limousine stopped outside the hotel, Katarina excused herself with a sweeping gesture and dashed for the hotel entrance. She had her key somewhere in her shoulder bag and started feverishly rummaging for it. Where the hell was the damned lift?

Her room was on the sixth floor and the lift seemed to take an eter-nity to get there. With growing panic, she managed to get the door open and without even taking off her cape she rushed into the bath-room and collapsed, head over the toilet bowl. She had eaten nothing all day, so only fluid came up, then bile – and tears blending with her mascara. She had never felt so terribly lonely before.

She wiped off the dark red lipstick on a tissue, rinsed her face in cold water and looked at herself in the mirror.

Not a pretty sight. Her mascara had smudged below her eyes and her hair was scruffy, dry and uncared for. That perm had clearly not been a good idea, especially as she was on tour and never had time to condition it.

Katarina examined her puffy complexion. The wrinkles round her eyes were clearly visible and her narrow mouth was thinner than ever without lipstick. She was starting to show her age. What was she going to do?

She cleansed her face thoroughly, and put on some Nivea cream. This was the beginning. Tomorrow she would start a new life. This couldn't go on much longer. She swallowed two Moga-don, without which she wouldn't have a hope of getting a wink of sleep.

She couldn't even be bothered to wonder where Rob was . . .

The telephone rang shrilly and Katarina searched vainly for it, then found it on the other side of the bed.

'Katarina, this is Sue Cameron. Alex suggested I should take you on a tour of LA, Beverly Hills, Universal Studios or whatever you'd like to see. Rob's going to be busy with radio interviews, so he suggested that I . . .'

The woman must be mad! Katarina couldn't get her head together. She felt round the bed for Rob, grimacing with nausea.

What had happened? Where was she?

'Hello? Are you still there?'

'Yes, yes. Meet me in the lobby in an hour. I've only just woken up.'

Her head pounding monstrously, she sat up carefully and gazed at the room. It looked as if a bomb had gone off, clothes absolutely everywhere, empty beer cans all over the place, ash-trays, carrier bags, half-open suitcases . . .

Where was Rob? She remembered he hadn't come up with her. She must have been sleeping so heavily, he hadn't been able to wake her when he had left that morning.

But she couldn't suppress the horrible feeling that he hadn't slept there at all. She stumbled round the bedroom and into the bathroom to see if she could find any trace of him, but how could she do that? The mess was like nothing on earth. Wet towels everywhere. The DO NOT DISTURB sign was on the door, so the maid hadn't been in and Katarina couldn't even remember what they had done before leaving yesterday.

What a stupid idea, meeting this woman. She was sure her head would soon blow apart. This certainly did not seem to be the right day to start a new life.

Katarina looked in the minibar for a beer, but it was empty, and there wasn't a drop left in any of the glasses. Hell, just when she needed a pick-me-up so badly.

She pulled out her purple velvet dress from the suitcase and hung it on the door in the bathroom hoping the steam from the shower would take out some of the creases. If she was to be ready by two, she had to get a move on.

After a critical glance in the mirror, she decided she was definitely a creature of the night and shouldn't be looked at in daylight, particularly in sunny California. Everyone here was blond, buxom and young.

On her way down in the lift, Katarina did a quick check in her little velvet bag. Yes, sunglasses, lipstick and Rob's American Express card still there, the things she needed most.

'Katarina, how are you?' The woman was disgustingly cheerful.

'OK, thanks.'

'So, what would you like to do? We could go out to Universal Studios – '

Katarina interrupted her.

'Have you heard from Alex today?'

Sue hesitated slightly before replying.

'I presume he's with Rob at the radio interview, but I'm not sure . . . Now maybe shopping in Beverly Hills? Or perhaps lunch?' Sue saw that lunch was the best suggestion. Katarina didn't look in particularly good shape for a trip.

Sue Cameron was one of those women it was impossible to put an age to. She could have been anything between twenty-five and forty. As they sat in the back of the limousine heading for the Beverly Hills Hotel the two women contrasted startlingly. Sue, trim in her short page-boy bob, cool linen suit and neat pumps, carried a flat briefcase under her arm and never let go of it. Katarina, her permed and dyed hair looking worse than ever, wore an over-large, long purple velvet dress and enormous black sunglasses. Aware of the unflattering contrast, Katarina was for a moment actually tempted to remove her glasses, but stopped at the memory of her swollen eyes reflected in the bathroom mirror.

Sue had booked a table at the Polo Lounge, and Katarina realised what good contacts the woman had when the head waiter greeted her warmly and showed them to one of the coveted booths on the left. They had a perfect view over the long bar, and Katarina searched vainly round for a famous face. She hardly touched her salad, but was far more interested in the Sauvignon Blanc Sue had ordered. Her mood improved with the drink and she leant back to enjoy the atmosphere.

What finally made Katarina take off her sunglasses was Warren Beatty coming in together with a short, rather plump man in a pink open-necked shirt. After exchanging cheek kisses with a few ladies, Katarina didn't recognise, the two men sat down in the next booth.

Sue couldn't help noticing Katarina's wide-eyed curiosity, and she told her that Mr Beatty often came here and the man with him was his agent. That was roughly the last thing Katarina heard Sue say, because after that she ignored Sue and concentrated on trying to hear what Warren and the little fat man were talking about.

God, how handsome he was. Katarina searched in her bag as she leant even further back in her seat. She thought she could hear something about a party, but where and when . . .

Where the hell was her compact? Suddenly she felt a little packet which might possibly contain quite a different kind of powder. Where had it come from? Katarina tried to pick the packet to see if there was anything left. Oh well, God knows.

'Excuse me for a moment, I must go to the ladies.' Uninhibitedly staring at the film star, Katarina almost collided with a woman in a vast cartwheel hat.

The ladies powder room was a dream in green and pink, but Katarina didn't notice, she went straight into the toilet and couldn't get the little packet out fast enough. There wasn't much in it, but enough for a line. She knelt down in front of the toilet lid and scraped the paper thoroughly with the credit card so as not to waste any. There was more than she had thought. She sniffed the whole lot at once, then licked the paper clean.

Sue couldn't help noticing what Mrs Hove had been up to in the powder room. Not only was she in a noticeably better mood, but she also kept snuffling. And though she'd had quite a lot to drink before, now there was no stopping her.

After lunch, almost exclusively liquid for Katarina, the time had come for shopping in Beverly Hills. Nothing really caught Katarina's eye, as all the clothes were far too American and far too elegant.

'I know something I think would interest you,' said Sue, as the limo turned on to Brighton Way and stopped at a small store called the Head Shop.

Katarina could hardly believe it. Everything, but everything to do with drugs. Elegant pipes, razor blades, tubes, spoons and mirrors in fourteen carat gold or silver. She felt like a child in a toyshop. Sue had certainly known what she was doing when she had brought her here.

Katarina bought a little set in gold for Rob, complete with razor blade, tube and mirror, all beautifully packed in a small box. For herself she bought a gold flask with a spoon fastened to the top. Perfect, no need to go on hacking away. Oh, how practical.

'Hi, darling. Had a good day with Sue?'

'Great!' Katarina, in a radiant mood, took Rob's beer away from him.

'I've bought you a present, sweetheart. What did you do last night, by the way?'

Rob was busy opening his parcel and didn't even look up as he told her he had had a drink with Alex in his room. Katarina had been out like a light, and today when he'd left, she'd been sleeping like a child.

She nodded vaguely. 'Oh, yeah . . . Do you like your present?'

'You bet. Let's try it straight away.'

'Have you got some?'

'You can bet your life I have.' Rob held up a small bag of coke.

Katarina went down on her knees in front of him and slowly unbuttoned his jeans. While he cut the coke with his new present, bought with his credit card, she gave him a blow job.

The twins of last night were even more excited in front of the stage that evening. No one in the audience could have missed seeing the two of them.

Again they wore identical clothes – black leather hotpants, high-heeled red patent-leather boots, tube tops that slid down over their busts when they danced and short leather jackets tied round their hips. Every rocker's dream girls, thought Katarina drily, with their enormous breasts and long blonde hair.

'Alex must have struck it lucky last night, not getting just one bimbo, but two,' she whispered thickly into Rob's ear, nodding at the two blondes, holding on to his arm with one hand, a joint in the other.

Alex had arranged a private party in his suite and the drink had flowed. Everything was a testament to their having taken Los Angeles by storm. Rob was now a hot name here.

Alex sat down close to her as he filled her glass.

'Katarina, I've been thinking about tomorrow. Our schedule in

214

San Diego is to say the least somewhat hectic – radio and news-paper interviews, so you might like to stay here during the two days we're away. It would give you a chance to go shopping and enjoy the sun instead of sitting on your own in a hotel room.'

Katarina did her best to focus on Rob to see what he thought, but he just sat there nodding rather meaningfully at Alex. Finally he made the point that as they were setting off for the interviews early the next morning, she would be able to sleep in.

'Wouldn't mind swapping with you,' he remarked.

The idea of not having to get up and cram into the bus attracted her. And this way she could have a good time tonight without worrying about tomorrow.

Suddenly Kevin came and hauled her up off the sofa.

'Come on, Kat. Let's dance.'

She smiled at him. 'Join you in a sec, Kev. Oh, by the way I have a surprise for you.'

Katarina wanted to show off her new coke bottle. Now she didn't even have to disappear into the ladies. All she had to do was to find a fairly dark corner where she could sniff the coke from the spoon.

Kevin was fascinated.

'I hear you're staying here tomorrow,' he said when she'd finished her demonstration. 'Can you get one for me?'

How the hell did he know I was going to stay here? thought Katarina. Alex had only mentioned it a few minutes ago, but her thoughts scattered with the lump of coke in her throat. She needed a drink. And quickly.

Katarina couldn't remember when she had last been on her own. This was only going to be for two days, but not knowing anyone except Sue, whom she hadn't any overwhelming desire to phone . . .

As usual she spent the hour after she'd woken reconstructing the day before. Yesterday evening they had gone on to the Rain-bow and then to an all-night party in some hotel, at least she thought that's what it was. It had annoyed her that after two o'clock in LA no one served alcohol and all the clubs closed, but

215

that was when parties normally started warming up.

There hadn't been any problems continuing the party last night. They had been at the other hotel until about six in the morning. How the hell had Rob and the others managed to get up to go to San Diego?

Katarina had one of Rob's old tour T-shirts on as she got up to get a beer out of the minibar. She took three aspirins and washed them down with cold beer.

'Hello, room service? This is Mrs Hove. Can I have some coffee and two packs of Marlboro? And quickly!'

There wasn't a single cigarette in the room. Katarina had dug about in the butts to find one she could light, but both she and Rob smoked them right down to the filters.

She took a shower while waiting for the cigarettes, then in the hotel's bathrobe, sat down at the table by the window. In the bright daylight, unmade-up, she looked like a tired forty year old.

Katarina felt a stab of anxiety. Most of her adult life she had been dependent on men, never really creating a life of her own. What would happen when she stopped being attractive, was no longer such fun? In all honesty Rob was not the greatest lover in the world, but they had good times together. And for once, he had been the one dependent on her, not the other way round. She had taught him how to dress, how to move on stage, which songs would work and which image was right. He seldom did anything without asking her advice first. He had been a bundle of nerves during the last few days in England. Katarina had tried to persuade him over and over again that it *wouldn't* be a fiasco and they would love him just as much in the US as they did in Europe.

Lately he had been able to see with his own eyes that what she told him was true, and the tour had actually all gone well beyond everyone's expectations. But why didn't he seem to want to spend time with her on their own as he had before, and why wasn't she allowed to go with him to press conferences and everything else Alex arranged?

Katarina frowned heavily.

How often had they had sex recently? And had he really come back the night before? She remembered Rob and Alex and the twins sitting in the car. Had they had that drink together with those two? Supposing they'd had a twin each? Or group sex . . .

'Room service. May I come in?'

Katarina was jolted out of her thoughts.

The taxi stopped on Sunset Boulevard outside Tower Records.

'There it is.'

The driver pointed down the street and Katarina paid and jumped out.

Tower Records had enormous posters of Rob and the band outside, but Katarina took no particular notice of them. Instead she popped yet another strong peppermint in her mouth so that she wouldn't smell of drink, and went into Budget Rent-a-Car.

'I'd like to hire a car. No, it doesn't matter, any car will do. Can I leave it in San Diego?'

It was almost ten at night. Katarina had been in her hotel room all day, room service providing her with an endless parade of waiters bringing beer, wine and Bloody Marys. Her thoughts had become more and more confused, not helped by the coke Rob had left behind for her.

Perhaps it was just imagination, but she had to find out what the situation really was or she would never have any peace. Why should she stay behind while the others went off? And how the hell had Kevin known she wasn't coming with them?

It was nearly half past two when Katarina finally turned off the 405 to San Diego. It hadn't been an easy drive. She had stopped for a beer once and lost her way getting back on the freeway. It was dark outside and Katarina was smoking like a chimney, her thoughts swirling round in her head. She accelerated. According to the signs there was not far to go. She pulled in at Union 76, a petrol station.

'Excuse me, do you know where the Hilton Inn is?'

'Yes, just round the corner. First turn on the right, and it's on the left, you can't miss it.'

Katarina rang the nightbell; a woman opened the door.

'Which is Rob Hove's room?' she asked, walking towards the reception desk.

'I'm afraid I can't tell you . . .'

Katarina interrupted the woman night porter by slapping her hand on the desk.

'For Christ's sake, I'm Mrs Hove, his wife, and I demand to know which room he's in.' They still used their own names, thank God.

'I'm terribly sorry, Mrs Hove, but have you any ID? As you know, we have the kids trying anything to get in.'

The porter looked suspiciously at Katarina. Not that she was a rock fan herself, but she did know enough to doubt this was the rock star Rob Hove's wife. The woman in a large black velvet cape and slouch hat was rummaging desperately in her bag for some kind of identity card, swearing to herself, and she was quite clearly not entirely sober. If she didn't come up with something, she'd get the guards to throw her out at once.

'Here. Come on, which room is he in.'

The woman behind the counter looked at the backstage pass and Rob's American Express Card that Katarina held up in front of her.

'I'm very sorry, Mrs Hove, but I hope you understand I had to—'

'Yes, yes, what number?'

'Mr Hove is in 1202, on the second floor.'

Five minutes later Katarina banged on the door like a madman.

'Go away. Piss off!'

She could hear Rob's voice, and others. Or was it her imagination? She went on banging and started to kick the door as well.

Rob's voice finally responded, 'Kevin? I fucking well told you, you can't join in. All right, then, you can have a look.'

Katarina's eyes widened when a stark naked Rob opened the door. She pushed past him into the room. To find the equally naked and giggling twins in the bed . . .

17

Surrounded by suitcases, Monica was on her way to Heathrow in a black cab.

Crispin had persuaded her to leave England as soon as possible and come and live with him in the south of France.

The scene with Gordon had been horrible, dirty, full of threats and humiliation. But this time he had not succeeded in persuading her to give a single inch. With her new man at her side, Monica had never been so certain before. It was an enormous relief in all that pain not to have to play along with Gordon.

He had insisted that she should leave Eaton Square the very same day, permitting her to take with her nothing but her clothes and some of her jewellery; she had also been allowed to keep the Mercedes. According to her bank statement, she had only three thousand pounds at her disposal, but for once that didn't worry her. She was so happy, money and material things had lost their power over her.

Without thinking, she had signed a paper to say she wanted nothing from her husband. Gordon had coldly suggested that if she signed a statement saying she would not set foot in Hewitt Hall for the next five years, then he would undertake to pay for Robert's education for the same length of time. He had even added a clause covering any possible extension when the time came. That was typical of Gordon, but that didn't worry her, either, in fact on the contrary – it solved all her problems, as it was Robert she had most worried about. And what did Hewitt Hall matter? It didn't worry her that the deal suited Gordon to perfection. He had built up a lot of his business round the Hall, and now he could go on parading all those things money could not buy.

There was nothing there she would miss, except possibly old Mrs McDonald. Monica had not even bothered to contact the old family solicitor, Sir Hugh Grenville, before signing Gordon's papers. When she had finally done so, he had tried to get her to change her mind in vain.

'What'll happen if this affair in the south of France comes to an end?' he asked. 'Where will you live? And what would you live off? You haven't worked for almost fifteen years. It wouldn't be easy for you to find employment again. Monica dear, I wish you would pull yourself together and look a little further than tomorrow. It really isn't like you to be so irrational. Particularly when it comes to money.'

Monica had just laughed.

'It won't come to an end, I promise you. This is real love like I've never had before.' For a brief moment Monica returned to reality and bit her lip, looking cautiously at Sir Hugh. 'Except for Edward, of course.'

Sir Hugh Grenville had been Edward's solicitor and Monica could feel herself flushing. Edward's had been a true love, but nothing to compare with this. Now there was passion, and love, and she was sure it would never die.

Dennis had packed up all her clothes and a tearful Maria had helped.

'Oh, Missa Clarke, I'm so sorry.'

Gordon had followed her like a guard dog, saying nothing, to check she didn't take anything with her that wasn't hers.

Some jewellery was missing from the safe, including the magnificent diamond necklace with matching earrings. Monica realised Gordon had weeded some things out, but not even that bothered her. The kind of life in which such things were needed was over as far as she was concerned. All the same, Monica couldn't help smiling at the thought of some of the jewellery still in her bank deposit at Coutt's; he couldn't get at that. Not that she wanted it, but the thought of cheating Gordon amused her.

She had deposited what Gordon had left of her jewellery at the bank the day after she had moved out, for she wouldn't need it in France. The only things she'd taken with her were a gold Rolex and the one-carat diamonds she wore in her ears. She hadn't bothered to check exactly what she had in the deposit box, but had just stuffed the lot in and left. Her old life lay there in Coutt's, a life she had left behind and would never go back to.

Going to Eton and telling Robert everything had been difficult. They had a long lunch together and trying to pluck up enough courage to tell him what had happened had been one of the most difficult things Monica had ever had to do.

It would have been so simple if she'd been able to explain exactly what the situation was, what it had been like in recent years with Gordon. Then Robert would have been pleased for her that it was over and his mother could live happily without constant fear of Georgina.

But Monica had no desire to drag her son into all that filth. Gordon had always treated Robert well, and Robert looked up to him. Everything they had done together had been exciting and fun. Gordon had encouraged him to expand his horizons, to undertake challenges that did not come naturally to him, but which he always drew satisfaction from.

Nor had telling him proved any easier than she'd anticipated. Poor Robert had turned deathly pale when Monica had tried to get him to understand that her love for this new man was so strong it was no use fighting it. She and Gordon had moved away from each other, she said, and this would anyhow have happened sooner or later.

It was quite impossible to tell him the whole truth all at once, so she left out the agreement over Hewitt Hall, thinking she would face that problem when the occasion arose.

She had felt a stab in her heart when Robert had looked appealingly at her and said: 'Mummy, how can you do this to Gordon?'

Robert simply couldn't understand it. Who was this new man in his mother's life? An artist? A man who painted pictures.

Monica knew that if only Robert could meet Crispin he would immediately like him. She could almost see them in front of her, and of course hoped he would spend all his holidays in France with them. In her turn, she promised to come and see him as often as possible.

It had certainly not been easy to leave a hurt and confused

Robert at school that day. She had seen him in the rear mirror as he stood there waving, and she thought about the lovely long hug before she'd left.

'It'll all work out, Robert,' she'd whispered. 'It's not as if I'm disappearing for ever. And I'll always love you.'

'And I love you, Mummy. I hope you know what you're doing.'

He was so understanding and oddly old fashioned, her son. She knew he was unhappy about her split with Gordon, but once he had met Crispin, everything would be all right. Crispin was so unlike Edward and Gordon. So full of life and surprises.

The day she had been to see Robert, she took the Mercedes and left it at the garage for storage. The truth was she couldn't afford to have it taken over to France at the moment, but that could be arranged later. As for her clothes she packed only summer dresses and simple suits. Chanel suits, evening dresses, crocodile bags, all went into store, her furs into cold storage at Harrods.

Now she was squashed in a taxi with four Gucci suitcases containing her whole life. How everything had changed. She would normally have had more luggage for a weekend visit, and Maria as well, of course. She hadn't been to Heathrow by taxi since her days as an air hostess, nor travelled tourist class since long before then.

On the plane, Monica looked for seat 24B along the narrow aisle on the plane. It must be further back than she remembered. She'd grown used to sitting in first class in the front part of the plane, to being shown to her seat and helped with her coat and hand luggage. Now she had to do all those things herself.

Crispin had sent her the ticket. The thought of seeing him again made her feel quite dizzy, like being a teenager again. She couldn't concentrate on anything except for his arms round her, his mouth on hers.

Monica found herself squashed between two women, one German, the other American, carrying on a lively discussion right across her, but they didn't really disturb her: her thoughts were elsewhere. A stewardess approached with lunch but Monica politely refused it, unable to eat a thing.

She hadn't seen Crispin for two weeks, though it felt like two years. She had moved in with him in his house in Hampstead after Gordon had thrown her out. Crispin had wanted her to come with him to France immediately, but that had been impossible; there were far too many things to arrange, the divorce, the storage of her possessions and not least going to see Robert.

Monica sipped at the white wine she had asked for. She hadn't touched any pills for over two months and she very seldom drank. She did have some wine with Crispin, but that was different – that was not to forget or relieve pain, but simply enjoyable. She had even begun to appreciate red wine.

Monica put her drink down, and pressed the button to call the stewardess. It suddenly seemed not all that long ago since she herself had been in the same job, and she remembered very clearly how awful it had been working in the tourist class. She asked for a glass of water. She certainly didn't want to smell of cheap wine when Crispin came to meet her.

The plane landed at Nice airport at half past four on the fourteenth of April and it was pouring with rain.

This was certainly not the first time she had been to the Riviera – she had been once with Edward and to Cap Ferrat with Gordon a few times. She had some memories from those latter visits. She'd been under the influence of drink or drugs, so they weren't quite clear.

When she came out of customs, he was waiting there with open arms, rushing up to her, lifting her up as if she had been a little bird and smothering her face with kisses.

'I've missed you, I've missed you, I've missed you . . .' he said over and over again.

Monica shuddered with happiness.

Crispin had a big dark blue American stationwagon. They said little throughout the journey; he held her hand and occasionally glanced at her, making her glow with happiness. Words were superfluous. The whole atmosphere in the car was permeated with love and desire. It was pouring with rain and the windscreen wipers were working overtime. The Riviera, the pearl of France, was hardly showing its best face, now grey and dismal, not entirely unlike the country she had just left, but it didn't matter.

Ten kilometres or so outside Nice, Crispin drove up towards Cagnes-sur-mer and finally to Vence. He stopped in front of a low white house that clung to the hillside, its roof tiled, creepers winding their way along the walls and roses climbing up espaliers everywhere.

'You can usually see right down to the sea from here,' he said with some pride in his voice.

The house was built in rustic style, the front door opening straight into a big room with a dark wooden floor, large white open fireplace, a long sofa opposite it covered with blankets, in front a table overflowing with newspapers, candlesticks and loose papers. A desk in the corner was even more laden with papers, magazines, pens and a telephone, and Monica could also see a well-stocked drinks table. In the kitchen was an enormous ancient stove and a large table with room for at least eight people.

He took her suitcases into the large, light south-facing bedroom. How wonderful to wake up here, thought Monica. Without a word, Crispin put down the cases, threw his arms round her and pulled her gently on to the bed. He took off her linen jacket and thin silk blouse.

What she had dreamt of was now going to happen. Her happiness was complete.

After they'd made love, he lay with his arms round her, neither of them saying anything. Monica had never experienced such fantastic sex as she had with Crispin, and at that moment it was hard to believe she'd ever been with another man. It was as if the years with Gordon had blown away. Here she was in a wonderful house with a man she would happily die for. She could barely believe how happy she was.

As Crispin dozed off, Monica got up, swept a towel round her and went off to explore what was going to be her new home. The walls of the living room were covered with paintings, in an abstract style but very interesting and quite beautiful. She stood looking out of the window. It had stopped raining and seemed to be clearing. The garden was fairly overgrown but, with its mass of rose bushes, beautiful. Winding stone steps led down to a patterned mosaic Jacuzzi she could hardly see; she would take a closer look later. Dreamily she imagined herself and Crispin down there toasting each other and their future.

'There you are, darling.'

Crispin emerged naked from the bedroom and threw his arms round her.

'Come with me, my love. I've something to show you.' He took her hand and led her back into the bedroom. 'The right side of the wardrobe is yours.'

Monica looked at him in surprise.

'Open it, and you'll see.'

Monica opened the wardrobe door a little and saw five or six dresses hanging inside. 'Oh, Crispin!' She ruffled through the dresses, one silk, one velvet, and several in the thinnest of cottons. They were all long and loosely cut, in a rather hippie style.

Monica took out one of them, a dress with a high waistline and an enormously wide skirt, then swung round with it in front of her. She also found a couple of chiffon scarves and two straw hats. She was delighted.

In the evening she wore a long, cream-coloured silk dress as she and Crispin sat down for dinner. He had prepared the meal himself and they drank to each other in champagne.

'To you, Monica. To us. Remember you need never doubt my love for you.'

Crispin did most of the talking that evening, and she was a good listener. Monica was so fascinated by this man, she couldn't get enough of him.

Days and weeks went by and Monica didn't regret for one moment giving up everything for the man she loved.

Crispin had a studio up in Saint-Paul consisting of a large room with a sofa, a toilet and shower, and a loft built in under the roof with a bed. He usually painted at night and rested in the mornings. Since Monica had appeared, however, he had changed his working programme, saying he wanted to go to bed with her, sleep with her and wake up with her.

She usually got up and had breakfast with him, and then he

went off to the studio and returned in the late afternoon. Monica spent her days walking in the countryside, tending the roses in an attempt to match those at Hewitt Hall, or preparing their evening meal, something she had to learn all over again, as she hadn't even boiled an egg for a decade. There were heaps of cookery books in the kitchen, some that had been there before and some she'd bought. It was fun doing something herself, and the labour involved definitely worth it when she saw her lover appreciatively sniffing the delicious aromas that wafted from the pans.

Some days Crispin stayed at home and then they spent practically all day in bed. His appetite for sex was colossal, and he knew precisely what to do to satisfy Monica. Sex had been a necessary evil to her in recent years, something she feared so much that she had to sedate herself first. How different it was with Crispin! They were as if created for each other, two pieces of the same puzzle.

Although she was thirty-seven, she discovered she was a novice when it came to sex. Crispin became her teacher and she a willing pupil. Experimenting together was sheer ecstasy.

Every morning they made love and after lunch, if Crispin was at home, twice, and at night they made love until they fell asleep. They had also made love in every conceivable place in the house, in the car, on the beach – his inventiveness and stamina were unlimited.

To Monica the days went by in transports of ecstasy. Sometimes they went out to dinner with some of Crispin's friends and played boules. And once or twice they went down to Cannes where he also had many friends. But most of the time they spent alone together.

Everything was so simple with Crispin. He was so unlike her previous men.

In only a few months, Monica's life had been radically changed: Chanel suits replaced by flowing dresses, her hair grown so that it hung straight round her heart-shaped face. Sometimes she knotted a chiffon scarf round her head or else she wore a straw hat, sandals on her feet.

Every week she telephoned Robert and told him about her new life in France, blithely unaware that he was finding it hard to understand her. She was full of plans for his summer holidays, when she wanted him to come and stay with them.

'Oh, Robert,' she assured him, 'you'll love the Riviera. And I know you and Crispin will get on well together. I'm so looking forward to seeing you, my love.'

Yes, now only Robert was missing. But he would soon be there and the last piece of the puzzle would fall into place – complete happiness.

Crispin had showed her where in Nice she could buy the freshest fish, the best bread and the best vegetables. He used the station wagon while Monica had to manage with his bright yellow Citroën *deux chevaux*. It was a funny little car, she thought happily, even if it didn't have the comfort of her Mercedes.

Always careful of her figure before, Monica no longer bothered about dieting. She quite simply ate when she was hungry. She did put on a little weight but it suited her. People round about were friendly and she would stop from time to time to talk to some of the neighbours.

Thank goodness she'd heard nothing from Gordon, and apart from Robert, she had very little contact with London in general. Papers arrived now and again from Sir Hugh for her to sign, which she did and returned, that was all. And she did see that William Hickey's column in the *Daily Express* had an item in it saying that the millionaire Gordon Clarke's beautiful Swedish wife Monica, the former Lady Hewitt, had left her husband for the recently discovered artist Crispin Que and now lived with him in the south of France.

All Monica wanted was that the divorce should go through as quickly as possible. Not that she wanted to remarry. On the contrary, she loved the freedom she had with Crispin. No, all she wanted was to erase Gordon completely from her life.

She had talked to Gerd a few times on the phone – Gerd was pleased for her daughter. She was aware Monica had not been happy with Gordon, not why, but in the way mothers knew she'd realised that all was not well. She hadn't heard her daughter so bubblingly happy for years.

Monica listened absently to what Gerd had to tell her, about her father and what had been happening on the home front. She was so absorbed in her new love, she found it hard to get involved in the lives of other people. Her life consisted of Monica and Crispin, Crispin and Monica.

Not until the end of May were they together at a major event. The Cannes Festival was in full swing and the telephone rang constantly. Lots of Crispin's friends had come to the Riviera and Sid Milestone, Crispin's agent in London, stayed with them for a few days. He owned the Milestone Gallery in Curzon Street, a gay man in his thirties. Monica liked him from the very start. He was full of life, talking and smoking all the time, a source of laughter. He had been the moving force behind a documentary film on Crispin which was now to be shown at the festival, and he reckoned it would be decisive to Crispin's career. He would now make a breakthrough for real.

And it seemed a breakthrough really was in the air. Crispin had just heard that a commission from Cannes city itself had been confirmed, and that meant not only money but honour and appreciation.

That evening Monica was looking forward to going to Monte Carlo. There was a party at Le Pirate and Crispin was full of enthusiasm when he told her about all the friends he would be introducing her to.

'Oh, Monica, they'll all love you, and you them,' he'd said when he told her about it. The weather had been marvellous and Monica was already quite tanned. To show this off, she decided to wear a full-length antique lace dress. Her hair had now grown below her shoulders and she wore it with a centre parting. With very little make-up she looked angelic as she went down to the Jacuzzi to join Crispin and Sid for a drink. For the first time since her arrival in France, she was wearing her gold Rolex and the diamond earrings.

'Monica, you look absolutely sensational!'

Sid even applauded.

'Come and sit here, darling,' said Crispin patting his knee.

'Oh, Crispin, you know I don't like you to smoke before you drive – supposing something happens.' Monica waved away the smoke from the joint Crispin had in his hand.

He actually smoked grass quite a lot, he liked it. Monica had tried it once, but she didn't like what it did to her. Her head had spun around violently and she felt as if she was losing her self-control. These days she appreciated having a clear head after all the years of fog with Gordon, so she hadn't tried again. But she didn't mind Crispin smoking and he had sworn it wasn't dangerous or addictive. All she wanted was for him not to drive when he'd been smoking – she had been so dizzy when she'd smoked it, she wouldn't have been able to drive at all.

'Don't worry, Mopsie,' he grinned.

He always called her Mopsie and they'd laughed when Monica had told him the only Mopsie she'd known had been a little pekingese dog belonging to her mother-in-law. It made him call her Mopsie even more.

On the whole, it was the period of her life she'd spent with Edward they talked about most whenever the past came up in the conversation, as well as her life in Sweden. They never talked about Gordon. They hadn't been happy together, was all she said. She would have been able to confide in Crispin, but she had buried Georgina so deep down, she didn't even think about it herself.

Le Pirate was on a cliff above the sea. One part of the restaurant was indoors, the other part out of doors under a thatched roof. Guests inside could see a large open fire outside on the right of the steps, the area where all the food was prepared. Waiters were dressed as pirates, with naked torsos and tight black trousers. Every table was supplied with olives, garlic bread and crudités, with jugs of sangria being consumed almost as quickly as the waiters could carry them to the tables.

The restaurant was crowded, a marvellous mixture of artistes, painters and actors. Monica felt slightly awkward among all these colourful people. They all seemed to know each other, and as far she could see they were all young and beautiful.

Crispin, seeming to read her thoughts, put his arm round her and kissed her cheek. He introduced her eagerly to everyone and was reassuringly affectionate to her in front of all these new people. Monica could feel the tension in her slowly giving way, though, used to being alone with Crispin for so much of the time, she still found it rather difficult to adapt. The people were so different from those she was used to, and before she had always been the centre of attraction. Extraordinary to think what clothes, jewels and the knowledge that you have money does for you. Now she was just Monica, Crispin's girl-friend.

Crispin sat holding her hand all through dinner, whispering in her ear. What an amazing amount of love the man had to give. He was in a great mood, but that was not unusual, though he was obviously enjoying seeing his friends again and introducing them to Monica. They were about ten or twelve round the table, the sangria flowing. For once Monica drank more than usual and was drawn into it all by the music and the atmosphere.

She listened and observed. The open, rather cheeky banter was something quite new to her. She saw a joint being passed round and practically all of them had a drag.

Who would have believed this could happen to her? The dinner parties she was used to were stiff and boring, with people poking at their food with silver cutlery. Here everyone was talking and laughing, drinking whenever they felt like it, without having to wait for someone else to propose a toast. They were happy to see each other and showed it.

A few hours later, Monica began to warm up and take a more active part in the conversation. And she was as enthusiastic as the rest when Sid said, 'Let's go to Jimmy's. What do you all say?'

The club was crowded and noisy when they made their entrance and squeezed their way to a corner table the tall, thin hostess showed them to.

'Come on, Monica, let's dance while we wait for our drinks.'

Sid pulled her by the hand and she was quick to agree, tossing back her head with a laugh. He was a fantastic dancer with a style entirely his own, swinging his arms round and shaking his head in time with the music, his footwork enough to make the most skilful dancer green with envy. ABBA'S 'Take a Chance on Me' was roaring out of the loudspeakers.

'Sid,' she panted finally. 'I need a drink.'

'What? I can't hear.'

The music was so loud, Monica realised it was useless even trying to make herself heard. So she pointed at their table and he nodded.

People who hadn't been there before had joined them, but there was no sign of Crispin.

'Have you seen Crispin?' Monica said, leaning over towards Pierre, a young actor who had been with them all evening.

'I think he's dancing.'

Monica looked across the dance floor, but could see no sign of him. It was so crowded it was hard to distinguish anyone.

Sid had ordered three bottles of Cristal, and Crispin had jokingly asked whether the money from his commission in Cannes was paying for it. Pierre filled Monica's glass. He was about twenty-five and, Monica discovered, just about to make his great breakthrough, in a French film which was being shown at the festival, and although he had only a small part in it, he'd had great reviews and a brilliant career in front of him.

With his dark hair and sensitive blue eyes, he reminded Monica slightly of Robert. They talked about everything under the sun and for a few minutes Monica forgot everything else.

Suddenly she spotted Crispin emerging from the crowded dance-floor hand in hand with a black girl who'd joined them during the evening. She was sensational. She couldn't have been more than seventeen, but was six foot tall, of which at least three must have consisted of leg. Her perfectly shaped head and long neck were further accentuated by her cropped hair. She appeared to have nothing on but a leopard-patterned shift, gold sandals laced up her legs, and gold jewellery round her neck and wrists.

They were sweating after the dance and laughing loudly. Monica felt a twinge inside her. Crispin had thrown her a kiss, but sat down with the black girl on the other side of the table. For a moment, her jealousy felt uncontrollable and she was about to rush over to him, but she stopped herself. Of course, dancing with another woman was no more peculiar than her sitting talking to the incredibly handsome Pierre. But she couldn't help glancing sideways across the table now and again to see what was happening. Pierre went on talking about his break with his girl-friend, but now Monica found it hard to concentrate, mostly nodding at what she thought suitable moments.

What were they up to? Crispin was whispering into the girl's ear and they both kept giggling. She saw him holding her hand as he lit her cigarette, and in the light of the flame she could see they were gazing into each other's eyes. This was another thing that was quite new to her. She couldn't remember ever feeling an ounce of jealousy since just before she married Edward and Margaret was around.

As soon as the black girl got up, Monica excused herself and went over to Crispin. He received her with open arms, and, like lightning, Sid took her place beside Pierre. Crispin kissed her as if nothing had happened and Monica was suddenly ashamed of having suspected anything and cursed herself for her unfounded jealousy. Crispin's earlier words rang in her ears: 'You need never doubt my love for you.'

As the Eagles played 'Hotel California', Crispin whispered: 'Come on, Mopsie? That's our song. Let's dance.'

It was so long since Monica had had a hangover she'd forgotten how awful it was. But for once it had been worth the headache. It had been an incredible evening, wonderful.

'Good morning, my darling.'

Crispin was as bright as a button. She looked at him, fascinated that there was not a single trace of his having been out until four in the morning. He was clearly one of those people who could do anything and still look shamelessly alert the next day.

'Breakfast's ready.'

Monica didn't know how she was going to get a single crumb down her. Perhaps a cup of strong coffee would allow her to rejoin the human race.

'Where's Sid? Did he come back?'

'No, he's just phoned. He ended up at Pierre's.' Crispin smiled rather mischievously.

'You don't mean . . .'

'Oh, yes, you can bet your bottom dollar on that.'

Monica gulped down some coffee. 'But I thought Pierre said he'd just split up with his girl-friend after four years.'

'Yes, he has. He isn't gay, but things probably worked out that way last night. Sid must be in a state of bliss.' Crispin kissed her on the cheek. 'I'll leave you for a while so you can wake up. Must go up to the studio to get some canvases for Sid when he gets back. He may be a while.' Crispin winked at her before disappearing out through the door.

He left a shocked Monica behind at the breakfast table.

In June, the summer really set in. The weather was wonderful and Monica had learnt to like the sun again. She had always avoided it like the plague since it had made her ill while pregnant, and because of warnings about the sun causing skin cancer and premature wrinkles. But now she didn't care, she loved it. She liked herself with a tan.

Monica had telephoned and written to Robert, suggesting that he should come to stay for the holidays. He had exams and term ended in July and so it would fit in well if he could come then. He had spent the Easter holidays at Hewitt Hall as usual, and Gordon had clearly been there. Now it was Monica's turn to be with him and she was counting the days, even the hours, until he arrived.

Not even Monica could help noticing from his voice on the phone how apprehensive he was about going to France, but that didn't really worry her. As long as he came and met Crispin and saw how wonderful things were for her, then everything would work out. She knew that.

There was so much for him here and Monica was looking forward to finding lots of things to do together, like a real family, things such as hiring a motorboat and going water skiing or having a picnic on the beach. There was so much she wanted to show him; they had a lot to catch up on. She missed him so.

Monica woke up feeling dreadfully sick, the nausea worsening so that for a moment she thought she was going to throw up. She simply daren't move.

She recognised the symptoms. There was no doubt whatsoever.

233

Cautiously, without moving her head, she poked at Crispin. He woke immediately with a jerk.

'Crispin, I'm feeling sick and I've got a splitting headache.'

He leant over her, resting on one elbow, stroking her cheek and smiling compassionately.

'Shall I get you an aspirin, darling?'

But Monica knew this was no ordinary headache. She lay there for a long time holding Crispin's hand without saying anything. She tried to smile – inside she felt happy – and she pressed his hand harder.

'Crispin, I'm pregnant.'

He opened his eyes wide and Monica realised what he was going to ask, so said quickly:

'Yes, darling, I'm certain.'

'But how long have you known?'

'About three minutes.'

Monica was on her way to the airport in the stationwagon to pick up Robert. It was half past two and the heat was oppressive. She was grateful she'd managed to get out of bed; today was the day she had looked forward to for so very long. Robert's summer holidays had begun and he was on his way.

Almost a month had gone by since she'd found out she was pregnant. The nausea had gone on as it had begun, and she found it very difficult to do anything at all before noon. The mornings were the worst, and she also felt terribly tired.

Crispin treated her like a delicate china doll, and although she was only in the early stages of pregnancy, he would not allow her to carry anything the slightest bit heavy. At thirty-four this was going to be his first child and he was truly looking forward to it.

Every time he looked at Monica, Crispin's handsome face radiated happiness. As she gazed back she'd think she'd never seen such eyes as his before – dark blue with black eyelashes and black eyebrows, his long dark hair and big generous mouth always smiling and showing his dazzling white teeth. To Monica he was the most handsome man she had ever seen.

But now she must concentrate on Robert. She'd decided not to tell him she was pregnant, for two reasons, really. One was that she was thirty-seven and you never knew, and also this holiday was Robert's and she didn't want anything else to distract him. There was quite enough already, with a new man and a new country. She was afraid he might feel left out if he knew they were having a new baby. Anyhow, she would wait. She parked the big car and went into the arrivals hall.

She knew Philip and Gordon had been to pick him up from Eton and had taken him out to dinner in Windsor that same evening to celebrate. But now the two of them were going to spend the next six weeks together.

All in all she was blissfully happy. She was expecting a child by the man she loved more than anyone else on earth next to her son, who would be arriving at any minute.

Filled with excitement she waited impatiently for Robert to come through customs, standing on tiptoe in an attempt to see through the doors.

There he was. He had a big bag slung over one shoulder. My God, how good-looking he was. His brown hair was short and slightly wavy, and he looked twenty although he was not yet sixteen. He had never been athletic, however much Gordon had tried to encourage him, and his tall gangling figure was clad in a dark blue college jersey and beige cotton trousers, black loafers on his feet.

When he saw her, he rushed at her shouting, 'Mother, Mother', so the whole airport turned round to see what was going on. They threw their arms round each other and she held on to him, tight.

'Oh, Robert, you've no idea how I've missed you.' She looked straight at him and saw the tears rising. He was such a sensitive boy. She took his hand and said: 'Come, let's go.'

They stepped out into the brilliant sunlight.

'Phew, it's hot,' said Robert, taking off the blue Eton jersey, his white short-sleeved cotton shirt underneath much more suited to the climate.

The air-conditioning in the car wasn't working, so Monica opened all the windows as they headed for Vence. The wind blew in their hair and it was difficult to hear, but Monica could see he was looking inquisitively around.

'Well, what do you think?'

'What?'

They wound up the windows to be able to hear better.

'What do you think?'

'I don't know. I'm glad to be here with you anyhow.'

'How were the exams?'

'All right, I think. I guess I did well in maths and English. Not so well in history and chemistry. We'll see when the results come. I'm more interested in languages and literature.'

Monica knew this. Gordon had not succeeded in getting him interested in science, but Monica was nonetheless tremendously proud her son was doing so well at school. She remembered how badly she herself had done. Robert must be a genius. Her maternal pride knew no bounds. As a glow of warmth filled her she wished she could tell him she was pregnant, but she sensed this was not the right moment.

'I'm proud of you. Your father would have been, too.'

It took them less than an hour to get back to the house, and before they went in, she took Robert's hand.

'Robert, I know you'll like Crispin. He's so totally unlike other men. All I want is for you two to be friends. I've really been looking forward to this holiday.'

'I promise, Mother. I'll do my best.'

She parked the car in the shade behind the garage, the sun blazing down.

'Crispin, Crispin, where are you? We're back.'

A smiling Crispin came towards them and gave Robert a hug.

'At last you're here. Your mother has told me so much about you, I'd almost begun to think you were a figment of her imagination.'

'How do you do,' said Robert, with some reserve, but just managing a smile.

Monica looked rather anxiously at her son.

'Come on, Robert, I'll show you your room.'

She went ahead of him to the guest room and he put his case

down on the bed before she took his hand to show him round the house.

'If you want to we can go down to Cannes and hire a motor boat and go water-skiiing. Tomorrow we were thinking of taking a picnic to Ile Ste Marguerite.'

Robert could see how much it meant to her that he should like Crispin.

'That sounds wonderful, but I'm so hot now, I must have a shower and change.'

Leaving him alone for a while, Monica went out on to the terrace and sat down under the big umbrella with Crispin.

'What a handsome son you've got.'

'Yes, I told you so.'

'Yes, but not that he was so good-looking and *adult*. You two look more like brother and sister.'

'Oh, come off it, Crispin.'

'I mean it. I had no idea he was so big. You talk about him as if he were a ten year old.'

'Hm, I suppose that's how I see him.'

'But he's almost a grown man.'

'Not to me. To me he's still my little boy.'

'I dare say, but not for long.' Crispin laughed. 'You'll soon have another little boy or girl.'

'Ssh, not so loud. I don't want Robert to know yet. This is his holiday. I'll tell him when he goes back.'

Crispin nodded in agreement.

When they went in, they found Robert now changed into shorts and looking at Crispin's paintings. Crispin went over and put his hand on the boy's shoulder, but Robert pulled away.

'What do you think of them?'

'I'm impressed. Though I'm not all that good on abstract art. I'm more into the old masters, so I can't really judge them properly.'

Robert however could see there was a message in Crispin's work and that a skilful artist had done these paintings. Not entirely to his taste, but he did his best to please Monica.

'They're good,' he said, nodding.

He took his time looking more closely at them, which seemed

to please Crispin, who took him around the room and explained what he was trying to express in certain paintings. Monica watched, with a mixture of anxiety and pleasure, the two men in her life talking to each other, side by side.

The three of them spent the rest of the afternoon down on the beach and that evening they celebrated his arrival with dinner at La Colombe d'Or.

Robert woke as usual at half past six. He was used to the early routines at Eton, and he got up as quietly as he could. He felt a stranger in this small house, creeping round on tiptoe so as not to wake Monica and Crispin as he put on his shorts and T-shirt.

His stomach was rumbling with hunger. The meal the night before had been good but so much had happened, he hadn't eaten enough. He slipped down the corridor to the kitchen.

His mother had said that if he was hungry, just go to the kitchen and help himself and she'd shown him where things were. There was so little in it what was there wasn't difficult to find.

The sun was just rising and it was cool; he was grateful, as the heat the day before had been almost unbearable. As he started his breakfast he thought about the events of yesterday.

He wasn't quite sure whether he understood his mother's choice of man. He liked Gordon and couldn't understand why she'd left him for this man. From the very beginning, Gordon had made it quite clear he was not going to discuss the matter, so Robert hadn't been able to do anything but accept Monica's explanation that they had grown apart from each other.

The paintings really were fascinating though, even if it disturbed him that the proportions weren't quite right. But the colours were strong and bold. Of course he preferred still-life, objects, figures, landscapes – traditional paintings. Crispin's were largely colourful daubs.

There was something about Crispin himself he couldn't really figure out. The way he looked, the mouth, always laughing. Robert could see he adored his mother. But he was so different from the kind of man Robert was used to and had grown up with.

Then there was his mother. He was used to seeing her in elegant suits, wearing lots of jewellery. And make-up, although he hadn't really liked the smell of it. Now she didn't use any, wore no jewellery and her clothes were peculiar. Long floppy dresses and big hats.

He decided to have a look round the garden and went down to the Jacuzzi. He studied the operating buttons considering taking a dip. He had never been in a Jacuzzi before. Gordon had talked about getting one but had changed his mind, saying only the *nouveau riche* had them. Robert pulled off his T-shirt and shorts and jumped in. The sun had risen and warmed him as he lay there. He pulled all the switches and suddenly jet streams of water erupted all around him. He laughed to himself. It seemed to tickle him all over – the overall effect was irresistibly sensual and he could feel his penis hardening under his pants as he started breathing more quickly.

His sexual development had been slow despite the fact that he had grown physically so early. His friends at Eton had started talking about sex two years ago and had slipped girlie magazines to each other. He'd felt left out and hadn't quite understood what they were talking about. He didn't even know what masturbation was until some of the boys had done it in the showers after a games session. He'd been shocked and at the same time egged on, though of course he hadn't dared do it there, but had gone back to the house and done it in private.

He enjoyed the Jacuzzi and wriggled out of his underpants to let the bubbles massage him, an indescribably sensuous feeling. He parted his legs and helped with his hand – he came quickly, he'd never felt an orgasm so strongly before.

He felt around for his underpants and put them back on under the water, then, dripping wet, he got out and went up to the house. He sank into a chair on the sun-filled terrace and fell asleep.

He woke with a start to find Monica in front of him.

'Did you sleep well? Have you had breakfast?'

'Yes, I've had a bit.'

'That's not enough. Come along, I'll make you a proper breakfast. Crispin may well want something, too.'

Robert was surprised. This must be the first time she'd made breakfast for him since he was a small boy. And he saw she was keen to do it. He didn't want to spoil her pleasure by refusing.

'Eggs and bacon, is that all right?' she asked.

'Smashing, thanks,' he smiled in return.

Crispin had hired a RIVA in Cannes and, full of anticipation, they set out for Ste Marguerite. Monica had fixed a picnic basket of cold chicken, bread, cheese, peaches, some bananas, a large bottle of Coca-Cola and two bottles of cold wine. Crispin put the basket in the boat and Robert willingly jumped in to help Monica who was wearing a long thin cotton dress with broderie anglaise at the neck and hem. As he busied himself with their picnic gear Robert glanced at his mother. He was still rather bewildered by her new appearance.

They left the marina in Cannes and raced at high speed across to the island and when the time came to pack up for the return to the mainland, all three felt they'd had a really wonderful day. Robert had thawed out a little in Crispin's company, Monica noted, although he clearly still had some reservations.

That evening Crispin and Robert played Monopoly, in French, as practice for Robert and Monica enjoyed watching them both getting absorbed in the game. She was proud at how fluent her son's French already was. But she was a little taken aback when at nine o'clock he got up and said he was tired. He kissed his mother and said goodnight to Crispin without looking him in the eye.

Monica went with him to the guest room.

'Is everything OK? Did you enjoy yourself today?'

'Oh, yes, I'm just tired. I was up early this morning. School habits still there, you see.' He kissed her lightly on the cheek and closed the door behind him.

As usual, Crispin could read her thoughts.

'Don't worry,' he said as she came back into the living room. 'Give the boy time to get used to it. You didn't think he'd be flinging his arms round my neck a day after he met me, did you?'

'Yes, as a matter of fact I did.'

They laughed and he kissed her.

The hot summer days flowed into each other and Robert enjoyed being alone at home with Monica. Crispin was in a very pro-ductive period and painted all day, occasionally reverting to his old habit of painting at night.

'Just to give you more time alone with Robert,' Crispin had said, and Monica hugged him for being so understanding and undemanding.

It hadn't been easy to hide from Robert how sick she was in the mornings. But she slept late and he was used to that, so didn't think it anything unusual. Sometimes she said she had a migraine, and there was no reason why Robert should doubt that either. And the floppy dresses she wore all the time hid her thickening waistline.

At the moment Monica's desire for sex was virtually non-existent. She loved Crispin so much, it almost hurt, but there was simply no desire there. He seemed to understand; she had tried to pretend as long as she could, but he'd felt their love-making wasn't satisfying her. He made no further demands and Monica, knowing full well his great urge, appreciated his sacrifice.

Every week he brought her big bunches of flowers with loving little messages inside. Monica felt that, even without sex, their love was growing stronger.

The third of August was Robert's birthday and Monica had plan-ned it in detail. She had ordered a cake in Nice with the Hewitt family coat-of-arms in marzipan on top of chocolate icing and whipped cream, and, of course, sixteen candles.

Crispin had booked a table at La Colombe d'Or for the evening, but Robert spent the day out on a boat with the scuba diving instructor.

Almost four weeks had gone by since Robert's arrival, and on the whole she thought they'd had a great time together. Crispin had bought him a set of painting things as a present, complete with oils, brushes and easel. She was sure Robert had creative talent.

Monica had bought him a set of underwater gear, a mask, rubber fins and harpoon. He had shown great interest in diving and she hoped he would appreciate the presents. He did, especially the painting gear but because it was so closely linked with Crispin, Robert felt reluctant to say how pleased he was with it.

241

Philip was the first to telephone on his birthday. Monica answered and they exchanged a few polite phrases before she handed the phone over to Robert. She found herself eavesdropping on their conversation. Robert looked up to Philip as a father-figure and was clearly pleased that he'd called. Monica tried to work out whether Philip was asking anything about Crispin, but it was difficult. An occasional 'yes' and 'no' and 'well, I dunno' seemed to be Robert's only answers and whether they were in response to anything to do with Crispin, she couldn't be sure.

Crispin was at the studio and Robert on the beach when the telephone rang again.

'Hello.'

'Can I speak to Robert?'

A cold wave went through her. She hadn't heard his voice since before she left England and had suppressed everything to do with him. He didn't even say who he was. He hadn't changed.

Monica's heart jumped. She had had no idea that just hearing the sound of his voice would be so difficult and she took a deep breath.

'Gordon, he's down on the beach. He'll be back in an hour.'

'I see.'

That was all. Then he put down the receiver without another word.

Suddenly so much came back to her that for a moment she was plunged into the years of terror again. She poured a glass of wine from the opened bottle in the fridge and took it with her out to the terrace. Her hand was shaking. To think that that man could make her feel she needed a drink just by saying a few short words. It was not surprising she'd been more or less an alcoholic during her marriage to him.

She could feel how tired she was. She'd been to her doctor in Cannes and he'd prescribed iron tablets for her, as she had turned out to be very anaemic.

She knew she had to change and make herself nice for the evening, but she didn't feel like it. In fact she wasn't feeling at all well. She threw out the rest of the wine. One sip had been enough.

Crispin had picked up Robert, who was thrilled with his day's diving.

'Look at these, Mother,' he said, flinging a plastic bag into the sink. He'd caught a dozen or so fish, not very big ones, but he was proud of them all the same. 'We'll have them for dinner tomorrow, won't we?'

'Yes, we will. By the way, Gordon phoned.'

'Oh, did he? What did he say?'

'He wanted to wish you many happy returns and said he would call again,' Monica lied, but she didn't want him to feel hurt.

'OK. I'll go and get ready. I'll just go and have a dip in the Jacuzzi first.'

Robert always made sure he was alone in the Jacuzzi. He knew they were getting ready for the evening, so he could take the opportunity for a pleasant spell on his own. He went there every day and knew exactly what to do to get the maximum enjoyment.

Crispin took Monica by the hand and led her into the shaded bedroom. He kissed her carefully.

'I missed you so.'

'But I'm here. I'm here all the time.'

He laughed mysteriously, and she realised what he meant. Suddenly Monica started feeling better, responding to his kiss. He put his arms round her and together they fell on the bed.

'Crispin, not now, in broad daylight. Think of Robert.'

'Calm down. It's almost evening. Anyway, he's down in the Jacuzzi.'

Monica gave in and they made love slowly, deliciously. Afterwards Monica felt a glow of sensual satisfaction she hadn't felt for some time.

A few hours later, all three of them were at the Colombe d'Or – a hotel as well as a restaurant. The beautiful room with its wooden walls and handful of tables provided just the right atmosphere for celebrating Robert's birthday.

Robert drank wine that evening, but Monica looked nervously at Crispin as he kept filling his glass.

'I don't think . . .' she began.

'Oh, Mopsie. Come off it. He's a grown man now.'

By ten o'clock, Monica was struggling against sleep.

'I'm not feeling too good. Do you two mind if I go home?' She was loath to break up her son's birthday party.

'What's the matter?' said Robert, looking at her uneasily.

'Nothing, darling. I've just got a migraine.'

Crispin looked at Robert.

'What do you say? Shall we go on? We can drive your mother home, then I'll show you a couple of places.'

Monica looked appealingly at Robert and he understood the signal. She wanted him to have a good birthday and the thought of him and Crispin together meant a lot to her.

'Of course, why not?'

'Good.'

Robert liked the taste of wine, but he was feeling slightly dizzy. He had only sipped at one of Philip's glasses before, and he needed time to decide whether he liked the effect of it. He closed his eyes as he sat in the back of the car and decided that he liked feeling relaxed like this.

They dropped Monica off. Although pale, she was smiling radiantly as she peered into the car to wave goodbye. Robert had climbed over and was now sitting by Crispin.

'Have a good time now,' she called.

'I'm sure we will.' Crispin winked at Robert.

They waited until she was inside the house before driving off.

'So, Robert. This is your day. What would you like to do with the last few hours?'

Feeling the effects of the wine, Robert just shrugged.

'I don't know.'

'I know. We'll drive down to Cannes. There are lots of fun clubs there.'

Crispin drove to the Whisky à Gogo. They parked the little yellow car and went in. The dance floor was full and the disco lights whirling.

'Oh, Monsieur Que, we're very full tonight, but I think I can find you a table,' smiled the head waiter before showing them to a small booth right by the dance floor.

'Shall I bring a bottle?'

Crispin laughed.

'What do you want to drink?'

Robert stared at him in despair. 'I'll have whatever you have.'

Whisky and two glasses appeared on the table, together with ice and soda.

'You can have it either with ice or with soda or both.'

Robert laughed with some embarrassment.

'I've never drunk whisky before, you see. I've no idea . . .'

'Then I suggest you have it with a little soda.'

While Crispin poured the whisky, Robert looked across the dance floor – it was swarming with people in the most amazing clothes he had ever seen, girls in shorts, high boots and low-cut tops, and boys in tight trousers with low waists and tight singlets laced at the neck with lots of scarves. They looked like hippies he had seen in photographs. It was all very unfamiliar and certainly no one he knew from Eton dressed like this.

He could feel his body tingling, the wine and the atmosphere having the same effect as the Jacuzzi. He and Crispin raised their glasses and unsuspecting, he took a great gulp, just as Crispin did.

It tasted foul and he grimaced as he swallowed, the whisky burning his throat. Coughing, tears came into his eyes and he almost threw up.

'What's the matter?'

'It's so strong. I don't like it.'

Wryly Crispin reckoned whisky was not right for Robert. 'Perhaps you'd better stick to wine. Wait a moment, and I'll order a bottle.

'Louis!' he called to the head waiter, who soon came hurrying through the crowd. 'I think our young friend here would prefer a little wine instead. Have you a good bottle of white?'

'Certainly, sir.'

Robert felt relieved. He had liked the wine and was looking forward to some more. But, despite Crispin's respite, the whisky was taking effect and things began spinning, not unpleasantly, in front of his eyes. He sat swaying in time with the music, thinking he'd really like to dance. Not that he knew how, but it looked fun with all those bouncing jumping people.

Crispin looked at him rather mischievously.

'I'm sure there's someone out there you like.'

He led him out on the dance floor over to two girls in hotpants and plastic boots and they willingly turned to him, gesturing for him to join them.

Robert had never danced before, but it wasn't long before he was drawn in by the music. Dancing wasn't all that difficult. He'd never had such fun before. He loved the feeling the alcohol gave him, and letting himself go to the music was great. He might be dizzy, but he still felt totally in control of himself.

After a while they went back to the table. Robert was sweating and thirsty, and took a great gulp of the cold wine.

He suddenly saw Crispin with new eyes. Perhaps he wasn't as strange as he had first thought – on the contrary, he thought he really liked the man sitting opposite him making everyone laugh. Robert took the initiative this time and raised his glass to Crispin.

'Shall we move on?' Crispin said. 'I know another place where they go on fairly late.'

Robert, curious to see what other places had to offer, could only agree. He took another drink before they left the table, deciding happily that he liked the taste more and more.

Crispin gave the head waiter some bank notes, then put his arm round Robert and led him out.

The yellow Citroën made its way along the little streets of Cannes, and Robert could hear music coming from somewhere. They parked the car and went down a narrow alley and found themselves facing a wooden door with iron fittings. Crispin knocked, the door opened and the music could be heard much more clearly. This was the best jazz club in Cannes, Crispin told him. Robert wasn't all that clear just what kind of jazz this was but he liked the sound of the rhythm.

Crispin ordered a bottle of white wine and Robert drank as if it were water. He felt as if he was floating on a cloud and life was wonderful. He talked and laughed all the time, opening up with Crispin in a way he hadn't done since he'd arrived.

'Enjoying yourself?'

He certainly was, no denying it. He had never done anything like it before. He wished his school friends could see him now. The warmth he felt all over his body was wonderful. He raised his glass to Crispin.

'Thanks,' he said. 'Thanks for a super evening.'

He had begun to understand his mother. Crispin was always laughing, a tremendously positive person. He had been wrong from the start, and slightly indistinctly Robert now started telling Crispin so, adding apologies for his behaviour during the first weeks.

Crispin put his arm round him and gave him a hug.

'Don't bother about that now. The main thing is that we're all here and everything's OK, isn't it?'

They sealed their friendship by clashing their glasses together.

He was glad to get out in the cool air.

'Shall we go up to my studio?' Crispin suggested. 'I'd like to show you some of my other canvases.'

Robert hadn't the slightest desire to go home to bed, so quickly agreed. They drove up to Saint-Paul and stopped outside the studio. Crispin switched on the light.

'More wine?' Without waiting for Robert to answer, he got out another bottle. 'I've got something here I don't think you've seen before.'

He switched on the television, and put in a video at the same time as he took what looked like a home-rolled cigarette from an inside pocket.

'Do you know what this is?'

'No, I can't say I do. Looks like a cigarette, but thinner.' Robert sat down heavily on the sofa.

'I'll show you how to smoke it. Have you ever smoked, for that matter?'

'No.'

Sitting down next to him, Crispin lit the joint and inhaled deeply, drawing the smoke down into his lungs and holding it there for what to Robert seemed an eternity. When he exhaled, there seemed to be hardly any smoke left. Robert could smell the sweetish scent of the smoke.

'Now it's your turn.' Crispin handed him the joint. 'All you have to do is inhale deeply and hold it there. Count to ten slowly.'

'What is it?'

'Marijuana. It'll make you feel even better.'

Robert, already long past knowing what he was doing, put the joint to his lips and inhaled.

'Hold it. No, don't let it go. Hold it in.'

Robert at first looked as if he were about to start coughing, but then the effect came almost immediately, settling like cotton wool round his brain. He looked at Crispin and burst out laughing. Everything seemed so funny. He didn't know what it was that was so funny, but he couldn't stop. He couldn't catch what Crispin was saying either, he was so totally absorbed in his own thoughts, laughing at jokes he had just thought up himself.

Suddenly Robert fell over on to Crispin's lap, helpless with laughter. Everything looked so funny. He looked round and his eyes fastened on a big painting above the television set, one of Crispin's typical abstracts. It was in the most amazing frame imaginable, laurel leaves, little berries and looped garlands forming a bizarre and deliberate pattern in gold leaf. He had a feeling he'd seen something similar before, but couldn't think where. The actual picture was of a clown in the usual Crispin style, painted in bright colours. The clown had a knife in his heart and blue blood was running down his costume. Robert knew deep down that it wasn't supposed to be comical, but he couldn't stop laughing. Literally doubled up with laughter, he made an attempt to point at the painting.

'What on earth are you laughing at?'

'The clown,' Robert managed to get out.

'Oh, it's my painting is it? I call it "the blue-blooded clown" blending the new with the old – the frame that is. My illustration of all upper-class buffoons. Though I'd better watch my tongue now I've got a real live lord on my sofa.'

They both howled with laughter. Crispin didn't approve of the upper classes and used to refer to them jokingly as incestuous, everyone related, sharing one brain between them for so long there would soon be none left at all. But he said nothing about that in Robert's presence.

Instead he switched on the video and Robert could see two naked women on a bed. The picture then vanished and suddenly there were two men doing the same thing. Again the picture vanished and then it was a man and woman lying on the bed.

His laughter faded and Robert tried to focus his eyes. He'd never seen a pornographic film before, and despite the state he was in he could sense that what he was seeing was arousing him.

Crispin moved closer and put one hand on Robert's knee.

'Have you any girl-friends?'

Robert didn't know where to look. 'No, I haven't,' he said carefully, laughing rather nervously.

Crispin laughed.

'Well, then, it's high time you started living a little.' He put his arm round Robert's shoulders. 'You see, I know how young men think.'

Before he knew what was happening, Crispin grabbed the hair on the back of his head and started kissing him. Robert was so far gone, he didn't really know what was happening, but Crispin soon had his tongue inside his mouth and his hand down on his crotch. Robert couldn't think clearly, but he groaned when Crispin undid his trousers, and a moment later he was kneeling in front of him taking him in his mouth.

Robert wasn't sure whether he was dreaming or not. All he knew was that it felt good and he didn't want it to stop. He groaned loudly, and Crispin looked up, smiling.

Robert could see him through a mist and again started laughing hysterically. The marijuana had plunged his brain into such a haze he was incapable of realising what was going on.

Crispin got back up beside him on the sofa and they kept watching the video. Still laughing, Crispin handed him the glass of wine, which Robert drank eagerly. Crispin took Robert's hand and put it over his own crotch as he whispered in his ear, 'You know this is all just for fun, nothing serious.'

Suddenly he pushed Robert over and at the same time pulled down his trousers.

'Don't worry. You'll like it,' he whispered.

Still in a daze, Robert didn't understand what was going on, and it wasn't until he felt the pain of Crispin's penetration that he became totally panic-stricken.

Up to then, it had all seemed like a game, both arousing and exciting. He had been influenced by all those stimulants, but now, in a flash, their effect was gone.

'Stop, stop, you're hurting me,' he cried out.

But Crispin was too far gone, his pace quickening. He clearly had no intention of stopping.

Robert could feel the tears rising and he cried out even louder.

'Don't, please, stop . . .'

Suddenly he felt Crispin's hand round his own still stiff penis.

'Don't you like this, either?' moaned Crispin.

Robert couldn't move. Crispin's hand was giving him pleasure, but the pain was unbearable. He screamed, but Crispin was as if possessed, his thrusts becoming longer and harder.

To Crispin it made no difference whether it was a man or a woman beneath him. No matter. He needed release and Robert happened to be there. He reckoned he had received signals that it would be OK with Robert, so what was the problem? This was Monica's son, yes, but Crispin was horny and couldn't resist it.

According to Crispin, sex and love were two widely separate things. He loved Monica, but that seemed no reason for him not to share his bed with someone else. He had an unusually strong sexual urge that had to be satisfied. It was that simple.

He hadn't even heard Robert crying and screaming. He could think of nothing but himself and his own pleasure.

He was nearly there. He put both hands round Robert's narrow hips and with a forceful thrust he came. He let out a bellow and collapsed on top of Robert, who was now lying sobbing with his head on a sofa cushion.

The pain had been insufferable and the degradation indescribable.

Crispin rose slowly and leant back on the sofa.

Robert pulled up his trousers and rushed into the shower-room where he threw up in the basin. He'd never been as sick as this before. This just couldn't be true. He turned on the cold water and with both hands splashed his face, desperate to rid himself of the

250

terrible nausea. He dried himself before finally he went back into the room.

Crispin was sitting on the sofa fully clad, a cigarette in his hand.

'Don't you feel well, Robert? Let's go home?'

His eyes were swollen from crying and he didn't look at Crispin. He knew now what had happened.

He could feel the pain burning still, but the shame and humiliation were burning him even more. His mother's man had raped him. But what was worse, he himself had enjoyed it to start with. Robert felt sick again, but managed to quell it.

Crispin picked up his jacket and put it round Robert's shoulders.

'It's been a good evening, but I think we drank too much. It's time to go home.'

They drove home in tense silence but as they swung up in front of the house Crispin turned to Robert.

'By the way, you'd better not tell Monica anything about this. You see, we're going to have a baby. She's three months' pregnant, and she'd be very upset if she knew about tonight. She'd take what happened quite the wrong way. She'd meant to tell you about the new baby, but wanted to save it as a surprise for you.'

Robert said nothing.

'Are we agreed? Look at it like this. Nothing has really happened. Just the two of us having a bit of fun.' Crispin laughed lightly.

Robert was rigid with shock. He had been raped and now he couldn't tell his mother. Who could he turn to?

He didn't fall asleep until early morning, just lay in bed crying and shaking as he relived the terrible thing that had happened to him that evening.

18

Robert could hear Crispin's voice in the kitchen. He and Monica were talking, but he couldn't make out what they were saying.

He'd been awake for several hours, his head aching horribly. He hoped it had all been a bad dream, but the pain reminded him of what had happened.

He wished he could just disappear, the nausea rising again. How could he even look at Crispin?

At last he heard what he'd been waiting for so impatiently – the sound of Crispin's car roaring away out of the drive.

It was almost eleven when Monica knocked on his door.

'Are you awake, Robert?'

'Yes, I am. Just coming,' said Robert, doing his best to sound normal.

'Good, then I'll get breakfast ready for you.'

Monica was frying eggs when Robert shuffled into the kitchen.

'Crispin has just told me what the two of you got up to last night, Robert, and I suppose I ought to be very cross with you both. But it was your birthday, so I'll just have to turn a blind eye.'

Robert went rigid with terror. Had Crispin told her? And she had taken it that calmly?

With ill-concealed delight, Monica attempted to admonish her son, telling him he was much too young to go to nightclubs, drinking wine all night, but she was glad he and Crispin had had such a good time together. Crispin had been honest enough to tell her they'd been drinking.

Robert felt a lump in his throat and couldn't bring himself to look at his mother. Monica put the plate down in front of him and ruffled his hair.

'I want this to be a once only event.'

Robert looked up and Monica saw how swollen his eyes were. 'Mother, I . . .'

At that moment they heard Crispin's car in the drive and before Robert could blink, Crispin himself was in the kitchen.

'Good morning, Robert. If you're feeling as bad as I am, then I'm sorry for you. I've confessed our sins to your mother.'

Robert didn't know which way to turn. He wanted more than anything to shout out what had really happened. He'd thought Crispin had left the house for the day as usual, but it turned out he had only gone to buy some fresh bread. It disgusted him to see Crispin putting his arm round his mother, the way she curled up in his arms.

'Robert, your mother and I have something to tell you.' Crispin stroked Monica's stomach.

'Crispin, what are you . . .'

He ran his hand over her shoulder with a calming gesture. 'Do you want to tell him yourself?'

Monica couldn't understand why he'd taken the initiative to tell Robert, but she presumed it was because her two men had got to know each other properly last night.

Robert sat looking down at his plate, fighting back tears.

'I've been waiting for the right moment to tell you Crispin and I are going to have a baby. You're going to have a little brother or sister.'

It was too much for Robert. Not only did he already know, but deep down he'd hoped it wasn't true, that it was something Crispin had said to keep him quiet. But now to hear it from his mother and at the same time see how happy she was – it was more than he could bear.

He pushed away his plate with a crash and rushed out of the kitchen and into his room, slammed the door shut and locked it, leaving behind him in the kitchen his astonished mother in the arms of the man who'd raped him.

Monica couldn't understand why he'd taken it so badly. She had hoped he would be pleased for her and even look forward to having a brother or sister. Of course, he'd been the only child so far and had had all the attention, but now he was so grown up, there didn't seem to be any reason for him to be so jealous.

She had dreamt about the moment when she would tell him, imagining him throwing himself into her arms. She remembered longing for a brother or sister herself when she was Robert's age.

Crispin had been a great support, explaining that Robert was at a sensitive age and at puberty boys were awkward, didn't like talking about their emotions, preferring to keep their feelings to themselves. He presumed Robert was going through a crisis because Monica was creating a new family and he was probably thinking there would be no room in it for him.

But worse was that Crispin blamed himself, saying he was the reason that things had worked out like this.

'If only I'd said nothing and let you choose the right moment,' he said. 'I'm sure it would have been better.'

But he said, he'd been feeling so elated after his night out with Robert, he'd thought it an excellent moment. Monica had assured him it wasn't his fault and that he really mustn't blame himself.

From the moment he was told, Robert changed utterly. Monica had tried approaching him, but it had been like talking to a wall. He'd shut himself in his room and when Monica had cautiously knocked on the door, he'd shouted that he wanted to be left alone. Then he would just disappear and not come back until evening. Monica sat up many evenings waiting for him, and once she'd just been about to go and look for him in the car when he appeared at two o'clock in the morning.

'We must talk about this, Robert,' Monica said, trying to confront him, tearfully asking him to meet her half way, but with no success.

Robert had suffered agonies. He knew his mother was miserable because he wouldn't talk. He wanted nothing more than to be able to cry in her arms and tell her everything, but that was impossible. First of all, he had participated to some extent to start with, and secondly, and most importantly, it would break her heart. He couldn't avoid seeing how happy she was with this man, and how wonderful she thought it was to be carrying his child. So he could do nothing but keep it to himself. It disgusted him to think of his mother with Crispin, and the thought of them in bed made him feel sick.

He knew it would destroy her if he told her what had happened, but he didn't realise how hurtful he was being to her by behaving as he did. He made sure he was in the house as little as possible, taking the bus to Nice or sitting in some café drinking wine or beer to numb the pain. Fortunately no one thought him being alone in a café on his own at all peculiar. He looked much older than his sixteen years.

It was all so confusing. He didn't know which was worse, the humiliation or the rape, that he had actually liked it at first, or that his mother was with Crispin. And there was no one he could talk to about it all.

Finally it was Monica who felt she could no longer handle the situation. She really had tried to talk to Robert but quite unsuccessfully. In the end she could think of nothing else but to call her mother and ask if Robert could come and spend some time with them in Sweden. Perhaps a change of environment would do him good and get him to see it wouldn't be such a disaster to have a little brother or sister.

Robert had greeted her suggestion with total apathy, but at least he hadn't said no. It seemed the best thing to do for all of them at the moment. And she genuinely wanted him to spend some time with his grandparents and get to know his Swedish roots a little better.

It had been a tearful farewell at the airport. For the first time for over a week, she thought she'd managed to break down the barrier a little. He'd given her a great hug, tears pouring down his cheeks.

'Robert, darling,' she'd said, almost in tears herself, 'the new baby won't mean I'll love you any less. You know that.'

He hadn't answered, just held tightly on to her, but he managed to say: 'I love you, Mother.' Then he'd gone through passport control without looking back.

Philip was at his typewriter, more or less driven to write. His deadline had been last Wednesday and his agent was calling every day.

'Philip, I don't understand what's happened? You of all people are usually so prompt, and we've always handed in the manuscript at least a week ahead of time before. There's a whole team devouring money for every day that passes. No one can do anything without your manuscript. When am I going to have it?'

'Jason, I'm totally exhausted. I'm writing late into the night.'

'Stay up all night if you have to. We don't want a writ on our hands. We've agreed the delivery date in writing. You know that.'

Every day, Philip had lulled his agent into false hopes that he had almost finished and that there was only a little polishing left to do. If only Jason had known how little had been done. The last bit he'd done was pure garbage. Perhaps he was too self-critical, but what he had in front of him was really no better than any other cheap thriller.

The television series had been a great success, but working on the conveyor-belt principle did not suit Philip at all. Being lashed on to produce something by a certain date simply gave him writer's block.

Then there was the fact that his thoughts were elsewhere. He couldn't stop worrying about Robert. The boy seemed to have changed beyond all recognition since he'd come back to England. Robert had spent a few days at Hewitt Hall before he had to return to Eton and Philip had been as pleased as punch to see his nephew again. Robert was like a son to him and as long as he could remember they had got on very well together. Robert had always brought his troubles to him, but now suddenly he couldn't get anywhere near him.

He'd hardly recognised the youth emerging from the taxi that late August day. It hadn't been all that long since they'd last met, so he found it difficult to believe. The always neat and tidy Robert had let his hair grow, the classic side parting now nothing but a memory, his hair unkempt and badly in need of a wash. He was also as white as a sheet, hardly to be expected of a teenage boy just back from a summer on the Riviera and the islands outside Stockholm.

Philip had received no response to his embrace, Robert simply stood looking down at the ground, and things had carried on that way until he'd gone back to school.

Mrs McDonald had cooked all Robert's favourite dishes during the few days he was at home, but he just poked at his food.

Philip remembered his own puberty, Edward's, too. He and his brother had been inseparable until Edward had turned sixteen, and then Edward had suddenly turned his back on Philip and the difference between their ages had created a huge gulf.

But this was not the same.

Although he hadn't been all that enthusiastic about calling Monica, he had steeled himself and done it. Not that he thought she would open her heart to him, after the way he'd treated her over the years, but . . .

He was right. Monica was short with him, but at least she told him she was pregnant, a fact Robert had not even mentioned. She clearly thought her pregnancy was a major factor in Robert's behaviour. And Philip agreed it must have been a shock to him, what with her first running away with a total stranger and then expecting his child without even being married.

So Philip had just waited and bided his time. Perhaps all this would turn out to be just temporary. But although he called Robert frequently at school, he still sensed something was very wrong. His nephew seemed distant during their conversations, as if simply wanting them to end.

Philip started to think that perhaps the fault was his, that he was refusing to see his little favourite was not so little any longer, but a young man in puberty. Perhaps he had been over-protective – wanting for his own sake to be the person Robert always turned to. Perhaps Monica was right when she said she thought he'd taken it too hard.

Once, after a conversation with Robert in which the boy had snapped at him, he'd even telephoned Gerd in Stockholm. Philip thought Gerd would be surprised. Over the years, he'd exchanged very few words with her, and he'd definitely never phoned her before. Yet he was glad he had, for despite Gerd's halting school English, he'd realised that his unease was justified. Over the crackling lines Gerd had made herself clear. 'Yes,' she'd said, 'he was . . .

how you say? Um, strange. No like he use to be. Want to be alone. All time, you understand? I am worry over him.'

If anything Gerd seemed to be more worried than Monica, though, Philip thought wistfully, you never knew with Monica. She had never confided in him . . .

'Philip, Philip. Can you hear me? Are you there? Hello!'

Philip was jolted out from his reflections on last week's conversation to the one in hand.

'Yes, I promise. You'll have the manuscript by Friday,' he said hastily.

'Friday? Are you mad? That's three days away. I want it tomorrow.'

However difficult it might be, there was nothing he could do but take a deep breath and get on with it. There was no way out.

And he really would have it done by Friday. Not just because of the agreement, but because Robert was coming for the weekend and he wanted to be with him as much as possible – to whatever extent he was allowed to be.

The Lord and the Con Man had been an immediate success and still was. The television series about the lord of the manor who teamed up with a wide boy had gone straight to viewers' hearts. But Philip had had no idea of how stressful it was writing for television and having to produce new material almost every week. They had done eight episodes the first year and sixteen the second. Now they had renewed his contract for yet another season, which meant eight more episodes, possibly even sixteen.

Writing on command was frustrating. He was not that kind of writer. He certainly knew his characters inside out, as well as the plot. It was just that it was so damned hard getting it all down on paper. If only they didn't want it in such a hurry. He'd always been so thorough when it came to quality and now he kept feeling dissatisfied whenever he handed in a manuscript.

But he had earned an amazing amount of money from television, even if deservedly so for it took up all his time. But the greater his success and the higher the ratings, the more he had to write. And he didn't even have the leisure to spend the money he earned.

Since Gordon had taken over the upkeep of the Hall, Philip had decided not to put his income into it. The arrangement between Monica and Gordon suited him down to a T. He didn't have to see Monica there and Gordon came only now and again to arrange pleasant dinner parties. The rest of the time he was alone with a staff of servants and the expensive maintenance of the Hall was paid for. He was keeping his fingers crossed that the contract between Gordon and Monica would be extended.

Philip had opened an account in Liechtenstein and against all expectations had managed to have half his income tax-free and paid directly into the bank account. He'd bought a small apartment in Vienna, as he loved everything about the city, its art, theatre and music. It was his investment for the future; Robert would take over Hewitt Hall one day and then where would he be, if he hadn't made careful provisions.

He also knew Gordon paid Robert's school fees, as Gordon enjoyed following Robert's progress and kept in close touch, so Philip was anxious he shouldn't see how wrong things seemed to be going at the moment. Philip hoped he would be able to put things right before Gordon realised anything was awry. Gordon would not understand what Robert was going through at the moment. He wanted to see the boy as a fighter, an eager beaver who fought and won.

They had actually phoned Philip from Eton once or twice to warn him that Robert's work would go drastically downhill if he didn't pull himself together. They had also told him that his concentration had gone, his personal hygiene was dubious and, well, the boy seemed to have gone through an obvious change. He was markedly different from his contemporaries and was apparently hanging around with a gang of older boys outside the school in his free time.

Philip had tried consulting Robert's housemaster, but he'd just said that puberty affected boys in different ways. In an effort to make things easier for the boy at school his uncle had told them that Robert's mother had left the family and moved abroad with another man, with whom she was also expecting a child. All he could do now was to bide his time and try to talk to Robert at the weekend.

Robert's love of his mother was certainly very great, sometimes almost ridiculously so, but a sixteen year old reacting like this – from a model pupil to a rebel in a few weeks! Philip shook his head. Something else, he guessed, was seriously wrong.

He worked away to get the last pages finished. He knew exactly how the episode was to end, so that was not really the problem. It was more how to get there . . . it felt like knowing what a certain place looks like but not knowing how to reach it.

In September, Gordon had held a large garden party at Hewitt Hall for all his employees in England and abroad. It had been one of the most luxurious events Philip had ever been at. Great tarpaulins had been erected across the rear courtyard of the Hall and from there Fortnum & Mason's catering department had served champagne, caviar, salmon and quantities of other delicacies, all beautifully displayed on silver dishes. The guests had arrived either by coach or helicopter.

Gordon had a new girl-friend. At least, she was new that day, a very young Thai girl with beautiful dark eyes and waist-long hair. And you could see that Gordon had spoilt her. Her name was Mia and she'd been wearing Chanel from top to toe, the obligatory gold Rolex dangling from her wrist.

But Philip was pleased. Hewitt Hall was flourishing, its standards of comfort and upkeep nowadays higher than it had been for half a century. He need no longer worry about it. Instead he was able to spend his free time in his apartment in Vienna and he was getting quite good at German now.

He finished the manuscript just in time, the messenger actually waiting in the hall as he wrote the last lines. Two more episodes were ready for filming.

Robert's train was getting in at twenty-five past two. Philip got out the Land Rover, which despite its age still ran very well indeed.

Soon Philip was waiting on the platform, prepared for anything. The reports from Eton had been both numerous and detailed, though unfortunately not very happy reading, and it was almost two months since he'd last seen his nephew. Despite this, Philip was shocked when he saw Robert ambling towards him from the train. Was this wild-looking youth his nephew, Lord Robert Hewitt? It couldn't be true.

His hair was now so long that it curled right down to his shoulders. He had certainly looked fairly unkempt when Philip had last seen him, but this was unbelievable. Robert even had the beginnings of a beard and moustache. He was wearing a colourful sweater, jeans, and, God help us, a suede waistcoat with a sheepskin lining.

Philip tried to appear normal and unshocked. He held out his arms. 'Robert!'

Robert walked straight past him without even looking at him. 'Where's the car?'

'Behind the station.'

'Well, what are we waiting for?'

Once in the Land Rover, Philip plucked up his courage and said: 'How are things going at school? I suppose you know your housemaster has phoned me a number of times.'

'Yeah, I know. I'll get by.'

Philip hesitated, but then decided to wait before taking the subject up again.

'Well, now, what do you want to do over the weekend? Maybe go to London . . .?'

'No, I'll stay at home.'

'Do you want me to arrange anything special?'

'No, I want to be alone.'

His answers were short and emphatically clear.

As soon as they got to the Hall, Robert took his bag and disappeared upstairs. Philip was hurt. Was this really the same boy as before?

He knocked on Robert's door. 'Dinner'll be at seven.'

'I don't want any dinner. Just leave me alone.'

Philip went down to the kitchen where Mrs McDonald was sitting at the big table, reading the evening paper.

'He's here now. I can't think what's happened to him. He doesn't want to come down to dinner and you should see what he looks like . . .'

'Teenagers,' said Mrs McDonald without raising her eyes from

262

the paper. 'It's just because you've never seen it before that you're so shocked. Don't worry, I'll talk to him later.'

'I know it's against our principles, but couldn't you take a tray of food up to him?' Philip was aware that her hip still hurt after the operation, but he was sure it would be better if she was the one to take the tray up.

'Robert, it's me, Mrs McDonald. I've got a bit of food for you.'

'Just leave it outside the door. I haven't time at the moment.'

She could hear music coming from his room, but she did as he asked. She was an understanding woman. She had seen both Edward and Philip go through this, though not quite as violently. But times were different today.

Philip sat alone with his thoughts in the big dining room, enjoying a bottle of red wine and Mrs McDonald's good food. He heard someone moving outside and presumed it was the housekeeper.

'I've not finished yet,' he called.

After his meal, he went and sat in the library. The fire was burning and it was relaxing listening to the wood crackling. He poured himself a small brandy. How should he handle Robert? He finished his glass. Perhaps his thoughts would clear if he had another?

He went across and picked up the other decanter, then looked at it in surprise. It was almost empty. He was sure it had been half full as recently as this morning.

'Mrs McDonald, can you come here for a moment,' he said, walking towards the hall.

She appeared in the door of the kitchen.

'When did you last fill the brandy decanter?'

'It was half full earlier today,' she replied. 'I was dusting in here, so I know that for sure.' She closed the kitchen door behind her.

Philip began to put two and two together.

'I'll have to speak to Robert. This is beginning to be very disturbing. First he doesn't come down to dinner and then there's brandy missing. It's scandalous.'

He could feel his anger mounting. It was clearly no use mollycoddling the boy. He would have a thing or two to say to him.

263

'Robert! Robert, open the door!'

Philip hammered on the door without much success. In the end he grabbed the door handle and the door opened immediately. He found himself in a dark room.

'Robert?'

He reached out to switch the light on.

Robert wasn't there, but there was a glass on his bedside table. Philip picked it up and sniffed it. As he had thought – brandy. Out of the corner of his eye he noticed an ashtray on the window sill. What? Did he smoke as well? He went over and picked up one of the cigarette ends and to his horror saw it was no ordinary cigarette. Suddenly his direst fears were confirmed.

This was worse than he could possibly have imagined. It simply couldn't be true. His face in his hands, he sank down on Robert's bed. What should he do?

He went back downstairs and asked in the kitchen if anyone had seen Robert, but no one had. He sat down by the fire again. He would wait until Robert came back, however late he was. This had to be dealt with here and now. If necessary he would physically knock a bit of sense into the boy's head. He put some large logs on the fire and leant back in the armchair.

Robert had grabbed a bottle of Château Margaux 1932 from the wine cellar and taken it with him. He'd already had a large glass of brandy and smoked a joint in his room. After that he had eaten the lamb cutlets Mrs McDonald had taken up to him. Smoking always made him ragingly hungry.

Then he'd had to get out for a while. With the bottle under his sheepskin waistcoat, he'd slipped out of the front door unnoticed. The raw November air struck his face and he'd pulled the waistcoat tighter round him on his way down to the ruins of his grandmother's cottage.

Even today he found it hard to grasp what had happened that evening, the tragedy that ended her life. He shuddered at the thought of her fighting the flames.

He quite often went down to the untouched ruins, just to sit there and think. The past term had been a torment. His marks were wretched. He just couldn't concentrate on anything any longer. He was hanging out with a couple of older boys who were using alcohol and marijuana. He had once only just escaped by the skin of his teeth getting caught. Two other boys had been expelled.

All his interest in school and school work had gone. He just wanted to be with his friends smoking and drinking himself silly. He knew he drank too much and he always felt ill afterwards, but what had happened in France had affected him on a deeper level. His memories and fears haunted him even as he slept. He knew that if he was not drunk or high by the time night came, panic would creep up on him, and with that his anguish. Not a night went by without him waking up sweating and shaking.

Just having to live with the knowledge that that man was there with his unsuspecting mother was unendurable. It was a horror talking to her on the phone and whenever she mentioned Crispin, it had felt like being stabbed in the stomach.

Feeling the old familiar sense of revulsion creep over him, he went into what had once been Lady Rose's dining room. Now there was nothing left but the walls. He sat down against one and drank straight out of the bottle. He laughed to himself when he thought of what Philip would say if he could see him with this vintage wine, to him an old family treasure. But it was his – and it was just alcohol to dull the pain. That's what getting drunk was really. Trying to buy time from the shadows.

He didn't often speak to his mother, but whenever he heard her voice, his insides contracted. He couldn't tell her anything. She was soon going to have a baby with the man who'd destroyed his life.

It was half past two in the morning. The wine, the marijuana and his sheepskin waistcoat had kept him warm and only a little was left in the bottle. He walked the long way back up to the Hall, feeling slightly sick. It was dark, but he knew the way so well he could have walked it blindfold. When he opened the front door the great hall was dark except for a small light above the stairs. It all seemed silent and calm, just as he wanted it to be. No Philip interfering.

He was just about to take off his shoes so as not to wake anyone, when he noticed the great painting hanging in the hall. What was it about it? Still with one shoe on and the empty bottle in his hand, he limped over and gazed trance-like at it.

The painting was of a young boy in a black velvet jacket, breeches and beret. Robert stood in front of it as if hypnotised. He knew it was of his great-great-grandfather or something, but it wasn't that. What was it? What was it? His mind cleared and he knew he was getting nearer. He closed his eyes and suddenly the clown was there in front of him.

A foolish clown with a knife in his heart, blue blood, Crispin's studio and that terrible night, the night that had destroyed his life.

He opened his eyes. Now he knew. It was an identical frame, an exact duplicate, the gold leaf, the laurel leaves and the garlands.

As if from a blow, Robert lost all control. Everything returned to reality. He let out a great wail and with all his strength threw the bottle straight at the picture. The bottle shattered and split the canvas. Splinters of glass flew back at him, but he didn't notice. Instead he fell to his knees in front of the picture, weeping uncontrollably, tears pouring so thickly down his cheeks he could hardly breathe. He was shaking violently, his hands over his face.

Suddenly he was aware of Philip kneeling down beside him, taking him by the shoulders.

'What is it?' Philip pulled the boy to him and held on tight, and for the first time since the summer felt a response, convulsive though it was.

Robert said nothing, so Philip just held him gently.

'Come on, Robert. Let's go into the kitchen. I'll make you a cup of tea.'

But Robert refused to budge.

Philip grasped him by the shoulders and literally lifted him up from the floor, then supported the still weeping boy towards the kitchen. He sat him down at the big table where Robert put his arms in front of him, hiding his face in his hands.

Philip was by now deeply troubled. He put the kettle on, thinking that at least this was a reaction. He didn't give the ruined picture a thought. This was about Robert. He made the tea, sat down by his sobbing nephew and put his arm round him.

'Robert, I know Monica's pregnancy has upset you, but . . . listen to me. You're a young man and you have to take responsibility for your own life. Your school work has gone to the dogs and anyone can see how self-destructive you've become. This simply can't go on. I really do want to give you all the support I can, but . . . Robert, look at me.'

But Robert kept his eyes firmly on his cup, mechanically stirring the tea. All Philip could hear were helpless sobs and it was impossible to see his face as his long hair was hanging in front of it. He was shaking more than ever now and Philip saw him wiping away the tears.

'Robert, this can't be just because of the new baby, can it? There must be something else troubling you. Is that so?'

Robert was trembling like a leaf.

'Robert, I wish you would confide in me.'

Philip leant over him and ran his hand over his head, cradling him as if he were a small child.

'Robert, Robert, what is it that's worrying you so?'

The trembling became a shuddering and Philip realised the boy would soon break. His sobs were loud now.

'Robert, what is—?'

With a jerk, Robert hit the cup and tea ran all over the table. He threw his head back and half rose, then hit the table so hard the teapot rattled.

'He raped me! That's what wrong!' Robert was scarlet in the face as he bawled it out, his eyes swollen and half closed from weeping.

Philip's mind went blank with shock.

'What are you saying?'

'I said he raped me.'

'Who? *Who* raped you? Robert, speak to me. Who raped you?'

Robert sat down, wiped his eyes on a table napkin and stared at Philip. In a perfectly steady voice, he said:

'My mother's boyfriend. He's the one who raped me.'

19

By the end of November, everything had returned to normal in the South of France after the hectic tourist season.

Monica was busy turning the guest room into a nursery. She and Crispin had repainted the room themselves in pale blue and yellow. Monica was huge and ungainly and not finding it easy to move around, but she very much wanted to do everything herself.

They still hadn't bought a crib. The baby was due in three weeks and never had there been such expectant parents as these two.

Crispin had continued to be so devoted to Monica that she was still floating in a haze of happiness. They hadn't had even one argument and her joy was of an intensity she'd never thought possible.

She very much wished Robert would come for Christmas, but it looked as if that dream would not come true. They still had problems communicating and Monica felt for him: he was having a difficult time getting through puberty.

She felt like an elephant, but Crispin was considerate enough to keep away when she wanted to be alone and to be there when she wanted him. It was as if he had a sixth sense. Monica was so in love with him that sometimes when he was up at the studio she sat looking at a photograph of him stroking the glass. He worked more and more at nights, sometimes not coming back home until four or five in the morning. She always woke then and held out her hand to feel he was there, and he always responded to the gesture with a kiss.

She never questioned why he worked so late and nor did she mind being alone at home. She was full of thoughts about the baby and what a wonderful family she was going to have. Crispin would be the best father in the world.

They had played with various names for the baby. Monica wanted a girl, and on balance that was Crispin's preference too. They'd call her Christine Marie, then she would have an initial from each of them. After all, she was a product of their love.

Monica's days were usually spent going down to Nice shopping, or to Cannes to see her doctor. She was far too big to get into the little Citroën, so Crispin took it and she had the stationwagon. The rest of the time she spent reading or watching television in bed, she tired easily these days.

Crispin had been tremendously productive. He'd had another commission, this time from Paris. He'd been there several times in recent months and Monica missed him when he was away overnight, but at the same time was proud his work was being appreciated. She ran her hand over her belly, certain there was another little artist inside there.

Despite being so busy with his Paris commission Crispin had painted a portrait of her leaning against one of the bedroom walls. Monica thought it looked like an elephant in pink and grey, and was secretly unimpressed by the yellow straw supposed to be her hair. But he had spent a lot of time on this portrait of his pregnant Monica and that's what had mattered to her.

When the phone rang and it was Philip, she was very surprised. She hadn't spoken to him since early autumn when he had rung to ask about Robert. His voice was even more full of tension than usual.

'Monica, we must meet, I've something very important to talk to you about. I've booked a flight for tomorrow and would like you to meet me at the Carlton Hotel in Cannes at seven o'clock. If you like, we can have dinner.'

'What do you want to talk to me about? Won't it do over the phone?' Monica hated it when he behaved so dictatorially. She hadn't the slightest desire to see or dine with him – the part of her life he represented lay behind her.

'I'm sorry, Monica, but what I have to discuss can't be done over the phone. So meet me at the Carlton at seven.' At that he put down the receiver.

Monica was uneasy. Philip knew about the agreement between her and Gordon. She was not to set foot in Hewitt Hall for the next five years, and in exchange Gordon would pay Robert's school fees. What had happened? Had Gordon suddenly stopped paying the fees? She still had her jewellery she could sell if that were so.

Crispin didn't get back until very late that night, so she couldn't tell him about the call until the next morning.

'Philip rang yesterday,' she said over breakfast. 'He wants to have dinner with me tonight in Cannes. It's something important. Probably about Robert's schooling or the Hall.'

'Darling, you oughtn't to drive about at night in your condition. Do you want me to come with you?'

Monica inclined her head. Typical of Crispin, considerate as usual.

'No, thanks, sweetheart, I have to cope with this myself.'

'I understand,' he said, stroking her stomach. 'As long as you're careful with Christine Marie.'

'I'll be back by ten or so. You needn't worry. I was going down to see Dr Rochelle anyhow.'

Her doctor had phoned and asked her to come in. The baby was in a breech position. He had assured her that there was no danger and there was plenty of time to turn it: it wouldn't necessarily be a breech birth.

Crispin kissed her before setting off for the studio.

'I love you.'

'And I love you.'

She watched him squeezing into the little yellow car. As he waved goodbye he let out his wonderful laugh.

Monica swept her big black cloak round her.

She went into Dr Rochelle's waiting room and sat down. There were two people before her. She hated waiting and she shifted restlessly in her chair. Why was Philip coming all the way here to disturb her? France was her territory and she didn't want to see him here.

Monica listened with only half an ear to what the doctor was saying, but heard enough to know she needn't worry. Nor was she

271

worrying. This child would be born perfect.

She had tried not to think about Amanda. She wanted only happy memories from this pregnancy and had wiped everything else out of her mind. When the doctor had finished, Monica walked to the big white building that was the Carlton Hotel and asked for Monsieur Philip Hewitt.

'He's expecting you, Madame,' the porter replied. 'Suite number 2201–3.'

Thirty minutes later the same hall porter saw the heavily pregnant woman he'd helped earlier stumble weeping through the lobby. For a moment he thought she was going to fall by the door but she only stumbled and dropped her bag.

What Philip had told Monica was beyond anything she could have imagined. She couldn't express her pain in words and she was trembling so violently she could hardly get the key into the keyhole of the car.

She drove off at speed, tears streaming down her cheeks, hardly able to see the road in front of her. Her heart was beating hard and she felt sick.

She couldn't believe it. Philip must have made it up. But why would he want to hurt her so, torment her like that? She'd agreed to everything, even turned down her share in the Hall to ensure Robert's education. Philip lived on there undisturbed.

It just couldn't be true. Was it revenge because she was at last happy, because she had found a man she loved and who loved her? Couldn't he accept that? What did he know about love anyhow? He had never loved anyone, apart, one supposed, from his mother and Edward.

Philip had asked her to sit down. He'd been very formal, shaking her hand when she'd come in. The horrible thing was that he had gone straight to the point without any polite phrases. All he'd said was that what he had to tell her would be very hard to believe, but he knew it was true. After that he had calmly and coolly told a stunned Monica what Robert had told him.

She had just sat there looking straight through him.

'Monica, it's true,' he'd insisted after what had seemed like an age of silence. 'Robert isn't lying. Are you listening? This is what has been tormenting him so dreadfully, what has changed him so suddenly.'

He'd gone on until Monica got up and screamed, 'Stop! Stop!' pressing her hands to her ears. Philip had been grateful to see at least some reaction and, despite all their previous differences, at that moment he had felt for her. Telling her had not been easy. He knew that he was pulling the rug from under her feet, destroying her whole world. But he had no choice, it was her or Robert.

When Philip had gone into detail she had whimpered with pain. 'You're lying, you're lying! You want to ruin my life here. You've always wanted to spoil things for me. You hated me from the very first moment. Nothing I've done has ever been good enough for you.'

'Monica.' Philip sounded very much under control. 'The past is behind us. We have to look ahead. I am here, perhaps not as your friend, but as someone who cares very much about Robert. And he needs you now. Otherwise he'll break. Are you listening? You're his mother.'

Tears were pouring down her face and her heart was racing. 'You're lying, and you've got Robert to lie too, you bastard.'

Monica had made her way to the door and for the first time Philip had raised his voice and called after her: 'For Robert's sake, Monica! For your son's sake!'

Monica sat in the car and screamed out aloud – dear Lord, it couldn't be true. When Philip had told her about Robert, she had just thought he was lying, but here in the car, alone and in the darkness, it was suddenly all quite clear to her.

Everything fitted. Robert's reaction the day after his birthday and Crispin suddenly telling him about the baby. Robert had told Philip that Crispin had persuaded him not to say anything to her because she was pregnant. Oh, God, yes, what Philip said made sense. She drove like a lunatic up the winding road towards Vence. But instead of going to the house, she went on, towards the studio. She wanted to look Crispin straight in the eye.

For one last moment, as she drove down the familiar little road to the studio, it struck her that it simply couldn't be true. Her beloved Crispin, her all . . . no, it wasn't possible.

The yellow Citroën was parked outside the studio. She clambered out of the car and opened the front door. It was dark inside except for a faint light from the loft.

'Crispin!' she shouted.

She could see two dark silhouettes outlined against the wall up there. Trembling, she fumbled for the light switch. This was too much to take in – Crispin was up there, naked, the black girl from the party in Monte Carlo with him, both apparently high. Monica recognised the sweet scent of marijuana.

'Monica, I . . .'

'How *could* you, I hate you! More than anything else on earth. You're the devil himself. How *could* you?'

Crispin swept the sheet round him and came down the steep stairs, the naked girl behind him. She rushed past Monica and started collecting up her clothes.

Crispin, ignoring her, grabbed Monica's arm desperately, 'Listen, Monica. She means nothing to me. Nothing. She's just a fuck. Don't you see? It's you I love.' He meant every word. She was the one he loved. The fact that he leapt into bed with other people meant nothing to him at all.

Monica slapped him so hard, for a moment she thought she'd cracked his eardrum. Then she spat straight into his face.

Moving quicker than she had for months, she left the studio and got into the car. When she got home, she went immediately into the bedroom and locked the door. She took a deep breath and closed her eyes, feeling as if she were about to fall apart completely. She knew she had to mobilise all her strength to stop herself going out of her mind. With trembling hands, she picked up the telephone and dialled. 'Hotel Carlton, can I help you?'

20

According to the nurses, Tanya Clarke had been the most beautiful baby any of them had ever seen, with thick black hair, dark lashes and dark eyebrows. She was born in Queen Charlotte's Hospital in London. The birth had been physically painless thanks to an epidural; anything but painless as far as the circumstances surrounding the birth were concerned.

They had asked Monica if she wanted to breast-feed the baby, but she'd said no. During the first twenty-four hours she'd hardly looked at her daughter and had fallen into a deep depression. Dr Johnson told her it was not at all unusual for new mothers to get postnatal depression and had prescribed antidepressants.

Monica lay in bed thinking that if Dr Johnson knew under what circumstances this child had come into the world, then he might understand why she was so depressed.

She remained in hospital for a week, then the time came for her to emerge into real life again, a life she would now have to work out for herself.

Philip had been very useful in a practical way. Through an acquaintance he had arranged for her to rent a small house in Elm Place in Fulham. It had two bedrooms and a bathroom on the top floor, a living room at street level, and dining room and kitchen below. There was also a small yard in the back with space for a few chairs and a table.

For the first in her life, Monica was on her own. She had always lived with someone else, first sharing a flat with Katarina after she'd left her parents' home, then living at Hewitt Hall with Edward, then after his death in Gordon's apartment, then at

275

Crispin's house. Now she was on her own.

After eleven months in the little house in London Monica was preparing to go home to Sweden with her daughter. They were going to celebrate Tanya's first birthday on 15 December at her parents' and then Tanya was going to stay with Gerd while Monica returned to London.

She was exhausted. She'd had no help with the baby for the whole year and the slightest adversity was likely to break her completely. Why couldn't she get rid of the memories of Crispin, the great sense of loss?

She had sold the engagement ring Gordon had given her and the thirty thousand pounds it had fetched in a Bond Street jewellers had been her starting capital. Monica knew it was worth at least a hundred and fifty thousand, but she'd had no choice.

Her divorce from Gordon had now finally gone through. Ironically enough, Tanya had been born within the marriage so bore Monica's surname – Clarke. Gordon had got the child he so fervently longed for, whether he wanted it or not; Monica had thought apathetically putting him down as the father, that at least the name was simple.

She spent very carefully although she had quite a bit of money. Sir Hugh Grenville had managed to extract a lump sum of fifty thousand pounds from Gordon despite the papers she had signed. But she had no regular source of income.

She was homesick for Sweden – she'd been terribly lonely in London over the last year. It seemed incredible that she had no friends in a city she'd lived in for almost two decades. Weeks could go by without the phone ringing even once.

Tanya had turned out to be a very independent child from the start. She could occupy herself for hours with some coloured blocks or small toys. Sometimes Monica could hardly bear to look at her daughter as all she could see in her was Crispin. Tanya was their love-child, the fruit of their happiness, a terrible reminder. She was looking forward to leaving her daughter in Sweden for a while in order to try to get some perspective on her life.

During this lonely year, Monica had thought about Amanda increasingly often. Although Amanda was not aware of the world around her, she was her child and Monica had seen her only that one time. She would like to go and see her first-born daughter, but she realised she wouldn't be able to cope at this particular moment.

Robert had been expelled from Eton when he was caught smoking a joint in the shower room. He'd spent Christmas at Hewitt Hall, and had visited his mother and baby sister in hospital.

He really had changed, Monica realised, and it would have been naive to think that it would all get better just because Monica had left Crispin. Monica blamed herself for not understanding what had happened to him, for not seeing the obvious signs though Robert assured her it wasn't her fault.

Monica had not seen Crispin since that dreadful night. He had desperately tried to find her, to explain, to make her understand that he had not seen the incident as betraying their love. He regarded the fact that he'd raped her son as an unfortunate mistake, something that had happened as a result of too much alcohol and drugs. Philip however had risen to the occasion and protected Monica. Crispin never got any further than Hewitt Hall, nor was he given any information as to where she was, and Monica's telephone number in Fulham was ex-directory.

Always physically rather weak, to everyone's surprise Robert had joined the Merchant Navy and gone to sea. Monica was afraid it would be too much for him, but Philip thought it was probably just what Robert needed. On that score, she felt she really could trust Philip. They did have this one thing in common – their love for Robert was genuine.

Monica and Philip spoke on the phone occasionally – he was still fairly curt, but now there was something in his voice she couldn't quite make out, perhaps pity? Or perhaps he was just being ingratiating: as Robert had left Eton, Monica's and Gordon's arrangement was now invalid. So the Hall was Robert's, and Philip was more dependent on the goodwill of Robert and Monica than ever.

She was busy packing for her visit to Sweden, looking forward to the reassuring traditions Christmas brought with it. Gerd had promised they would bake ginger cookies and that they would go to the Christmas market at Skansen. Monica was eager to leave.

Three weeks later, alone and a little stronger, Monica was back in England. It had been relaxing to be in Sweden, where Gerd had agreed to take her beloved little granddaughter for an indefinite period of time. Monica had realised she simply had to stop living like a hermit. She needed a break. She told her mother she didn't know when she'd be back for Tanya.

The only time she ever went out on her own was when she went to her hairdresser, Roger who had a very trendy salon only a few blocks away from her house. They had somehow found each other and Monica always looked forward to going there. Roger was gay but she didn't mind. Before Christmas he'd suggested they'd go out and have a meal together. At the time she had had Tanya to think about, but now it was easier. So when Roger offered her a part-time job helping in the reception area she accepted eagerly.

She looked forward to the mornings. The people who worked in the salon were so young and interesting, nothing snobbish or artificial about any of them. And they produced some of the most fantastic hair colours and styles. Punk was flourishing, but Monica stuck to the style she'd worn for the last three years, her long hair straight down round her face. Some things, she thought wryly, would never change.

William Hickey noted in the *Daily Express*:
'Monica Clarke, previously Lady Hewitt, who left her husband the multi-millionaire Gordon Clarke for the gifted artist Crispin Que to live with him in the South of France, has been seen working part-time at the trendy hairdressing salon Mr Roger on the Fulham Road. What can have brought about this sudden change? For surely it can't be lack of money?'

It was true, she always felt a trifle old when she went out with her colleagues. However, 'the gay crowd' who had become her friends always treated her appreciatively, and gradually she began to relax in their company. But when it was time to go to some club, she always politely refused, telling Roger she'd never liked nightclubs and parties. She would rather go home to her bottle of wine, alone.

One evening, after a determined assault from Roger, she rather reluctantly allowed herself to be persuaded to go with them to Munckberry's in Jermyn Street.

Munckberry's was the in-place for people in the music business, he informed her, Monica knew nothing about music except what she heard on the radio, and she couldn't help feel a little curious.

She put on a pair of tight pants and a short black velvet jacket cut very low, emphasising her full bust. Despite herself, she was tingling all over. This was the first time for ages she had gone out and she was looking forward to it.

When Monica opened the door of her little house in response to Roger's ring her friend's mouth fell open in amazement.

'Monica, I'm struck dumb.' He put his hands on his head in a gesture of astonishment. 'You look gorgeous.'

Monica laughed, embarrassed. It was a long time since anyone had paid her a compliment.

Munckberry's was different from any other club she had ever seen before. They left their coats at the reception, where the ticket desk was, and after walking through the packed dining room entered the disco with its mirrored walls and suede couches, a wooden dance floor at one end of the room and at the back, a small stage. The whole place had a Moroccan feel to it.

'I'll just ask the hostess if she can fix us a table. She's Swedish, too, by the way,' Roger shouted through the noise of the music.

'Oh, is she? Where is she?'

'I can't see her at the moment. Come on, let's have a drink first.'

Roger took her arm and fought his way to the bar. He ordered wine for both of them.

Suddenly Roger bawled in her ear.

'Look over there, in the corner. That's Britt Ekland with a whole bunch of toy boys.'

'Where? I can't see her.'

'No, there. In the corner on the left.' Roger resolutely turned her head in the right direction.

Then she saw her. Unmistakable. It was her, in the company of seven or eight young men.

'You see, Monica. Nothing left of her famous hair. She almost has a crew-cut.'

Monica nodded. 'She looks more like a boy.'

'Talking about Swedes, there she is. Katarina, the hostess.'

Monica was startled – it couldn't be possible.

The two women stood facing each other. Neither said a word, but they were obviously trying to recover their composure.

'Do you know each other?' said Roger in amazement.

Katarina broke the ice. 'Monica, I don't believe it!' The two women fell into each other's arms.

'Katarina! It must be almost twenty years ago!'

'Ssh,' she said. 'Not so loud. Someone might think we're ancient monuments.' Then she laughed.

Heavens, Monica thought, looking at her old flatmate, how thin Katarina was. And she did look old, her face quite white, with scarlet lips and long straight purple hair, though it could have been the disco lights.

Monica was speechless for a few moments, so confused she didn't know what to say. Was this her best friend and flat-mate?

'Katarina, I didn't recognise you. You look so . . . different.'

'Well, I've been through quite a bit, too.'

Suddenly Monica remembered the article about Katarina and her life, including the night with Gordon.

'Come on and I'll fix a table for you.'

Katarina took them to one of the corners and cheerfully drove away the unfortunates already sitting there.

'Here you are. Do take a seat. What would you like to drink? No, I'll fix it. It'll be champagne, on the house. It's not every day you find an old friend.'

She turned to one of the waiters. 'Mario, champagne.'

Monica and Katarina had so much to talk about, they didn't know where to start. Katarina couldn't control her delight at seeing her old friend again and was like a boisterous puppy, infecting Monica as they drank to each other.

Monica filled her glass and tried to keep up with Katarina's stories. They kept laughing uncontrollably and Monica could feel the effects of the champagne creeping over her. Perhaps she was drinking too much? But when she tried to say no Katarina just grinned.

'Come with me, I've got something that'll fix that.'

Katarina took her by the hand and marched through the crowd to the ladies. There was a long queue waiting, so she changed direction and they ended up in the kitchen.

'It's only me,' she called to the chef and the waiters, none of whom took the slightest notice.

There they found themselves in the staff bathroom where the bright light really did reveal that Katarina was no spring chicken. For a moment Monica hoped she wouldn't age so quickly. Katarina was only two years older than her.

Once inside, Katarina took out her little gold bottle with its spoon.

She thrust the spoon into the full bottle, drew it out and pushed it up into one nostril then sniffed.

'Katarina, I've never . . . I haven't . . .'

'Never taken cocaine? Then you're in for a real surprise. I'll show you what you do.' She repeated the procedure in the other nostril. 'As long as you breathe it in with a jerk, like that.'

Monica had always been very much against illegal drugs and had refused to smoke marijuana. She had tried it once with Crispin, but that was all.

'Come on, then,' Katarina said impatiently. 'We can't stay here half the night.'

Uncertainly, Monica bent over the bottle.

'That's it, you'll love it,' Katarina smiled, putting the spoon into Monica's nostril. Monica breathed in. It stung right up to her brain. She coughed and a bitter taste came into her mouth.

'Here, take the other one now.'

Katarina held out the spoon, like a mother trying to get her child to eat.

'No, I don't think . . .'

'Oh, don't be silly. There you are, nothing to it.'

Monica looked at Katarina and suddenly felt tremendously exhilarated, her heart beating faster. She felt an urgent desire to go back to the music. But she wanted to talk to Katarina too. They had so much to say to each other! Suddenly life seemed playfully easy. Monica laughed and took Katarina's hand.

'See! I knew you'd like it. Come on, let's go and dance. This place is great, full of young, good-looking guys. Not the old men you're used to.'

As Monica walked jauntily back to their table she realised she really liked the effect of the cocaine. It gave her a self-confidence she'd never felt before. All her inhibitions seemed to have vanished and she let her body sway to the music.

A few minutes later a young man sat down beside her. No more than twenty-five or twenty-six, he had long black hair and the thinnest face she'd ever seen, with deep-set eyes, high cheekbones and skin as white as porcelain.

He put his bottle of beer on the table.

'Is this the first time you've been to Munckberry's?'

Monica could feel the excitement growing in her. He was cute and there was something special about him. He was wearing a white lace shirt and a black jacket with the sleeves rolled up.

The DJ announced that the time had come for the evening's performance. A female impersonator was taking the stage with an act called the 'Fiona Boss Show'.

In came an almost six-foot-tall black 'woman' dressed as Diana Ross, wearing a skin-tight red sequinned dress, a large white fox fur and shoes with such high heels it was almost impossible to understand how he could stand upright in them. Apart from his height the impersonator looked very like his model and he sang the whole Ross repertoire from the days when she'd been with The Supremes.

Monica was so into the show that she didn't notice that her nameless admirer had put his arm round her shoulders. But when she did, she didn't mind. For once she felt free.

Katarina winked meaningfully at her from the other side of the table.

'Shall we go and have another?'

Monica agreed at once. She excused herself, saying she'd be back soon.

In the ladies Katarina gleefully encouraged her to get to know him better.

'But he's so young,' Monica protested, blushing.

'All the better,' Katarina pronounced, helping her to another spoonful of cocaine.

When they got back, the show was over and the dance floor crowded again. The young man was still at their table and Monica made herself comfortable next to him.

She had been sitting with her head against his shoulder for half an hour, when he finally introduced himself. 'My name's Daniel. What's yours?' He looked into her eyes. 'Shall we have breakfast together tomorrow?'

Monica didn't know what to say to such an odd question, but he went on before she had had time to think.

'Shall I phone you? Or just give you a nudge.'

Monica laughed and he gently eased her to her feet.

On her way to the cloakroom, she felt Katarina's hand on her shoulder.

'Don't you dare go without leaving me your phone number. Sophie, have you a piece of paper?' she said to the elderly woman in the cloakroom. She wrote down her number and tore the piece of paper in half. 'Write down yours . . .'

Monica put the paper with Katarina's number inside her bra.

'Take it easy tonight,' Katarina said in Swedish, and Daniel looked questioningly at them both. 'Do you need a taxi?'

Daniel shook his head. 'No, we'll walk.'

They went out into the early summer morning. Monica had no idea what the time was, but it was already getting light.

'I was only joking about walking,' Daniel said. 'I just wanted to get out of there. Shall we take a taxi? Except I haven't any money.'

Monica laughed. 'If we take a taxi, then I'll pay.'

'Where shall we go then?'

'Well . . .' Monica hesitated.

'I mean, where do you live?'

'Elm Place, just off the Fulham Road.'

Daniel looked round the little house. 'Well, this suits me fine. I feel at home here. Where's the fridge?'

Monica pointed at the kitchen.

Daniel at once went and opened the refrigerator.

'No beer?' he said.

'No, only wine. I don't drink beer.'

He took out the half-empty bottle of wine and went straight to the point.

'Where's the bedroom?'

'Upstairs.'

'Let's go then,' he said, pulling her gently up the stairs.

He put the bottle on the bedside table and without even switching on the light took off his jacket, shirt and trousers, suddenly standing there in front of her, stark naked.

'Now it's your turn.'

As she undressed Monica hadn't the slightest idea why she was doing this. She had never seen him before and they hadn't even kissed.

Something had happened to her that evening to make her behave like this. As she sank down on her bed, she felt this was the beginning of another life . . .

Daniel quickly settled down in her house. He was a musician, but hadn't played anywhere for a while. Monica liked having him around, and the sex was great.

Katarina had been right. Once she'd tried cocaine, there was no return. In the past, she'd always taken pills and liquor to forget. Now she drank and sniffed coke to laugh and enjoy herself, and Daniel had become the link between her and the pushers.

Some evenings they didn't go out at all, but stayed home and drank and did coke until early morning, then slept all day.

At first Monica had been shocked at how quickly things had developed. She was going to be thirty-nine soon and here she was with a twenty-six year old. She wasn't in the least in love with him;

she didn't think she was capable of such feelings.

The evenings they didn't stay home doing coke, she went with Daniel wherever his new band was playing, or she went down to see Katarina at Munckberry's. Otherwise they went to Legends or the Embassy in Bond Street. At the Embassy they'd go up to the office. The manager was gay and had his eye on Daniel, so was always very generous with the cocaine.

These days Monica slept until three or four in the afternoon. As soon as she got up, she'd search through her pockets and handbag to see if there was anything left from the day before. If not, Daniel had to go out and get some more.

Cocaine cost fifty pounds a gram and she was spending several hundred pounds a week. But she'd never felt so free as she did now, fully in control of her life. She decided and she paid. She worked at the salon only once or twice a month now, but that was only to oblige Roger.

Her friendship with Katarina was again strengthened, whether it was drugs or their old friendship binding them together she didn't care. You always had fun with Katarina. She knew everyone and all the clubs.

Katarina had told her about her life, particularly about her marriage to Rob Hove. He'd not only humiliated her and betrayed her, but when they'd returned to England he'd grown completely blatant, sometimes even asking her to move into the spare room so he could carry on with his latest slut in their bedroom. But she had been desperate. As she had neither money nor a job, she had had to put up with it.

Rob had become more and more cynical, constantly putting down other rock stars. Katarina got bored stiff listening to what a miracle it was every time another artist got into the top ten.

But then one day the dam burst. He'd come home and said he wanted a divorce. She could keep the flat and he would pay her maintenance for a year. It turned out that the young blonde he'd been with for a couple of months was pregnant and he was in love.

'Fuck him,' Katarina had said about it all, but she hated it when they played his records at Munckberry's and was always nagging the DJs not to.

She and Monica spent innumerable nights in a frenzy of cocaine and alcohol, telling each other their life stories. It wasn't long before the subject of Baby Gordon came up. He gave them one of the best laughs of all.

One afternoon, when Monica woke up before Daniel, she put his clothes and his toiletries into a plastic bag.

'Daniel, Daniel. Wake up. Time to go.'

He slowly opened his eyes.

'Up you get.' She was speaking to him as if to a dog. 'Up!'

Daniel couldn't make out what it was all about. Monica helped him on with his shirt and stood waving his trousers about.

'Here are your trousers. On with them.'

When he was at last dressed, she gave him the plastic bag.

''Bye.'

She pushed him out through the door and closed it behind him.

They had been together for almost a year. Nothing special had happened, but that morning she felt she'd had enough. She was quite simply tired of him, tired of paying for everything. She had woken up and looked at the sleeping Daniel and thought: out he goes!

'Is that you, Katarina? I got rid of him.'

'You haven't!?'

'Yes, I have.'

'Then I know what we'll do. We'll go to Paris.'

'To Paris?'

'Yes, I'll see if I can get hold of a car. Yours is too small. It takes only two hours to Dover, and another two on the ferry. We can be there in six hours! I'll just check whether I can get hold of a car. I'll call you back.'

Just what Monica was feeling like. She was open to anything these days.

Katarina didn't take long to get hold of a Ford Escort and the two friends put the little luggage they had in the boot. Monica drove at first while Katarina waved a small bottle of champagne in front of her.

Gloria Gaynor's 'I Will Survive' was booming out of the loud-speakers. Although it was two years old, it was their signature tune and the two women sang along with it at the tops of their voices.

They had booked in at Hotel Montalembert off Rue St Germain, an exquisitely beautiful old building, its rooms clean but small, crammed with antique furniture and not at all expensive – amazing for Paris.

Monica had never been to a nightclub before in Paris, but Katarina knew exactly where to go. They went to the Palace, a huge disco with a roller-skating rink in the basement, where they met an eager Frenchman whom they took back to their hotel with them. Their new companion had to work double time that night, a new experience for Monica. But she hadn't hesitated for a moment when Katarina had suggested a *ménage à trois*. After all, she thought mischievously, they were in France.

Monica's life had become one long party. The fact that her new and expensive habits were devastating her bank account didn't worry her in the slightest. She knew there was some jewellery left in the bank deposit which she could always sell if necessary. She didn't give a thought to either Robert or Tanya at this time, apart from phoning now and again. It was her turn to live, she told herself, and she had no desire to burden her life with a guilty conscience.

Robert had decided to leave the Merchant Navy and take a course in agriculture in Gatton, Queensland, not far from Brisbane. He was living with a young Australian, and Monica's intuition told her that he was his lover. If that was the direction he had chosen to go, after what had happened, then she would no doubt have to accept it. She had long since ceased feeling any sense of responsibility for everything that happened around her. *Her* life was what was most important. She loved her children, but they were not going to stand in the way of her own fulfilment.

Tanya, now four, was in good hands and spoke perfect Swedish. Monica went to see her at least twice a year and Gerd also brought her to London, where they'd spent a whole month together.

Monica had to admit that although they were her own mother and daughter, she'd been quite happy when they had gone back to Sweden.

It was the end of June 1980, and Wimbledon was just about to begin. Monica knew nothing about tennis but liked watching it on television, leering lightheartedly at the tight shorts of the players.

One night Katarina suggested they go to the Hard Rock Café in Park Lane. There was going to be a party for the Wimbledon players there and Monica, who always fell in with plans for a good party, agreed at once.

It was ten o'clock at night. They'd had a few lines and shared a bottle of wine back at Monica's house before leaving. When they arrived, there were crowds of people outside and a guard on the door with a guest list, as well as photographers everywhere.

The guard ticked their names off the list and they went in. Monica looked around. It was very crowded and cramped and she didn't know a soul.

A group of women and two men were sitting in one booth. They must be the players, all apparently health freaks. Her glance fell on a short-haired blonde woman of about twenty and she noticed the woman's eyes were on her.

'Katarina, who are these people?'

'The fair one with short hair is Chenka Chaneci, the famous Romanian tennis player. She's lesbian.'

Monica was tempted. This was something quite new. She'd had quite a lot of affairs but she was a novice in this particular field.

'I must have a drink. You can flirt with her later.'

'No, let's go to the ladies first.' Insistent, Monica turned to go to the ladies, and noticed the young woman's eyes following them.

In the ladies, Katarina took out her little bottle. Monica was on top form.

'Shit!' she said impatiently. 'You're messing about with that little spoon. Give me the bottle.'

Monica clenched her hand round her thumb and poured a little cocaine between her thumb and forefinger. Then she raised her hand to her nose and sniffed up the powder.

'Monica, you pig. You're worse than I am. That was at least half the bottle. You're a vacuum cleaner, that's what you are.'

Seconds later Monica took as much again in the other nostril. 'You've got some more,' she said when Katarina protested. 'Why are you so keen on that bottle anyway?'

'Because it looks so nice.'

'Nice and useful are two quite different things,' Monica laughed as she went over to the basin to wet her finger. 'The coke gets stuck in your nose with it.'

She pushed the cocaine up her nose and rubbed her gums with the rest of the powder. She made sure no trace of it would show round her nose. That was the worst thing she knew. Talking to someone taller so that you could see the coke inside the nostril – ugh! Now she felt she could conquer the whole world.

With Monica in the lead, they went over to Chenka's table.

'Hi, do you mind if we sit down?'

There was a bottle of champagne on the table.

'Do athletes really drink?' Monica asked, smiling. Then she took Chenka's empty glass and poured some champagne for herself.

Monica looked closely at her. She was wearing diamond studs and a gold Rolex with diamonds round the face. Phew, she must earn big money. Given how successful Katarina said she was, Monica was sure this young woman had bought them herself.

Monica wanted to dance and have fun. She found it difficult to sit still. She kept on talking though somewhere at the back of her mind she wasn't certain anyone was keeping up with her. But Katarina laughed now and again.

'Shall we go somewhere else?' Monica said, turning to Katarina and Chenka.

'We could go to Tramps.'

'No, too many old men.'

'I know,' said Katarina. 'We'll go back to your place.' She winked at Monica.

Chenka had no objections. 'Why not? I'm not playing tomorrow. This is just a party for the players and the newspapers. I really hate these things.'

She told them about her career, how she started in Romania

and then went round the world. She now lived in Nevada and was ranked number seven among women tennis players.

Katarina got the vodka and lime from the refrigerator.

'I presume you don't drink?'

'No, I don't touch liquor. But I'd like a joint if you've got one.'

Katarina searched through her handbag. The gold bottle with coke, some Mandrax and two joints appeared. 'So pick your poison,' she offered.

Chenka lit the joint with a practised hand and let it go round, though Monica refused.

'I've never really liked it,' she smiled, moving across the room to put the Gloria Gaynor tape on instead. Chenka looked at her.

'How beautiful you are,' she said wistfully.

'Am I?'

'Yes. When you came into the restaurant tonight you seemed to be the only person there.'

'Thanks,' said Monica, sniffing a line of cocaine.

'But why do you take so much of that stuff?'

'Because it's fun. It's the greatest fun I've ever had. Maybe I can tempt you to a little? No, how stupid of me. You're an athlete.'

Chenka shook her head. 'No thanks, though I know a lot of my colleagues do. But I don't.'

'Here's to you, Chenka. I hope you win.'

Katarina had taken a Mandrax and smoked a whole joint herself, and was now semi-comatose in the corner of the sofa.

'Where's your bathroom?'

'Come on, I'll show you.'

Monica took Chenka upstairs and pointed to the door. She went into the bedroom and switched on the bedside lamp. She knew what was going to happen and that it would be new and exciting. She took off her clothes and put on a long silk dressing-gown with a large orange bird on the back. When she turned round, Chenka was standing in the doorway looking at her.

'What a lovely dressing-gown,' she said, closing the door behind her.

'One of my ex-husbands, I don't remember which, bought it for me.' Monica laughed and lay down on the bed.

Chenka lay down beside her and started cautiously kissing her.

Am I really kissing a woman, Monica thought, running her hand through Chenka's short hair.

Chenka took off her white tennis shirt and navy trousers. 'Have you ever made love with a woman?'

Monica shook her head.

Chenka played with Monica's big breasts, lifting them gently out of the silk dressing gown. 'I've always loved breasts,' she whispered. 'I've never had any.'

'Is that why you became a lesbian?' Reaching out, Monica caressed Chenka's small breast.

'No,' laughed Chenka. 'I've always preferred women.'

It was lovely, lying there talking, caressing each other. None of the frenzy Monica had experienced with men. She shuddered. It was pleasant, but difficult to feel really aroused after all the coke she'd taken.

Willing herself to concentrate, Monica explored Chenka's muscular body. Her breasts were not much more than two stiff nipples and there wasn't a scrap of fat on her.

Then Monica let her hand graze lower. It was so odd not feeling anything down there. It was just empty. But she was curious. Slowly she let her fingers slide between Chenka's legs and felt how moist she was.

Chenka kept kissing her, nibbling down her stomach. Then she took hold of Monica's hips. She let one hand glide in under her bottom to lift her up and with the other she parted her legs.

It was arousing and at the same time slightly ridiculous. Somehow it didn't seem right, Monica thought as she lay back, letting the waves of pleasure trickle through her. There was nothing serious about making love to a woman. But by the time she'd finished Chenka'd more than satisfied her . . .

When Chenka left, she asked if Monica would like to come and see her play.

'I'm in the doubles on Friday afternoon. I'll get my coach to pick you up and get you in. There are so many rules at Wimbledon. He'll look after you. Promise me you'll come?'

'Yes, I promise.'

They kissed goodbye.

Monica went down to the living room and put a blanket over Katarina. This new experience was not at all bad, she reflected. Monica took two of her friend's Mandrax and patted her on the head.

'Goodnight, Katarina,' she said fondly. 'I'll tell you all about it in the morning.'

They were together almost all of the ten days Chenka spent in London. Chenka's coach, Jockum, was not particularly pleased to find his protégée had a distraction, but wisely realised that it was as well that what Chenka wanted, she got.

Chenka had taken Monica to Cartier, where she'd bought them identical gold rings. Monica hadn't been to Cartier since her days with Gordon, and the assistant raised his eyebrows slightly when he saw her.

'Nice to see you again, Mrs Clarke,' he said politely but his surprise was obvious. Together Monica and Chenka made a conspicuous pair, both wearing linen suits, blue and white striped jerseys and white panama hats from Herbert Johnson in Bond Street – another of Chenka's ideas.

As they left the shop Monica couldn't help but laugh at the whole situation. What would they think? Gordon Clarke's ex-wife together with the tennis star buying rings at Cartier. For ten days the two of them had played an amusing game but Monica knew she didn't want to live like this for ever. It had been fun, however, even if she'd had to reduce her intake of cocaine during the last ten days – Chenka didn't like it – and Monica was finding it rather difficult to function. She was willing to keep off it, just for a while.

Chenka knew Monica wouldn't go with her on tour, so the night before Chenka left, she gave Monica a gold cross and her address in the States.

'If you ever come to Las Vegas, give me a call. I'd really like to see you again,' she smiled.

Monica kissed her goodbye. Somehow she was glad it was over.

21

Monica decided to go to Sweden. She missed her daughter and the time had come when she was beginning to wish she lived a more normal life.

She'd been in a permanent haze recently and realised there were great gaps in her memory: sometimes whole weeks were quite blank. She found herself calling Katarina, asking where she'd been and what she'd done, in order to reconstruct the days that had passed. It was extremely unpleasant not recognising situations or people, not even when they were retold to her.

She also found she had a splitting headache when she woke up, worse than migraine, and she was taking huge amounts of painkillers. Her depression at her state of health was unbearable and she ached all over. She didn't know whether it was her age, the drugs or the lack of food, but she knew she was now in desperate need of a break from this kind of life.

As she got off the familiar SAS flight she began to look back on the last few years. Everything had gone too quickly. She was forty-one and she'd been living like a woman in her twenties. How had Katarina managed to survive for so long?

When she saw her mother waiting for her at the other side of customs, Monica thought Gerd had aged in only a few months. She had clearly looked after Tanya wonderfully though, and Monica was eternally grateful to her for that.

Tanya's beauty was truly striking. She was so like her father, it brought tears to Monica's eyes. She took her hand to walk to the car.

* * *

She spent almost the whole of her first week in Stockholm in bed with headache, cramps, diarrhoea and nausea.

'It's only 'flu. It'll pass,' she tried to reassure her mother but Gerd was worried. Monica couldn't very well tell her she was suffering from withdrawal symptoms though.

Once she managed to get out of bed, she decided she must look after her daughter. She took her to Skansen, to Gröna Lund and they went out to the islands. Whatever she suggested Tanya was always pleased, happy just to be out with her mother.

Tanya spoke perfect Swedish but Monica wanted her to learn English as well.

'Speak Swedish, Mamma,' she kept saying, but Monica insisted they spoke English. She was beginning to realise she'd been in danger of losing her daughter.

Monica stayed in Sweden all through September and when she went back to England, she took Tanya with her. She had decided. She'd get a job and send Tanya to nursery school.

After a few weeks she found a nursery she liked and took Tanya there at eight every morning and then picked her up at six in the evening. Roger had asked her to come back for, as the salon's popularity had grown, he needed more people in reception. Her salary was modest, but she realised she simply had to attempt to earn a living: a letter from Mr Benton, her bank manager, had informed her that her overdraft at the bank was almost three thousand five hundred pounds. The time had come for a visit to the bank deposit.

Monica took Tanya with her. Her daughter gazed at the glittering jewels with astonishment. To her they were the jewels of a princess.

'What do you think? Shall we take this one?' Monica asked, kneeling down in front of her daughter and holding up a magnificent diamond and emerald necklace.

Tanya smiled at her.

'Well, it'll have to be that one then.'

Monica had no appointment at the Bond Street jewellers, but they received her all the same.

'Exquisite workmanship, but unfortunately we can't pay more than the value of the stones. I'm afraid the settings are worth nothing to us here. I can give you five thousand for it.'

Monica felt desperate and Tanya running around banging on the show case did not make things any easier.

'Tanya! Stop it. Don't do that!' she scolded as she fingered the glittering necklace. She knew it was worth ten times as much.

'You say five thousand. But I know it's worth more and you know it, too.'

'Yes, but times are bad. And as I said, the stones . . .'

'I want fifteen thousand for it. Otherwise I'll take it to Sotheby's . . .' Monica looked steadily at the little man.

'Then I must go and consult my brother first.'

The elderly man disappeared into the office at the rear.

'We'll say fifteen thousand then.'

Monica put the cheque into her bag, thanked him and, taking Tanya by the hand, went out on to Bond Street.

'Now, Tanya, it's your turn. Let's go to Hamley's and you can choose whatever you want. Taxi!'

She seldom went out these days, and when she did she always drank very moderately. She took a few lines with Katarina occasionally, but it always stopped at that.

She was glad she had Tanya. Without her, she would certainly have gone under. Monica really enjoyed her company now, although she was sometimes tryingly inquisitive, but if Monica said she was tired and wanted a bit of peace, Tanya respected that and went to get a puzzle or some other toy, happily playing on her own while Monica rested.

When Monica occasionally planned to go out, she took Tanya to Hewitt Hall. Tanya loved the Hall and thought it was just like being in a fairy tale. Mrs McDonald, though now very elderly, was still robust and wonderful with children, so Monica knew Tanya would be in safe hands.

Tanya quickly got on well with Philip and when she returned from Hewitt Hall she'd tell Monica everything about Uncle Philip and what they had done. Philip would never mention any of it. Monica laughed at it all. Typical Philip. He loved children, but didn't want Monica to know that he liked her daughter. He remained a very complicated person.

Monica had to admit that his detective show on television was very good. She normally never watched television and had sat through the first episode just because Philip had written it, but now she was hooked.

Monica felt she was sufficiently stable to be able to invite Gerd and Gunnar over for Christmas. It would be rather a squash, but Tanya could sleep in her room for the week. She wanted to give them a good Christmas after all they had done for her. And Tanya was delighted her grandparents were coming to see them. When the time came the holiday was a great success. Together, they all went to see the lights in Trafalgar Square and Harrods. Christmas in London was so different from Stockholm, and Monica loved seeing Tanya so happy, at one with her mother and grandparents.

Not until March did Katarina succeed in tempting her out on a spree again. Katarina had also been taking it easy recently. The bridge of her nose had collapsed, corroded away after all those years of abuse, so she'd had to have an operation for a new septum. She persuaded Monica she needed cheering up after the ordeal.

'Come off it, Monica. It's been such a long time,' she pleaded. 'We need one of our old jolly evenings.'

Monica was tempted, longing to be out among people, to drink a little wine and have a laugh.

'There's a party for the television premiere of "The Family" and the male star is here on a promotion campaign. I can't remember his name, but you know, that tall good-looking one . . . typically American, looks as if he spent his life on the beach. Anyway, he's going to be there, together with some of the others in the series. And the press, of course.'

'And where is this fantastic party taking place?'

'At Tramps, and yes, I know what you think, but this time it'll be different.'

'Thursday. Hm. I'll try to get a sitter.'

'That can't be all that difficult, Monica. Take her to Hewitt Hall. She does nothing but talk about what fun she has there.'

Although Katarina didn't like children, she got on very well with Tanya, sometimes taking her out for a few hours to give Monica some peace. Tanya regarded Katarina more as a big sister than an auntie, as with her she was allowed to have as much ice-cream as she liked, and as many sweets as she wanted, all the things her mother would not allow.

'All right, Katarina,' Monica agreed at last. 'I'll phone Mrs McDonald. I'll let you know later.'

Monica was wearing a new outfit in leopard-skin print, designed by Ninva Khoma. Tight leopard leggings, low-cut short tunic and a jacket in the same pattern, she felt great.

It was just like the good old days. Monica had even hunted out the Gloria Gaynor tape and was playing it at full blast when Katarina arrived.

'Oh, what do I hear? Does that mean you're feeling horny tonight? And look at you!'

'Maybe. But I'm well under control, thank you. By tomorrow morning I'll be my old respectable self.'

'Afternoon, you mean . . .'

The club was packed when they got there and Luigi informed them that there wasn't a single vacant table.

They looked into the dining room.

'There, there he is.' Katarina pointed into the midst of the crowded room.

'Who?'

'The guy in "The Family". Who do you think?'

Katarina had spotted him at once. He was sitting at the long table by the back wall. Both table and wall were wooden and the tall, deeply suntanned man with blow-waved locks looked as if he were in some medieval banqueting hall.

'Isn't he good-looking?'

Brad Jordan, the star of 'The Family', was surrounded by a flock of long-haired and short-haired, big-busted and flat-chested, long-legged girls. All kinds had been summoned to entertain the star during the advertising campaign in Europe.

The television series was immensely popular in the US. It had

297

begun as a mini-series four years earlier and its great success had taken everyone by surprise.

'Do you see that smile?' Katarina was lyrical.

'His teeth are capped. Bet you not one of them is his own.'

'Lay off. What about his tan?'

'Looks like one of my old Louis Vuitton suitcases.' Monica took Katarina by the arm and pulled her away. 'Come on, he's not my type.'

'What are you saying?' protested Katarina. 'On the scale from one to ten, he comes fifteen.'

'Fifteen times too American, yes.'

But even if she wasn't impressed by Brad Jordan Monica was pleased Katarina had persuaded her to come with her. She enjoyed being out among people again, relaxing a little. And although Katarina had dived into the ladies numerous times, Monica had gone with her only once.

But where had she got to now? she asked herself. She'd been gone almost twenty minutes. The queue couldn't be that long. For a moment she regretted she hadn't gone with her. A couple of lines would have been great. She ordered a vodka and lime and stayed by the bar to wait.

'Excuse me.'

'Oh, I'm sorry. Am I in the way?'

'No, not at all.'

Brad Jordan looked at her and fired off a dazzling smile. Monica had never seen such white teeth, or so many, in one mouth.

'I saw you before.'

'Really?'

'What's your name?'

'Monica. Monica Clarke. And yours?'

Monica couldn't help it. She was sure he presumed everyone knew who he was as the party was in his honour, so she simply had to ask.

'My name's Brad Jordan.'

He had that kind of broad American accent that Monica detested.

'And I'm the star of "The Family". That's why I'm surrounded with girls and champagne,' he laughed.

'Is that so?'

Monica was surprised at her own superior attitude to him, but she had an irresistible desire to bring him down to earth a little.

'Where do you come from?'

'Chelsea.'

'I mean, from the start. I seem to hear a slight accent.'

Monica did not reply.

'May I offer you a drink?'

'Look, Mr Jordan . . .'

'Call me Brad.'

'OK, Brad. I already have one.'

Monica raised her glass of vodka.

'Uhuh, then maybe I can tempt you with a little coke,'

Brad made a gesture towards his top pocket.

Had she heard right? Monica almost choked over his straight-forward question. When she'd recovered from her coughing attack, she laughed and smiled at him for the first time.

'Yes, please, that'd be nice.'

The ice was broken.

'Glad to hear it. But although we've only known each other a few minutes, we've got a bit of a problem.'

'Have we? What kind of problem?'

'Well, if you look around, we've got around five hundred pairs of eyes staring at us at this moment, and there would be even more if we went to the toilet together.'

She reached out and felt the little packet in her hand.

'Is that all you've got?'

'Yes, it is, so I'm counting on you not to run away and leave me alone here.'

'Don't you be too sure.'

Brad watched her head for the ladies.

What a woman! He had been attracted by her as soon as he'd seen her, and his interest had only been increased by her cool attitude. He was used to women doing absolutely anything to get near him. He had become truly bored with all the bimbos the PR people supplied him with. They just sat there pouting and agreeing with everything he said. He used to test them, saying the most controversial things and nine out of ten of them still agreed with him.

Brad had made sure Brian, his personal assistant and good friend, was entertaining Katarina so that he could approach this woman. It was impossible to guess her age, but he assumed she was about the same age as him, perhaps even a few years older. Whatever, she was sensationally beautiful.

He'd even tried to find out something about her, but all he had managed was that she'd been married to some Englishman who was rolling in dough and that she was now divorced. That suited him perfectly.

Monica went into the ladies, past the old woman who sat there with every cosmetic under the sun in front of her ready in case one of the guests needed them. She went into the lavatory, opened the envelope and laid two lines on the lid. Then she flushed the toilet and as the water rushed in she sniffed a line. The water wasn't so loud on the second flush: that was always the trouble with the second line.

Monica had never seen or heard of Brad Jordan before Katarina had mentioned him. He was certainly not her type, but all the same there was something interesting about him. She'd thought he would be offended and leave when she asked him his name, but that hadn't seemed to stop him. On the contrary.

He was still waiting by the bar where she'd left him. For the first time she noticed his clothes. He was wearing worn jeans and cowboy boots, a white cowboy shirt and a suède jacket. At least they weren't too ostentatious.

'Ah, there you are. For a few moments I thought you'd carried out your threat.'

Quietly, Monica returned the packet.

'Was it to your satisfaction?'

'Oh, yes. I can't feel my teeth at all, so it must have been good.'

'I'm glad . . . I've taken the liberty of ordering you another.' He winked meaningfully. He knew how thirsty coke made you.

Brad didn't leave her side all evening. He was fascinated by this woman and her cutting tone, which at the same time was almost kind; it amused him to bandy words with her.

'So, Monica, what do you say about taking a look inside the Dorchester?'

'I've already seen it,' she said nonchalantly. Really, however, she felt no hesitation – it was so long ago, Tanya was away, and going with Brad would make Katarina green with envy. Where was she, for that matter?

Five minutes later Monica was in the back of Brad Jordan's silver-coloured limousine. He asked the driver to close the dark partition, then he opened a bottle of champagne and drew up some lines on a mirror he had in a compartment.

'Have you told the driver where we're going?'

'No.'

Brad took her glass away, put it down on the tray and pulled Monica towards him. She could feel his breath caressing her mouth as he said: 'He'll drive round and round until I tell him to stop.'

Monica had never made love in a limousine before, a new experience.

Two hours later when Brad dropped a dazed Monica off at Elm Place, she was quite convinced she'd never see him again.

'I'll call you,' he said gravely.

'Great.'

Monica saw him waving goodbye in the faintly lit back of the car. She stood watching the limousine disappear.

Five months later, the house in Elm Place was let again and Tanya left her nursery school.

The two of them had moved to LA.

22

Monica was driving her white Volkswagen Rabbit cabriolet along the Pacific Coast Highway. She had just picked up Tanya from the Montessori school in Santa Monica.

It was twenty past three and they were on their way home.

It had been a great day. Earlier in the day she'd been to a meeting at the Twentieth-Century-Fox lot, where 'The Family', one of the most popular soaps in the US, was being filmed.

'Dallas', 'Dynasty', 'The Family' and 'Falcon Crest' in that order had had the highest viewer ratings for some time now.

Brad was immensely popular in the States and this was his fifth year in the series. Fan mail arrived by the sackful every day, almost all of it from women.

He was in a position to demand anything he liked – and did so. Outside Studio 17, 'The Family's' permanent set, he had a large trailer with a bedroom, living room, dressing room and bathroom, the refrigerator always packed with fruit, vegetables and various kinds of juice.

Brad had a personal dresser, a coach and Brian, his assistant, all on twenty-four hour call. He was also surrounded by a number of buddies who mostly sat around all day.

Monica had moved to California only five months after she'd met Brad. She'd never been to Los Angeles before, but had agreed at once when Brad had suggested she should join him. She would miss nothing in London. All she had to do was to pack up Elm Place, take her suitcases and Tanya and leave for LA.

Six months later they were married and she still felt like a newly-wed. Brad was very good with Tanya and gave her everything she pointed at, but there was no mistaking that he wanted a child of his own. Monica wanted to wait though she knew her age might be a problem.

Today she was unusually happy. She had been to a meeting with Linda Mansfield, head of PR for 'The Family', who had suggested that instead of sitting around watching her husband all day, waiting for him to finish, she might as well do something useful and start working with her.

When Linda had made her proposal, Monica couldn't believe it. She was sick and tired of having nothing to do. She could sunbathe, of course, but that soon palled, and she'd had enough of shopping during her time with Gordon.

Linda thought Monica had all the qualities needed to deal with people, and said she thought it would be terrible to allow such talent to go to waste. Monica was an outgoing person, her shyness now gone, and everyone appreciated her openness, honesty and helpfulness. Linda pointed out how different she was from showbiz people, who usually took the first possible opportunity to stab someone in the back as soon as they left the room.

Monica was going to start her new job the following day. She had to spend the first week at all the meetings to learn how the advertising campaign round 'The Family' was drawn up. She was having nothing to do with Brad's publicity but was to spend her time on the female characters. As the action always centred on Brad and the other male characters, they had been neglected. Competing series had Joan Collins, Linda Evans, Linda Gray, Victoria Principal and Jane Wyman, so Monica's assignment was now to bring the women in 'The Family' to the fore in roughly the same way. Monica felt confident she could rise to the challenge.

It was September and the sun was blazing. Monica considered putting the hood down, but knew it would make little difference. Despite the trying heat, life was good, everything so free, open and healthy here in California.

She swung to the right at Big Rock and drove up the steep road above Malibu. Their house was less than half a mile from Olivia Newton John's, and they could see her stables and the paddock where the horses were. They had a magnificent view over the ocean and on really clear days, they could see Catalina Island, or so Brad said.

She had moved into Brad's house, what they called a log cabin, with its dark beams and stone and tiled walls, an enormous open fireplace in the living room and opposite it a picture window facing out on to the wide view. Outside was a balcony suspended over the steep hillside.

Animal hides lay everywhere and various weapons hung on the walls. Brad had a collection of pistols he was very proud of. Monica had changed very little in the house, except to add something of the Santa Fé look she'd come to like since she'd moved to California.

They had four cars in the garage and Brad also had two Harley Davidson motorcycles though he usually used his big black Willy Jeep. Apart from that, there was a 1962 Corvette, an open-top Mustang and the little Volkswagen Rabbit he had bought for Monica.

She loved her car. It was considered very chic to have a small car and now only the nouveaux riches had expensive sports cars. A small foreign car was the first sign that things were going well for a television star and there was quite a number of them in the studio's parking lot.

Brad loved the outdoor life – shooting, fishing and then weight training. He'd turned half the garage into a gym and his personal trainer usually came up from Malibu to train with him. He had to keep his famous body in trim. Monica had occasionally gone to a work-out at Lotte Berk's in London, but now she'd begun weight training too.

Brad's image was built round his well-trained chest, his bare torso displayed on dozens of advertising photos, adorned only with worn jeans, shorts, swimming trunks or just a towel. He had a PR agent of his own to make sure his name and photograph appeared regularly in newspapers and magazines. The agent also tipped off the press on where they were and what they were doing, leaking both true and untrue stories. It didn't matter what they wrote, the main thing was that they wrote it. The law of the jungle ruled in Hollywood and Monica was soon aware of it.

She herself had certainly been mentioned in the press during her marriages to both Edward and Gordon, but that had been mostly on the social pages. Here it was something quite different, and Monica found it hard to put up with almost every single thing they did, and more, appearing in the press the following week. But that was what Brad wanted.

The day after Monica met Brad, she was sure she'd never see him again, but the very next morning he'd phoned three times and insisted they should spend every single minute of his remaining two days in London together. When Monica had laughingly pointed out that she was a little old for him, he'd declared that the ten years difference in their ages was nothing.

Monica had actually lived in the belief that she *was* ten years older until she'd happened to find his well-hidden passport. Out of sheer inquisitiveness, she'd opened it to look at the photograph and then she'd found that he was actually thirty-eight, only six years younger than she was. She had never let on that she knew his real date of birth, but went on celebrating the birthday he'd chosen. It wasn't enough to be rich, famous and successful in Hollywood. You also had to be young.

On the other hand, no one had made anything of her being older than him. Most people thought they were the same age. At forty-four, she was extremely well preserved and looked thirty-five even in strong sunlight.

Their relationship had attracted great attention in the American press, but privately they lived very modestly. Living in Malibu was like living in a world of its own. Almost everyone was rich and famous, and there they escaped the hysterical fans and autograph hunters and their cameras.

Monica loved Malibu. It was so free, with the beach and the ocean. Carbon Beach, Malibu Colony, Broad Beach. Some of the houses were built on piles along the shore and to get down to the water they had to climb down steps or ladders. The only snag was the traffic when they had to go into town. It could take hours to get to or from Hollywood.

Their social life in the hills consisted mainly of barbecues by the pool with grilled chicken, spare ribs, lobster, corn on the cobs and baked potatoes; plus plenty of beer, wine and Coca-Cola in coolers.

There was always a constant stream of people coming and going in their house. Once every two weeks a woman came from Vidal Sassoon in Beverly Hills and put highlights in Brad's hair and dyed his eyebrows and lashes. After that, a Vietnamese woman came to give him a manicure and pedicure, and then there was Sitva, a large Swedish woman who came and gave him the most fantastic body massage. Whatever they wanted, all they had to do was to pick up the phone. People came and washed the cars, brought in food or clothes to try on, anything anyone could desire.

Naturally the risk of becoming lazy and apathetic from spending her days by the pool was great, so Monica was glad she now had something meaningful to occupy her.

From the first day Monica truly relished her new job, and she was pleased to hear she was considered an asset to the company. She was just the right person to handle the female stars in the series, beautiful, but no threat to them, partly because she was older than they were. She and Linda Mansfield had become close friends, and after never really having many friends before, Monica found she had several, all of them extroverted and easy-going, making her feel special.

And family life was so good, too. They had given Tanya a little Norwegian elkhound puppy for her eighth birthday, grey with a black nose and black ears, and for some unfathomable reason she had christened him Björn Borg, though everyone called him BB.

It was wonderful to see the two of them playing on the beach, Tanya first and BB behind with his greyish white tail curled up his back. It would be hard to find a more obstinate dog. He worshipped his toys above all else. Tanya could fling one into the pool and BB would stand stock still gazing at it until it floated to the edge and he could get hold of it. Then he would run round the garden in a lap of honour.

For the first time for ages Monica was feeling in full control of her life. She was happily married and Tanya was the most beautiful and affectionate child imaginable. She hadn't yet started asking questions about her father; among her school friends it was more usual for parents to be divorced than married. But she knew that Brad was not her real father.

Monica didn't have anything to do with drugs, and quite recently she'd also decided to give up drinking. She'd started to go to Alcoholics Anonymous meetings, and that had not been easy, but she was absolutely determined not to give in.

Her only worry was Brad. For long periods he went without drugs or drink, but then he would suddenly take to them in a big way. He usually consulted her on everything – but not on this.

When he had these spells, living any kind of social life was difficult. He sat up all night, taking cocaine and drinking vodka, then, if not needed at the studio, slept all day. Monica found it easier to understand than most, for she herself had been addicted and knew what it meant.

Brad needed Monica and that she found reassuring. He left almost everything in her hands despite her own work. She went with him to all the photo calls and made sure he looked all right. Recently they had been doing large ads for 'The Family' for magazines and billboards – Brad with bared torso, suntanned and smiling, in leather trousers and boots, leaning against his Harley Davidson.

Monica had also taken on the task of handling his finances. Brad wanted her to see where his money went. Almost at once she found that enormous sums were being paid to people who really had no function whatsoever beyond drawing a salary to occasionally entertain Brad between takes. Monica had a great clear-out and made sure he appointed only *one* person who did several things, functioning as secretary and chauffeur, seeing to the fanmail and generally being Brad's right-hand man.

She couldn't help being fascinated by Los Angeles. It was so unlike what Katarina had told her. Her friend had seen nothing but hotel rooms and nightclubs, but for Monica it was exactly the opposite. There were unique views here – Hollywood Hills, where the houses appeared to be glued on to the mountains and, further down, Beverly Hills, with its enormous houses on tiny sites. Then there was exclusive Bel Air with the houses tucked away from view.

Monica often spoke to Robert on the phone. He was back at
Hewitt Hall after his three-year stint at agricultural college in
Australia, and now having supervised the gradual reclaiming of
their land from tenants, was going to start real farming in his own
right at the Hall.

Monica longed to be able to give her son a hug. It had been ages.
She could hear from his voice that he was much happier than he'd
been for a long time and, from his conversation, also much more
mature.

Brad's contract ran out in the autumn of 1983, and the time had
come to negotiate a new one, not easy for Brad's manager, Tom
Cohen. Brad had achieved everything he had set out to, his name
now one of the biggest in the history of soaps, exposed in the press
more often than Joan Collins, his fan mail heavier than the mailman could carry. But he wanted more.

He was tired of having to get up at half past three in the morning
when they were filming. He also disliked television stars not having
the same status as film stars. He wanted to be in films and make a
name for himself as a serious actor.

Brad had had an offer to make an action film in Mexico but Tom
was doing his utmost to convince him that he couldn't just leave the
television series. Brad was having none of it.

'What you must do, Tom, is to demand such an outrageous
amount of money that they simply won't be able to agree,' he
insisted. 'If against all expectations they do agree, then okay, I'll
stay for another season.'

'Are you quite sure, Brad, that you want to take this step?'

'Yes. I know you worry and it's "The Family" that's made me
famous, but I want out, I want to do movies.'

Monica also tried to persuade him to stay for another season, but
he wouldn't listen to her, either. He was already full of plans for his
film career and spent days reading his script, marking dialogue and
situations he thought needed altering.

Because Brad was already receiving an incredibly high salary his
demand came as a shock to the producers. They were certainly prepared to negotiate, but not for the kind of money he wanted. Tom
tried to mediate, but Brad refused to give in. So in the last episode

of the season, the character Brad played was seen to leave for Europe, thus leaving it open whether he would come back or not.

When Tom told him the negotiations had broken down and he was no longer on the cast list for the following season Brad didn't bat an eyelid. He was already absorbed in his new project, *Jungle Heat*, as the film was called. It was an action film with all the classical ingredients. He was 'the good guy' battling against 'the bad guys'. Filming was going to start early the following year and Brad had recruited all his old buddies as co-stars and stunt coordinators so that they could go to Mexico with him. He was like a child with a new toy.

Monica did wonder whether he'd taken the right decision, but was grateful that some good seemed to be coming of it – he touched neither drugs nor alcohol, but lived on juice, salads and tuna fish. His trainer came to Malibu every day now and they kept up iron-hard routines and ran for miles along the beach and up the mountain roads. He wanted to be on top form for the film.

Although Brad had left 'The Family', the decision was to be kept quiet until January and Monica was continuing as before in the PR department. At the moment however she was also free, grateful to be able to just relax in the calm before the storm of the film shooting and that when he wasn't training, they could spend almost all their time together.

At the end of January, Jay Stein, his press agent, issued a statement which confirmed the rumours circulating in Hollywood that Brad Jordan was not coming back to 'The Family' next season, as the producers were not prepared to pay the salary he felt he was worth after five years in the series. The studio immediately issued a denial stating that this was not true, but that Brad had suddenly demanded an amount too high for the Network to even consider.

Jay was pleased. This verbal warfare would certainly keep Brad in the headlines for at least a week. Photographers and journalists flocked outside their house, waiting for just a glimpse of Brad, and preferably some comment. But on Jay's advice he kept them on tenterhooks.

As Jay had predicted, there was a public outcry against the studio. Everyone wanted Brad back and the newspapers also wrote mile-long columns on the film he was going to make. Everything was going entirely according to plan.

Monica stayed at home when Brad went down to Mexico to start filming. She had her own work to think about, now more than ever. She had to get the advertising campaign straightened out after Brad's departure.

Brad phoned her every day and talked about his part and the filming. Monica was pleased for him and had started to write down what he told her in a diary. Her memory had recently let her down on several occasions and once or twice she had completely forgotten what she'd done or was going to do. Sometimes she would have a blackout and couldn't for the life of her remember the names of people she worked with every day, and once she'd had to think quite hard to remember even Brad's name.

Monica knew she had to get Brad to realise how dangerous drugs were. She was sure she'd damaged her brain and this loss of memory was the price she had to pay. She couldn't bear to see him going the same way.

Suddenly there was complete silence from Mexico. Brad didn't phone for a whole week, and in the end Monica had to look in her diary to check when he'd last telephoned. She'd been busy herself and she thought perhaps he'd been the same but this was getting worrying.

Monday, Tuesday, Wednesday . . . she went on turning the pages. No, no sign of life since last week. Extraordinary!

Monica phoned Tom, but it turned out that he had also gone down to Mexico. That was even more extraordinary. Tom wouldn't have done that unless something had happened.

A few more days went by, then Brad suddenly phoned. The money had run out and the production had not been able to go on. They had looked for a backer, but with no success. The filming had taken longer and everything had been more expensive than expected. They needed money now. So Brad was thinking of putting two hundred thousand dollars of his own capital into the film.

Monica did everything to get him to change his mind. She had arranged for his money to be invested properly, and if he touched it now, he would lose all the interest. And that was what they had to live on. To her despair, he refused to listen.

Time passed and the gaps between his calls grew longer. Finally Tom told her that the money had again run out and they had been forced to close down the production. They just couldn't complete the film.

'Brad will be back in a few days,' Tom told her, 'but, Monica, take it easy with him. He's staked all on this film. And I don't just mean money . . .'

He came back, but not to her. He locked himself in the cutting-room and stayed there for weeks trying to put together what they had, then just filming as few scenes as possible in and around Los Angeles to keep down the costs. But there were far too many important scenes missing, and they had to abandon the project and wait for better times to come.

Brad was desperate. He shut himself up in the gym for days and nights at a stretch and Monica didn't know what was going on in there. He drank vodka and took cocaine, and she saw him only occasionally. He looked dreadful. Every personal advance he'd made for the film he was now about to destroy.

Monica now knew she was pregnant again, and she also knew Brad very much wanted to have a child, but she could see this was not the right moment to tell him.

She really wanted this child. She was forty-four and this was her last chance. She felt she had a stable marriage and they had a housekeeper, as she had no desire to give up the work she loved. She also wanted to give Brad a child before it was too late.

One night Brad collapsed and Monica had to drive him at top speed to St John's Hospital in Santa Monica. The doctor asked her whether he took drugs, and with her usual candidness she said yes. She was told Brad had alcohol poisoning and was very close to an overdose, so they had to pump his stomach.

Naturally it was no use trying to keep it out of the press. Only a few hours after he'd been admitted, the hospital was besieged by reporters and the newspapers were speculating wildly on why he was there. The crowd of pressmen when he left hospital was enormous. A host of people had been into his private room to fix his appearance so that he should look as healthy as possible, and he did look as if he'd come directly from a holiday in the sun. His hair was blow-waved, fake tan had done the job and he wore his usual fairly casual but expensive clothes.

Officially he was said to be suffering from overwork, hence the collapse, but the press didn't accept that and the speculation continued unabated.

After his return home, he spent most of the day on the telephone to Tom, trying to work out a strategy for what he should do to get things back on track.

'Brad, you're a television star,' Tom said, time after time, 'why can't you accept it? All the offers you get come from television, and I'm sure I can get you back into "The Family".'

But Brad was adamant. 'I'd rather die. I'll never go back. Never!'

He was quite unmovable and, her heart torn by how much he was suffering, Monica did everything she could to care for and console him.

One evening, a few days after he'd come out of hospital, they were sitting on the balcony watching the sunset. For once he was fairly calm and Monica knew she couldn't leave it much longer to tell him, so she took his hand and knelt down in front of him, almost without realising it, putting her head in his lap in a gesture of supplication.

'Brad, we're going to have a baby,' she said quietly.

At first he looked at her shocked, but almost immediately a broad smile spread over his face.

He took her head in his hands. 'You've given me what I so very much wanted, Monica. All those other things don't matter. We're going to have a baby, you and me, Monica. That's all that matters.'

The news and the shock of going to hospital meant that for the first time Brad had a real motive to give up drink and drugs. At least that was Monica's dearest hope.

Monica was in her eighth month. Her pregnancy had been relatively easy, but she presumed that was simply because she hadn't been able to spend it in bed. Brad needed her. He was still deeply

313

depressed, although happy about the baby.

He had more or less given up hope of *Jungle Heat* ever getting distribution, and to his distress 'The Family' managed perfectly well without him. They had signed up another star, Brendan Rook, who'd soon become the new idol.

At Jay's prompting *Vanity Fair* had asked Tom whether they could do an article on the happy parents-to-be, and even though Monica had no desire whatsoever to be photographed in her condition, she saw the importance to Brad. He needed all the publicity he could get, and it would also help to disperse all the speculations. He'd simply taken time off to be with his pregnant wife.

Over and over again, Tom and Jay went through with them what they were to say, convinced this might turn his setbacks into success.

The photographs were lovely, Monica heavily pregnant and Brad from every possible angle, and the text was more than they could have hoped for. Brad must have charmed the journalist, as she had written just what he'd said. And for *Vanity Fair*, the article was relatively free of allusions to their pasts. Jay Stein had performed a miracle.

While *Vanity Fair* was on the magazine racks all over the USA, with Monica and Brad on the cover, the future parents in the article were at home in Malibu in the very depths of grief. Their little boy had been strangled by the umbilical cord during the birth and neither Monica nor Brad knew how to cope.

This was Brad's first child and he'd been present during the birth, and for Monica it was the second time she'd left the delivery room without having her baby with her.

The shock was so great to them both that several days went by before they even said a word to each other. Brad drank as if there were no tomorrow and probably also took coke. But Monica was forced to remain sober and strong, for both Tanya's and Brad's sake.

Why should she be made to suffer so? Hadn't she been tried enough already? Every time her future began to look bright, fate struck again and crushed her happiness.

She spent a lot of time on the balcony thinking about what had happened in her life. It wasn't easy. There were gaps everywhere and she had to think really hard, but one thing kept coming back to her. She found herself constantly wondering where she would be if she'd been off-duty that day Edward Hewitt had been on her flight – probably still in Sweden with a husband and children. She had never really yearned for the world beyond her former existence and would almost certainly have gone back to her own country once she'd stopped flying.

Monica had called Robert at Hewitt Hall and told him what had happened. To her horror, just as he'd answered, she found she'd forgotten whom she'd been calling. She'd rambled on a bit and he'd asked whether she'd been drinking. As so often when innocent, she'd tried too hard to explain, and sounded even more guilty.

Their grief was not made any easier by telegrams and congratulations pouring in as a result of the article in *Vanity Fair*. Monica knew they had to put an end to it, and when Tom phoned and said that Joan Lunden wanted them on 'Good Morning America', she was the one who was keenest.

Joan wanted them to talk about the child they had lost and Monica saw that there could be no more effective way of putting an end to the stream of congratulations. Every time the mailman came, it was like a stab in her heart. The newspapers were also full of articles about their expected baby; it would be just as well to tell the truth before the gossip columnists put their stamp on what had happened.

Brad wasn't so sure. He was exhausted and didn't think he looked good enough to appear on a programme to be broadcast all over the States. His career was in shreds and he'd lost his much longed-for child. But he agreed to the interview for Monica's sake.

Monica had never given a television interview before. But she was calm, and in spite of everything, in control of the situation. In her PR work, she had instructed actresses and actors on how to appear on television and somehow it was as if everything she'd learnt and in turn taught to others fell into place when she found herself in front of the camera. Suddenly everything fitted and as the cameras began to roll she found that she and Joan were the ones doing all the talking. The interview was all Joan Lunden had wanted it to be; the moving story of a couple who had lost their longed-for child. And, quite unplanned, Monica revealed her drinking and drug-taking in the past, because she thought it fitted in with the context of the show. She also talked about how because of her age she'd had an amniocentesis and everything had been all right, so she and the doctors had been optimistic that the birth would be without complications.

After the programme, the producer came down to the studio, took both Monica's hands in his and just looked at her.

'Mrs Jordan, I'm at a loss for words. Your strength, your courage and your directness were amazing. This gripping story of yours went straight to our hearts. And the camera loves you.'

Taking part in the programme had clearly been the right decision and it was amazing what attention it aroused. Monica felt stronger. Letters of sympathy and admiration poured into their house in Malibu and to Tom's office, addressed either to Mr and Mrs Jordan or just to Monica.

Monica read them and replied to most. The compassion shown to them was incredible and with each letter Monica felt herself overcoming her crisis.

But Brad did not cope so well. He was still drinking heavily and their sex life, never particularly active, had as good as ceased.

Nor did Monica miss it. She threw herself wholeheartedly into her PR work; the tables were suddenly turned. Now it was Brad sitting at home waiting for Monica. She knew he drank during the day and knowing that, it wasn't easy to leave him in the mornings. But she had a job to do.

The autumn went by and nothing much changed. Brad was taking no drugs, but was drinking more heavily than ever. He had now given up all hope of *Jungle Heat* ever being completed.

One day Tom called and asked them to come to his office. Brad said he had sounded terribly secretive and wouldn't say on the phone what it was about.

Monica was excited, sensing it was something positive. She could see Brad was pleased, that something was in the air. She knew just how the fact that offers had faded since he'd left 'The Family' had affected his psyche. As they drove to Tom's office she felt that

316

gradually light was dawning on the horizon.

'Sun comes after the rain, think about that, darling,' she said, squeezing his hand.

Tom asked him to listen to the whole proposal before refusing it. They could tell by his expression that it was a television project. Brad interrupted him before he'd even finished the sentence.

'Now, Tom, don't tell me you've got us to come all the way here to talk about television deals. We've gone through that hundreds of times. I'm through with TV, and that's it.' He stood up to leave.

'Brad, I asked you to listen, so sit down.' He looked at Monica.

'Darling, you might at least listen to what Tom has to say.'

'It doesn't make any difference. If it's TV, that says it all. I won't do it.' Reluctantly, he sat down again.

'Brad, I've said it before and I'll say it again. You're a TV star whether you like it or not.' Tom suddenly sounded much more authoritative.

Brad was clearly not going to like what Tom was about to say, but he did agree to listen. Deep down he knew that Tom was right.

'You've given films a chance and it hasn't worked out. *Jungle Heat* can't be completed, and you know it. No one who's seen the dailies is willing to back it, and no other decent offers have come from the film industry. They've all come from television, and unfortunately they haven't always been all that brilliant, either. Up until now. Now something really good has come up. So, Brad, for your own sake, listen to me. This is good.'

Brad straightened up in his chair.

'OK, Tom. Lay it on me!' he nodded, clearly chastened.

The offer involved a new television series called 'Fairfield High', the action set in a high school in Santa Monica. Brad's role was as a football coach who was going to turn a bunch of nerds into a winning team. The production company had a good reputation and there was a decent budget for the pilot now being planned.

Tom explained that if this show was picked up, Brad would take all his old fans with him and also a whole new young audience, as it was a series aimed at the young.

'You'll earn good money, Brad, but we'll ask for a percentage as well. You'll soon be on top again. Put your movie career on hold and make the most of this.'

'I'll think about it. Give me the script, and I'll read it. I'll let you know.'

'Yes, but don't take too long. And for God's sake start training again. No one wants a fat football coach.'

Brad glanced at his tight white T-shirt. Tom's words had struck home. Monica nodded, entirely on Tom's side. These days she and Tom were in agreement on most things.

Before long the preparations for the pilot were underway. One of the many telephone calls however was for Monica. It was a producer from Channel 5 on the line. They wanted to see her in their office as soon as possible.

She had no idea who he was. He'd been very secretive and Monica presumed they wanted to tempt her away from 'The Family' to another network.

She was not particularly enthusiastic. Linda had given her a chance and Monica really did not want to let her and the rest of the cast down, even if it did mean more money. She also knew the actors in 'The Family' so well she hadn't the slightest desire to start again with a new cast.

Brad was the only one to encourage her to at least go and meet them.

'Why not?' he said, 'you've nothing to lose, have you? Find out what they want and ask for double what you're getting now.'

Nothing would please Brad more than if she turned her back on 'The Family', Monica knew that. She understood very well why Brad was so enthusiastic about this meeting at Channel 5.

'Brad, Brad. Where are you?' Monica called but received no reply. She found him out on the balcony in the evening sun.

He was fighting back on the fitness front and spent hours with his trainer, winding down by sitting in the sun to get back the obligatory tan. But he hadn't stopped drinking vodka, although these days he diluted it with lime and lots of crushed ice.

He smiled at her and Monica saw that self-confident Brad Jordan smile she hadn't seen for a long time.

318

He'd been to a meeting with the producer of 'Fairfield High' earlier in the day and he seemed suddenly to have forgotten all about being a movie star. He was full of the new series and how they would take the US by storm. He would show that Brendan Rook just who was a star with a capital S.

'Brad . . .'

He had been so busy telling her about 'Fairfield' she had to interrupt him.

'Oh honey, I'm sorry. What happened, what did they want?'

'I can't believe it, Brad. It had nothing to do with PR.'

'No?'

'You know that morning programme on Channel 5. Called "At Home?" '

Brad nodded, even though he didn't know the show. But he saw how excited Monica was.

'It was the producer of that. He had seen us on "Good Morning America" and been so impressed by me that he wants me in a permanent slot on "At Home". Well, of course he wants me to audition first. But he's convinced I'm right for his show . . .'

'Hang on, darling. I'm not with you. What exactly are you going to do?'

'Every morning, they want me to talk about something moving that's happened in real life. He is giving me a research team who'll find gripping and tragic events for me to cover. Can you imagine? And I'd have my own office and secretary.'

Brad was in two minds. Of course he wanted her to leave 'The Family', but one of them in front of the camera was enough. Suddenly he felt threatened by the thought of his wife competing with him. Not that he didn't want her to be successful, but . . .

He took a sip of his drink and tried to hide his displeasure as long as possible.

'Don't get your hopes up too high. You have to do the audition before you'll know if you get it. Never plan anything until you've got the signed contract in your hand. And God knows if it's really safe even then.'

A few weeks later, Monica had her own slot in 'At Home'. She could choose from the alternatives the research team handed in.

She had her own secretary, Rita, who handled the administration and her personal life. Suddenly it was Monica who was the one in demand. For although her pieces were short, they always attracted a lot of attention and Rita was busy making appointments for everyone who wanted to meet her.

Brad had gradually adapted to Monica working in front of the camera instead of behind it, but at first he hadn't been able to hide his antagonism. Fortunately he had plenty to do to get himself back on form. Because there were a number of scenes in which he had to appear with his chest bared or in a T-shirt and shorts, his trainer seemed to live at their house.

Monica loved her show. Linda had been very understanding about her leaving, so she had not lost a friend and she was now so successful, she was no longer known just as Mrs Brad Jordan, she was Monica Clarke. She used that name because it was short and easy.

It was a joy to go to work, although she had to leave at an ungodly hour in the morning. Luckily their housekeeper, Concita, drove Tanya to school and back. And Monica was now back from the studio earlier in the afternoon and could usually go down to the beach with Tanya and BB, and throw tennis balls which he chewed up. They were constantly having to buy new ones – Björn Borg had to live up to his reputation.

Everything pointed to Brad's pilot being picked up and as things looked now, they would start filming next year, January 1985.

All round, things were looking good. They celebrated Christmas in Aspen, and stayed at the Hotel Jerome on Main Street. It was a wonderful Christmas and Robert was the only person Monica missed. She had invited him, but he had so much to do on the farm that he hadn't the time. Monica knew from his voice that he was really sorry, though at the same time he was proud of his achievements at Hewitt Hall and felt he really couldn't leave it now.

They spent their days skiing and ate at different restaurants at night. Aspen was a skiers' paradise. Monica had finally overcome her fear of skiing and now loved it.

The new year began if possible even better than the old had ended. Monica had only just got back from her holiday when she was called in for yet another meeting.

The response to her slot in 'At Home' had been beyond expectations, so the production company were planning a morning programme of her own. Everything went so quickly, Monica found it hard to keep up. The executives believed in her and were prepared to do a pilot for 'This is LA', a morning chat show hosted by Monica. They were planning to start in May, and Monica's time was taken up with fittings, going through research and PR photo calls.

Things were still going well for Brad too. The pilot had been picked up and Brad was preparing to start shooting the first five shows.

'This is LA' was an instant success for Monica – she was a natural talent, the critics agreed and it seemed incredible she'd had no experience at all when she'd started on 'At Home'.

Brad's attorney had negotiated her contract as well, and Monica couldn't believe her ears when she heard what they had agreed on. She was getting seven thousand dollars a week plus an office of her own, a dressing room, and on top of that, her own hairdresser and make-up artist. The company was also paying for the clothes she wore on the screen and any other expenses she might have in connection with the programme. When Monica thought back to her days in London, when except for her part-time job at Roger's she had done nothing, she could hardly believe it was true.

Suddenly she realised she was in a new phase of her life – career woman. It was hard to find the time to be mother, wife and a hard-working, gainfully employed woman.

She had a permanent guilty conscience because she was home so late, but consoled herself that it would be better as soon as the programme got going properly. The planning for the first couple of shows was extremely tight and as Monica regarded 'This is LA' as her own baby, she supervised everything. Later she would have more regular hours.

She was so absorbed in her work and so utterly exhausted when she got home in the afternoons, she didn't notice the tell-tale signs she ought to have been familiar with by now. Brad was under such pressure. He knew there was a lot at stake. If the series turned out to be a flop, that would really be the end of him. The newspapers were full of his come-back and the frenzy had begun again.

BRAD JORDAN – NOW IT'S WIN OR OUT, ran one of the headlines.

The publicity had affected Brad badly, and combined with the pressure of filming had become too much for him. He had again started drinking and taking drugs. All the classic symptoms were there – twitching round the mouth and trembling hands. Monica just didn't notice them. As soon as Monica left for the studio and Concita had taken Tanya to school, he would mix his first vodka.

His ordinary pusher had for a while thought he'd lost his best customer, but now he was back. Every day he came to the house and Brad was using more and more.

Tanya was spending the weekend with a friend from school, and for once Monica dragged herself away early from the studio to do some shopping. She thought the two of them should take the opportunity to enjoy a few days on their own.

She knew he was at a fitting until quite late and that would give her a chance to prepare supper.

On the way home, she stopped at Georgio's in Beverly Hills and bought a cream-coloured silk teddy and dressing gown with exquisite lacework. She wanted to surprise Brad. She was tingling all over.

She'd been stuck in a traffic jam on the Pacific Coast Highway for an hour, and breathed a sigh of relief when she finally turned off at Big Rock. As long as Brad hadn't got home yet, she thought, but she couldn't see his car in the driveway up to the garage.

Monica was struggling with bags and trying to get the key out of her handbag. She could hear the telephone ringing and dropped the bags as soon as she got inside. Maybe it was Brad.

The answerphone had just started but she stopped it by lifting the receiver.

'Hello.'

'Monica, at last someone answering. Where's Brad?'

'Tom, you know perfectly well he's got a fitting today. He's been there . . .'

'That's just what he hasn't. There are three wardrobe people and two stylists who've been waiting all day, and I can't get hold of him

322

anywhere. Could he have forgotten?'

'No, he couldn't have. He was awake when I left this morning and we talked about it then.'

'So you've no idea where he is? Has he been home during the day, do you know?'

'I don't know. I've only just got in. Can you hang on a minute and I'll go and see if there's a note or anything?'

'Of course.'

Monica put the receiver down on the basketry table and went to the kitchen. When she got to the living room even Tom heard her scream. He also heard her knocking into something on her way back to the phone and something crash to the floor. By the time she reached the phone she was so out of breath, he could hardly hear what she was saying.

'Tom, call an ambulance.'

'Wait, Monica, what are you saying?'

'He's . . . He's quite lifeless – lying on the sofa. Brad's . . .'

'Calm down, Monica. Is he breathing?'

'I think so. There's a bottle of vodka beside him and there's cocaine on the table.'

'Monica, listen to me. Hello, can you hear me?'

'Yes.'

'Go and see if he's breathing and then come back to the phone. I can be with you in half an hour. We must avoid calling an ambulance unless it's absolutely necessary. If you phone, you'll have the newspapers there in next to no time. He won't survive another scandal now.'

'How can you worry about things like that now?' she gasped. 'He's unconscious.'

'Do as I say.'

Brad was breathing but otherwise showed no sign of life. Waiting for Tom was terrible. She bathed Brad's forehead with ice-cold water and did all she could to bring him round, but with no success, he didn't even open his eyes. His car was in the garage, so he had clearly never left the house at all that day. As she knelt beside him, Monica wept and screamed alternately. He simply couldn't die on her.

Tom must have known a short cut for he was with them in the

promised half an hour, although it seemed like light years. Together they managed to carry Brad's lifeless body to his car and they set off to St John's Hospital in Santa Monica. Tom drove and Monica sat in the back bathing Brad's forehead. He was breathing heavily and unevenly.

Tom stayed with Monica in the waiting room while the doctors examined Brad, and it seemed an eternity before anyone appeared in the corridor. One of the doctors showed them into his office and judging from his expression, the situation was serious.

'Mrs Jordan, your husband's life is no longer in danger, but we mustn't ignore the seriousness of the situation. He has taken an overdose of cocaine and vodka, and is at the moment being stomach-pumped and treated with electric shocks. We're going to keep him under observation, so why don't you go home now and phone us in the morning. Unfortunately, it seems to have already been leaked to the press that Mr Jordan is here, there's a mass of photographers and reporters outside the hospital.'

Tom couldn't control himself and leapt up, thumping his fist on the desk.

'Who the hell have you got here leaking things like that? For Christ's sake, he's only been here a few hours!'

'I'm sorry, Mr Cohen, but it's pretty well impossible to gag the whole staff. With a famous person like Mr Jordan, rumour spreads like wildfire all over the hospital and before you know where you are, someone's tipped off the press. Most unfortunate.'

He was right. The very next day the headlines were there.

BRAD JORDAN 'DIES' IN DRUG BINGE

Brad Jordan 'died' and was then brought back to life by a team of doctors after an overdose of drugs and booze. The soap star's heart stopped beating after he had a fit and crashed out at his luxurious Malibu home. Brad was reported to have over-dosed on a cocktail of cocaine, marijuana and vodka. He was only saved because his beautiful wife, 'talk-show-host',

Monica Clarke, found him and took him to St John's Hospital. Doctors administered a series of electric shocks to get his heart going again.

Monica was not allowed to see him until later that afternoon. Meanwhile both the house in Malibu and the hospital were besieged by reporters and photographers.

Brad was devastated, he'd lost control over how much he had taken, he told her, and after that he could remember nothing. As Monica talked over what had happened with him, this time she was sure he really did want to give up.

Monica realised now that he'd been under terrible pressure. In less than a month, he was starting to shoot the new series.

Although Monica was in the middle of the hectic business of starting her own programme, she knew she had to take time out to help Brad get back on his feet. She was grateful her daughter was as independent as she was, for there simply was no time for her at all.

Monica drove Brad home in her new blue BMW. They had left through the underground garage to avoid the photographers as much as possible. The car had been parked in the basement where the doctors left theirs. In a black wig, Brad in a wheelchair and a blanket over his head, Monica managed to evade the scandal-hungry press.

Despite Brad's protests that he'd made a mistake, Monica couldn't help wondering whether he could possibly be harbouring some kind of death wish. But Brad assured her that was absolutely untrue. He had everything to live for.

Tanya was afraid Brad was going to die, but Monica had explained that Brad had used some pills that his body couldn't take.

'Don't worry, darling. He's not going to die. I promise you.'

The next day Monica turned the house upside-down in her search for drugs. Brad even had to agree to her looking in his back pocket.

'Monica, there isn't any left. I took everything I had.'

Monica could see that this time Brad realised how close to death he'd been and was prepared to do something about it. They went to his first AA meeting together.

'You don't have to say anything,' Monica whispered into his ear as they sat at the back of the room.

Brad was fascinated by what he heard. People got up and confessed to being alcoholics or drug addicts, and told the most terrible stories. He held tight on to Monica's hand. He knew he could never get up on to that little platform and talk. He stayed for Monica's sake, not his own.

An hour later they were at Ma Maison, Patrick Terrail's popular restaurant, to have lunch together.

'Brad, Monica . . .' Patrick held out his arms and kissed them both, then showed them to a table.

Everyone in the industry was there, Zsa Zsa Gabor sitting by the entrance as usual, and up the few steps Orson Welles at his regular table, the only one indoors.

'She must come here every day. It can't be just chance that she's here every time we decide to lunch here,' Monica remarked as they were shown to their table.

They had hot duck salad but without the usual Kir Royale. This time it was mineral water.

On their way back home, they picked up Tanya and then stopped off at St John's Hospital where Brad had to go and see Dr Mann. The results of some tests they had done had come and he wanted to talk to Brad.

Monica and Tanya went and had an ice-cream while they were waiting, Monica anxiously wondering what news they might bring.

'Mr Jordan, we've done a number of comprehensive test nd have found that your blood count is very irregular. Your white blood cells are not behaving as we should like them to and the red blood corpuscles have an irregular sedimentation rate. We would like to do another test. It's called HTLV-III.'

'What the hell's HTLV-III?'

'Well, it's a new test . . .' The doctor didn't finish the sentence.

Brad had no idea what all these tests meant. All he knew was that he was run down after all he had gone through and that he needed rest. So he didn't reflect much on what the doctor said. The new test probably had something to do with his liver.

He left a blood sample and then hurried down to Monica and Tanya.

'Sorry you've had to wait so long, but he wanted more blood, that vampire!' he said with a laugh.

'What was it about this time?'

'I don't really know. Some liver check-up, I think.'

'What about the other results?'

'OK. He said my sedimentation rate was rather high, but otherwise fine.'

He didn't really want to tell Monica what the doctor had said, and anyhow, he couldn't remember it all. Monica would only worry if he said anything.

On the way home Tanya could talk about nothing except that she wanted a horse. According to her, every single one of her school friends had a horse of their own. And she knew exactly how she was going to look after it. Monica had tried to explain to her that since they couldn't build a stable where they lived – there just wasn't enough room – Concita would have to drive her to the stables every time she wanted to go riding. But at best, Monica thought as they drew up to the house, she didn't seem to be worrying about Brad quite so much.

A week later, Dr Mann telephoned. He had the results of the new test and wanted Brad to come to see him.

'Why can't we do it on the phone? Do I really have to come all the way to the hospital?'

Brad was used to people coming to him, not the other way round.

The doctor was adamant. 'I'm sorry, but I need to see you. We have a few things to discuss.'

Brad sat down at the desk, opposite Dr Mann.

'We've gone through the test results twice, Mr Jordan. But first of all I must ask you a few questions. I hope you don't mind that some of them are of a rather personal nature.'

327

Brad looked at Dr Mann in surprise.

'Have you ever had an operation in which you've had a blood transfusion?'

Brad was quite certain. 'No, I haven't.'

'Have you ever had . . .' Dr Mann straightened his glasses and hesitated for a moment before going on, '. . . a homosexual relationship?'

Brad glared angrily at him and said sharply: 'No, I'm no fucking queer. What are you getting at?'

'I know you use drugs, have you ever used syringes?'

Was the man crazy? What did he mean?

'Mr Jordan. Please answer my question.'

'Well, I don't know. Yeah, some time in the seventies when I was working as a waiter in New York to pay for my drama school. I was sharing an apartment with three other guys, and now and again, yeah, we did shoot heroin. But only for a few months. I'm sure you understand, Dr Mann . . .'

'Did you share needles?'

'Well, I guess so. I don't really remember. It was a long time ago.'

'There's a new disease. It largely afflicts homosexuals, but also drug addicts who use needles.'

'Dr Mann, I am not a drug addict.'

'I'm sorry, Mr Jordan, but unfortunately once can be enough if you have bad luck on your side. You are HTLV-III positive. You're carrying a very serious virus.'

'What does that mean?'

'Have you ever heard of GRID – Gay Related Immune Deficiency?'

Brad suddenly understood the seriousness of it all. 'Do you mean that it's a fatal disease?'

Dr Mann looked him straight in the eye.

'Yes, unfortunately at present there is no cure for it.'

'Tell me . . .' He swallowed hard. 'How long have I got?'

'We still don't know enough about this disease. All we know is that most people who have tested positive for this seem to die quite quickly, and we know for certain that people die of the complications the virus brings with it. We also know the infection comes from sexual contact, blood transfusions and hypodermic needles.'

Brad covered his face with his hands. My God, I'm going to die . . .

'Don't give up, Mr Jordan. There's still a lot to do.'

He stared into Dr Mann's eyes.

'You said infection. And my wife? What'll happen to my wife?'

'I was coming to that. It is essential that Mrs Jordan comes in for the same test, and as soon as possible. She may not be infected, but we have to check. You, Mr Jordan, at present have no problems. You have a strong physique and I would advise you to change your lifestyle fairly radically. You must live as healthily as possible and try to avoid alcohol, and naturally also drugs. And you ought to use condoms.'

Brad heard all this in a fog. It just couldn't be true. He wanted to wake up from this bad dream and go on with his life. He was going to die of a disease that afflicted homosexuals, and it was possible that his wife was also infected. How could he possibly tell her that?

From this day on their lives would be changed for ever.

Dr Mann went with him to the door.

'Ask your wife to come in for a test. On Monday. It's important. I'm very sorry, Mr Jordan. Are you all right?'

Brad mumbled something and avoided the doctor's eyes as he left the office, Dr Mann's words echoing in his ears. In less than an hour, his whole world had collapsed.

It was six o'clock and as usual on a Friday evening the traffic was heavy. Brad drove down Wilshire Boulevard to Santa Monica and turned left on Main Street. He parked the car and went into Chez Jay, a small fish restaurant very popular with the industry. He needed a drink to get his head together.

'Vodka and lime, please. A double.'

'Brad!' The bartender stared at him. 'Haven't seen you for a while.'

'No, I've been busy. New TV series coming up.'

'Good. We've missed you on the screen.'

Brad knocked back the double vodka and ordered two more. He put two twenty dollar bills down on the counter.

'See ya!'

He could feel the drink taking effect.

He got into his red open top Corvette and headed for Malibu on the Pacific Coast Highway past the turn off for Big Rock, Moon Shadows restaurant, Malibu Pier, the Colony, Pepperdine University and up Malibu Canyon Road. He drove at a furious speed past the great brick castle some mad dentist had built in the '70s. Suddenly he knew the solution to his problems.

It had grown dark. Brad switched on the lights and accelerated. The car was heavy but immensely fast. He loved the feeling of control.

The curves were sharp, with the mountain on one side of the road and on the other a sheer drop.

As he came to a straight bit of road, he put his foot down. At the next bend the red Corvette flew soundlessly over the steep edge, then apparently hung suspended for a moment or two in the air before falling the six hundred feet straight down into the ravine. As it hit the ground the petrol tank exploded and in a few seconds the car was engulfed in a mass of flames.

Monica sat up waiting all night. She couldn't understand what had happened to Brad. She hadn't heard a word from him. She knew he went to see Dr Mann that afternoon, but it wasn't like him to go out on a Friday night without telling her.

Monica was sick with worry. Perhaps he'd had a relapse and crashed out somewhere. She knew it was very late, but she had to phone Tom. Perhaps he'd heard something.

'Don't worry. He's probably out drinking with some friends.' Tom sounded unconcerned.

Monica could do nothing but wait. She roamed uneasily round the house. Where could he be? In the end she went to bed.

At half past four in the morning, the telephone ringing woke her. Sleepily, she fumbled for the receiver, but was at once wide awake when she saw that Brad's side of the bed was empty.

'Mrs Jordan? This is Captain Ronson. Highway Patrol. There's been an accident . . .'

The front page of the *LA Times* carried a photo of the wreckage and details of the accident in the Sunday edition. It had already been on the news on all the channels on the Saturday and the fans had poured into the ravine where the accident had happened.

Monica had to be strong. She had Tanya to think of, who was devastated with grief. Brad had been like a father to her and it hadn't been possible to hide the truth from her. They only had to switch on the radio or television to hear all the terrible details.

Monica also had to cope with her show on Monday morning. She needed all the strength she could summon. Her team had been wonderfully supportive and her producer had asked if she really felt she could go on.

But worst of all had been the photographers waiting outside the studio for the grieving widow going to work only two days after her husband's death.

How could they be so cruel? Couldn't they leave her alone?

Tom was at her side all the time, and he'd helped her get into the studio and kept away intrusive photographers.

Her show, already a great success, was expected to get its highest ratings ever on that day. The whole of California would be watching her. Would she collapse? Would it show that she'd been crying?

But Monica got through without breaking down. She couldn't allow her personal tragedy to affect her work. Afterwards, she collapsed in her office, crying.

'Monica, telephone for you.'

'Not now, Rita.' Monica tried to stop the tears.

'It's very important. It's Dr Mann.'

Monica went to the phone at once.

'Mrs Jordan, we must have a talk. Could you come here as soon as possible? It's very important.'

'Is it about Brad?'

'Yes, in a way. But it also very much concerns you.'

Monica left the car outside Dr Mann's surgery and took a taxi home without giving a thought to how she was to get it back. All she knew was that she was not in a fit state to drive.

The tan faded from her face, she was white with shock. So it hadn't been an accident. He had taken his own life. He hadn't been able to face her.

Monica felt sick. All she could think about was Tanya. Supposing she, too, had been infected? With GRID.

She had read about the disease in *People Magazine*. The article showed a photograph of a man with sores all over his body and had said it was apparently a new type of cancer that affected homosexual men.

This was a nightmare.

Dr Mann had insisted that Monica took the test at once, and now she had to wait a whole week for a result which might be a death sentence.

When Monica got back home, Tanya at once rushed up to her, but she couldn't take any more.

'Tanya, sweetheart. I need to be alone for a while. Could you go in to Concita for a bit?'

As usual, Tanya was understanding and did as Monica had asked her. It hurt to have to reject her daughter when she knew she was suffering just as much as she was herself.

Monica went into the bathroom and with trembling hands opened the bathroom cupboard. She took some pills out of a bottle and mechanically walked to the bar in the living room to pour herself a glass of vodka. She grimaced as she washed down the three Valium.

23

'Could you please call Carla and ask her to come to the office today. I haven't seen her for a week or two now, and you know what it usually means when they avoid coming here.'

'That they're fat.'

'Something like that, yes. Just see she gets here. Think up anything you like.'

'By the way, have you got a moment?'

'Certainly not, but OK. What is it?'

'I was thinking about Sonja . . .'

'What's the matter with her now?'

'I think she's homesick. Nothing much has happened for her, and rumour has it she's giving up. She wants to go back to Germany.'

'Over my dead body. We've already paid for her flight and her keep. She's staying until she's earned what she owes us. I'll call her this afternoon and say we've got a suggestion for a Calvin Klein ad . . . I'll think up something else. We'll tell her the job is in three weeks' time. Then we can always say they changed their minds. Just see to it that I know what's going on with her.'

The Brook Model Agency was buzzing with life, five full-time staff sitting round the booking table with the classic roundabout of all the models' files in the middle. The telephones were ringing ceaselessly and a stream of assistants and messengers kept coming in and out. The only thing missing were the models.

No model, however famous, ventured into the heart of the agency, the actual booking room. They went there if they were summoned, but hardly even then, as each model usually had

333

individual conversations with her own booking agent in a neigh-bouring room.

It was five in the evening and the telephones were humming. Between five and six the models phoned in to find out if they had a job or whether they had some 'go-sees' the following day.

When a hundred and fifty models called in at the same time it was total chaos and it was also always the models with the least work who were most likely to phone. The agents had to chase up the others like mad to get hold of them. Usually they had to follow them up at home, sometimes trying all night to get hold of them.

Lisa looked uneasily at her watch. She had to be finished by six when they were all to meet up at Marlene's.

She knew exactly what these meetings were about. They were to ensure 'the coming generation', i.e. the new young models the agent would be living off in the future. Those decorating the covers of today's fashion mags would soon be too old.

Once past twenty, things could only go downhill. Every agent had his or her own plant file, as they called the file in which they collected young girls from eight upwards. Then they had to follow up their development and see how they shaped up. It was unusual for the one for whom they had the highest hopes to develop in the wrong direction.

Things had been stressful lately, to say the least. Time was run-ning out and there would soon be only two weeks left to come up with new faces for the Dior make-up campaign. Such a presen-tation happened about once in four years; landing a contract as big as this meant the agency could carry on for at least another year.

Over recent weeks it had been thrashed out which girls were to be presented. Talent scouts were scouring the US. What was demanded was an entirely unknown quantity in the context of modelling and that she should be as young as possible. The make-up photographs were often so close that the least little wrinkle could spoil everything.

There were certainly candidates to present, but Marlene was not entirely satisfied. There was always something wrong. Top of the list was a fourteen year old from Texas, but the negotiations had fallen through as her parents had refused to let the girl go through with a nose-job. There was actually nothing whatsoever wrong with her nose when you looked at her, but it came out in the photographs. A shadow or two on the tip of her nose put an end to a promising future. It was one of the first things Lisa had learnt when she'd started at the agency as an assistant five years ago. No hopes should ever be put into a model until you had her – and her nose – on a photograph. A passport photo was often sufficient.

In the end, they had found it difficult to distinguish between one scared fourteen year old and the next after looking at the hundreds of Polaroids supplied by the talent scouts. As Lisa set off for Marlene's she wasn't hopeful of any kind of real breakthrough.

A booking agent's loyalty lay between the client and the model. It was her job to know the market, keep contact with photographers, stylists and clients, as well as placing the right model for the right product and negotiating the contract. She was quite simply responsible for the model's career and often worked twelve hours a day.

Lisa tried to spend as little time as possible on the telephone in her leisure time, as she was so heartily sick of sitting with the receiver clamped between her shoulder and her ear. Before, she had been able to sit for hours like that, but these days she had become extremely curt.

As she'd expected, the meeting hadn't really told Lisa anything she didn't already know. It was the same old story – the hourglass was running out and they simply had to come up with a few names.

Lisa stepped out into the cold New York air. Her reflection in the lift mirror had not been a pleasant one. Being a booking agent, apart from total devotion to the telephone, also entailed endless cups of coffee and cigarettes every day. There were plenty of assistants and apprentices, and without thinking about it, another cup would be supplied. Then it became a cigarette per telephone call. Sometimes Lisa had three cigarettes on the go at once.

Lisa thought that half an hour in the solarium would perhaps hide her sins. Portofino Sun on Fifth Street was open until nine at night. It was easier to get up in the morning if you had a bit of a tan.

Lisa struggled up the steep stairs. All model agents had a

335

discount there. A sunbed usually cost a fortune.

'Hi, any sunbeds free?'

'When?'

'Well, now actually. Don't tell me you haven't. You can see I'm in urgent need of treatment.'

The girl behind the desk laughed. The woman was right.

'You can have number five, but it won't be ready for twenty minutes. Sit yourself down with a mag in the meantime.'

Lisa sat down and poured a cup of coffee from the thermos on the table in front of her.

She absently riffled through the heap of magazines. *Vogue*? No, not another fashion magazine. Not in her free time. That was a hard and fast rule. That was what they did all day, looking for models in magazines, tearing out pages and putting them into a file. No, *National Inquirer* was better. A little smutty gossip was just what she needed.

She lit a cigarette and smiled to herself as she leafed through the paper. It really was beyond belief.

Suddenly her eyes fell on a report on the opening of some restaurant in Los Angeles. She couldn't take her eyes off what she saw. She kind of slid to her feet, the paper still in her hand. In all the years in her profession, Lisa had never seen anyone quite so beautiful.

Long dark hair, classic beauty. And, as far as she could see, the most perfect body and incredibly long legs.

Lisa even found it hard to tear her eyes away from the photo to find out who she was. She couldn't be anything else but a model. 'Talk show host Monica Clarke with daughter at opening of . . .'

'Your sunbed's ready.'

'I'm . . . er, I'm sorry. I can't . . . I mean, can I borrow your phone?'

The girl looked in surprise as the confused woman desperately collected up her belongings from the sofa. Holding the solarium's paper firmly clamped in her hand, she went over to the phone, and her fingers drummed angrily on the table as she waited for a reply.

'Thank God you haven't left. No, nothing's happened. Yes, actually, something has. I've found her.'

'Who? Who've you found?'

'Of course we've got to investigate whether she's got a contract with anyone, but if she had it would have said so.'

'Lisa, may I ask what you're talking about?'

Maggie, their office manager, sounded bewildered.

'Stay right where you are. I'll be at the office in half an hour. No, I'll take a cab. I'll be there in fifteen minutes.'

Without even explaining to the receptionist why she couldn't stay and why in God's name she was stealing their paper, Lisa raced down the stairs, out on to the street, and hailed a cab.

Maggie was just as entranced as Lisa by what she saw. She knew all about Monica Clarke and was a walking encyclopaedia when it came to her life. Miss Clarke had a TV show in California called 'This is LA' and she'd been married to Brad Jordan, the soap star who had been killed in a car accident a few years ago.

'Lisa, you must remember – he was in "The Family"? Tall, stunning-looking, sun-tanned, you know.'

'Maggie, that could be any star from LA.'

'Yes, but he was . . .'

Lisa nodded. 'Maggie, I was only joking. Of course I know who he was. He was my great love when I was a teenager. It just didn't click. Her name's Clarke.'

'Yes, that was something . . . she must've used her maiden name for her show or something.'

'How long is it since he died?'

'I think he was killed in 1984, so that's three years ago. They say he was up to the eyeballs with drugs when it happened.'

Research on the girl began that very same evening. Maggie rang round all the contacts she had on the west coast and they'd never even heard of her.

'As long as she hasn't an agent already.'

'Don't be too hopeful. With those looks it'd be a miracle if she didn't have an agent in every town in the States and Europe.'

It was the dream of all agents to be the first to find a star. Then they became what was called a Mother agent and had the right to decide in which agencies the new star should be placed in other countries. Most important of all, as Mother agents, they received a

337

percentage of all the star's fees wherever she was working, for ever. That is, as long as she was working as a model. The agent could make big money without having anything to do with bookings.

Maggie crumpled up yet another empty cigarette pack. It was late now and not easy to get hold of anyone, but this couldn't wait until morning. Now what were they to do? The *National Inquirer* had come out the day before, so hundreds of agents would be on the telephone by now. She saw Lisa waving at her from the other side of the table.

She had piled her long hair up into a knot on the top of her head and then stuck a pencil in it. The telephone receiver was as usual jammed between ear and shoulder, and now she was holding up her thumb. Then she scribbled something down on a piece of paper and triumphantly held it up.

'Her name's Tanya.'

Before they went home that night, they had all the information they wanted. They knew that Monica Clarke would be in the studio early the next morning.

It turned out not to be all that easy to get Miss Clarke on the line. 'This is LA' was very successful and the presenter employed underlings whose main task was to keep unwelcome telephone calls and visitors at bay.

'Who did you say you were? Have you a telephone appointment with Miss Clarke? What is it about? Have you anything to do with the show?'

After several hours on the phone, they managed to get as far as one of Miss Clarke's two personal secretaries, Rita. This Rita was very formal, but informed them that the Brook Model Agency was well known to her; unfortunately Miss Clarke was extremely busy, though she promised to tell her that they had telephoned.

The only thing they could do was to fly over there. Without the slightest hesitation, Marlene gave her approval.

'I'll sign any expense sheet as long as you bring back the girl's name on a contract. We'll buy up all the copies of the *National Inquirer* if we have to. That girl's ours!'

With nothing but a vague promise of a moment with Monica

Clarke on Tuesday afternoon, Lisa and Maggie were booked on a flight to Los Angeles.

Monica settled into the black limousine. Her chauffeur, Manny, who'd driven her for two and a half years, turned round.

'Home, Miss Clarke, or . . .'

'Yes, home, and quickly. I've an appointment with some people to whom I have absolutely nothing to say.'

Monica's television show had turned into a huge success. The content of the programme was so mixed that it was impossible to say whether it was following a certain pattern. Perhaps that was the key to its success. The programme had never become routine, so no one knew from one programme to the next what was going to happen.

She'd had a mother and son on one of her shows, the son HIV positive, a very controversial subject. A public outcry had arisen when Monica had told viewers that she too had lived with an infected man and what horror that had entailed. She had not said his name and as a result the newspapers were full of speculations. Naturally, the ratings soared.

Linda, her old boss, begged and prayed.

'Can't we do an interview? I promise you'll have the front page of *Life, People, Vanity Fair*, well, anyone we go to.'

'No, Linda. I can't go any further than that. What I said had a direct connection with the programme. I won't be doing anything more on the subject.'

What had happened three years ago still pained her. The horror of losing her husband and the possibility that she or Tanya had tested positive had paralysed her. She had been so dazed with Valium the day she'd been back to see Dr Mann that she could hardly remember what he'd said.

Monica often took up subjects she herself had experienced and she was now in the middle of planning a programme on transvestites. She spent a vast amount of time with the research team. Perhaps now that so many years had gone by, she could find a way to put Gordon's behaviour into perspective a little more, and learn to understand why.

It was painful to talk about such things, but she needed to for her own personal development. She had been through so much pain in her life that she was no longer afraid of working on her problems, if necessary in public.

And that made Monica very popular. The show was still put on between ten and half past on Wednesday mornings, when housewives and those a little older might be watching television. She had a large audience, but now they were negotiating to move her to an evening slot. They were convinced they would then have an even larger audience. Monica looked forward to the challenge. She wanted to reach as many people as possible.

Her life since Brad's death had consisted of work, work and more work. And Tanya, of course. Tanya had spent eighteen months at a boarding school up in the mountains near Palm Springs, two hours by car from Los Angeles. The school had thought a ten year old rather young to board, but as Tanya was unusually mature for her age, they had accepted her. Tanya was not happy to leave home, but when Monica promised her a horse of her own, she forgot all her objections.

But after eighteen months Monica couldn't stand it any longer. She wanted the company of her daughter and Tanya was overjoyed to be heading home at last.

'Both BB and I are longing to see you,' Monica had told her, trying to fight back the tears. 'Do you know he still sleeps on your bed every night?'

The only trouble had been the horse, but Monica found stables in Brentwood. Tanya's homecoming was the high point of the year.

Now Monica was on her way home. It took her half an hour from the studio to her home in Bel Air. As they drove along Bel Air Road, she noticed a strange red hire car outside her house. Just as well her secretary Rita lived with her so that she could look after these people in the meantime.

'See you tomorrow, Manny. I won't be needing you any more today.'

''Bye Miss Clarke.' Manny gave her a discreet salute, touching the peak of his cap.

Monica blew him a kiss.

She still had the figure of a teenager although she was now forty-nine. She was dressed all in black, the narrow pants accentuating her perfect figure even more, the high-heeled shoes making her look taller than she really was.

There was no doubt about it, the woman who got out of the car was indeed a beauty, always elegantly dressed, usually slightly soberly for her show. She wore her hair short these days, and today she was wearing a big black cartwheel hat. She picked up her suede bag and saw Rita coming out of the house.

'They've come.'

'Who are they again?' Monica couldn't for the life of her remember who she was supposed to meet, although Rita had told her over the phone just before she'd left the studio.

'They're from the Brook Model Agency in New York.'

That still didn't ring a bell with Monica, and Rita, used to having to remind Monica about most things, carefully repeated what they'd come about. She knew how embarrassed Monica was about constantly forgetting things.

'It's about Tanya,' Rita said. 'I wanted to prepare you. One's called Lisa. That's the young one with long dark hair. And the fat blonde one's called Maggie.'

Monica tried to memorise them: dark hair, Lisa, fair hair, Maggie. She repeated it several times to herself as she went on in.

She hated meeting new people. When she was working she used the auto-cue. Names were the worst, and recently she was finding it difficult to keep places apart, too. But there was always help at hand at the studio and if the worst came to the worst she could hear the producer in her ear. She had a small coil which was always in contact with the control room where he was sitting.

Monica went into the living room and across to the two women on the sofa by the fire. That was it. One with long dark hair, the other is short and fair, but which was which? She listened carefully when the women got up to introduce themselves, trying to concentrate and memorise their names.

Concita came in.

'What would you like to drink, Miss Clarke?'

Monica looked at her guests enquiringly and they accepted

their hostess's suggestion for a cup of English tea.

Monica handed her Louis Vuitton briefcase to Rita who disappeared into the next room with it.

The two women wasted no time, and after a brief comment on Monica's show, they went straight to the point.

'Miss Clarke, we've seen a photograph of your daughter Tanya in the *National Inquirer* and we can assure you everyone at the Brook Model Agency is enchanted by her. I suppose you've heard of us?'

Monica nodded and sipped her tea.

They went on to explain how their organisation worked and how seriously they took it. Monica began to wonder whether they would ever stop. She did her best to appear as interested as possible, smiling and nodding whenever it seemed appropriate. It all seemed to be about some kind of make-up contract for Christian Dior, and these women were sure that Tanya would be the right one for the job, although they had seen only a photograph in a gossip mag.

'Are you aware that my daughter won't be twelve until December?'

It was perfectly clear from both Maggie's and Lisa's expressions that they were not. Maggie broke the silence that had settled on the room.

'To be honest, no. From the photographs we took her to be at least two years older.'

'My daughter is very mature for her age, both physically and mentally.'

'Miss Clarke, is your daughter here? Could we possibly see her?'

Monica got up and excused herself for a moment.

'What do you think?' said Lisa thoughtfully.

Maggie shrugged. 'Hard to say. Seems rather vague. Impossible to say whether we've convinced her or not. If it doesn't work with the daughter, we could always use her. How old do you think she is?'

'They say she's pushing fifty.'

'Can't be possible. She looks about thirty-five.'

'Must be a face lift.'

The two women tittered. A moment later a black and grey dog

with a tennis ball in its mouth came tearing into the room. And behind it came The Girl.

Maggie had been worried to hear Tanya was so young. Perhaps their trip had been a waste of time. But now she was astounded. Tanya was if anything even more beautiful in real life than they could have imagined.

BB's paws were suddenly up on Maggie's plump knees and Tanya rushed forward to squat down in front of her.

'Please excuse BB. He loves strangers. He'd really be the very worst possible guard dog.'

Maggie couldn't believe it. She had never in her life before seen such blue eyes. And her complexion ... like a peach. Maggie just stared.

'Is everything OK?' said Tanya uneasily.

'Yes, yes, forgive me. I wasn't thinking.'

Maggie got up and introduced herself and Lisa.

Monica came up behind Tanya and put one hand on her daughter's shoulder.

'Tanya, they have come from ... sorry, I forgot ...'

Rita intervened from behind.

'The Brook Model Agency.'

Maggie and Lisa explained what a model agency was and showed them their prospectus. They had even brought with them various composites, a model's visiting card on which she showed as many sides of herself as possible, full face on the front and one or two full-length figures on the back of the card together with all her measurements.

Tanya gazed in amazement at all the material. She knew some of the models the Brook agency represented, and had read about the agency as well. Like many young girls her dream was to become a model. She found it difficult to hide her enthusiasm.

'I'm very pleased to have met you and hope to see you again soon,' she said politely, then left the room to allow the two women to go on talking to Monica.

'If we were to accept your proposal to make Tanya into a model, what would that entail, in practical terms?'

Monica was used to advantageous contracts, but was still surprised at the offer. They were willing to contract Tanya for a year and over that period would guarantee her a minimum income of two hundred thousand dollars, regardless of whether she were working or not. Added to that, they would pay for all her flights to and from New York and hotel bills for both her and the guardian who came with her. They would also pay for a private tutor so that Tanya did not miss out on any schooling.

All she had to do was to stay in New York for four weeks. They would pay for the car that would take Tanya to and from client contacts. There would be only a few clients. The first week would be spent taking various test photographs, so they could put together a portfolio.

After a month, she would be quite free to go home again in order to go to direct bookings. The client would then fly Tanya specially to the job she was to do. On those trips, the same circumstances would prevail, private tutor and so on.

Monica thanked the women and said she would talk to Tanya and then come back to them. Maggie and Lisa told her they were staying on for a few days to await their decision.

Monica heaved a sigh of relief after they had gone. She was suddenly desperate for a drink and she headed for the bar.

The car was hardly out of the driveway when Tanya and BB came rushing in.

'Mother, Mother! Can I be a model? Please!?'

Monica sipped at her drink. She still liked vodka but tried to keep her drinking to a minimum. She was acutely aware of the rumours going around that she was a secret drinker, but they weren't true. She had fallen by the wayside for a while after Brad's death, and in the end had been unable to hide it, but she now drank only very moderately. What was difficult was getting rid of the reputation. No one said anything directly to her, but she couldn't help noticing that people were talking. Sometimes there were even hints in the papers.

What she was really worried about was what the drugs had done to her. There was so much that didn't come out as it should when she was talking and she had difficulties concentrating. She reckoned her brain was not functioning as it ought to. She was quite convinced she would never have managed without Rita and Doris.

The fact was that the studio had appointed Doris just because of this. Monica needed two personal secretaries. She kept forgetting so many things, so they had to be around all the time.

The executives on her show knew she had a drinking problem but her show was a great success. They had raised no objections to increasing her budget to appoint a second secretary.

Monica looked at her lovely daughter. 'Tanya, is this really what you want to do? Do you understand what they want? They're some kind of model agency.'

'Monica,' Rita broke in. 'They're the most famous model agency in the whole world!'

Monica glanced at her, then at Tanya.

'Yes, Mother. I'd be as famous as you are.'

Monica shook her head and moved towards her bedroom.

'It's true, Mother.'

'We'll talk about it tomorrow, Tanya. First I must have my attorney go through the contract. Then we can discuss it further.'

'But I want to do it, Mother.'

'It's no good going on about it, Tanya,' she called over her shoulder. 'I've told you I'll think about it.'

Monica knew her daughter was beautiful, but that they were prepared to offer that kind of money to a child was unbelievable. She closed the door behind her and went to lie down.

Tanya followed her mother to the door, but then she rushed back to the living room and threw her arms round Rita's neck.

'Rita, you must persuade Mother. I want to be in the magazines, in beautiful photographs. Please, Rita, talk to her.'

Rita nodded patiently. 'Yes, but not today. Your mother's tired and needs rest.'

Monica's bedroom was a symphony in blue and white. This was the first real home she had owned and paid for herself. She had chosen the décor for all the rooms and was extremely proud of the result.

After Brad's death she'd put their home up for sale. She had inherited it and a third of his royalties, plus a lump sum of money. The rest had gone to his family, his mother and father and a younger sister in Ohio. Monica still kept up sporadic contact with his parents.

There had been a very short funeral service and according to his wishes his ashes had been scattered over the Pacific ocean.

Monica had rented an apartment on Wilshire Boulevard. It had top security, with a doorman and a swimming pool and gym. She had lived there with Concita until she'd found the house in Bel Air: 1782 Bel Air Road.

Her home now consisted of four bedrooms plus a room for Concita, a large living room with a fireplace, separate dining room and three bathrooms. The swimming pool was quite small and kidney-shaped, with a waterfall, the area round it fitted with wooden duckboards.

She had abandoned the Santa-Fé style she'd favoured with Brad and filled her home with Swedish antiques. From Gordon she had acquired a taste for art-glass and there were photographs of her family in silver frames everywhere. She loved her home and often had friends back for dinner. Concita turned out to be a great cook.

Monica still had the Bonniers cookbook Gerd had given her as a wedding present when she'd married Edward. It was in Swedish, of course, but Monica would stand beside Concita and translate for her.

She took great care of herself. She had a trainer who came to her home. Together, they ran up and down Bel Air Road, and then did sit ups, push ups, weights and finally stretching exercises.

Sometimes she thought how ironic it was that her life had become so like Brad's. Two Vietnamese girls came every other week to give her a manicure and pedicure, and Sitva had continued to give her massage over the years. The only thing she did outside her home, apart from the gym, was going to the hairdresser, Cale and Cale, in Beverly Hills. Jonathan, the English colourist, and Monica would spend most of the one and a half hours it took him to put highlights in her hair talking about London, complaining about how long it had been since they both had been there.

346

Monica was very much in demand. She had recently hosted 'The Best TV' Awards, and at the moment she was appearing in a commercial for Swedish Herb Shampoo. She was also involved in several different charities.

She'd had many admirers wanting to take her out to dinner, but she was concentrating everything on her career. In the past she had devoted all her time to the men in her life, but now it was different, although according to rumour, she had a relationship with the head of KTLA 5, Robert Levine, forty-two, dark and so handsome, no one could understand why he wasn't an actor. He was incredibly clever and had raised Channel 5 from being just another channel among many to being virtually pre-eminent.

Although there was a lot of talk about them, Monica didn't take it very seriously, ignoring the fact that, prompted by the appearance of the two of them at an AIDS gala Channel 5 had arranged, the rumours floating around them had increased substantially.

The telephone rang and, as usual, Rita answered.

'Monica, it's long distance. A Mr Philip Hewitt.'

Monica couldn't help wondering what on earth he wanted. She hadn't spoken to him for years. There was no mistaking his rather superior tone of voice.

Monica chatted rather absently with him, then asked him what he wanted.

'Amanda is dead, Monica. They rang me from the clinic this morning. She lived an unusually long time for someone so severely handicapped.'

She felt a stab in her heart. She'd always hoped to be able to visit her daughter one day, and now it was too late. She was both relieved and at the same time pained. She'd lived with the shadow of Amanda for so many years, unable to free herself from her guilt, which went back to the time they had lied to everyone about the child's existence.

'I must warn you, Monica,' Philip went on, 'apparently some American journalist has been snooping around. They were afraid someone had sold the information to the American press.'

347

'What are you saying? How could that have happened?'

'I don't know much more, but I want you to be prepared for a photograph to be published.'

'Photo? There aren't any photographs.'

'Well, apparently an old group photograph is missing from the wall in the day room. It's all rather extraordinary.'

Monica struggled with the cable to get it to reach as far as the bar. Her throat was dry and she needed a drink. What would they say in the papers? And what would the consequences of the scandal be? Philip went on talking about a discreet funeral, but Monica's thoughts were far away. Severely brain-damaged children rarely lived longer than twelve years, but Amanda had been twenty-three.

When Monica put the receiver down, she collapsed like a small child. Amazingly, she was almost angry. Angry with herself for not having accommodated her daughter into her life, angry with Amanda for dying. She hoped the headlines wouldn't be too terrible and that they would not spread to England. What would Robert say?

Philip had assured her that Robert knew nothing and he'd advised her not to talk about it unless absolutely necessary. He would keep an eye on the papers there and let her know if anything appeared. Monica was grateful. When it came to Robert, he was extremely loyal.

She decided to go to England and stay at Hewitt Hall as soon as she could take the time off. In many ways she longed to be there, not just to see Robert, but to be back at the Hall that had been her home for so many years.

The next day there were photographs in the *National Inquirer*, the *Globe* and the *Star*, the same blurred picture of ten or so young handicapped children in a typical school class group, with a ring round a girl whose features were barely discernible.

THIS IS WHAT SHE LEFT BEHIND was the headline that hit Monica when Rita brought in the papers. Rita patted her comfortingly on the back.

'Aren't they bastards. It must be very hard for you.'

Monica stared at the blurred photograph. This was all she had ever seen of her daughter, who couldn't have been more than five or six when it was taken. Having tossed and turned all night Monica no longer felt any guilt. She knew Amanda wouldn't have been able to comprehend where or who she was, but the way it looked in the newspaper was terrible, just what she didn't need at this moment.

Jay Stein, who saw to her PR now, came by in the afternoon and they discussed what measures should be taken. They agreed it would be best to ignore it for the time being.

When she arrived at the studio there were inevitably reporters outside, but Monica made no comment. She had already found a way to confront them. She would make a programme on severely brain-damaged children. She was all enthusiasm and at once set her research team to work. Why hadn't she thought of that immediately?

Jay put out a press statement saying that Miss Clarke had no comment to make, but the subject of her next programme was to be just that.

The producers rubbed their hands. This was sure to produce record ratings.

Monica's attorney called, but she couldn't for the life of her think what contract he was talking about. Model agencies and Tanya? What was it all about? She had to tell him she'd call back.

'Rita, do you know anything about a model agency wanting Tanya?'

That kind of thing happened more and more often now. Some things vanished completely from her memory. On one occasion, fortunately after the show, she had disappeared from the studio. Rita had found her in a state of confusion out on the street, and Monica had no idea what she was doing there.

Rita and Doris had been instructed to make sure she didn't drink at work, and in fact they had never seen her touch a drop or noticed the smell of alcohol on her breath. If Monica drank, then she was certainly very discreet about it.

Once she'd had the situation explained to her again Monica could see no objection to Tanya signing on with the agency if that was what she wanted. It was decided that Rita should go to New York with her for the first week. Then Megan, her private tutor, would take over the responsibility. It was only for a month and Tanya was so excited.

She would be back in time for Christmas, which they would spend in Aspen as usual. Originally Monica had planned to go to England, but there hadn't been time, she was so busy. She hadn't been for so long, and she really missed it. Thankfully, it looked as if Robert would be able to get away and come to Colorado.

Robert and Katarina were the only people in England with whom she kept regular contact. She was making plans to invite Katarina over to LA and spoke to her on the phone at least once a month.

Katarina had done an about-turn in her life, no doubt very necessary. She now did yoga and was working in a health-food store, having given up all drugs and alcohol. She lived in Notting Hill Gate. Rita typed out Monica's dictated letters to Katarina for her, because Monica found writing difficult as she was unable to collect her thoughts sufficiently. All her concentration went on making one good programme a week and working in the office almost every single day. She hadn't had a holiday for a whole year, but that was her own choice. She was content as long as she had peace and quiet in her free time.

Christmas had been quite wonderful. Not only had Robert come, but he had also brought his girl-friend, Sarah Dimbleby, which had pleased Monica. She was the daughter of one of the Queen's private secretaries. Sarah and Robert suited each other perfectly.

They had all stayed in Aspen for a week and then Robert came with her to Los Angeles. Sarah had to go back to England, which suited Monica, not because they didn't get on well, on the contrary, but it was wonderful to have her son all to herself.

Relations had at first been slightly strained between Robert and Tanya. They didn't really know each other, but had gradually made friends.

She had talked to Robert about Amanda. The scandal had hit England just as he was leaving. They sat up all night talking; he'd been very upset that he'd lived with a lie all that time.

Monica had done everything to keep her wits together. There were so many gaps in her memory from that period in her life, but she'd explained that it had been his father's decision. She was not proud of agreeing to it, but she had been very young and hadn't known any better.

Tearfully, Monica said that she realised he might find it difficult to like Tanya when there was so much of Crispin in her. Robert gently put his fingers to her lips and looked straight at her.

'That's forgotten now, Mother,' he said firmly. 'It's behind me. It took a long time, but I'm free of it now. It has absolutely nothing to do with Tanya. She's a wonderful girl.'

Monica was flooded with relief: it had been the conversation she should have had with him several years ago. She loved her son so much and was grateful that they had found their way back to each other.

Tanya's spell in New York had been like a dream. She'd had to do only one test photo. The camera loved her, and Marlene and her husband Harry had looked after her as if she'd been their own child. Her face had no bad angles and the photographer said she was probably the most easily photographed model he had ever worked with. She was a natural.

In February, Maggie flew in from New York to confirm that the Dior contract would be Tanya's if she could lose fourteen pounds. Monica thought she was mad, honestly, fourteen pounds, Tanya was already very thin. But Maggie had explained that the camera always adds ten pounds and that Tanya still had some of the baby fat in her face so common in girls of that age. They had calculated that the weight loss would bring out her cheekbones.

A contract of that kind was worth several millions, Maggie explained, but it also demanded sole right to her for a year.

Monica thought hard about it. To allow a thirteen year old to lose that much weight could not be good for her health. But Maggie had protested that it would be no problem. She had invited Tanya to New York where they would put her on a carefully controlled nutritional diet. It would be best if she stayed for

351

a month because it was not good to lose weight quickly.

Monica considered what Maggie was proposing insane, however much money was involved. She knew it wouldn't be easy to tell Tanya, but as her mother she had to be hard and not give in. Tanya's career as a model would have to wait.

Maggie was waiting at JFK. She had a limousine ready to take Tanya and Megan to Marlene and Harry's house. They were going to live there during their stay in New York. They were not alone, for the house was full of young models.

On the very first day, Tanya had to meet a dietician and her personal coach. Her diet consisted of half a grapefruit and a cup of tea every morning, an extremely sparse salad for lunch and if she were really lucky a piece of cooked meat. Dinner was not much better. Once a week it consisted of half a chicken breast with no skin and that was a feast. After a while Tanya felt sick at the very thought of haricots verts or pineapple, which seemed to come with every meal except breakfast. She lied to Monica every time she phoned, saying it wasn't all that bad and she was allowed to eat as much as she felt like.

She spent most of her free time with Megan and her school work, but there was also time to go out. Everything was so big in New York. Tanya almost got a crick in her neck looking up at all the skyscrapers. Best of all she liked the department stores. Tanya loved going to the cosmetic counters, where one day her picture would be advertising the product.

On their way home she used to stop outside restaurants and cafés, just gazing longingly, her mouth watering at the very thought of food. She had always eaten when she was hungry and was used to a full fridge at home in Bel Air. Being hungry was a new experience. Not a day went by without her getting a headache from tension and she nearly always felt sick during her training sessions. But she wanted to lose those pounds so that she would be perfect.

She began to compare herself with every girl she saw. She took armfuls of the fashion magazines lying around the house into her room and then sat sighing over the pencil-slim models. She looked at herself in the mirror. Why hadn't she noticed before? Her face really was fat, and there were only three weeks left until the next photo test.

Tanya started spending more time at the agency, fascinated by everything that went on in that world. She saw models she recognised from the fashion magazines coming and going; they were almost unrecognisable without any make-up.

Usually Tanya didn't finish everything on her plate, as if it made her feel guilty to eat that little piece of lamb with haricots verts. The fewer mouthfuls, the fewer calories. The fewer calories, the slimmer she would be. It was worst in the evenings. During the day so much was happening, but in the evenings the pangs of hunger came, her stomach ached, and so did her head.

In the daytime, she went jogging in Central Park with Karen, her trainer, then they set off for Ragu, the gym where they worked with weights for an hour. She'd also tried skating in Central Park. She had never skated before, but to Karen's delight, she liked it and it was excellent exercise for her calves and thighs.

Tanya also had to give up chewing gum, which she loved above all else. But her dietician told her that made her hunger worse.

One day when Tanya was in a drug store buying some soap and talcum powder, the temptation was too great, she took a Mars Bar, looked round so that no one should see, then slipped it into her pocket. She hadn't meant to steal, but Karen was waiting for her at the check-out.

Tanya and Karen walked down 72nd Street past the Ralph Lauren boutique. Cautiously, Tanya felt the chocolate in her pocket. No, she wouldn't eat it, she thought luxuriously, it was enough to feel it.

It turned out just as she had thought. That night the pangs of hunger again got their claws into her and she couldn't stop herself. She got up and fumbled for the jacket. There it was. Without a second's thought, half of the Mars Bar was in her mouth. Oh, how good it was. She simply couldn't control herself and, cramming the rest in, closed her eyes with pleasure as she munched the toffee and chocolate.

The moment she had swallowed, panic seized her. What had she done? They had told her about the well-balanced diet she was on and how important it was not to eat anything beyond it. Supposing she had spoilt everything now? Two weeks wasted! Supposing they began wondering why she wasn't losing weight?

Tanya was stricken with panic and shame. Suddenly she knew what she should do. Of course. Why hadn't she thought of it before?

She went to the bathroom, turned on the hot and the cold taps and knelt down in front of the toilet bowl. Then she stuck two fingers down her throat. Tears spurting down her cheeks, she pressed them even further down . . . at last.

Tanya had found a way of getting rid of those calories.

'How do you like it here in New York?' said Lisa, looking at Tanya as they sat in the model room for their regular once-a-week conversation. They had talked about how much weight she'd lost, and the make-up artist had made a sketch of her face showing which cosmetics they should use for the test.

'It's fine,' Tanya smiled. These 'chats' always made her a little nervous.

'Your training, then? Do you think you're making any progress? By the way, have you had time to see anything of New York, or has it been all work?'

'It depends what you mean by "see". I've been and looked round the stores.'

'No, I meant the sights, museums and so on.'

'No, but I . . .'

Lisa suddenly thought she had neglected the poor little thing. Everyone was so keen that she should eat properly and train that they'd forgotten to bother about her social life.

'Have you been to SoHo, Tanya?'

'Where?'

'Oh, you'd love it. It's all boutiques and little cafés and galleries. I'm thinking of going to some exhibitions there on Saturday. If you like, we could go together. Though maybe you're not interested in art?'

'Oh, yes, I've painted ever since I was a kid.'

'Good! At least three artists are having private views on Saturday. I think you'd like it. Then I'll take you to Chinatown and Little Italy so that you can see that, too. They're quite close by.'

Tanya was looking forward to going out with Lisa. She felt grown up when she thought about the two of them going out as friends. Lisa was ancient, of course, at least twenty-four or -five, but still, it would be a welcome change. So far the highlight in her day had been her secret candy bar. She made it a routine every day to take something from a store and put it into her pocket. She then ate it in secret and got rid of it in the bathroom immediately afterwards. It wasn't too bad any longer. Only the first time had been really awful. Once she knew the technique, it went really well. All day she looked forward to the highpoint when she could eat what she had taken, usually in the bathroom. Recently she had gobbled candies on several occasions and then thrown up. She didn't actually have to be at home. There were public conveniences as well.

At last Saturday came. They started at a little café called Dean and DeLuca. Lisa had ordered a cappuccino and Tanya wanted one as well. She didn't drink coffee, but today she had decided to start – though because of the diet it would have to be espresso. But at least that was more sophisticated than a soda.

Lisa, drawing on her cigarette and glancing up from her glossy preview brochures, smiled at her as they sat by the big window facing the street. It looked grown up to smoke and for a moment Tanya thought of asking for a cigarette, but then she changed her mind.

'I was wrong, Tanya,' Lisa said, blowing out a stream of smoke. 'There are only two private shows today. The third one isn't until next week.' She fingered the two invites. 'One of the artists is called Brian O'Neill and the other Quintin, no, I read that wrong, Crispin Que.'

24

'This is LA' was going out in an evening slot for the first time. The idea had been to move the show much earlier, but negotiations had dragged on and the rumours about Monica's alcohol and drugs problems had been one of the reasons it had been postponed.

No one knew for sure when she drank because, other than her memory lapses and confused speech, there were few signs and nothing could be smelt on her breath. But of course it could be as some people said – she took pills which helped her hide it.

They hadn't been certain whether they dared risk her on an evening show. She'd become more and more confused and could ask the same question three or four times within a conversation. She had even got lost in the building. It was Rita who found her. She had more or less become Monica's shadow.

The run-throughs before each programme were long and thorough, as they seemed to have to hammer information into Monica. Rita, who had always protected Monica, not telling anyone how bad things really were, was increasingly worried.

Monica had spoken to Tanya on the phone that day. She seemed to be enjoying herself in New York and clearly her diet wasn't quite as bad as she had first thought. Tanya assured her she got enough to eat, and she and Lisa had become friends. Tanya had been very excited by a trip to SoHo they were planning together.

Monica wished she had time to be with her daughter in New York, but right now, a week before the premiere, it was difficult even to find the time to phone. The run-throughs lasted almost all day and then there were the photo sessions and trailers that had

357

to be done. The coverage of her was enormous.

Jay, paying one of his increasingly frequent visits to the house, rubbed his hands in glee as they surveyed the advance publicity.

'Incredible what an impact you've made.'

Both he and Tom were real PR geniuses, that had to be admitted. They always managed to turn the worst information which had one way or another leaked out into something positive on her behalf. As Rita showed Jay out of the house, their meeting finished, she had to admit he was effective – although secretly she suspected Jay of supplying the newspapers with material about Monica's increasing drink problem, just to keep her name coming up more and more often in their columns.

Monica knew eyes were always on her; Rita hated to see her so tense. Monica never drank in public, not even a glass of wine. A recent photograph of her with a glass in her hand had made the front page of all the gossip rags. So Monica made sure she never took anything until she got home, but then she made the best of it. She actually needed little to wind down, but she herself had begun to wonder. She noticed quite a lot of the vodka had gone from the bottle, but she couldn't remember whether she'd just had a drink.

'Rita, did I have a drink, or not?' she asked.

'Yes, you've had two as far as I've seen.'

'Have I really?'

Rita bit her lip anxiously. Were things as bad as the *Star* and the *Globe* made out?

Tanya and Lisa had been to Brian O'Neill's private view and then moved on.

'Shall we go straight to the other one, or would you like a coffee first?'

Tanya wanted nothing better than to extend the afternoon and nodded in agreement when Lisa suggested a coffee.

'By the way, Tanya, tomorrow I think we'll have the final result of your latest test. Don't look so worried. The pics were wonderful. You're so beautiful it's not true, and we even managed to find your cheekbones.'

Lisa pinched her cheeks and Tanya flushed slightly. She wanted

Lisa to talk to her like an adult, not pinching her cheeks in public.

Tanya was so hungry she felt sick. Coffee clearly was not the right cure for hunger. Then she spotted a drug store across the street.

'I have to pop in to the drug store, Lisa,' she said. 'I think it's an emergency.'

Lisa laughed and said she'd wait. She had no idea that when Tanya came back she had three Mars Bars in her pocket, nor that she had both eaten and brought up two of them by the time she'd returned from the ladies room.

'Do you want your coffee, or shall we go?'

Tanya was ready for more paintings.

The Green Gallery was crowded when they got there. Lisa couldn't help commenting on how unusual it was to offer only red wine at a private view.

'Let's see now. His name is . . . Crispin Que, and he lives in the South of France. He's very well known in Europe for his abstracts and this is his first exhibition in the States.'

'Let me see. Is there a picture of him?' Tanya pulled inquisitively at the brochure.

'No, there isn't, but he ought to be around here somewhere. Maybe we'll see him later. Let's take a look at the paintings now.'

A buzz ran through the crowd and there was a lot of tut-tutting about the abstracts. Tanya didn't understand this kind of art, but was nevertheless fascinated. She gazed for a long time at a large painting called 'A Pregnant Woman in Vence'. Tanya laughed. She thought it should be called 'Pregnant Elephant in Vence'.

The next picture was a clown with a knife through his heart, blue blood pouring down his costume. Lisa thought it unusual for an abstract work of art to have such an elaborate frame.

Without exception, his paintings were remarkable. He seemed to find inspiration in the most peculiar motifs. One was of an empty cot and called 'The Lost Child'.

They went round the gallery studying the striking but strange paintings.

'I'd like to see what the man behind these pictures looks like,' Lisa murmured.

'So would I,' said Tanya.

She had one Mars Bar left and asked where the ladies room was. A guard showed her where to go.

There was a queue outside and Tanya stamped her foot with impatience, which made the woman in front of her turn round and stare at her. Tanya looked down at her clothes to see if anything was wrong, but everything seemed in order. Then the woman put her hand on her arm and with a smile leant towards her, breathing a waft of red wine over her.

'And this is young Miss Que, I suppose?'

Tanya must have looked astonished, because the woman suddenly stopped.

'Aren't you Crispin Que's daughter?'

Tanya laughed with some embarrassment. 'No, I've never even met him.'

'Oh, I'm sorry. I thought you looked so like him.'

Tanya was dying for the chocolate that was now melting. Inside the toilet she did her usual routine.

'Oh, there you are,' Lisa said, waiting for her outside the ladies room. 'You must see the artist.'

'Did you?'

'Yes, he's here.'

'Does he look like me?'

'Well, now you come to mention it, he did, a little. But how do you know that? I thought you'd never met him.'

'No, but some woman in the ladies thought I was his daughter.'

'Oh, wait a minute. Where is he now?' Lisa looked around, but couldn't see him anywhere. 'There. There he is. Look.'

'Where, where?'

'Now you've missed him. He just went out through the door.'

Tanya shrugged. 'Oh well, it doesn't matter. We've seen his pictures, that's enough for me.'

The next day Tanya was told that the contract was hers. The following week, they were going to photograph her every day so that they had as much material as possible. No fewer than seven different make-up artists were doing her face. It was so exciting, she could hardly believe it was true.

Tanya had some real doubts over the last few days. She still thought her face was too fat and she'd been panicky when it turned out she'd lost only eight pounds. She couldn't understand it. On the whole she had eaten nothing. But the dietician had explained that that was just the problem. She had to eat as much as she was told to, not leave things on her plate as she had been doing. Her body was reacting to starvation, putting its own reserve store into use, which meant her weight remained the same.

But now the contract was hers and she could always lose a couple of pounds for other jobs. She was so happy, she had to share it with someone.

'Hi, Rita. It's Tanya. I got it, I got it!'

'The contract?'

'Yes, it's mine.'

'Wonderful. I'm so happy for your sake.'

'Is Mother there?'

'Yes, but she's . . .'

'What?'

'Well, rather tired. Wait a minute and I'll ask her.'

Tanya waited for what seemed like an eternity. She could hear Rita and her mother whispering in the background.

'It's Tanya. Tanya, Monica. Can you take it?'

'Tanya, sweetheart!'

'Mother! The contract's signed.'

Again she heard Rita whispering something and Monica came back to the phone. Tanya hardly recognised her voice.

'I'm so happy for you. Is everything all right?'

'Yes, couldn't be better. Photographing all next week and yesterday Lisa and I went to a private view and saw some artists called O'Neill and Crisp—'

'I'm not feeling too well, Tanya. Can I call you back a little later?'

Tanya was disappointed. She'd been longing to tell her mother everything that had happened, but she knew it was no use going on when Monica said no.

'OK. Call me later. Promise.'

'I love you,' her mother said quietly.

'And I you.'

* * *

361

Monica had been behaving oddly all day and neither Rita nor Doris had let her out of their sight for a moment. 'This is LA' was going out for the first time in the evening.

The show centred around Nicaragua, where there had been a major earthquake. The US had sent aid, but according to the Nicaraguan president, who was in the studio, not enough. The aid convoy was leaving from LA, and the producer wanted the show to cover this important story.

It was made for colossal ratings.

The first ten minutes flowed smoothly, but the floor manager was sweating. The little red light telling Monica which camera was on her and where she had to look was no longer sufficient, he had to wave his arms to attract her attention. The auto-cue had been enlarged to make it easier for her to read.

Monica was concentrating. The moment for the conversation with the president arrived and Rita and Doris at once joined her during the commercials to assure her everything would go well. They also took the opportunity to remind her of a few essential points she had jotted on her pad.

Monica began by asking the president how much aid he considered the area afflicted by the earthquake would need. He didn't have time to reply. She suddenly seemed to change, her eyes no longer focusing, she appeared to be staring into thin air.

'Yes, it's them. They. No, I can't. They're the ones who decide.'

The president looked at her, desperately trying to work out whether this was a question.

Monica went on: 'No, them. They can see up there. It's not them and I can't because they hold on to me if they don't want to. Now you can see, I must go.'

Gregor, her producer, acted immediately, slotting in a commercial. He had plenty at his disposal as all advertising space had long since been sold out.

'Monica, what's happened?' he demanded.

Rita and Doris ran across the studio floor, Doris to deal with the bewildered president.

Gregor held on to Monica tightly.

'What's wrong?'

'Them. They've got control, but I can, can succeed, I can't see . . . No, no.'

Rita whispered something into Gregor's ear about it not being possible to go on. It was clear Monica had had a breakdown.

Carefully, they led her out, the studio now in a state of total confusion. Gregor scrambled together an explanation to be sent out on the screens:

WE WISH TO APOLOGISE BUT MONICA CLARKE HAS COLLAPSED DUE TO STRESS. WE WILL BE BACK SOON.

Rita went with Monica as Manny drove back to Bel Air. Once home, a dazed Monica sat down on the big sofa in front of the fire. It had all been too much for her Rita realised, what with the stress of the programme, rumours of drug and alcohol abuse and the accusations in the press about abandoning her handicapped child. Brad . . .

'Is there anything I can do for you?' Rita asked gently.

'No, no. I'm . . . No.'

She kept repeating no, no, all the time.

Rita went out to Concita in the kitchen. She needed something strong. It was impossible to say whether Monica had had anything to drink, but she didn't smell of alcohol. Rita sat down at the kitchen table with Concita, but suddenly they heard a terrible wail coming from the living room.

The two women rushed in immediately.

Monica had pulled all the cushions off the sofa and was lying on the floor punching them.

'You bastard, you bastard. How dare you?' She was punching the cushions as if they were real people. 'You've let me down. I hate you.' Tears were pouring down her face. 'How could . . . I hate . . . You're a Crispin, you . . .'

Her sentences remained unfinished – she seemed to be utterly possessed – they simply couldn't get through to her.

She was now throwing the cushions all over the place, calling them names: Gordon, Crispin, Philip, Edward . . . all her past lying there among the cushions.

Rita saw that this was no ordinary breakdown. Asking Concita to stay with Monica, she went and phoned Gregor.

'What do I do?' she asked, panic rising as the sound of Monica's shouting went on.

'I'll call a doctor and send him to Bel Air as soon as possible. Wait there for the time being.'

Twenty minutes later, Dr Waltman, a young Jewish psychiatrist working at the Cedars of Sinai Hospital, arrived. As he came into the living room he bent down beside Monica and started talking; she took no notice of him. She had collapsed, exhausted and sweating on the cushions.

As the doctor couldn't get through to her, he called for an ambulance. He then gave her an injection which instantly calmed her down. Rita sat next to her on the floor holding her hand, waiting for the ambulance to arrive.

She was taken to the Cedars of Sinai where she was admitted for observation. For ten days she was sedated while various tests were carried out.

Meanwhile the TV station put out repeats of 'This is LA', as most of the evening viewers had not seen them.

The headlines were not amusing:

DRUNKEN MONICA CLARKE FORCED OUT OF SHOW

It was not much better on the news, the judgements more or less the same. They said she had been so drunk, she hadn't been able to read the auto-cue. Her drinking had finally resulted in a nervous breakdown.

Tanya was in the middle of a shoot in New York when she heard the news and flew to LA as soon as her photo session was over. She didn't understand. What was wrong with her mother?

Jay Stein released an official statement that confirmed a nervous breakdown, but denied that it was linked to alcohol and drugs. It meant nothing. The media had a field day speculating about Monica's condition.

Rita had informed Robert of his mother's breakdown and they were in daily contact. She didn't feel it necessary for him to come over as long as Monica remained stable. She promised to phone as soon as she knew anything more.

The doctors did test after test, but could find nothing wrong during the first week. Then they decided to do a brain scan. When the results came through they asked to speak to Rita, who was closest to her.

'We've found a disease caused by a virus that is common among the old, but now seems to be affecting younger people,' they informed her, 'men as well as women. Monica Clarke is suffering from Alzheimer's, a mentally debilitating disease, and there is no cure.'

Conversations between Bel Air and Hewitt Hall intensified. Robert was devastated and offered to come to Los Angeles, but after many discussions, he decided to look after his mother at the Hall. She needed peace and quiet and California wasn't the best place for that. Philip, he said, was in total agreement.

Jay made another press statement confirming that Monica Clarke was suffering from Alzheimer's disease, which in its early stages could often be confused with alcoholism.

The papers were now full of comparisons between what had happened to Monica and Rita Hayworth. The media had labelled both as alcoholics before it had been confirmed what they were really suffering from. The fact that it was the papers themselves that had jumped to the wrong conclusion didn't appear to concern them.

* * *

Rita, Doris and Tanya flew with her to England and took her to Hewitt Hall. Only Tanya had ever been there before. As money was no problem, they employed two full-time nurses to look after Monica.

In the time that followed, Monica seemed to be in a trance. Philip seemed to mean nothing to her but she smiled every time she saw Robert, though he wasn't quite sure whether she really knew who he was. She wandered around the Hall like a lost soul.

365

Months went by and her behaviour patterns became more and more incomprehensible. She started hiding things everywhere and if the nurses didn't watch her very carefully, all kinds of objects disappeared: clocks, soap, food, jewellery. She also disappeared herself at the first possible opportunity, and it sometimes took them several hours to find her. Often the nurse only had to go to the bathroom for Monica to take the opportunity to disappear. Or she slipped out at night.

Sometimes they would find her far out in the fields. And once Philip, who behind his controlled façade was clearly upset by Monica's state, found her sitting in the ruins of the lodge talking to someone or something. She could stand talking for hours on end to a painting.

It was difficult to get her to eat, but she loved sweet things, so the sugar bowl had to be kept hidden. She paid no attention to personal hygiene at all, the nurses did everything for her.

Rita, Doris and Tanya had flown back to California, but they phoned every two or three days to hear how things were going. Robert's fiancée Sarah was not finding it easy. She had barely known Monica when she'd been her usual self: unlike Robert she didn't have a store of affection to keep her going when Monica was at her most difficult. Sometimes Monica's behaviour was almost normal, but then she would suddenly change completely. She could be violent and sometimes even fought those around her, summoning up incredible strength.

Monica stayed at Hewitt Hall for six months, a difficult time for Robert and Sarah. He was suffering so much for his mother, and it also profoundly affected his relationship with Sarah. Monica talked a great deal but it was not possible to make out what she was saying and then she heard voices inside her telling her what to do. It was so hard to understand what was going on inside her head.

Gerd and Gunnar came and stayed at the Hall for a month which made things considerably easier for the nurses, as Gerd spent all her waking hours with Monica. Either she or Robert sat with her, talking to her or just holding her hand. Sometimes they went on long walks.

Often Philip would stand watching them from a distance. A

certain calm seemed to settle on her when either Gerd or Robert was with her. It was as if she felt their presence and their love, but it was impossible to know for certain. The strange thing was that her appearance barely altered. She was still just as beautiful, and the nurses were instructed always to dress her well and do her hair. Robert made sure she was never allowed to slide into physical decay. The mother he'd known over the last decade would have hated that.

Monica still owned the house in Bel Air and Rita went on living there to look after Tanya and accompany her on her modelling assignments. Now that others were taking care of Monica, Rita knew her priority was Tanya. She was very much in demand. The agency had added two years to her age, so officially she was sixteen and was allowed to travel round as a model.

She had already spent lots of time in New York and was on the covers of several major fashion magazines nationwide.

Tanya was slimmer than ever and Rita did everything in her power to get her to eat, but it was hopeless. Food was her greatest enemy and all she talked about was how fat she was. Rita found her worries about Tanya's mother being replaced in her mind by fears for her daughter. She knew something of Monica's turbulent history. She just hoped Tanya would not make the same mistakes.

Gerd fairly soon realised that the situation at Hewitt Hall was becoming untenable. Monica grew more and more ill tempered and they were all beginning to feel the strain. She and Robert spent most of their waking time near her but that was a great strain on their patience and it was easy to get angry with her. For the sake of them all, especially her grandson, Gerd began to talk about taking Monica home with her and getting her into a hospital in Sweden. At first Robert wouldn't hear of it, but as time went by he realised that even with the nurses he would not be able to cope with looking after Monica much longer.

Gerd made some enquiries at Danderyds Hospital in Sweden, at first without Robert's knowledge, but when she finally told him even he had to see the seriousness of the situation. Monica needed hospital nursing and it hurt him that they couldn't give what she needed at Hewitt Hall.

The day they left Robert looked at his mother – she was still amazingly beautiful, even though her hair was slightly grey without the highlights – and her eyes were sunken and without focus.

In May 1989, Monica was admitted to the closed ward in Danderyds Hospital. Robert planned to visit her as soon as he had the time. He knew Gerd went every day, not an easy thing for the mother of an adult daughter. Monica – so young and independent, was now helpless in a mental ward. Gerd wished it had been her instead.

Occasionally Monica was so aggressive they had to tie her down. Sometimes she fought with the other patients and it would end with them chasing each other up and down the corridor. This was all symptomatic of the disease. Gerd knew she had done the right thing by placing her there. It wouldn't have been fair to Robert and Sarah to have had to cope with all this.

Tanya went on to Stockholm after she'd done a six-page layout in Paris for *Vogue*. It was only a two-hour journey, and she and Rita stayed for a week.

Monica didn't recognise Tanya, just laughed slightly when she saw her. It was hard for Tanya to take. During the week they were in Stockholm, Monica fell and broke her thigh, so was confined to bed. Gerd wondered uneasily just how much her granddaughter could bear. Her mother was as thin as a little bird, she refused to eat. No one knew whether this was deliberate, but she just lay there staring at the ceiling and pursed her mouth when offered food. They were finally forced to give her a drip so she would have some nourishment.

'It's them. They tell me. No, I can't . . . It's they who decide.' Her speech was now totally incomprehensible.

'Them' and 'they' were the cornerstone of her monologue. Always 'they' who decided and it was pointless asking who they were. She had gone into a world of her own and no one knew to whom she was talking. The winter months saw a rapid deterioration in her condition.

The following August, when Tanya was returning from another

visit to Sweden, she stopped off in London for a few days. She'd
had a booking with Vivienne Westwood; the shoot had been one
of the most original she'd done and they had fixed her up with
plaits that stood straight out, and high platform shoes. She'd found
it exciting, and for a while she could forget the trauma her family
was suffering.

It hadn't been easy for her to leave Gerd and Monica again, but
she'd had no choice and she would be back the next week. She
had talked to Robert on the phone and they had decided to go to
Stockholm together to be with their mother on her birthday.

It would mean a great deal to Gerd to have her two grand-
children with her then, and Robert, who had not seen Monica for
a couple of months, wanted to make the most of it. He was getting
married in September and after that he knew there wouldn't be
much time to visit her.

'Hewitt Hall.'
　'May I speak to Philip Hewitt?'
　'Who's speaking, please?'
　'Sir Hugh Grenville.'
　Philip went to the phone.
　'Hugh, how are you?'
　'Fine, thanks. Dreadful, what happened to Gordon.'
　'Yes, it was a shock to us all. He was here at Hewitt Hall two
years ago to celebrate his birthday . . .'
　'Yes, a real tragedy.'
The event had been reported on the news. Gordon's helicopter
had been taking him and his girl-friend from his yacht off Sardinia
to a restaurant in the mountains. He had been so proud of his
helicopter, he'd had a landing platform built on top of the hundred
and fifty foot *Gordanza*.

They had been on their way to a charity dinner in Porto Cervo,
where the guests included Princess Caroline of Monaco. As they
were coming in to land, the rotor blade had caught a cable. The
helicopter had exploded and there had been no survivors. It had
certainly come as a great shock.

　'Gordon's solicitor contacted me yesterday,' Grenville went on.
'The only heir they could find is a certain Tanya Clarke, born

during his marriage to Monica Hewitt.'

'But Tanya's—'

'I know, Philip. But she was born within the marriage and Gordon left no will. Nor had he any other relatives. He was an only child and he had no other children of his own.'

'But that's incredible. How is it possible for a man in Gordon's position not to have made a will?'

'He had made one in favour of his parents, but as you know they both died last year, one shortly after the other. A new will had been drawn up in which he had actually left quite a sum to Robert. But the bulk was to go to various research centres and charities. But for some reason he never got around to signing it.'

'But can Tanya Clarke really inherit from him?'

'Yes, I've looked into it. All that's needed is verification that the girl was born during their marriage. As the only surviving relative, she will now inherit his fortune.'

This wasn't just a matter of money. There was the penthouse in Eaton Square, the chalet in St Moritz, the villa in St-Jean-Cap-Ferrat, the apartment at the Carlyle Hotel in New York and the property in Bermuda. Plus all his investments and personal property. The assets exceeded two hundred million pounds.

Philip felt faint.

Tanya was staying at Blake's Hotel in Chelsea with Rita. He and Robert, together with Sir Hugh, would break the news to her personally.

25

Robert and Tanya were on the plane to Stockholm. It was 19th of August and tomorrow was Monica's fifty-first birthday. They took a taxi directly from Arlanda airport to Gerd and Gunnar's apartment.

A great deal had happened to Tanya in the last few days. She could hardly believe what it meant to have so much money. They had never lacked for money in the States and had always had an extremely comfortable life. But it wasn't entirely easy suddenly becoming heiress to such an enormous fortune. They hadn't yet told Gerd and Gunnar; they were waiting for a suitable opportunity.

Rita was left in London, waiting for Tanya to return so they could go back to the States together. She now worked full-time for Tanya and they had decided to keep the house in Bel Air and use it as their base. When they went on modelling assignments, Tanya's private tutor came with them so she wouldn't miss any schooling.

The British newspapers were full of the Cinderella story of a top model inheriting a fortune from a father she'd never known, Gordon Clarke, and Philip was extremely worried. With Tanya's face in every newspaper, it wouldn't be long before Crispin tried to find her.

In silence Tanya and Robert took the lift down. Their grandparents had already left the hospital; they wanted the children to have a moment alone with their mother.

Robert looked at his young sister and felt an enormous

371

tenderness for this tall, slim fourteen year old. Despite her youth, she was already an established model. He had seen her in magazines such as *Vogue* and *Harper's* and in the major Dior campaign which no one could escape noticing. And now she was one of the richest women in the world, and still only a teenager.

He wrapped his arms around her thin body and she leant her head on his shoulder, crying. Robert fought back his own tears.

Monica who had been so beautiful and clever, who had been through so much in her life and whose sweetness everyone had loved, had been unrecognisable, incapable of looking after herself, totally unaware of the grief and sorrow her children were feeling.

The lift came to a halt and, with their arms still round each other, they went out and across to the car park. Tanya looked at her brother. He was so beautiful, but his eyes were filled with sadness. Her mother had had unusually dark children for someone as fair as she was. She took a packet of Kleenex from her Maud Frizon bag, gave one to Robert and blew her nose on another.

'Where do you want to go? Straight back to Grandmother's?'

On their way to the car, he asked whether she would like to stay at Hewitt Hall for a few days. It was the first time he had invited her there without Monica. He knew that now and in the future they must become rock-like supports for each other.

He still had his arm round Tanya as he searched his pockets for the car keys. Neither of them saw the man in a dark blue cashmere coat, a briefcase in his hand, hurry through the glass doors of the hospital the moment Tanya and Robert's car had disappeared.

He looked at the piece of paper in his hand – Ward 5B. He took the lift up to the fourth floor, walked towards the closed door on the left and knocked on it.

A young male nurse in white hospital clothes opened the door.

'I am Monica Clarke's husband. I have come to see my wife.'

Mikael, the orderly, stared at the man. Earlier that day, both her parents and two children had been there, and now the husband . . .

'You are . . .?'

'Mr Clarke.'

The young orderly took him through another locked door, past a dining room and along a corridor, then opened the door into one of the bedrooms. Inside were two beds. One was empty, and Monica was lying in the one on the left, fresh flowers on her bedside table.

'Thank you. I would appreciate it if we could be left alone.'

Mikael smiled with understanding and closed the door behind him.

The man took off his coat and sat down on the chair beside Monica's bed. He sat there looking at her for a long time without touching her. She was laughing, not with or at him, for her gaze was elsewhere.

Then he took her hand: 'Monica, can you hear me?'

She sank back on the pillows and stared straight up at the ceiling, her eyes flickering.

'Monica, Monica, do you remember me?' He did not expect an answer, but he wanted to make quite sure.

He sat there for quite a while, holding her hand and talking to her. There were so many things he had never said but he said them now, knowing it was too late. She would not understand, perhaps never would have.

Then he put his briefcase on the bed and took out a small packet wrapped in a silk handkerchief. He unwrapped a syringe filled with ricin. He looked round, although he knew only he and Monica were there. The door was closed.

He stood up, and turned her head to one side, tucked her greying hair behind her ear and with a swift jab, pressed the syringe into her hairline. He withdrew the syringe, wrapped it in the silk handkerchief and put the little packet back in his briefcase.

Philip looked at Monica. Her eyes rolled back and she took a few rattling breaths. Then she was quite still.

Her eyes were staring straight ahead. He closed them with his forefinger, leant over her and pulled the sheet up to her throat.

'It took me all these years,' he whispered into her ear, 'to realise that I love you. I am sorry about everything you've had to go through, but now you have peace. You can sleep. Happy birthday, Monica . . .'